Deadly Cargo: A
terrorism

Rich Johnson

Table of Contents

Prologue

October 1571

A cloud of dust lifted suddenly off the Saharan floor, stirred by the spin of a small whirlwind that seemed to come out of nowhere. Nothing else moved. Every creature that lived in this desert had long since heeded powerful survival instincts, taking shelter from blistering sun, hiding under rocks, down holes in the soil or in whatever shade it could find. Heat waves shimmered, creating a wavy distortion above the sun-tortured earth.

Far away beyond the edge of the land, the cool blue of the Atlantic offered visual relief. Or it would have if anyone had been there to see it. But on this day, in late summer of the year 1571, there was no one on this unsettled coast of northwest Africa to feel the stifling heat or hear the wind or see dust rise in a whirling shaft.

A thousand miles south, in the Gulf of Guinea, monsoon rains fell as if the belly of the clouds had been slit. A torrent poured from the sky, washing the coastal jungle, filling rivers to flood stage and beyond. Humid air hung like a wet sheet of gauze, waiting for the afternoon's rising convection currents to carry the moisture aloft. Eighteen thousand feet up, the tropical jet stream steered the moist air of Guinea to the north, where it collided with the hot Saharan air mass, and a meteorological bomb started to tick. Hot updrafts and cold downdrafts began a cyclonic dance, whirling to the screaming music of an ever-increasing symphony of violent wind.

Every year, during the heat of late summer, this was where some of the world's most serious weather was born. It began as a tropical wave in the atmosphere, evolved into a tropical depression, then to a storm – then, if all the conditions were just right, it became a hurricane. This time, all the conditions were in balance. Seventeen days later, a powerful hurricane carved its way across the north Atlantic, ripping trees off the Windward Islands of the Caribbean, slashing the southern edge of Cuba, and slamming into the east coast of Guatemala. It was an era before government weather agencies existed and attached names to storms, but in legends created by early explorers, this storm was known by the name of 'O Gigante'.

For the ancient mariners, there was little warning of 'O Gigante's' coming. In native villages along the Rio Dulce, though, it was different. Tribal elders who could read the signs of the sky and understood the queer behaviours of birds, insects and forest animals, quietly gathered their clans and moved inland to higher ground away from the river and its tributaries. But they did not say a word to the white men from the large ships. Those men had come peacefully enough, a full cycle of the seasons before, but were now wearing out their welcome. They took unwanted liberties with the women of the villages and took unfair advantage of the natives' generosity. They hunted game that was needed for food for the villagers, killing too many animals and driving away those that weren't killed. The white men were vulgar, dirty and loud. They had no reverence for the land or regard for the people. It was clear that these men did not want to learn the native ways; they wanted only to learn about the gold that came from the high mountains far inland.

Guillermo Ascente, the Portuguese captain of the brigantine *Tesoro do Rei,* awoke to find the bay gently rolling and the breeze fresh. Broken clouds specked the eastern sky. The ship's launch had just come alongside and the coxswain brought a strange report that the river villages were empty of people. A puzzled expression spread across Ascente's face, and in his momentary confusion he reverted to his native tongue. "A onde forem?" he asked, then realising that his men didn't understand, he translated for his rough British crewman – "Where have they gone?"

The coxswain shook his head slowly and held out open hands below shrugged shoulders. This needed no translation.

Ascente turned and looked over the rail toward the distant jungle. "We have been here long enough – perhaps too long. We have what we came for," he said slowly. "There is nothing more for us here. Prepare the crew to get underway. We will take what we have and go home."

In the cargo hold of the massive wooden brigantine there was gold enough to satisfy the profiteers who financed this voyage of plunder. Guillermo was smooth of tongue, as well when promoting his business in the streets, shops and banks of Europe as when meeting with native elders. He knew when to bow and when to stand tall, when to avert his eyes and when to bore through the gaze of his opponent. He understood when to play the humble role and when to wield the sword to get what he wanted. He was good at this game – some said he was the best there ever was.

The call went out across the decks, and men scrambled. No one wanted to stay here any longer than it took to ensure their share of a fine take. There was plenty of treasure in the hold and to a man they were satisfied with the loot and ready to make sail toward home, especially now that the villages were strangely empty and there was no more entertainment for them ashore. Under the best conditions, the voyage back to Europe would take months, so Guillermo Ascente made the decision – today was as good a time as any to get started.

Three days later, in the wide waters of the Caribbean Sea, 'O Gigante' bore down on the Tesoro do Rei. A month after the storm passed and the villagers had returned to the Rio Dulce, the ship's name-board drifted onto the beach near the mouth of the river. The elders convened a conference and all agreed that their God had heard their prayers.

Chapter One

September 2007 – Northern Afghanistan

A fiery late September wind picked up brittle grains of sand and shot them across the lifeless desert floor like so many shards of glass. Two human forms, one wearing desert camouflage and the other an ankle-length black robe, pushed slowly through the blowing sand towards a large military-style tent. The woman's head was covered by a large black shawl. In a storm like this, it was nearly impossible to breathe without inhaling tiny fragments of sand dust. If viewed through a microscope, these seemingly harmless bits of soil would show razor edges. Instant blindness and the agonising pain of eyes lacerated by tiny silica knives awaited anyone unlucky enough to be caught without eye protection. The man wore desert combat goggles and held a cloth across his mouth. The sandstorm was nature's relentless weapon in this war.

Howling wind thrummed the taut fabric of the camouflage-coloured tent, cancelling any hope of hearing someone approach. The first indication that anyone approached was when the tent wall parted and an old woman stepped inside the 12x20-foot enclosure. Her shawl was wrapped tightly around her covered head and face, and her shapeless black dress hung to her shoe tops. She turned her back on the two men who sat at the table, just long enough to re-tie the tent flap that served as a door. Then she slowly turned around to face them, and removed the shawl from her face.

"You have him?" Husam al Din asked.

She nodded, "He is outside."

"Are you sure about him?"

"I am sure," she answered, keeping her eyes low. "Love and hate are only a heartbeat apart, and when the one turns to the other, the heart is ready to find a new reason to live."

"And his reason now?"

"It is beyond hate: it is revenge. I am sure about matters of the heart," she said, "and his heart is ready."

Husam al Din stood. "You have done your part, old woman. May you now die in peace."

"That is my prayer," she said, backing away from the young man's path as he strode toward the tent flap.

"Show him in," al Din commanded. "Then go."

The old woman wrapped the long shawl around her face once again, untied the tent flap and went out. A hand reached through the opening, then an arm covered by US military desert camouflage clothing. Josh Adams stepped inside and removed his goggles.

"Please," Husam al Din said, "take a seat over there." He motioned to a folding chair on the opposite side of the small table. He tied the tent flap and returned to his own chair.

Adams stood, his hands on the chair back, waiting for his host to complete the introductions. Al Din stared at him for a moment, then realised why the soldier was still standing. "Ah, yes," he said, "western customs. Let me introduce everyone. Staff Sergeant Josh Adams, this is Sorgei Groschenko. Sorgei, Josh Adams," motioning from one to the other.

The two men each searched the eyes of the other, then reached across the table and shook hands. They bowed ever so slightly as was done in formal company, but their eyes never left the eyes of the other, almost like the beginning of a martial arts battle.

"Mr Groschenko," Josh said.

"Staff Sergeant Adams," the Russian said slowly.

"You can call me Josh."

"Call me Sorgei," the Russian said without emotion.

Josh turned to look directly at Husam al Din. "But I don't know you. All I know is that the old woman said she knew someone I should meet. Someone who can help me with a certain personal problem I have."

"And you trust her?" the Arab asked.

"No reason not to. Not yet anyway," Josh replied.

"You Americans are such—" he stopped himself in mid-sentence, catching the bitter hatred before it spilled from his lips.

"Such what?" Josh asked.

Husam al Din coughed. "I was just going to say that you Americans are such trusting people." He forced a cold smile, even though he would rather have drawn the dagger that was in his waistband and plunged it through the American's heart. He coughed again. "Ach, this dust … it is enough to choke a Saudi lizard." The comment broke the tension and all three men chuckled politely at the joke. "Now, let us sit." The Arab motioned to the chairs and the two men took their seats at the table.

Josh did not move. "I will sit at your table only after I know who you are."

"So perhaps you do not trust the old woman?"

"No reason to," Josh said. "At least not yet."

"Very well. I am Husam al Din." His black eyes stared hard at Josh Adams.

"Sword of the faith," Josh translated.

"You know the Arabic language," al Din smiled. "It is one of the reasons we chose you."

"You chose me?" Josh asked.

"Yes. You are not here by accident, or by mere circumstance. Now, please sit down. We have much to discuss."

While the sandstorm raged outside, the three men talked and listened and watched each other's expressions and mannerisms. It was like the first round of a prizefight, when the combatants feel each other out before committing to a personal fighting style. Josh watched the eyes, looking for hints of deception. Both Husam al Din and Sorgei Groschenko studied Josh as if they were examining an expensive item before handing over the cash.

It began slowly, but over the next few hours, each got to know a little bit about the other – at least as much as they were willing to reveal. It was quickly obvious that much was being left unsaid, as each man strained to conceal deep personal motives. It was a dance of lies mixed with truth, but behind each man's story were secrets that would not be revealed. Some of the secrets, in fact, were hidden even from the men themselves, as is true of everyone. A man knows only what he remembers or has been told, even though there is much more to a personal history than is openly recognized. For Sorgei Groschenko and Husam al Din, pieces of the unseen past had been laid together as paving stones to create a path that led to this desert tent. For Josh Adams, most of his life had been wrapped up in a lie. Between the lies and the truth, destiny had thrown these three together as comrades in an horrific plot against the United States.

Husam al Din began, "Just so we are all clear about who we are, why we are here and what we are going to be doing, I want us to tell each other about ourselves. Sorgei, you go first, please." He nodded toward the Russian. "We are all in this together and we must be able to …" he looked at Josh and flashed a cold smile, "… to trust each other. Right?"

Chapter Two

Late December 1991 – Yakutsk, Siberia

A dim bulb gently swung from a pair of twisted wires that hung from the high ceiling and flickered in the cold room. Outside the frosted window, wind howled and snow flew sideways. The wind was so strong that it shook the building, setting the light bulb into motion. The light flickered again, and Sorgei Groschenko looked up at the bulb, muttered something under his breath and wrapped the woolen blanket more tightly around his shoulders. Then he bent over the table once again and studied the figures he had been calculating.

It's insane, he thought, *that the government expects me to do my best work under these terrible conditions.* At least they could have the decency to provide enough heat so he didn't have to huddle beneath a blanket to work. How did the military expect him to develop a new strain of bacteria when he was freezing to death?

His thought faded away to the time he spent on the beach along the Black Sea two summers ago. Oh, that was pleasant! The sun was warm in Sochi. Even the water was warm enough for swimming. The city was like a garden of subtropical trees and plants, and the sun shone 200 days each year. It was like heaven, to his mind … the closest thing to heaven he could imagine right now. He wanted to be back there, baking under the August sunshine, not holed up in this Siberian no-man's land, trapped in a frozen hellish exile working on a secret new form of germ warfare.

Of course, if he succeeded, all this misery was worth it. He stared at the lightbulb for a moment, and the dream came alive in his mind. He would be lauded by his peers, praised by the government, and undoubtedly be rewarded with a vacation in Sochi again. Food … good food, lots of food. Women to entertain him. The warmth of the sun. Ah yes, for all that, he worked his heart out in this lonely dungeon in the depths of the frozen wasteland. The dream was strong. It was the dream of every Soviet military scientist. He knew that if he developed the breakthrough, there would be missile warheads named after him. Generations of schoolchildren would learn his name. Maybe even a monument to his honour in Red Square. The thought brought a smile to his face.

His reverie was cut short by the sudden jangle of the telephone. It was an old phone, black and heavy, with a rotary dial and an annoying bell that scared the mice right out of the building, even on a horrid night such as this. The phone rang again before he was able to reach it and pick up the handset.

"Alo?" he half yelled into the mouthpiece. This piece of junk telephone was so bad that he and whoever was on the other end of the call had to shout to be heard.

"Da, this is Sorgei Groschenko. Da. I will bring them and come." He rested the handset back on the cradle, but his mind was troubled. What now? What could they possibly want with all these papers at this time of night?

He scooped his papers into a ragged satchel, then went to a cabinet and removed all the files. Those, too, were stuffed into the fat satchel. He pulled the blanket from his shoulders, folded it double and tossed it over the back of the chair, struggled into a huge winter coat. Beside the door, he kicked off his shoes and stepped into tall mukluks, blew hot breath into his hands and then pulled on a pair of mittens. He flipped the fur-lined hood over his head, grabbed the satchel and went out the door into the blizzard.

It seemed to Sorgei that it was always winter in Yakutsk, and always night. He could not remember ever being at this military research outpost under any other conditions. Or maybe it just seemed that way to him. This past few months were so long and slow-moving. And at this high latitude, the winter nights were endless and the days ... well, he didn't know what happened to the days. Right now he remembered no days, only nights, only cold, only blizzards.

Against the merciless Siberian wind, he pulled the side of his hood close to his face and crossed the frozen pavement through ankle-deep snow that swirled around his feet. A single bulb beneath a rattling metal shield lighted the door that led into the other building. He wrapped his mittened hand around the knob, turned and pulled the door open. A flood of light made him squint, and his face felt welcome warmth. It was another world in here, with far more light and more heat than in the place they had given him as his office. *I should have become an officer,* he thought, *instead of being a scientist.*

He shook off the snow, removed his mittens and the parka and hung them on a hook against the wall. With no shoes to wear, he kept the mukluks on his feet. He was sure he would be back out in the cold and snow soon enough anyway, trudging to his frigid quarters, so he didn't bother to bring his shoes.

Down the hall, a soldier with a rifle slung over his shoulder stood outside the office door where Sorgei needed to go. As he stepped in front of the soldier, the man came to attention and asked to see his ID. Sorgei pulled out the card from inside his shirt, where it hung around his neck on a piece of string. The soldier inspected the card, looked Sorgei up and down and then returned the card to him.

This is ridiculous, Sorgei thought. *Who else would be up here in this frozen Siberian purgatory pretending to be me?* The soldier moved aside; Sorgei turned the door handle and stepped into the warmth of the commandant's office. His glasses immediately steamed up, temporarily blinding him behind a gray fog.

"Excuse me, sir," Sorgei said as he removed his glasses and wiped them dry with a handkerchief. "It's the warmth. Marvellous!"

Commandant Schmernov didn't notice what Sorgei was doing, because he didn't even look up at the man as he entered the office. "Take a seat," the commandant barked. "This won't take long." He continued to write for another minute before setting his pen aside and raising his eyes to meet the scientist's gaze. The great bulk of the base commander filled all the space behind the desk. His red face and veined bulb nose told of too many years under the influence of a vodka bottle.

How do men like this end up in command of anything? Sorgei wondered. *They can't even take control of their own lives.* One thing he was thankful for was that the Groschenko family did not allow alcohol in their home. His father taught the children that vodka was poison for the brain, and Sorgei took that to heart. Not being an athlete for the state, he knew that if anything were going to move him up the ladder of success, it would have to be his brain, so he made sure he never poisoned it.

Sorgei took the seat, as commanded, and waited to find out why he had been summoned.

"I'll get right to the point," the commandant said. "You're out of a job."

The news took Sorgei's breath away. "Wh– what?" was all he came up with.

"Moscow wants you out of here immediately. I will take all your papers. A car is waiting outside. You are dismissed."

It took a moment for it to sink in. Sorgei felt suddenly weak all over, and a wave of nausea swept over him. As he spoke, his head was spinning. "What am I to do?"

"I don't care what you do," the commandant barked. "Just leave that satchel and get out of this office. I have work to do."

Almost too weak to stand, Sorgei gripped the arms of the chair and lifted himself to his feet. The commandant motioned to the soldier through the glass pane in his office door, and the guard came and took Sorgei by the arm to escort him out. "I don't understand," Sorgei whimpered to the soldier, "I just don't understand."

"Get him out of here," the commandant yelled. The guard hauled Sorgei down the hall to the door leading outside, took the parka and mittens off the hook and handed them to the scientist, then opened the exit door and pushed him out into the cold. Sorgei heard the door slam behind him, then heard a car engine start. Headlights came at him from the right, and the car stopped directly ahead. The rear door opened, and someone pulled him inside, then the car sped away into the night blizzard.

Inside the commandant's office, the big man in charge pulled down the privacy shade to cover the glass panel in the door. He ripped open the satchel and dumped the contents onto the floor. "What a shame," he muttered. "Months of work. Groschenko was supposed to be the most brilliant biologist for this kind of thing. I hope Moscow knows what they're doing." He picked up the first piece of paper, studied it long and hard, as if he hated to let it go, then he fed it into the shredder.

Twenty minutes later, the commandant picked up the phone, pressed a speed dial number and waited. When the line picked up, he said only three words, "It is done."

Someone on the other end of the line spoke, and the commandant listened. "Da. I will do that." He hung up the phone, emptied the shredder into a plastic trash bag, tied the top and carried the bundle out of his office. The soldier came to attention and saluted as the commandant left his office, turned left and walked down the hall toward the back of the building. He opened the door to the furnace room, and stepped back as the heat of the coal-fired boiler rushed at him. Then he stepped inside, opened the furnace door and tossed the bag into the flames.

Moments later, he placed another call and spoke the same three words as before.

****

Two days later, after a midnight flight from Yakutsk in an old DC3 propeller-driven airplane that had the appearance of being rescued from the scrap pile, Sorgei Groschenko found himself standing on the frozen streets of Moscow. He had no job and no place to go. There would be no fame, no fortune, no peer adulation, no heritage, and no monument in Red Square. Worst of all, there would be no vacation in the sun on the Black Sea. The Soviet Union was being dismantled in favour of a new Russia. The old Soviet military, along with its secret efforts to develop ever more deadly strains of germ warfare, was finished. Not only finished, but it was under orders and scrambling to destroy all evidence that it was ever working on biological weapons of mass destruction. All his research, all his effort – it was all gone, shredded, burned, destroyed to hide it from the probing inquiries of the United States and her allies in Europe.

For the first time in his life, Sorgei Groschenko and a vast number of other scientists were out of a job. He was on his own, and he didn't have a clue how he was going to support himself. If it weren't for the cursed United States, none of this would have happened, he reasoned. All his life, he knew that America was the enemy of his homeland, but now it was more personal. Now America was his own enemy. Her interference cost him his career, his future, and he hated the USA now more than ever.

****

For the next eight years, Sorgei Groschenko worked two part-time night jobs; one in the late evening sweeping out a grain warehouse, and one during the early morning hours restocking shelves at a store. He slept during the day in a room in an old, rundown hotel in a poor section of the city, paying by the week and hoping to afford the next rent payment. Most of the time, there was no heat for his dreary room.

During the long winter months, he wore a sweater and thin wool gloves all the time, even when he slept. The dull yellow walls were stained brown where water had leaked from somewhere above. The floor was rough wood, but that didn't matter much because it was so cold that he rarely took off his shoes. There was no lock on the door, but he didn't worry because he owned nothing worth stealing. Down the hall was the only bathroom on the entire third floor, and it was shared by thirty-one other residents of the hotel, both men and women, each having to wait to take their turn. Finding the bathroom unoccupied was rare, so Sorgei found a discarded one-gallon tin can and kept it under his bed for emergencies.

One bitter winter morning in February 2000, after leaving work at the store, he walked to a coffee house he used to frequent when he was studying at the university. A tiny bell above the door announced his arrival as he stepped inside, and it seemed that every person turned to look at him. In their eyes he sensed the despair. A political change of this magnitude had reached deep into society and rocked the lives of many of the most educated. Men and women who once had bright futures were now wondering how to make their way through life.

He took a seat at the counter and decided to spend a little of what he had left. "Black, please," he said to the waiter. Soon, the steaming cup appeared, and he gripped it with cold fingers, then pressed it to his lips. It felt good going down. He closed his eyes and savoured the feeling of the warm liquid melting its way into the cold cavern of his body.

An olive-skinned man took a seat on the counter stool next to him and spoke in a quiet voice. "Are you Sorgei Groschenko?" It was a voice with a foreign accent – an Arab accent, if Sorgei were not mistaken.

Chapter Three

May 1984 – Lashkar Gah, Afghanistan

The western horizon was red as embers, the colour coming from a combination of dust-filled sky and setting sun. In the east the moon would rise soon, appearing, as it were, out of the ground full and round and red. It was an omen; at least it seemed like one to Najia, as she lay sweating on a table in a little room, waiting for the midwife.

A bitter cramp gripped her abdomen and she cried out, but muffled her scream with her own hand cupped across her mouth. No one must hear her anguish. It was too dangerous. Already, her father was waiting to catch her if she came home. But she was not going home. She had not been near her family's house for more than three months, ever since her pregnancy started to show. Unwed mothers were not only a burden, they were also a shame in this society – a dishonour that was made to disappear. It happened before; she heard the stories. They were called honour killings, and they were normally carried out by the father, brother or uncle of the offending girl. The usual method was to slit the throat, a form of blood sacrifice that was meant to restore the lost honour to the family.

The midwife was an older girl, a friend of a friend who agreed to see her through the birth. Najia was thankful for her friends, even though she could not stay with them because they were known to the family and their homes were the most obvious places to look for Najia. It would place them in danger if they were caught harbouring an unwed pregnant girl. So it was friends of her friends, older girls who were out on their own, who shared their rooms and food with the unlucky Najia, quietly pitying her for the terrible situation she was in.

These girls were a true blessing. They were all at risk, if word of this got out, so everything had to be done in secrecy. The one who would be her midwife had been through this very thing herself, giving birth to a child when she had no husband. An older woman helped her through the ordeal, just as she would now help Najia. Even though it was illegal, even though it was forbidden and considered immoral, there was a covert sisterhood among the women that reached beyond what was socially acceptable. Nobody spoke of these things, yet when the need arose, there was always someone there to lend assistance.

The room was an empty storage space at the back of an old machine shop that went out of business. It smelled of grease and oil, and the dirt floor was stained black from years of soaking up spilled fluids. Najia was told that this was the place, and so she had come. She waited for more than an hour, lying alone with her pain and fears on a table that was nothing more than a scrap of oil-stained plywood laid over some old wooden boxes. It was the longest hour of her life as she lay waiting in the dark corner of this hidden room on a backstreet of Lashkar Gah – waiting for the girl, her midwife, hoping she would not abandon her just as the baby's father had.

A shadow crossed the doorway, and a black shape stepped inside. The girl said nothing as she walked to the table and removed the veil from her burkah. Najia smiled at first, then grimaced and clasped her hand across her mouth as another contraction swept over her. The girl rested her hand on the swollen abdomen and spoke soft words of comfort. "You will get through this. I will help you. Relax and let the baby come to us."

Outside, the end of the day had come. The sky turned a deeper, darker red.

On the table, blood and water spread across the bare plywood and spilled onto the floor. Najia struggled through the pain. The baby began to come, then seemed to hesitate, and the young mother gasped for breath, but it was as if there was not enough air.

In the west, the sun died at the very moment that the moon appeared in the east.

****

"We will name him Husam al Din," the old man said, as he took the baby in his arms. "Sword of the Faith – it is a good name, and we will train him to fulfill his destiny for the faith."

"It is a tragedy," the girl said. "To be alone in the world without mother or father. He will be in good hands here at the madrassa orphanage."

"Husam al Din," the old man smiled. "Yes, it is a good name. I can see it in his eyes. Too bad his mother died in childbirth, after losing her husband in battle with the Soviets, as you said." He probed the girl's face with his eyes.

"Yes." She turned her eyes to the floor in an attempt to hide the lie. "Yes, that is a tragedy."

"And no other living relatives, you say?"

"None." She regained her composure and looked him straight in the eye this time. "The madrassa is the only chance for him."

"Then he will have his chance," the old man said. "I will personally see that he has the best education."

"Thank you, Imam Waziri," she said, "may your life be blessed." Then she turned and left.

****

Five times each day, the call to prayer brought everyone to his knees. From the time he was old enough to walk, Husam al Din had his own prayer rug, and he kept it rolled and close to him at all times. The worst thing he could think of was to be caught without the prayer rug when the call to prayer was sounded. The mat kept him clean as he stood and knelt, placing his hands and his forehead on the ground. Being clean for his prayers was an absolute necessity.

Five times each day, beginning at dawn and extending until about two hours after sunset, prayer was the pattern of life for him, and he had known nothing else since his birth. The ritual pleased him. It was comforting to have no question about what he was to do with his time, and to know that no matter where he went somebody kept track of the time and issue the call to prayer at just the right moment. Then all he had to do was to unroll his rug, place it on the ground with the niche facing in the direction toward Mecca and begin the Salaat, his ritual prayer.

Before he began Salaat, there was much to do. His body and clothing must be clean, and he must perform wudu, the ritual ablution or washing. Then, standing erect but with his head down and hands at his sides, he recited his own personal call to prayer. "Allaahu Akbar," it began, being rehearsed four times. "Ashhadu Allah ilaaha illa-Lah," twice repeated, bearing witness that God is great and that there is none worthy of worship except God.

The prayers themselves were memorised, and that also gave him comfort. He didn't need to figure out what to pray about – it was all written down for him. There was no need for him to develop a personal relationship with his god, Allah, just repeat the mantra five times each day, like clockwork. There was no question about the rightness of the ritual – it was as natural a part of his life as was breathing or eating or sleeping.

At first, it was difficult for him to get all the parts of the Salaat right, and there were many times when he was required to excuse himself from his prayers and exit the mosque, then re-enter and begin the process all over again. To err in the words was shameful.

His daily existence was so regimented that it was unnecessary for him to wonder what he wanted to do with his life. From the day he learned to understand the spoken language, he was taught his mission – jihad – holy war.

****

In his eighth year at the madrassa, Husam al Din was given a dagger made of fine polished steel. It had an edge like a razor and the sides of the blade were engraved with Arabesque geometric designs. The curved blade was protected inside an oiled leather scabbard. On one side of the hilt was engraved his name, and on the other side was the name of the madrassa.

"Let this dagger remind you of your destiny," Imam Waziri told him. "Until you are old enough to carry a sword to avenge the faith, let the point of this blade stir up your heart in eternal hatred against the enemy."

"Who is the enemy?"

"Satan is the enemy. But the enemy is also anyone who is not of the faith, because they are an offence against Islam and are the agents of Satan," his mentor said with great conviction. "There is only one true faith, and all who are not believers are infidels. We must wage war against the infidels, first in our heart and then in whatever place we find them. Do not ever forget this, Husam al Din. It is the destiny of your life, indeed the destiny of your very name, to plunge the point of the sword into the heart of the infidels."

"How am I to do that, being only a child?" he asked.

"You will find a way. It will be shown to you what you must do. But for now you must prepare yourself in every way."

"When must I begin?"

"Begin today," the Imam taught, "to train up your heart in anger and hatred against the infidels. When you are twelve years old, we will begin to train you in other ways."

"Then I will hate them already," Husam al Din promised, taking the dagger from its scabbard and smiling at the gleaming blade. "Thank you for this wonderful gift. It feels good in my hand. And the hatred already feels good in my heart."

****

When he was twelve, al Din received the promised sword. It was a weapon of beauty, a Saif with a silver hilt patterned after the shape of a pistol grip, and an ornately tooled guard and pommel. The polished blade curved wickedly toward a deadly point, and a matching curved silver scabbard held a loop meant for a belt or waist sash.

"This sword is after the fashion of the old Arab blades from the classic era when Arabia ruled the world," Imam Waziri told him.

"Arabia ruled the world?" Husam al Din asked, not as a challenge, but merely as a matter of awe.

"Nearly so," the old man said. "The Arabs established a vast empire, which in its classic period stretched from the Atlantic Ocean, across North Africa and the Middle East, to central Asia." Then, with a faraway look in his eyes, he said, "The empire will rise again, one way or another. Out of Arabia came Islam, and Islam is destined to rule the world. And you, my son, for you are as a son to me … you will help that to happen."

****

When he was 14, Husam al Din was given a Kalashnikov automatic rifle and the training to shoot it with a high degree of accuracy. From then on, part of each day was spent on the firing range. Some days, he went with his trainers into the western desert wilderness to practice shooting and moving, shooting and moving, as if he were facing an enemy force of many men. He carried the rifle held horizontally out in front of him as he ran an obstacle course of boulders and logs. The training was rigorous and, at first, his muscles ached and quivered with exhaustion.

"It is good," he was told. "It is meant to build your arm and shoulder muscles, and the burn and trembling mean that your muscles are being torn down so they can be built even stronger."

In the midday heat, he ran along the tops of logs that were suspended high above the ground, to develop his balance and endurance. To teach flexibility and balance on the beam, three trainers at once threw rocks at him, and he was forced to either dodge the rocks or suffer the pain of failure. Bruises were common, but as he continued with his training, the bruises became fewer in number. His goal was to pass through an entire training session without falling from a beam and to dodge every stone.

One day, he reached that goal, and he was openly praised by his trainers in front of all the other boys. It was a day he never forgot, and it made him think how fine it would feel to one day hear the praise of Allah for having done a good job with his mission of jihad. Although he was not large of stature, Husam al Din developed powerful muscles, quickness on his feet, and an uncanny sense of incoming weapons. Because of his excellent efforts, among all the boys at the madrassa, Husam al Din was the favorite of Imam Waziri.

"You are the pride of the madrassa," the old man told him, "but you must beware of pride in your heart."

Husam al Din thought about that advice for a long moment. "That is a hard thing," he said to his mentor. "How do I do that?"

"Pride is poison for the heart and is a thief of your strength. Stand with honour before Allah in all things. Defend the faith with all the vigour of your soul. But do it all for Allah, not for your own personal gratification. That is how you will defeat pride."
****

It was the end of September when a new boy came to the madrassa. Ali was sullen and he intentionally picked fights with the other boys.

"His heart may seem cold, but his life has been difficult," Imam Waziri told the students privately when Ali was not present. "His family lived in Qandahar and his parents were killed in an accident, as they travelled on the road to Qalat. Ali was spared but now that his parents are gone, he has no one to care for him, so he was sent to the madrassa orphanage here in Lashkar Gah because there is no other family member to take him in. For the sake of courtesy, let none of you speak of these things," Imam Waziri commanded the students. It would be too difficult for Ali to think about – at least for a while.
****

Ramadan was about to begin, the holy month of fasting, a time of worship and personal contemplation, a time when most Muslims draw close to family and community. But neither Husam al Din nor Ali, nor many of the other students at the madrassa, had families. They were their own community, secure behind protective walls that kept out the world. They were safe here – safe from the influences of the world, safe from contamination from outside, safe to preach and practice the traditions of Islam in exactly the way Imam Waziri wanted it to be taught and practiced.

"Not everyone who professes Islam is a true Muslim," the old man taught his class. "There are false Muslims who follow another path, and you must be watchful of them. It is an old conflict that dates back many hundreds of years, to a time just after the Prophet was carried into heaven, and there were those who wanted to steal the faith and change it to suit their own desires. They are kafir, and as much to be despised as any other infidel."

The words of Imam Waziri thrilled the heart of Husam al Din. There was no question what was right and what was wrong, and he had the madrassa to thank for teaching him these things that kept him safely on the right path. Ramadan, he decided, would be a special month for him when he would fast and pray and give thanks to Allah for showing him the way.

On the first day of Ramadan, in the chilly morning air, as the boys were standing at the water pump waiting their turn for the ablution before prayer, Husam al Din spoke to Ali. "You have lived all your life, until now, outside the madrassa. I have lived since the time of my birth inside these walls. The only times I have been outside, I was with teachers. Tell me, what is it like?"

The new boy had never looked happy since coming to the madrassa. His shoulders were rounded and slumped, and his face downcast. "Ah yes, life before this prison," Ali whined, "I played soccer and had many friends. Some of them travelled to other countries and they told me about those places and the things they saw. And I had many books to read. It wasn't anything like the madrassa. There is nothing interesting to do here."

"You should be thankful for the madrassa," Husam al Din said. "The Imam took you in. It is a safe place, and there are people here who will take care of you."

Ali's eyes flashed. "There are people here who beat me when I do things wrong," he complained under his breath, so the other boys could not hear what he said. "I hate it here."

"I do not," Husam al Din said. "This is my home."

"That is because you have never known anything else."

"What else do I need to know? Here I have the Holy Koran. The Imam leads me in the way I must live. I have the mosque and my prayers, food and a bed. What else do I need?"

"You need—" Ali began, then broke off his words when the way suddenly cleared for him to step into the shallow puddle below the pump and perform his ablution. "Ah," he bitterly spit, "never mind. You wouldn't understand."

"Do not be so sure of what I would or would not understand," Husam al Din said. "I may be an orphan from birth, and have not seen all the things you have seen in the world outside the madrassa, but I am not stupid."

Ali quickly made a pass at his ablution, a hit-and-miss sprinkling and spattering, but no serious cleansing. And as Husam al Din watched, he knew that Ali's heart was not in it. Ablution was one of the most holy rites before prayer, and yet Ali was just rushing through it as if it did not matter.

"How can you approach Allah when you are still unclean?" Husam al Din challenged.

"Hah!" Ali turned to face him with a scowl. "You worry about your approach to Allah, and I will worry about mine. Okay?"

"You mock Allah. I hear it in your voice."

Ali pointed a finger and hissed through clenched teeth, "Allah allowed my whole family to be killed and left me an orphan. Do not lecture me about how great Allah is or how I say my prayers." Then he turned back to the pump and slapped a little more water on his hands.

"Do not say such things. That is blasphemy."

"I can say whatever I want," Ali insisted, "and there is nothing you can do to stop me. What are you going to do, tell the Imam so he can beat me again? Someday I will get out of this hole and I will be free."

An ugly thought rose in Husam al Din's mind. "You are not truly Muslim," he blurted. It was out before he realised it.

Ali turned on him. "What do you mean I'm not Muslim. Of course I am."

"I said you are not *truly* Muslim. Not in your heart. You may be Muslim from the lips outward, but not in your heart. You are an infidel of the worst kind, because you pretend to be what you are not. How dare you stand here in the waters of ablution, at the very doorway to the mosque, and yet in your heart you are kafir!"

Without further thought, Husam al Din gripped his dagger, slid it from its scabbard, crouched low and lunged. The clean upward thrust of the blade split the fabric of Ali's shirt and sunk easily into the soft flesh just below the breastbone, penetrating Ali's heart. The boy's head jerked forward, butting into al Din's eyebrow, but the sudden pain only made al Din more determined. Blood flooded over the dagger's guard and down the hilt into Husam al Din's hand, past his wrist and up his forearm to his elbow. He felt the warmth and watched the red drops fall from his bent elbow and mingle with the water of ablution at the base of the pump.

How fitting, he thought, as he watched how the blood ran all the way to his elbow, but no farther. The ritual washing required cleansing to the elbows. *I will have to wash that arm carefully, to cleanse myself from the blood of this infidel.*

He dragged the body away from the pump, then calmly washed himself in preparation for prayer. Intentionally, he left a trace of blood on the hilt of his dagger, where the stain would remind him of his first infidel kill. Then he inserted the knife into the scabbard at his waistband, stroked it as other boys might pet a dog, and smiled. "Jihad feels good," he whispered to himself.

****

Imam Waziri sat with a serious face as Husam al Din entered the room. The old man was bent with age, but his mind was sharp and his eyes clear. "It is time for you to leave the madrassa."

"I am sorry if you think I have done something wrong," Husam al Din began.

"Do not apologise. I do not hold it against you." The old man shifted in his chair, looking for the right words. "You have been trained from birth to defend the faith. What you did at the pump of ablution will be spoken of by all who remain and all who follow. It will be a long time before anyone will disrespect Allah again in this madrassa. You have begun a legacy that will live on after you are gone."

"Why must I leave?"

"It is time for you to receive further training and preparation. We have done all we can do for you."

The boy stood before his revered teacher. "It is my only desire to serve my mission of jihad," he said. "Tell me what I am to do."

"You will be sent to the tribal land, and there you will receive your final preparation."

"I am ready, but I will miss this place. It is all I have known from my birth."

The old man smiled. "I will miss you, my son. But it is for the greater good. Tomorrow morning, after first prayer, a man will come to escort you. You must do as he says, even as you have done here."

He bowed his head in humility and repeated his mantra. "I am Husam al Din. I am the Sword of the Faith. My life is for jihad. I will prepare in every way."

****

The next morning, after prayer, a man drove a Land Cruiser to the front of the madrassa. Husam al Din had rolled his few clothes inside his prayer rug and tied it with a string. With his head up and shoulders back, as a real man should stand, he went out to meet the one who had come for him. Inside the car were two other men, and Husam al Din crawled into the empty space in the back seat, closed the door and the Land Cruiser sped away northward.

All day they travelled, and Husam al Din sat looking out the window at sights he had never seen. One of the men gave him a hard piece of bread, a bit of cheese and a flask of water. At the appropriate hours, they stopped for prayers, unrolled their prayer rugs toward Mecca, then afterward they continued their travels. Sunset came, then darkness embraced everything. In the middle of the blackest night he had ever known, and with headlights switched off, they crossed a high mountain pass and descended into the tribal area that spread across the ragged mountains between Afghanistan and Pakistan.

Many hours later, the Land Cruiser came to a stop in a small dusty village where the air was thin and the night was very cold. One of the men in the car gave Husam al Din a wool blanket, and he wrapped it around himself and was led to a small house made of mud brick. A hard bed awaited him, and he spread his blanket and slept the first night of his new life.

In the village, he met men who had fought the Soviets. These men were lean and hard. They wore their skin like leather, and not one of them showed a smile. These were warriors who had slept out on the unforgiving ground among scattered rocks, living in crags and caves when everything froze solid. They had gone days without food or water, hiking the high passes on ragged shoes and bloody feet, fighting with antique weapons that were scavenged, rebuilt and pressed into service. These men were giants in Husam al Din's eyes, and those who were wounded bore the scars of war like a badge of honour. It was these men who would be his trainers.

****

Months passed, then years. Each day was the same as the last, filled with prayer and training. Weapons from all around the world were there for his study, and he learned to dismantle and re-assemble rifles, shotguns and handguns in the dark of night or while his eyes were covered. From scattered components thrown on the dusty ground, he was able, by touch alone, to pick out the right pieces, clean them and assemble a weapon.

It was the same with explosive devices, firing systems and booby traps. On the training range, anti-tank and anti-personnel mines were booby-trapped and buried, and he was required to locate and disarm them. Then he devised a different way to use the same components to booby-trap the mine and lay it for the next trainee to locate and disarm. The mines were dummies, but the blasting caps and booby-traps were live, and a mistake could be painful and possibly even disabling. Dangerous as the training was, humiliation from his peers was the biggest deterrent to failure. As part of his demolition training, he was taught how to use everyday household products to formulate and detonate improvised explosive devices.

During his second year in the village, he was schooled as a driver and mechanic, and was taught how to defeat automobile security systems and steal a car without getting caught. High-speed attack driving techniques were part of the curriculum, as well as counter-attack methods, the first training him to chase another vehicle and run it off the road and then how to avoid being the victim of the same thing.

In his third year, he was taken to a remote beach in southern Pakistan and taught powerboat operations, to prepare him in every way to conduct a suicide mission against enemy ships, if he were ever called upon to do so. The training was comprehensive, including the use of radar, GPS, electronic chart plotters and the use of paper charts and rudimentary navigation tools in case electronics were not available. He learned to operate marine radio systems and to rig up an emergency antenna.

Regardless of the nature of the military training Husam al Din was undergoing while at the village high in the mountains of the tribal territory, every day included strict adherence to the schedule of prayer and the study of Islamic fundamentalist doctrine. With what he considered to be a righteous pride for his people, he looked upon the old men, the weathered warriors of the Soviet conflict. They were his teachers, his mentors, his idols. He listened to their stories and admired their scars. *Someday,* he vowed to himself, *I will wear the scars and be a hero. Perhaps one day, a martyr. I will be the Sword of the Faith, as my name has destined.*

****

In October, 2001, the Americans invaded Afghanistan and for Husam al Din the reality was that the infidels of the new holy war were the Americans.

Chapter Four

September, 2007 – Northern Afghanistan

"Sergeant Adams," the voice called from across the empty street. "I've got mail for you." Josh Adams had been in Afghanistan for seven months, and it seemed that incoming mail was never frequent enough.

"Thanks, corporal," Adams shouted as he sprinted across to meet the young troop who handed him the envelope. "Ah, good, it's from Rachel," he said as he held the envelope to his face and inhaled. "Hmmm, she must have forgotten the perfume this time. Well, no matter, at least it's a letter. I do love to hear from that girl." He grinned at the corporal. "Now you better run off and deliver the rest of the mail. I'm going to sit down here in the shade and enjoy myself."

"Right, sergeant," the corporal half shouted. He was young and was new to the unit, so he was a bit intimidated by sergeants and tended to come to attention and shout in their presence.

Josh laughed at the corporal. "Stick around; you'll get over that."

"What?" the corporal asked.

"Ah, never mind." Josh laughed again. "I was just joking."

"That's one of the things I like about you, sergeant," the corporal said. "You have a great sense of humor. Over here, I think that's very important."

"Why thanks, corporal. Better keep moving. Lots of other guys waiting for their mail." He pulled out his Special Forces combat knife and carefully slit the envelope open, then pulled out the single sheet of paper. There wasn't much writing on it, and that worried Josh right away.

Dear Josh,

I don't quite know how to say this, so I better just get it over with. You and I have been together so long, but it seems like the time we're apart is even longer than the time we've spent together. The army is your life. I understand that. But I have to have a life, too. And I just can't have it with you. Rand Stroppe has proposed marriage – something you never seemed to get around to. I have accepted. We will be getting married next month. I'm sorry to have to break it to you this way, but I couldn't think of anything else to say.

Goodbye,

Rachel

He pushed his helmet back and sat in stunned silence, collapsed back against the wall as if all the air had gone out of him. The sheet of paper rustled in the breeze, held by loose fingers of a hand that lay limp on the ground. Two of the village men walked by and looked at him, but he didn't even pay attention to them. The men found that very strange, because these Special Forces soldiers were always sharp and aware of everything that went on around them.

"Marhaba, Sergeant Adams," one of the men said, meaning hello. Josh ignored him. "Kayfa haluk?"

Without looking up, Josh muttered, "Bihey. I am fine."

"You do not appear to be fine," the man continued.

Sergeant Adams was the A-team O&I specialist. All operations and intelligence men were trained as interpreters, so he was fluent in the Arabic language. He finally looked up into the watery eyes of an old man. The younger man stood back a little ways, allowing the elder gentleman to do the talking. "Well, I'm not really fine," the sergeant admitted. "My girlfriend back home has sent me a letter."

"Oh," the old man said, smiling. "That must make you happy."

"Normally, it would. But this letter is to tell me ma'assalama – goodbye."

The old man's gaze fell to the ground, and he wiped his eyes. "Oh," he said softly, "that is too bad. A sad day for you."

"Yes, very sad," Sergeant Adams agreed.

"I am sorry for you," the old man said. "May Allah bless you."

"Shukran, shukran," Josh said softly, thanking the man twice for his kind wishes, then lowering his head as if to sleep. But he did not sleep, he just thought about the letter.

One thing Josh Adams had discovered while in Afghanistan is that the rural folks in this unfortunate country were just as nice as the folks in his rural home in South Carolina. These people were caught in a bad situation, and had been for decades. But now the Special Forces teams were in the villages trying to befriend the people and help them recover from the devastation of the wars. There were schools to build, water and sanitation systems to repair, and bad feelings to mend.

A primary mission for his A-team was termed 'public affairs', which was just another way of saying public relations – helping the indigenous population come to understand that the United States was not their enemy, but was there to help them. His ability to speak their language went a long way toward fostering trust between them. He taught basic English classes to the school-age children, and that placed him right in the beam of the village spotlight because everybody wanted to learn English, even the older folks. It seemed that the whole village knew Sergeant Josh Adams, and most of the people liked him.

Beneath the surface, his work with the villagers had another purpose. As the people came to trust him, he asked them for their help in finding out who was setting improvised explosive devices along the roads to ambush American soldiers. "The sooner we get rid of the insurgents," Josh told the people, "the sooner life can become safe and normal in your village."

Most of the villagers seemed to trust the Americans, but there were always a few who held back, keeping to the shadows. The strange thing was that among the friendlies, nobody was willing to talk about those men. Josh saw fear in the eyes of the women and children, and men averted their eyes so Josh could see nothing there at all.

Major Alan Covington, the team commanding officer, found Josh sitting in the shade, his head down, the letter in his limp hand. "Hey!" the major said, "On your feet, sergeant. We've got work to do."

Josh raised his head and stared at his CO, then lowered his head again.

"I said on your feet, soldier!" Covington shouted in his most powerful command voice. "I want you on your feet now!"

This time, without even raising his head, Josh muttered, "Meaning no disrespect, but I don't feel like it, sir."

Major Covington squatted down and yanked Josh's head back so he could look him in the eyes. "You been taking drugs, boy?"

"No sir."

"You been shot?"

"Nope."

"Then what's wrong with you? Get on your feet. Show some respect. How do you expect the villagers to respect us if we don't show respect to each other?"

Josh looked up. "I honestly don't care, sir. You can take this war and shove ..."

"Shut your mouth, son, or I will shut it for you," Covington warned through gritted teeth. He stood, grabbed Josh by the shirt and lifted him to his feet, then slammed him back against the wall and shoved his nose right up in Josh's face. "When I tell you to do something, you do it. You got that?"

A small crowd of villagers gathered to watch what was going on. Old men muttered among themselves, and women whispered to each other. Children stood with wide eyes, staring at their trusted teacher being dragged to his feet by the major. Hearing the murmur behind them, Covington turned to look at the crowd. He waved his arm as if to sweep them away. "Go on now. Keep moving," he yelled in English. But they didn't move. They just pointed and talked among themselves about what was happening. "Tell them to get out of here," the CO commanded Josh. "You know their language."

"You're so smart, sir, you tell them yourself. The way I figure it, this is their town; they ought to be free to stand there if they want to."

"I'll have you up on charges of insubordination," the major threatened.

"Go right ahead, sir," Josh said. "I don't want to be in this man's army anymore anyway. It's done nothing but ruin my life." He waved the letter in front of the major's face.

"What's that?"

"A letter from my girl, sir. She's dumped me 'cause I'm not around much anymore. It's hard to be there for her and here for you and *all* of them," – he swept his arm toward the crowd – "all at the same time. And I sure don't love you or them as much as I love her. So go ahead and write me up and send me home so I can take care of more important business. 'Cause I don't care about any of this anymore."

Major Covington let go of Josh's shirt, stepped back and dusted the sergeant off. "Listen, kid," – he changed his tone – "you're just upset because some cheatin' chick back home is whining about not having you around. Give it a day or two, you'll get over it. Take my word, you're better off without a girl who dumps you just because she's lonely. If she's got no more grit than that, you're lucky to find it out this early in the game. Now go clean yourself up. You've got an English class to teach."

"Yes, sir," Josh said, putting his helmet on and bringing his right hand up in a slow salute that had no heart in it. Then he turned and walked away, leaving Covington alone on the street where the crowd still stood watching. Shaking his head, the major turned and walked in the opposite direction.

An hour later, Josh sat in a small dusty room, surrounded by villagers of all ages and both genders. One of the women noticed his downcast expression and asked, "What is the matter Joshua?" The villagers always called him by his full first name. It was easy for them, because it was a name right out of their scriptures, the leader who came after the prophet Moses. They knew of his girlfriend, Rachel – another name from their scriptures, the wife of Issac, son of the prophet Abraham. These were links that endeared Josh Adams to the people of the village, because they felt as if he were somehow one of their own.

"Ah," he said to the woman, "it is nothing to bother you about."

"Please," she said, "sometimes a burden shared becomes lighter."

He hesitated, then took the letter from his pocket. "I received this from Rachel today. She says she no longer loves me and she is going to marry another."

The woman broke into tears and sobbed, as if she were mourning for her own son. Josh reached out and touched her shoulder. "There is no need for tears. It is something I can do nothing about," he said.

"What would you do, if you could do something?" one of the men asked.

"Go home and fight for her heart," Josh answered.

"As any real man would," the man said, and the crowd murmured agreement.

"As much as I want to help your village, I am sorry to say that I no longer want to be here. I no longer want to be in the army. If it were not for the army, I would be home with Rachel and everything would be okay." He stopped for a moment, then put the letter back in his pocket. "But right now, it is time for your English lesson."
****

Class went well that day, but everyone was a little downcast in spirit. It was apparent that they all felt bad for Joshua, their teacher.

That evening, as Josh was hanging his uniform shirt next to his bunk at the barracks where the American team slept, he faced unrelenting lack of sympathy from his fellow soldiers. The story had gotten around about the incident after mail call that day, and the men were not about to let him off easy.

"Hey Josh," the weapons specialist Tony Blanco yelled across the room, "what's the matter, couldn't hold onto your baby?" The room erupted with laughter.

"Where did you guys get that from?" Josh challenged, knowing full well that Covington must have spilled the story to the rest of the team members. It wasn't necessarily a cruel thing to do because the major knew that the team came to feel like a band of brothers, and even though brothers give each other a hard time, they still support one another.

While Josh's attention was focused on Tony, one of the guys sneaked around behind his bunk and grabbed the letter from the shirt pocket. Waving it like a victory flag, he pretended to read it, using a falsetto voice to mock Rachel. "Dear Josh," he screeched, "I don't love you anymore."

Josh charged through the crowd of men as the one with the letter retreated for safety, then threw the sheet of paper and escaped out the door. Josh gathered up the wrinkled letter, folded it and placed it in his pants pocket, to the enthusiastic razzing of the men. "You'll pay for this, all of you," Josh shouted above the noise.

In the dimly lighted corner of the room, an Afghani boy who was hired by the team to keep their quarters clean laid aside a broom and dustpan. As the ruckus kept everyone's attention on the other end of the room, slowly he inched along the wall toward the door. His eyes were wide and staring at the fracas. When he reached the door, he quietly slipped outside and disappeared into the night.

Major Covington stepped through a door at the other end of the room. Almost immediately the place fell silent as he held up his hands and waved the noise level down. To a man, they all swung their heads to look at the open door, then their eyes turned back to Josh and then to the major.

"Good job, guys," Covington said. "A convincing act. I think we're off and running."

For the next several days, Josh was sullen and found reasons to be apart from the rest of his team. He ate alone, worked on the school building alone, refused to talk with the other soldiers. His face was no longer jovial, and his sense of humor seemed to have died. The change in his demeanor did not escape the notice of his English class members. When one of the women asked him how he was doing, he almost spit his answer.

"I hate the army and what it has done to my life. I'd do anything to get out of here, and when I go, I'll make sure they are sorry for what they've done to me."

The woman patted his arm in sympathy, and retreated quietly. From a place in the shade, Josh saw her later talking with a man he did not recognize, as they stood in the shadow at the corner of a building. The woman looked around nervously and seemed to be talking fast. The unknown man had thin eyes beneath bushy black eyebrows. His face was bony and covered with leathery skin. He reminded Josh of a shadowy figure that hangs around the dark perimeter, like a hungry wolf that shuns the light of the campfire, always waiting until the right moment to attack.

The next afternoon, that man came to Josh's English class, took a chair and sat quietly in the corner. After class, all the villagers left the room, but the stranger stayed.

"Can I help you?" Josh asked in Arabic.

"I believe I can help you," the man answered. "I understand you want to get out of my country and return to your home."

"Yes," Josh said.

"There is a woman I want you to meet."

"I don't need a woman," Josh said.

"No," the man smiled thinly, "not that kind of woman. She is old, and she can help you."

"How can she help me?" Josh asked.

"She knows people who can get you out of Afghanistan so you can go home, but you must confide in her your true feelings so she can decide how best to assist you."

"An old woman?" Josh asked. "A mother figure for me to talk to?"

"Exactly," the man said.

"I don't need a mother figure to talk to." Josh stood up as if to leave.

"You will find this woman helpful," the man said, and handed Josh a piece of paper. "This is how you will find her."

Josh looked quickly at the paper, then hearing someone enter the room, he folded it quickly and tucked it in his pocket. "Sergeant Adams," the voice called from the doorway. Josh recognized it as Covington. "I need a word with you." The major looked long and hard at the stranger. "Who's this guy?"

"Nobody. Just a fellow who thought he might like to learn English. But I don't think this class is what he's looking for." Josh shook the man's hand and said in Arabic, "I will seek her out. Thank you." The man lowered his head, bowed slightly and brushed by Covington on his way out the door, and he was not seen again in the village.

That night, Josh hit the bunk as usual and lights went out at 2200 hours. At 0400, one of the team members up for an early run to the toilet noticed that Josh's bunk was empty. A search of the compound turned up nothing. Sergeant Josh Adams was missing.

Chapter Five

Fierce wind beat against the tent walls, thrumming the taut material and whistling around the guy lines. Bits of sand made a speckling noise against the fabric as the desert storm raged. Inside, Sorgei Groschenko looked from one to the other of the two men seated at the table. Then he began. "I am a scientist. I worked in the field of weaponry until the collapse of the Soviet Union. That is all you need to know."

Husam al Din shook his head. "That is not all. Tell us about your motive for being here. I know these things, of course, but Sergeant Adams does not. And I am sure he will feel more comfortable about his role in all this if he understands your level of commitment."

Groschenko was quiet. Sensing the Russian's reluctance, Husam al Din turned to Josh Adams and continued. "He is here because he hates America for their interference in his country's affairs. It ruined his career. So, now that he has nothing else, he is here for the money. Everyone has a price, and our people are willing to pay it."

Josh Adams nodded. "Yeah, well I don't hate America, but I hate what America is doing here. We have no business even being here in the first place. The politics involved in this war are sickening. I'm only here because I have to be. I've got a contract with the army, but they've messed up my life plenty."

"Yes," Husam al Din said. "They deployed you to a war zone where you are very isolated, and now your girlfriend, Rachel, feels abandoned, but there is nothing you can do about it. Last week, you received a letter from her. She has plans to marry your old friend Randall Stroppe, who lives at 1547 Huntington Avenue in Palm Harbor, Florida. Am I correct so far?"

A look of bewilderment crossed Josh's face. "How do you know all of that? And how is it you speak English so well?"

Al Din showed his teeth through a cold smile. "As to the second question, I have had good teachers who believe it is important to know everything about the enemy, including his language. As to the first, it is my business to know what I need to know. And I know everything about you, Joshua Paul Adams. I know where you were born, where you went to school, where you have worked, your favorite foods, everything. Do you understand?"

"What does that have to do with anything? I only came here because I want out of the army. The old woman said you could help me. That is why I am here."

Husam al Din shook his head. "You are here because you were chosen. I chose you."

Josh stared across the table at al Din. "That's the second time you've said that. What do you mean that I was chosen?"

Husam al Din's smile disappeared and his eyes closed half way, showing dead pupils behind lowered lids. "You were chosen because of your special talents. If you refuse to cooperate with what I am about to tell you, I will simply find another to replace you. Someday your remains might be discovered along the Afghan–Pakistan border, a frozen and dehydrated mummy."

Josh stood up and slapped his hand on the table. "That sounds like a threat, and I don't like being threatened."

Husam al Din jumped to his feet, his eyes flashed and in his hand was the dagger. In a blur of motion the dagger came down hard; the point buried itself in the wood less than an inch from Josh Adams' splayed fingers. Josh leaped back with a startled yelp and at the sudden sound, two men stepped in through the tent door with AK47's pointed at his chest.

"Before you get yourself killed," Husam al Din warned through clenched jaws, "I suggest you sit back down and listen. You have a decision to make. If you decide to cooperate, you will eventually be set free and will be given a very large sum of money. You will be out of the army, and can go anywhere in the world you choose. If vengeance is in your heart, you can take care of Rachel and Randall Stroppe yourself or pay to have it done. Cooperate with me and maybe I can even work something out in that regard. We have people everywhere, even in Palm Harbor, Florida."

Josh shot an angry look at Husam al Din, glanced over his shoulder at the two men then rubbed his jaw and sat down. "What exactly is going on here?"

"It is very simple," Husam al Din said. "You have been kidnapped as easily as offering candy to a child to lure her into a stranger's car."

"You've got to be kidding!" Josh exclaimed.

"Don't look so surprised. It has happened many times before. Do you remember the reporter who was kidnapped and then was released six weeks later? What do you think he was doing for those six weeks? What happens to you after you are released depends upon you. If you are smart, you will take your money and keep your mouth shut. Just say you were not mistreated and let it go at that. You will be interrogated by your own government, but I am sure your Special Forces training will prepare you to handle that."

"How much money?" Josh asked.

"Seven hundred and fifty thousand American dollars," Husam al Din said without blinking.

"Whew," Josh whistled. "That's a pretty bright nickel. People would notice if I had that kind of money. How do I explain my sudden wealth?"

"Do not be a fool. The money will be placed in a secret account, so it cannot be traced. After we release you, we will give you the code to gain access to the account. Let some time pass before you start using the money. Let it trickle into your life. Develop a legitimate reason for having the income and no one will notice."

"How can you be sure I won't just go to the authorities and tell them everything?"

"There are two reasons you will not do that. First, if you try to double-cross us, we will set up the cash transfer and leak information that will make it look like you sold security secrets to your nation's enemy. You will get nothing, and you will be branded a traitor. The second reason is that it won't matter anyway because my plan will already be carried out by then."

Josh inhaled deeply, sat back in the chair and interlocked his fingers behind his head. "It looks like you've covered all your bases."

"I am an expert. We run a very sophisticated operation that you Americans have badly underestimated. You think that just because we live in a more primitive condition that we are not capable of planning such things as this. Trust me when I tell you that we are very well organized. We have satellite phones and computers. We have people in every country and in almost every city. Our motives are more important than life itself. If you doubt that, ask yourself why there are martyrs that you call suicide bombers."

"Well what do you want from me?" Josh asked.

Husam al Din relaxed his hand from the dagger, and sat back down. "I want some very specific information. Before you joined the army, you worked in the security division at the shipping harbor in Miami, Florida. You know the routine there for loading and unloading shipping containers, and you are familiar with all the security procedures. I brought you here to tell me everything you know about those things."

"Why do you want to know about that?"

"I have my reasons," al Din said flatly.

"That's it? All you want is for me to tell you about port security?"

Husam al Din nodded.

"If you know everything else about me, how is it you can't find out about those things?"

"Information comes to me one bit at a time, gathered from one person at a time. It is the same with this. I will gather this information one bit at a time from one person. Right now, you are that person."

Josh sat back and quietly studied the cold, emotionless eyes of Husam al Din.

"The fact is, you already know too much to back out and avoid the consequences," Husam al Din said. "You know about Sorgei Groschenko and you know about me. It is already too late to disappoint me and still remain alive, but I will leave the decision to you. I can always find another. The rewards for you will be great, but if you fail me … well, I have already told you what will happen. I do not have much time for you to try to negotiate. I need an answer now. What is your decision?"

Josh was quiet. His face displayed the uncertainty of a man caught in a trap with no easy way out. He stared at Husam al Din, then lowered his eyes to the table and pondered the situation in silence.

Husam al Din's eyes narrowed to slits. "Sergeant Adams," – he spoke slowly – "do not mess with me." He pried the tip of the dagger out of the table, held the point toward Josh and spun it in his hand so the blade glinted in the light. The two men stared at each other, neither one flinching.

After a prolonged, uncomfortable silence, Sorgei Groschenko cleared his throat. "Gentlemen, are we going to work as a team or not?"

Without shifting his eyes, Husam al Din said, "That depends upon Sergeant Adams. Right now, I am not sure he can be trusted."

Josh shot back. "My question is, how do I know that *you* can be trusted?"

"Because I am a true Muslim," Husam al Din replied. "Unlike your society, where a man may give his word and then not honor it, the Holy Koran teaches that Muslims must honor our word. We must act in fairness in all our business dealings. We must speak the truth."

"If you are so honorable, why are you attacking America?"

"Honor is a matter of fulfilling our duty, it has nothing to do with our choice of an enemy. We will be the most honorable enemy America has ever had, but an enemy we must be. American society was not always as it is today. Today it is an affront to Muslim values. Yours is a godless country, and your country spreads indecency across the world like a vile stench through your vulgar movies and magazines, immodest clothing, greed – these are the things that threaten and offend the Muslim world. Your government has a nasty habit of interfering in the affairs of nations that prefer to be left alone. We cannot allow your country to contaminate our people. So we will stop you."

"So that's the great plan?" Josh asked. "You're going to clean up the world by getting rid of America?"

Husam al Din nodded his agreement. "A difficult task, but one that must be done."

"Well good luck, buddy." Josh laughed. "Even if you wiped out America, have you taken a look at the stuff that's going on in the rest of the world? What about the fashion industry in France or Italy, or the loose lifestyle of the Danish. Or the Rossebuurt district of Amsterdam, with their public solicitation of prostitutes behind picture windows on their main streets. And maybe I should clue you into what's going on throughout Asia with children for sale. Listen, I'll admit we have our share of problems, but if you think America has the corner on filth and corruption, you need to wake up and take a look around."

"Yes," Husam al Din agreed. "The whole world is evil. Let me assure you that we will deal with that one step at a time. Right now, America is the enemy I am focusing on, for reasons other than moral decadence and failure to honor Allah. There is the Palestinian issue."

"Hey, that issue has nothing to do with the families in Northwoods, Iowa who go to church every Sunday and contribute to charities to help starving children they've never even met in some Third World country. Yeah, we've got our share of rascals, but American's are, for the most part, good and charitable God-fearing people. And there's nothing honorable about attacking innocent women and children who are non-combatants. In fact, that Holy Koran of yours even forbids it."

"What do you know of the Holy Koran?"

"Enough to know that what you are doing now would be an outrage to Mohammed."

"The Prophet Mohammed, Salla Allahu 'Alaihi Wa Sallam, would agree with what we are doing now. It is only to protect Islam from the pollutions of your world. I don't expect you to understand, or to agree with it. You are not Muslim. You are contaminated by your society. But even as you do not want us to attack your world, we do not want the pollutions of your world to attack ours. We are courageous enough to do something about it. In your country, there is too much concern about political correctness for you to be able to solve your own problems. So we will do it for you. The world will be a better place after the jihad."

"If I might ask," – Josh looked over at Sorgei then back at al Din – "why do you need him? You guys seem to be capable of building your own weapons and bombs."

"Sorgei has special talents. Just as you have special talents," Husam al Din said.

"So you have this jihad plan that involves Sorgei and me. From what Sorgei said of his background, and from what you're asking of me, I'm guessing your jihad is an attack on the Port of Miami, using a shipping container to deliver some kind of special weapon that Sorgei developed. And you're hoping my expertise will help get you past port security. That about right?"

"You are quick to understand, Sergeant Adams," Husam al Din said.

"Why pick on Miami?" Josh asked.

"I have done research, and Miami is a very decadent society that represents all that is offensive to Islam."

"Yeah, but did you ever stop to think that there are lots of Muslims who live in Miami? It's a big city, you know, and there are mosques there and I'm sure the population of Muslims is substantial."

Husam al Din smiled. "I see what you are trying to do, Sergeant Adams, but it will not work. I am not persuaded to avoid attacking America simply because there are Muslims there who will be killed along with the kafir. We will all die someday. It does not matter how we die, only how we live. And it does not matter how long we live, only what we do while we are alive. Innocent Muslims who are casualties in our jihad will be rewarded by Allah. Jihad is a purification process for the world. America is on the wrong path, and it must be cleansed."

"And you expect me to buy into that?"

"You admit that your political leaders are corrupt. They interfere in parts of the world where they have no business. Your foreign policy has ruined the way of life of so many in other countries. It must be stopped."

Sorgei Groschenko stood up and walked around the table, stretching his back and arms. "If you guys want to argue politics and religion all night, that's your business. Frankly I didn't come here for this. Let's get down to it."

"You are right," Husam al Din agreed, then looked again at Josh. "Sorgei and I have worked together for a while. But you are new to this. We need to be sure about your involvement. As they say in your country, the ball is in your court."

Josh squirmed in his chair, then stood and walked around the inside of the large tent. Each step of the way, he was followed by the eyes of the two guards and muzzles of their AK47s. The fabric of the tent began to relax; the wind was quieting. Outside, the sandstorm was blowing itself out. After an uneasy moment, he sat back down and placed his forehead in his hands on the table.

"You are suffering with your decision," Husam al Din said. "Do not waste your time or mine. Consider the suffering you will bring upon yourself if you make the wrong decision. Allow me to clarify things: you can either have your life and lots of money; or you can die tonight."

"I have trouble with the concept of selling my loyalty at any price."

"I do not expect you to sell your loyalty. I need only to be able to trust the information you give me. In exchange for that, you will have your life. When this is over, you will have enough money to be wealthy. This is a simple business deal. You get what you want and I get what I want. The choice is before you. Trust me when I tell you that if you do not cooperate, we will get rid of you tonight, and then we will simply find another to replace you. My plan might be delayed a short time," – he shrugged as if it were a small matter – "but it will still go forward. You are merely a convenient way to learn what I need, but you are not the only way. I will do this with or without you. There is no way you can stop it by refusing to save yourself."

Josh shifted in his chair and looked off into space. "You're right about one thing. I have no doubt that our leaders are misguided. Some say they're corrupt, but I think they're just being stupid."

"You are correct," Husam al Din agreed. "They are stupid, but they are also power-hungry and corrupt. They want to police the world, but they have no right."

"I know it isn't right what they're doing. They not only screwed up my personal life, they've done a lot worse than that. Our true system of government was bypassed to get this war started, and unless something is done things are going to get worse. I wish I knew how to stop the violation of our Constitution, but I am only one man – and the government won't listen to only one voice."

"You are right in feeling that way," al Din nodded again. "Your government is deaf to your concerns, but there is a way to open their ears."

"Not that I agree with your methods, but maybe a little attack on the port can shake things up enough to make people stop and think about what's going on. Blow up a few containers, damage a ship and the terminal – maybe then they will start worrying about security at home and quit starting wars abroad. After what happened on September 11th, everybody pulled together for a while, but then the same old political wrangling started again. And now here we are. Something needs to happen."

"You are beginning to think clearly," Husam al Din said. "Perhaps you are thinking clearly enough to save your own life." He turned to look at Sorgei, who at first shrugged his shoulders but then finally nodded. He turned to face Josh Adams and raised his eyebrows in question.

Josh stared at the table, then raised his eyes to meet those of Husam al Din, and he quietly nodded.

Husam al Din pushed back from the table and stood up. "Come, gentlemen, the Land Cruiser is concealed in a distant canyon. We have many hours to travel before we sleep."

****

Late that night, the Land Cruiser approached the summit of a high pass. Armed men appeared from behind a cluster of boulders that narrowed the roadway from both sides, creating a natural gateway that was an ideal place for an ambush. The men stepped in front of the vehicle and trained their weapons through the windows. Husam al Din identified himself and spoke for a few moments with the men, who then moved aside and let the vehicle pass. In the early morning hours, deep in tribal territories, the three men arrived at a plain-looking, mud brick house. They were greeted by armed men, then shown inside where rooms had been prepared for them.

As he dropped from consciousness into sleep, Husam al Din thanked Allah for hating America as much as he did. A man needs purpose in life, a vision, a goal, and his was clear – to destroy America, at least as much of it as he could. If he died in the process, which he fully intended, so much the better. Eternal life as a martyr was the highest glory. He hated all Americans, even though he never actually met one in person until Josh Adams stepped into the tent only hours earlier. He found the young sergeant strangely affable and actually enjoyed arguing with him. It was an entertaining mental exercise, and only strengthened his love of Islam and the tenets of the Holy Koran.

Still, no matter how much he enjoyed his brief debate with the American, it was at the same time disgusting, for he was dealing with an enemy. America was an enemy to be destroyed, not converted through debate and reason. America was more than merely an infidel nation: it represented all that was evil in the world. Offensive as it was for Husam al Din to be in such close contact with an American, to achieve his goal he would, if necessary, exploit an American like Josh Adams. His final thought before sleep overtook him was that being able to use one American to kill thousands, perhaps millions, of other Americans was going to be especially sweet.

Chapter Six

San Blas Islands, Eastern Caribbean

"Maria Elena, it is time to go." The small woman's voice carried from the edge of the palm forest, across the beach to shallow water where two girls stood knee deep looking for tiny cone shells. Her straight black hair was cut across her forehead, leaving a hard line of bangs. From her nose hung the traditional gold Cuna nose ring and the ridge of her nose wore a straight line that ran from bridge to tip. She was dressed in a bright red mola blouse and a blue skirt that hung to her sandaled feet.

"Oh, Cadee, I will miss you," the brown-skinned Indian girl moaned. "You are the best friend I have."

Cadee Plover opened her arms wide and the two girls hugged. "And I shall miss you, too," Cadee moaned. "But who knows, maybe my dad and mom will want to come back here again. This is such a beautiful place."

"Maria Elena," the woman said softly as she walked into the water to join the girls, hiking her skirt to her knees. "It's almost time for your lessons. The school will not wait."

"I know, Mama," the girl bowed her head in submission to the schedule. Then she brightened. "Cadee said maybe her family can come back again sometime. Wouldn't that be nice?"

"Yes, it would," the older woman said. "Cadee, I have made a gift for your family. Will you please give this to your mother?" She unfolded a large square of cotton cloth that was hand-decorated with intricate reverse-stitch embroidery. "This mola tells of our family history. Maybe when you look at it you will remember us."

"Oh, thank you. This is so beautiful. We will never forget you," Cadee cried as she hugged the woman. "You have been so kind to us. I know my mom and dad and my brother Jacob wanted to be here to say goodbye, but they went to buy provisions for the next leg of our voyage. I'm supposed to meet them at the pier in an hour. Actually, I think Jacob wanted to say goodbye to the store owner's daughter." She laughed.

"Ah, yes," said Mrs Morales, "she is a nice girl. I have seen the interest in Jacob's eyes when he looks at her." This set them all to giggling. "Now, we must go. We have far to walk to get back to the village school. I know it is hard to say goodbye, but don't be long, my daughter." The woman turned and walked back up the beach, put on her sandals and disappeared into the cluster of palms.

"I'll be right there, Mama," the girl called. Then she turned to Cadee with a look of serious concern. "I know I am only 10 and you are 11, and you may think of me as only a child, but ..."

"No I don't," Cadee insisted. "I know what it feels like to be treated like a child. Jacob does that to me sometimes. Being 17, he thinks he is so grown up." She rolled her eyes.

"I must tell you something important," Maria Elena interrupted. "Be careful where you are going. There are islands where there is no law, no government protection. There are pirates."

Cadee looked surprised. "You're kidding. Pirates of the Caribbean?" She laughed. But Maria Elena didn't laugh, and Cadee saw that her friend hadn't caught the humor in it. "You know, Pirates of the Caribbean – like at Disneyland. It's a joke."

"I am not telling a joke," Maria Elena said, more serious than before. "I do not know about this place you call Disneyland, but there are very bad pirates out in some of those islands where you will be sailing. You must be careful. Do not stop at those islands."

"What do the pirates do?" Cadee asked as the girls walked back up the beach and slipped into their sandals.

"They steal everything. I have been told that they even steal children, then sell them. And if you try to stop them, they will kill you. They have machetes and guns, and they have no soul."

Cadee was quiet for a moment, thinking about all this. She looked into the eyes of her new friend, then wrapped her arms around her again. "Thank you for warning me. This is a very serious matter, and I will tell all this to my father. I promise."

"Tell your mother and your brother, too. They all must know of the danger. I do not want anything bad to happen to your family."

"I will," Cadee whispered as they hugged.

"You will be in my prayers every night and every morning," Maria Elena promised.

"And you will be in mine," Cadee agreed. "If we pray for each other, we should be able to stay out of trouble, don't you think?"

"I believe that will help," Maria Elena said. "Now, I must hurry to my lessons. God be with you." The young Cuna girl turned and ran into the cluster of palms, clutching her hands to her face, hiding the tears.

"And with you," Cadee said under her breath, as she waved at the spot where her friend had disappeared through the foliage.

Chapter Seven

"So, you're heading for the Rio Dulce?" Sven Nielsen was the proprietor of the closest thing to a store on Ychutupu island, a crossroads for cruising sailors passing through this tropic archipelago. The store was just a large palm-thatched hut, blending perfectly with local architecture, but a rough sign hung out front that read 'Viking Mall'. Sven had been in the San Blas for twenty-two years, after leaving his native Denmark on a 32-foot ketch, with a dream of sailing around the world. He got this far, looked around and decided he'd gone as far as he needed to go. *Why go looking for paradise when I'm already here?* he reasoned.

"Yeah, that's the plan," Dan Plover nodded as he laid his list on the counter. "We need to stock up on a few more things before we get so far up the jungle river that we can't get back for a re-supply. Nicole hates running out of stuff like toothpaste and floss," Dan smiled.

"If it were me," – Sven looked up from the list – "I'd wait a while before leaving."

Dan forgot about the list and looked at the tall Dane. "Sounds like you're trying to tell me something."

"I know your *Gemini* is a good, seaworthy boat, and she rides nice and comfortable on the water, being a cruising catamaran, but I still wouldn't risk it with the storm. Especially with a family on board."

"What storm?" Dan asked. "I must have missed something."

"Well, there is no storm yet. Maybe there won't be one."

A tone of concern was in Dan's voice. "I thought most of the tropical storms this time of year were farther east and north."

"That is true. But this is a quirky time of year, and you just never know."

"So, if there's no storm, what are you worried about?"

"I've been here, let's see …" – he stared at the ceiling and started counting on his fingers – "… what year is it anyway? I tend to lose count. Oh yeah, I got it. I've been here twenty-two years, and in that time I've kept track of the bad blows that swept through the area where you're heading. Right here, we're far enough south to be out of the storm track, but farther north you could get hammered. I'm just saying I wouldn't go right now. But you know what they say about advice: it's free, and maybe it's worth what you pay for it."

"No, no, no." Dan waved off Sven's comment. "Local knowledge is worth a ton, and anybody who ignores it deserves all the grief that comes to him."

"Well, I don't know about that," Swen said, "but there have been some huge late-season storms in this area before. They're not the norm, but they do happen every once in a while. Myself, I like to lay low from the 1st of June to the end of November. Just kind of hide out and plan my long-range sailing for the winter."

"Hey," Dan said, "your daughter Kirsten didn't put you up to this just to keep Jacob around, did she?"

"Heh-heh," Sven chuckled. "That girl of ours has taken a liking to your boy. Normally, I'd be more than a little worried about something like that, being a protective dad and all. But you folks have been here for nearly three months now and I've come to know your Jacob pretty well. He's a fine lad. Good upbringing, I'd say. And Kirsten is a good girl with solid values, so I don't worry too much about them. They're more friends than anything."

"When we left Seattle, Jacob was barely 14," Dan said. "He used to help us at the clinic. He seemed to have a good rapport with the young students who were struggling to learn sign language. When we first got the clinic going, Nicole and I practiced sign all the time around the house, and Jake picked it up. Then later on, he got involved with us after school, teaching our younger students, and he never had time to go on a date. In fact, he hated girls back then. Well, maybe he didn't really hate them. Guys just talk like that, but he had no real interest in girls until now."

Sven nodded. "Yeah, I've noticed that he does have an interest now."

Both men nodded, and Dan turned to look out the door at the crystal blue cove. "A healthy interest, I'd say. But I don't know how interested Kirsten is."

Sven stepped around from behind the counter. "You can imagine what it's been like for Kirsten, growing up here on the islands. Her only friends are the Cuna and a few kids who have passed through the area on their way to someplace else. Kids come and go so fast that she has learned to be very careful not to let her heart get away from her. Friendships come easily to her, but then they tend to disappear over the horizon just as easily."

"Same with Jacob," Dan said. "Then along comes Kirsten. It's still just a great friendship, but I can see the possibilities."

"Good thing these kids of ours have a strong foundation," Sven said.

"Yeah, Kirsten has been out to our boat a couple of times. Jake's been teaching her sign language, and she seems to be picking it up real well. The kids go snorkeling together, and they always invite Cadee to go with them. It's great to see them all get along so well together. Talk about good upbringing, I'd say you and Grendel have done a great job."

"She's a good wife, my Grendel," Sven beamed. "Never thought I'd meet somebody like her way out here in the middle of nowhere."

"That was pretty lucky, I'd say. And to think a gorgeous blonde Swede like that gave up her own dreams of a solo circumnavigation just to settle down with the likes of you." Dan jabbed the big Dane on the shoulder with his fist.

"Guess I was irresistible."

"Oh, hah! That's a good one," Dan laughed. "Well, I guess that's the game, isn't it? We ugly men have to do our best to keep our pretty women thinking we're irresistible."

"Yah," Sven reverted to his Danish accent, "and imagine how hard that is for a Swede and a Dane, with our inbred competing Viking interests and all."

"What a match!" Dan laughed again. "But you two seem to have united Scandinavia here in the tropics. I don't suppose you tell too many crazy Swede jokes?"

"I've forgotten all about Swede jokes. Survival and self-preservation," Sven said. "And she's pretty good about not picking on the Danes too much. I call her my Swedeheart, and she calls me her Great Dane."

"That's a good one," Dan said as he looked nervously at his watch. "Nicole's supposed to meet me here pretty soon. Jacob and Kirsten are down by the pier saying their goodbyes. But dang! Now you've got me thinking that maybe we better lay over here for a while longer and let the storm season close out before we head north."

Sven shrugged his shoulders. "What do you want to do about this list?"

Dan picked up the paper, folded it and stuffed it in his pocket. "Guess we've got enough toothpaste and floss to see us through. And we know where to come and buy more when we need it."

"Hmmm, seems like I've talked you out of leaving any of your money with me today." Sven smiled. "But I'll get it eventually."

"I have no doubt that you will, my friend." Dan reached out his hand and Sven clasped it in their familiar strong handshake, gripping each other's thumbs in arm wrestler fashion and jacking their hands back and forth as if they were on opposite ends of a two-man crosscut saw. "Guess it's time for an executive decision," Dan said. "The admiral's not here, so it's left to the captain. But I'm sure she'll agree one hundred percent. Nicole is not one who enjoys heavy weather sailing."

"Well, you're only talking about another two months until the end of the hurricane season. When you're cruising, you're not supposed to be on the clock anyway. Right?"

"Are you sure you're not trying to get us to stick around so we will buy more stuff from you?"

Sven grinned. "Clever plan, don't you think? In the meantime, you can cruise up and down the island chain and see the rest of our 360 some odd bits of paradise."

"Okay, you've convinced me. Hey, why don't you bring Grendel and Kirsten out to the boat this evening. We can throw some fresh fish on the grill, the kids can play three-handed cribbage in the main salon, and we adults can lay out the cockpit pads on the foredeck and watch the sun go down.

"Can't think of anything we'd rather do," Sven said. "How about if we bring a fruit salad?"

"Perfect. I have a hunch the kids are going to be delighted. Cadee has been moping around for the last two days. Her little friend Maria Elena has been the closest thing Cadee's ever had to a bosom buddy. It's been hard on her to think of moving on."

"If you'll watch the store for me for a few minutes, I'll run over and let Grendel know about tonight. By the way, do you have your fish yet?"

"Nope."

"After I close up, let's grab our Hawaiian slings and I'll show you a little place where the fish are fat and willing. If we're lucky, maybe we can snag a couple of nice lobsters."

Chapter Eight

October 3rd – The Land Without Laws

Early October was cold in the village, but at an elevation of more than 8,000 feet, that was expected. Already snow had fallen on the higher peaks. Summer was over, and a long winter lay ahead. Sunrise came late and the sun disappeared over the western mountains by mid-afternoon. The growing season was short in these mountains, and some years it was non-existent, as early frosts killed garden vegetables even in mid-summer. In a good year, the people who chose to live here could grow only a portion of their own food in the few lower pastoral valleys. The rest came from outside. But food was the least of their concerns.

Those who lived in this forsaken no-man's land did so primarily because of the autonomous status of this mountainous buffer zone that lay between Afghanistan and Pakistan. Officially, the region comprised seven tribal zones known collectively as the Federally Administered Tribal Areas, but in the local language it was simply called 'ilaqa ghair', the Land Without Laws.

By an agreement that had been struck after a long history of bloodshed, the Pashtun people of the tribal areas formally became part of Pakistan. While they were granted a seat in parliament, tribal laws forbade the existence of political parties, so only the tribal elders were allowed to vote. In every case, they passionately rejected any government interference that threatened their autonomy. Even though the region received financial support from Pakistan, the people refused to submit to Pakistani laws.

It was an arrangement that suited the society of gangsters, weapons dealers and drug lords perfectly. Opium was their cash crop, produced and processed into heroin, then distributed through a network that fed the drugs into the international market. Money from the sale of narcotics was converted into whatever staples the people needed. Besides drugs, the second most important industry was weapons. Tribal law and social custom required that every man have a gun, and the area flourished as a center of arms production, both for local use and to supply terror organizations such as al-Qaeda. There were no taxes collected on money earned or goods sold. Internal fighting was a way of life, as rival clans warred against each other for power and control of the weapons and narcotics industries, and disputes were most often settled with guns and axes. The bloodstained landscape was a monument of pride and honor among the men, and the children were raised with battle and bloodshed in their hearts.

Sorgei Groschenko was not happy living in such a barbarous society. Coming from a strictly controlled Soviet nation, this unstructured culture struck him as being completely unhinged and disconnected as it operated seemingly without rules or direction. He longed for structure and order, and in this place nobody knew from one day to the next who was in charge or what the rules were. It disturbed him greatly as he labored in his makeshift lab.

Not only that, but he was cold again. There was no heat or insulation in the tiny mud brick house where he worked, and he was beginning to remember the worst days of Siberia all over again. Bitter cold penetrated the walls during the day, and at night it was worse as he shivered himself to sleep on the thinly padded pallet, covered only by a single wool blanket.

Why couldn't these terrorists set up shop on the warm shores of the Black Sea, he wondered. Why did they always choose the most inhospitable patch of ground on the planet to hide out? But at least he was well paid, and for that he was grateful. There was nothing about this project that he wanted his name attached to – no fame or glory this time – so the money had to be sufficient to fill the hole in his inadequately gratified ego. The sooner this project was completed and he got out of this frozen purgatory, the better.

"How is it coming?" Husam al Din asked as he stepped into the small room that Sorgei used as a lab.

"Slow," Sorgei replied, without taking his eyes away from the microscope. The counter was scattered with an assortment of Petri dishes, beakers, a small butane burner and an incubator for growing his crop of deadly bacteria. "The secret is to get the biotoxin to pace its growth after it is released, so no one even suspects it is there until it has a chance to spread from person to person. If people start getting sick too quickly, the government will issue a quarantine to contain it, then the impact will not be so great."

"Yes," Husam al Din agreed. "But when do you think you will have it?"

Sorgei Groschenko looked up from the microscope, massaged his tired eyes with his fingers and heaved a sigh of frustration. "I wish I could tell you that I have it already."

"Yes, but when? There are many plans to be set into motion, but I can do nothing until you are ready with the toxin."

Sorgei looked up from the microscope. "Well, I'm doing all I can do. I'm working around the clock, as if there were anything else to do in this paradise resort."

"You are supposed to be the best." Husam al Din was agitated. "You are being well paid."

"Look, these experiments take time. Each strain must be fully developed, then tested to see how they respond."

"Yes," the Arab agreed, "for the plan to work, the toxin must travel unnoticed from host to host by direct contact. It must have a long incubation period so it will not show itself too quickly. There must be enough time for the germ to spread across a wide area before even the first host becomes ill."

"The way I am designing this bacteria, anyone who comes in contact with it either by touch or by inhaling it, will become a host. Once inside a host, the bacteria will become active and begin to work, but there will be no symptoms for many hours. Anyone else who comes into contact with the host will become infected. And the disease will be passed along from person to person by carriers traveling on airplanes, trains or buses across the country. By the time the illness begins to manifest, a few days will have elapsed, and by that time thousands will be infected without knowing it. The germ will spread like a deadly wind, impossible to stop and moving so fast that no one will be able to determine where it came from."

Husam al Din nodded. "That is the beauty of this weapon. Before anyone realizes the disease has arrived, it will be too late to do anything about it."

Sorgei Groschenko smiled and looked into the twin microscope eyepieces again. "This is the culmination of the work I was doing before the Soviet Union fell. I am anxious to see it in operation."

"I, too, am anxious," Husam al Din reminded the scientist by tapping on his wristwatch.

Soregi raised his head. "I can't rush any faster than I am going." He hesitated, then continued, "But I am making progress. I can't promise anything, but I believe I will have what you need within a few days."

"A few days," Husam al Din repeated. "Then I will begin preparations for five days from tomorrow. I am generous." He turned and left the room, closing the door behind him and headed over to Asman Massud's shanty.

Asman Massud bent over his workbench, safety glasses protecting his eyes from tiny fragments of aluminum being sprayed from the working end of a high-speed rotary tool that buzzed in his hand. An overhead light hung low over the aluminum tube he was concentrating on. He flipped the switch and the tool went silent. Laying it aside, he picked up a thin aluminum disc that was shaped with beveled edges and tested to see if it fit in the end of the tube. He fidgeted with it, pulling it out and pushing it in several times, testing the resistance and fit.

A cold wind hit Massud in the back as the door swung open and Husam al Din stepped into the shop. The workplace was nothing more than a back room in a small house across the street from the mud brick structure with the lab where Sorgei was at work. And that one was only a little way from the one where Josh Adams was housed. Husam al Din was careful to keep the key players separated into their own spaces; no need to let Sorgei and sergeant Adams discuss anything without his supervision.

The machinist felt the breeze and heard a rustle behind him and turned to see al Din. "Ah, good," he said, "I have been wanting to ask you some questions about the vial that will hold the toxin. It will have a bearing on how I attach the explosive device."

Husam al Din clapped his hand on Massud's shoulder. "It is good to have such a thoughtful man working on this project – someone I can trust."

The machinist smiled at the comment. In this part of the world, smiles and compliments were rare. Conditions of life were too bitter for the frivolity of smiles. Relationships, even between husband and wife, survived more out of interdependence than love. Those who might be friends under different circumstances had to be satisfied with relationships of mutual misery, working toward a common objective such as a planned martyrdom to create a bond of mutual support that kept everyone going.

"It is good to be appreciated," Asman Massud said.

"As for this," Husam al Din said, picking up the tube, "I will be carrying two copies of this flashlight in a small duffel bag. They will be hidden among what will appear to be my personal items and clothing. Tell me how you are planning to rig it."

Asman Massud took the aluminum body of the flashlight from al Din. "This disc" – he laid the thin aluminum piece in his palm – "will become a false bottom, turning what was once a three-battery flashlight into one that uses only two batteries, and it will be wired so that it will not turn on the light. The vial and the blasting cap will be concealed in the end of the flashlight behind the false bottom. When the cap explodes, it will shatter the vial and pressurize the tube, forcing the toxin out through small holes that I will drill in the end cap. I only need to know the size of the vial."

Husam al Din unbuttoned his chest pocket and took something out and held it up in the light. "I will use this to serve as the vial. It was made especially for this purpose, with glass that is thin and brittle."

Asman Massud took the glass tube in his fingers, held it up to the light and examined it closely. Then he picked up a small caliper and checked the dimensions. "This will be perfect," he said, handing the vial back to Husam al Din. "I will use two small nylon cable ties to secure the blasting cap to the vial."

"I do not want anyone to hear the explosion," Husam al Din said. "I want the release to be as quiet as possible. You will need to insulate the flashlight body some way."

"I can do that," Asman Massud said proudly. "I can make it so the exploding cap will make no sound. All you will need to do is turn on the flashlight, and the batteries will fire the blasting cap, shattering the vial and releasing the toxin. In your hand, you will feel the detonation, but there will be almost no noise. Perhaps just a dull thud, but you can cover the sound of it with a cough."

"It is a good plan." Husam al Din smiled. "I want you to prepare two of these for me, so I will have a back-up. The time cannot come soon enough."

Chapter Nine

Josh Adams sat at an aged wooden table with legs that wobbled as he leaned over a large-scale nautical chart of the Port of Miami that was stretched out in front of him. Using a plastic sheet as an overlay, he marked three squares and labeled them – one was the US Customs office; the second was the Coast Guard station; and the third was the Port Security office.

Husam al Din leaned over the table and watched. "Where will the containers be removed from the ship?"

Josh used the marker pen to indicate the area of giant cranes. "This is the terminal where the containers come off the ship. One at a time, they are lifted from the ship's top deck, then the rest are pulled from the cargo holds. Depending upon the size of the ship, the top deck containers might be stacked as much as six high and ten wide."

"Then what happens?"

"The cranes lower the containers onto waiting flatbed trucks that haul them away."

"How long does the process take?"

"To unload an entire ship can take hours. How long it takes to unload your particular container depends upon where it is on the ship. The ones on deck come off first."

"An estimate?"

"From the time the crane hooks up until the time the container is on the truck, about six minutes. Twice that long, if the box is in the cargo hold. But you have to allow for breaks in the process. These guys are union workers."

"Tell me about the inspection process, from the time the ship approaches the harbor until the container is on the ground."

"Even before the ship enters the harbor, it might be boarded by the Coast Guard or Customs to check the manifest and look around. They are free to open and inspect any container they deem suspect. After the ship docks, that same process can happen again, although it is not likely, if the ship has already been inspected at sea. Once the containers start coming off, they hate to slow things down for inspections, although you can't eliminate the possibility of an inspection once the box is on the truck. There are new radiation screening processes they're putting the boxes through."

"From what you saw while working there, what do you think are the chances of an inspection?"

"Radiation screening is a sure thing. A physical inspection with the container getting opened, the percentage is low. A lot depends upon the ship. Container ships are rated according to the TEU capacity. A TEU is a 20-foot equivalent unit. Cargo containers come in 20-foot and 40-foot sizes."

"Keep going."

"Well, depending upon which ship we're talking about, it might be rated at anywhere from 1,500–9,000 TEU capacity. You have to consider that more than 30,000 shipping containers are processed into the US every day, each of them carrying thousands of containers, and there's not enough manpower to take a look at all of them. Only a very small percentage can be inspected. And only if a container is suspicious will it be deeply inspected."

"So how do I eliminate the chance of being among even that small percentage? There must be a way. There must be something the authorities look for when they are deciding what to inspect."

"Yeah," Josh exhaled, "that's true. There are key things they watch for, like drugs. They use drug-sniffing dogs for that. And radiation; they use detectors. And irregularities in the manifest. If the cargo is listed as something to be expected, bananas from Costa Rica, for example, they don't worry too much, especially if the container seal has not been tampered with. If the manifest lists a solid gold Rolls Royce from the Emir of Oman, they might take a look."

"Then we must create a manifest that will appear to be very normal, so no one will suspect anything. I have a plan for what will be on the manifest, and can get that handled by our people at the point of departure, without any problem."

"So, where are you shipping from?" Josh asked.

Husam al Din stared hard at him. "I am not sure I want to tell you that."

"Don't trust me, huh?" Josh said.

"I haven't known you long enough. I'm not sure I want to know you long enough. You are an American, an infidel. You are the enemy of my people and of my soul. I will pay you for your information, but that is all."

"Does Sorgei know?"

"He knows only what I want him to know. That is enough."

"But I'll bet he knows more than I do."

"I have worked with Sorgei before. He has been with our organization for several years," Husam al Din said. "Still, I tell him only what is necessary. He is a resource. If I need to have him make special arrangements, then I give him the details."

"How can you trust any Russian after what the Soviets did to Afghanistan?" Josh asked. "We were even helping your guys fight those Soviets – supplying weapons, giving clandestine training to your people."

Husam al Din looked straight at Josh. "The war with the Soviets is over. The war with America is not. Sorgei hates America. Have you not heard the ancient Pashtun proverb that says the enemy of my enemy is my friend?"

"So you consider me to be your enemy?" Josh asked.

"Are you Muslim?"

"No."

"Then you are an infidel. You are my enemy."

"Isn't Sorgei also an infidel?"

Husam al Din nodded. "He is indeed."

"Then how can you justify working with either of us?"

"An infidel might be used to help accomplish my greater purposes," Husam al Din said, "but he is still an infidel."

"If that is what you believe and you are sworn to kill infidels, how do I get out of this alive?"

"You will live only because I have decided to let you live. But if I die, you have no promise among my brothers. They are not bound by my oath."

"Then I better keep you alive as long as I can," Josh said.

"That is amusing." Husam al Din smiled. What he didn't say was that in less than a month, he intended to be dead – a martyr for his cause, as he personally delivered the deadly toxin in the container.

Chapter Ten

October 11th – Eastern Caribbean

October 11th dawned warm and calm in the tiny hidden anchorage of Waisaladup in the San Blas Islands. Palm trees on the encircling beach waved a friendly greeting to Nicole Plover as she poked her head through the forward hatch above the main stateroom bed.

"Ahhh," she yawned to Dan, "another gorgeous day in paradise."

Without waiting for an answer from her still-snoozing husband, she squirmed up through the hatch and onto the foredeck, then went to the bow seat on the starboard side and plopped down facing the sunrise. The world and all its problems seemed so far away as she soaked up the warmth of pink sunlight and listened to the birds and felt the gentle rocking motion of the boat on the water.

It's great to be a morning person, she thought, reveling in the quiet time she enjoyed while Dan and the kids were still asleep. *This must be what it was like for Eve when she woke up before Adam in the Garden of Eden.* It was a vision that brought a smile to her lips. Looking around and seeing no one, she eased over the side and into the warm velvet water. The kids were late sleepers, so she pretended to have Eden all to herself.

Nicole was just gliding past the port bow on her way around the boat for a counterclockwise lap when she heard a deep voice. "Why hello there Mrs Plover. Nice to see you this morning."

"Eeek!" The sound burst out of her throat before she could stop it.

"Ha!" Dan laughed. "I got you. You thought I was still asleep, didn't you? Thought you could sneak out for a little morning swim without me?"

She splashed him as he moved in to surround her with his arms. "How did you get in the water so quietly?"

"That's my secret weapon," he said "I can't tell you, or I might never have another opportunity like this again."

"How long do you think the kids will sleep?" she asked, cuddling in his hug.

"I drugged them. They're out for the whole day," he joked. "Why? What did you have in mind, Mrs Plover?" He hiked his eyebrows twice when he said her name.

"Hmm," – she smiled her best come-hither smile – "well, since you've drugged the children, maybe we have time for …"

"Hi mom. Hi dad," came the bright childish voice of Cadee. "What are you doing swimming so early in the morning?"

Nicole darted beneath the bridge deck between the bows and pulled Dan in after her. "Uh, oh, hi honey," she replied. "What are you doing up so early?" She scowled at Dan. "I thought your father drugged you."

"What?" Cadee said. "What did you say?"

Nicole poked Dan. "I said, is Jacob still asleep?"

"Yeah, he's snoring his brains out," Cadee answered.

"Well, here's a plan," Nicole said, "why don't you go jump in the shower and I'll come and get breakfast started."

"Okay," Cadee said, and disappeared inside.

"Drugged the kids," Nicole chided. "That will teach me not to believe everything I hear from a good-looking man."

"Want me to go get you a towel?"

"That would be very nice," she smiled.

"It'll cost."

"What's the price?" She raised her eyebrows as he had earlier.

"Hmmm." He hesitated, looked away and then looked back as if he were thinking about how high a price to ask. "Okay, a kiss for now, and your undying love forever."

"I can manage that," She wrapped her arms around him and pressed her soft lips against his.

"Umm, that was nice."

"Now, Mr Plover, my towel?"

"Right," he said. They swam to the back of the boat and climbed the steps. Then he wrapped her in a nice warm towel and they stood in the cockpit and watched the rest of the sunrise together.

Chapter Eleven

October 11th – The Land Without Laws

A frosty Autumn wind whistled under the eaves as Josh Adams sat on his hard bunk in the mud brick house. His wristwatch told him it was October 11th, but it felt like the middle of January. He was a prisoner in this bitter and uninsulated house. A small sheepherder stove made of thin sheet metal glowed red as he stoked the fire and tried to warm the room. His morning and noon meals consisted of goat milk and hard bread – for supper, his captors brought him hot soup. The drinking water smelled stale, and Josh wondered which pasture creek it came from, where years of animal dung might have polluted it.

It had been two days since Husam al Din last talked with Josh. At the end of that visit, the Arab rolled up the chart of the Port of Miami together with the overlay drawing and all the papers Josh used to write descriptions of the target area. Then he left the house and Josh did not see him again.

Two days and nights came and went, and the only contact Josh had with anyone was when food and water were brought. *It's exactly like being in solitary confinement in a prison,* Josh thought. *Food shoved through the door, then the door slammed and locked.* Josh rehearsed in his mind all that happened since his arrival in this forsaken place. Weeks passed, yet he had not been allowed outside. His windows were boarded up with rough planks, but by pressing his eyes close to the slits between the planks he could see a little of the narrow dirt road that ran in front of the tiny house. A couple of times, he caught a glimpse of Husam al Din walking between this house and the one across the way, and he wondered if that was where Sorgei Groschenko was housed.

Now, there was a mystery, Josh thought. *Why did al-Qaeda need to reach into Russia for a weapons expert to help them with their jihad?* These were people who seemed to be able to take a couple of firecrackers and a cell phone and come up with an improvised explosive device that they could set off at their pleasure. So why did they need somebody like

Sorgei? It was a puzzle – one that Josh wanted to solve. Maybe with Husam al Din out of the way for a while he could figure out how to spend some time with Sorgei and pick the Russian's brain.

The other thing he wanted to find out was exactly what Husam al Din meant to do in the Port of Miami. Yes, Josh had cooperated by telling him about port security ... but not all. He didn't tell everything – not the most important things. He revealed just enough to make the Arab believe he was getting the whole story. *Just enough to keep myself alive, without giving away the farm,* he told himself.

The sound of voices speaking Arabic penetrated the window from outside the front of the house. Josh leaned close and listened. He hoped Husam al Din had neglected to tell the rest of the men in camp that the American soldier was fluent in Arabic. As the men talked, he studied their words. A sudden chill ran the length of his spine, as he heard the message.

"Here is the food. Feed the dog. Husam al Din has taken the weapon. His jihad begins. We will keep these two alive only until we receive word that the mission has succeeded, in case we need to get more information out of them. Then we will take their heads."

Josh moved away from the window when he heard the hard metallic sound of a key being inserted into a padlock. The door swung open and a plate was set on the floor, then the door slammed shut.

Josh pressed his face against the window and squinted into the bright overcast dawn through the crack between the boards. From a distance, he heard the call to prayer, and several men walked past, all heading in the same direction. A few moments later, the narrow lane was empty. The realization struck him: *everybody's gone for prayer.* He called out for the guard, but there was no response. "Maybe even the guard has gone to the mosque. This might be my chance," he whispered under his breath.

Two other rooms in the house had windows that were also boarded, and one of them faced onto an empty field where there was nothing but dead brush and weeds. In that back room Josh squinted between the boards and saw only empty wilderness that stretched away to distant mountain peaks. He gave a shove with his shoulder and the nails in one of the boards squawked. He shoved again, and the board popped free and fell to the ground outside. For a moment, he waited, peeking around then ducking back, to see if anyone outside heard the noise. No one came.

With the butt of his hands, he hit the second board, and it came loose. Two more smacks and it was off, giving him room to escape.

Once outside, he loosely replaced the boards. On quiet feet, he moved to the corner and peered around. The rutted path that served as a road was still empty. As silently as he could, he sprinted across to the other small house. Boards covered all the windows. This had to be where Sorgei was being kept … or perhaps someone else being held hostage. These two houses were POW quarters, Josh guessed, and he also figured that he and Sorgei were the most recent prisoners. He stepped to the window and banged on the wood covering.

"Sorgei," he called in a loud, half whispered voice, "are you there?"

"I am," came the reply. "Is it you, Josh?"

"Yes. Can you let me in? We need to talk."

"The door is locked from the outside. It is only opened when they bring food."

"I know. Listen, put your weight hard against these boards. See if they will come loose."

Sorgei pushed with his shoulder, but he was slight of build and didn't have the strength Josh had. The board refused to budge. "I cannot loosen it," Sorgei sighed after several attempts.

"Kick it with the bottom of your foot," Josh said. "Quick, before somebody comes."

"Sorgei backed away from the window just enough to allow him to raise his foot and kick with all his strength. The old rusted nails complained with a loud squawk.

"Good," Josh said. "Try it again. I'll pull from this side."

Sorgei gave it another kick, and Josh pulled the board free. "That's enough," Josh said. "I think I can crawl through this opening. Then we need to pull this board back on, so nobody will notice that it has been removed."

"You would make a good Russian criminal," Sorgei said.

"I'm not quite sure how to take that," Josh answered as he scrambled through the opening and with fingers in the cracks between the planks pulled the board hard enough to stick the nails back into their original holes, "but I'll take it as a compliment."

"What are you doing here?" Sorgei asked.

"We're in trouble," Josh answered. "I don't know exactly what your deal is with Husam al Din, but he's gone off and left us swinging in the breeze."

"Do you think he is not coming back?"

Josh stepped over to the table and sat down. "I suppose that depends. Did you give him what he wanted?"

"Yes, he has the toxin. I finished its development three days ago."

"What toxin?" Josh leaped to his feet. "I thought you were a weapons scientist."

"A bioweapons scientist," Sorgei corrected. "I developed a weapons grade bacteria. His plan is to smuggle himself aboard a shipping container, then release the toxin when he arrives in Miami."

"Oh, crap! I thought he was planning to just blow up something at the container terminal, not release a biological weapon into the city."

"It won't be just the city," Sorgei said. "This toxin is designed to spread across the whole country."

Josh moved close to Sorgei, so he could look him directly in the eyes. "Listen man, you must tell me. What is his plan? What kind of toxin is it?"

"All I know about his plan is that he intends to conceal himself and the toxin in the shipping container. When he arrives at the Port of Miami, he will release the bacteria into the population."

"How does it work? How is it spread?"

"I designed it so that it must have a living host, or it cannot reproduce. If it is inhaled, that person will then serve as the host. The bacteria will live for a few hours inside the host before the host develops a cough that will spread the germ. You would not believe the power of a cough to disperse a disease, and yet this one will appear at first to be nothing more than a cough from a cold."

"So, if one guy at the port becomes a host, and he carries it home to his family, and they go to the store or to school or to church, they spread it."

"Exactly," Sorgei said.

"And before the original victim even knows he's got something, the disease will have been disseminated to an ever-widening circle of people, who in turn keep spreading it."

"That is the design. Before anybody gets sick enough to die and arouse the attention of medical people, the disease will be moving like a wildfire across the country. According to our computer model, within ninety days, ten percent of the population will be infected."

"So what happens to the original host?" Josh asked.

"After two days, he becomes feverish. Two more days and he is deathly ill. The bacteria are designed to break down the cell walls, first in the lungs and then in all the major organs and muscle tissue. As the cell walls break down, fluids leak throughout the body. The victim virtually turns to jelly inside. You have heard of necrotizing faciitis, perhaps – the flesh eating bacteria? This is something like that, but better."

"After he's dead, does the disease keep spreading?"

"No," Sorgei said, "when the host dies, within a few hours the bacteria is dead. It cannot live more than four hours in open air, so it is totally dependent upon a living host."

"My gosh, man, what were you thinking when you designed such a thing as this?"

"Nothing." Sorgei stared at Josh with blank eyes. "That is the worst part of my life. In this business, I had to learn to not think of the consequences. It was just my job." He blinked, but showed no emotion. "I suppose it is not much different than the pilot of a B-52 dropping bombs from 20,000 feet, totally disconnected from what is happening on the ground."

"Yeah," Josh said barely above a whisper, "I suppose not. It's an unfortunate world we live in."

"That it is," Sorgei agreed.

"Do you have any information about how Husam al Din plans to smuggle himself into the container?"

"No. I have told you everything I know."

Josh laid a hand on Sorgei's shoulder. "Listen, I am not your enemy. The United States is not the enemy of your country."

Sorgei interrupted him. "Because of your country, the Soviet Union fell apart and my career was ruined. I hate America."

"Think about who is attacking your homeland now. Think about the attack on the theater in Moscow and the University library, and the bus depot and the children's school. None of that was from America. You and I are fighting the same enemy, and right now we need to be working together, or neither of us will get out of here alive. I overheard men talking outside my room. In a matter of days, as soon as they receive word that Husam al Din's mission has succeeded, they intend to kill us."

A surprised look crossed the Russian's face. "You know that for sure?"

"Heard it with my own ears. I don't think those guys know I speak Arabic, or they'd be more careful what they say."

"I am disappointed." Sorgei shrugged with dejection. "After all the time we spent working together on other projects, now he decides to cheat me out of my money and my life."

"Disappointed?" Josh asked. "I think this would go a lot farther than disappointment."

"You are not Russian. You have not lived in Siberia. Disappointment is a way of life for me. It is harsh to live as I have lived."

"Well, unless you're ready to die a disappointed man, I suggest that we team up and get out of here."

Sorgei thought about that for a moment. "I am a man who is willing to take hold of an opportunity," he said. "Obviously … or I wouldn't be here now. I sold myself to the highest bidder."

"Then grab onto this opportunity. My people need to know more about this toxin you've developed. I don't have anything to offer, except a chance to save your life. We have to get out of here, and we need to do it together. Two sets of eyes are better than one during an escape."

"How do you propose to escape?"

Josh got up and paced around the room. "I'm working on it. Are you with me?"

Sorgei reached out a hand and Josh took it. "Okay, I am with you. Let me know what you want me to do."

"Just get yourself ready to leave. When I come back tonight, be wearing your best walking shoes and all the clothes you can put on. It's going to be cold out there. Hide your food in your pockets today." Josh moved to the window and peered out. Then he removed the board and crawled out through the opening. "Under the cover of darkness will be best. Tonight, during last prayer I'll be back." Then he disappeared across the narrow road and behind the tiny house where he was kept as a prisoner.

Chapter Twelve

October 11th – Peshawar, Pakistan

A dusty five-hour drive on dirt roads carved from the barren mountainsides took Husam al Din from the tribal frontier village to the crowded city of Peshawar. He rode in the back seat, shuttled by a driver and protected by an armed bodyguard. His only luggage was a medium-sized carry-on duffle bag that held a few changes of clothing and what appeared to be two well-used black metal flashlights rolled up inside his prayer rug. In the space created by a false floor in the bottom of the duffle, he concealed his dagger.

"At the airport," the bodyguard said, "you will be watched for. It has been pre-arranged for your carry-on luggage to be inspected and approved by one of our people who is positioned as security."

From Peshawar International Airport, it would take two days for Husam al Din to travel by a series of flights, first to Karachi then to Calcutta and on to Singapore before the final jump to Manila. His plan was known within al-Qaeda's upper echelon, and someone, he knew not who, had taken care of all his travel arrangements, documents and airport security issues.

After hours of travel, when they came to a halt in the airport parking lot at Peshawar, the driver turned to him. "To minimize the risk of detection, after you pass through security at this airport, you will de-plane into secure areas at each airport along the route. When you get on the ground, do not leave the secure area, or you will have to pass through security again. The less of that, the better."

Husam al Din nodded. "I understand. I have brought the Holy Koran to read during layovers, so I will not need to go anywhere."

"There will be places to buy food and there will be restrooms within the secure area, so you should have everything you need," the bodyguard said. Then he reached over the seatback and offered his hand to Husam al Din. "Smile at everyone you see. Be friendly and courteous to all the security people. May Allah lead you."

"And you, my brothers," al Din said. He opened the car door, got out, put a smile on his face and walked into the airport lobby, duffel bag in hand

October 13th – Manila, Philippines

A hot October squall swept through Manila, rattling the sky with thunder and lightning, and flooding a few of the bustling city streets to ankle depth. Each leg of the trip had been rough, and Husam al Din was thankful to be on the ground. He did not like flying, he decided. If he were to die, he would rather do it without falling from 30,000 feet. He wanted to be more in control of his final destiny than to be a helpless passenger in an airplane that was being ripped apart by a storm.

The other thing he did not like was the heat and thick moist air. For the past six years, he had lived high in the cold, arid mountains of Pakistan, and he was not accustomed to the scalding humidity of a tropical island. *Soon enough, I will be dead, and this will not matter*, he consoled himself with the thought. With the duffel bag strap slung over his shoulder, he drew his last breath of air-conditioned air and stepped through the door that led onto the sidewalk in front of the airport, haled a cab and slid into the back seat. "Hotel Bali," he said to the driver, and they sped away, melting into the flow of traffic. Three hours later, bathed and fed and having attended to his evening prayer, he left the hotel, determined to see what city life in Manila was all about.

Even though it was evening, the tropic air was saturated with humidity and he sweat profusely as he made his way through the bustling streets. Dressed in western clothing, his intent was to blend in with the teeming populace. Gone were the black turban and heavy beard. Now, clean-shaven for the first time since he was able to grow hair on his face as a badge of manhood, and wearing blue jeans and a cotton t-shirt, he played the chameleon among people who never suspected his true nature.

Had anyone been watching him, though, the expression on his face would have revealed the deception, as his first exposure to the bright lights and flashy fashions of the modern city at night left him staring with eyes wide and mouth agape. He was as a child of poverty being exposed to his first Christmas tree surrounded by brightly wrapped gifts and knowing that it was all his for the taking. His eyes flicked from side to side, straining to absorb the color and texture of the clothing, city lights, garish advertising signs, and the rushing vehicles. His ears were unaccustomed to the loud music, the noise of people all seeming to talk at once, and laughter that filled the night air. His head buzzed with the overload of activity and motion and glare of lights against the night sky.

But more than anything, it was the women that stunned him. Never had he seen so much of a woman's body exposed to view – bare shoulders and arms, flowing hair and faces made up with cosmetics, and legs all the way above the knees. At first, he tried to look away, but it was too beautiful to resist, and finally he gave in and stared without blinking, afraid of missing something. The scene rocked his senses. At one and the same moment, he was filled with pulse-racing desire and overwhelmed by a wave of holy disgust.

A short distance from the hotel, he found a grassy park with benches beneath a canopy of trees. In an attempt to calm his racing heart, he sat, closed his eyes and tried to think back to the lessons he learned in the madrassa.

Out of the darkness, a woman's voice broke his meditation, "May I sit with you?"

He opened his eyes and inhaled sharply when he saw the woman's bare midriff. Catching his breath, he lifted his gaze to her face. Her full red lips parted and turned slowly up at the corners, showing pearl-white teeth through a perfect smile. Her eyes were blue and round, and they seemed to dance from behind a parted veil of blonde hair. "Are you alone?" she asked.

"I am alone," he said, his eyes moving down from her face to take in the full image of the beautiful woman who stood before him.

"Would you like some company?" She smiled and held out her delicate white hand.

A hot desire swept over him. There was something he wanted to do before he left this life, and he intended to do it tonight. The men in the car when Husam al Din left the madrassa so many years before spoke about this very thing, but there had been no opportunity for him until now. Without stopping, the men had taken him from the madrassa and injected him directly into the most rigid part of Muslim fundamentalist society. It was a culture where boys and girls did not date and fall in love. It was a world where marriage was arranged and women kept themselves covered beneath heavy, shapeless burkas with mesh across the eyes, so no men except husband or immediate family could see them. The women were not to look into the eyes of a man to whom they were not married, and it was forbidden for a woman to be intimate before marriage. Honor killing was the accepted penalty for violation of the law. For the men, none of those rules applied. Men were free to enjoy relationships of any nature with as many women as they desired. The only problem was finding women to accommodate them, but that was solved by travel to regions of the world where there were more lenient cultures. It was something Husam al Din had never done.

"My name is Annette." Her voice jarred him back from his thoughts.

He looked again into her eyes, and thought they were more beautiful than anything he had ever seen. *Like sapphire gemstones,* he thought. He took her hand in his and stood up. "I am Stephan," he lied. "I would enjoy your company tonight."

In his lifetime, the only travel Husam al Din had done was for the purpose of warfare training in remote and deserted sites. It was never for pleasure. There had been no women. But today he was away from all that, and he intended to release himself into a part of life that was, up until now, denied him.

Afterward, he decided, *I will return honor to this girl's family – I will kill her myself.*

****

At eight o'clock the next morning, according to the arrangements made by al-Qaeda leaders operating in Islamabad, there was a black Lincoln Town Car parked at the curb across the street from the hotel. Husam al Din had been told what to do. He stepped onto the sidewalk, reached in his pocket, pulled out a gold coin and flashed it in the bright sunlight, then transferred it to the opposite pocket. At this signal, the driver climbed out, pushed a button on the key fob and the trunk lid popped open.

Glancing both ways to find a break in traffic, he stepped from the curb and crossed the street. "You have the shipping container ready?" Husam al Din asked in Arabic, skipping any pleasantries of conversation as he stowed his luggage and the trunk lid was closed.

"It is at the warehouse. We are going there now. Are you ready?"

"I am," Husam al Din replied. Then he climbed into the front passenger seat and slammed the door. "I am ready."

The Lincoln pulled into traffic and wound its way through the crowded city streets. Husam al Din stared out the window at the seemingly endless wealth of color and commercialism. It made him dizzy, but still he kept his eyes focused out the window, marveling at the garish scenes before him.

Gradually, the high-rise city gave way to lower buildings, then to poor houses, then to an industrial district. Half an hour after leaving the hotel, they were on the outskirts of town near the waterfront, in a derelict industrial area where warehouses constructed of rusting corrugated steel stretched away in the distance. The driver picked up a two-way radio and spoke to someone. A hundred yards ahead, the giant door on one of the buildings started to slide open, and the Lincoln sped ahead and made the turn into the opening.

Dry bearings squealed as two men pushed the door shut again on its crusted steel wheels, and everything went dark. Only a dim light glowed from a distant spot that looked like an enormous box, but from the passenger seat of the car Husam al Din could not tell what it was.

He stepped out of the Lincoln and heard the electric crack of a large power switch being thrown. There was a flicker, then bright bulbs came to life above him, and the warehouse became light.

"There it is," the driver said, pointing. Then he shouted, "He's here. Show him what we've got."

The door of an RV travel trailer swung open. A woman wearing khaki coveralls and black work shoes stepped out, and Husam al Din stopped in his tracks. In spite of her workmanlike clothing, she wore long, flowing auburn hair and her eyes were like green fire.

"What is this?" He turned to face the driver with a hint of anger in his voice.

The woman stepped in close, waved a dismissing hand as if swatting at a fly, and the driver turned on his heels and walked back to the car. She was, he guessed, in her mid-thirties, a good ten years his senior. Her stride was long and powerful, and every aspect of her bearing was that of a commander.

"What is this?" Husam al Din repeated, looking around as if suddenly everything had gone wrong.

"What's the matter," the woman asked, "haven't you ever seen a woman before?"

"Of course I have. But …"

"But where you come from, the women keep themselves covered and hide themselves away. Only men do the important work. Is that it?"

"Who are you? What are you doing?" Husam al Din barked, sounding suddenly defiant.

"Listen," she growled, "where you come from, things are different. But you aren't there now … you're here and you'll deal with me. My name is Alicia Gomez. I run the show in Manila. Do you have a problem with that?"

Husam al Din knew how to handle men, even tough men. But nothing in his experience prepared him to handle a tough woman. "Why was I not told?"

"Because you didn't need to know," she said.

"Alicia Gomez?" he asked. "Is that right?"

"Yes. That is my name."

"Alicia Gomez. I have never heard of you."

Her eyes flared. "There's a lot you've never heard of, because of where you've spent your life. Let me clue you in: it's a big world and you are a very small piece of a very big puzzle."

He glared hard at her, grinding his teeth, but said nothing. Suspecting that her hot Filipino attitude might have taken her too far, she stepped back and softened. "I do not mean to disrespect your importance to the cause," she said. "Your plan is a good one. Your sacrifice will benefit us all." She held out her hand, "Let me begin again. I am in charge of operations in Manila. It makes sense, does it not? Who would suspect a woman?" She smiled.

He found himself smiling back. "Yes, it does make sense. If the devil actually had horns and carried a pitchfork, no one would fall for his tricks."

"Okay," she said, her smile disappearing, "I'm not sure I appreciate the analogy, but your point is well taken. Now that we have that settled, let me show you what we have for you." She turned and climbed the two steps into the trailer, and he followed.

"This 26-foot travel trailer will conceal you and will give you everything you need to stay alive during the passage to Miami," Alicia Gomez said. "Before it is placed inside the shipping container, you will be hidden inside this area beneath the floor." She lifted the carpet and raised a trapdoor. "We removed the wastewater storage tank and replaced it with this compartment to serve as your hiding place. If the port authorities inspect the inside of the container and examine the trailer, inside or out, everything will appear to be normal. After the shipping container is sealed, you will be free to come out of hiding and live comfortably in the trailer."

Even in the muggy heat a cold shiver ran up Husam al Din's back. The thought of being locked inside a box no larger than a coffin brought back bad memories of the punishment closet in the madrassa, where he was tied up hand and foot and left for twelve hours because he forgot to bring his prayer rug to the mosque. It was a lesson he never had to repeat, but one that locked into his mind a deep fear of enclosed places.

Alicia Gomez noticed the involuntary shiver and the change in his expression. "Is there something bothering you?"

He shook it off, looked her in the eyes and lied, "No, it is nothing." But his pride was stung by her question. Perhaps she had seen his fear and thought him a coward. The question gnawed at him, and his pride quickly turned to bitterness.

"Come," she said, "I will show you all the features of this trailer. Light switches are here, and the fan switch is here." She pointed to the control panels. "The refrigerator is stocked with food and will operate on the oversized 12-volt battery system we installed. Canned and boxed foods are stored beneath the dinette seat. Dishes and utensils are in the cabinets and drawers. We have hidden drinking water beneath the bed in five-liter plastic jugs. The toilet is here." She pointed into the small enclosed lavatory, "and paper supplies and soap are in the cabinet under the sink. The bed is comfortable. You will have everything you need for the three-week voyage. Any questions?"

"Yes, I have one," Husam al Din said. "Will there be enough air in the container?"

"A good question. Shipping containers are tight enough to protect against water damage. You wouldn't believe how big the storm waves can get at sea. And sometimes those waves break over the bow of the ship, so the containers are sealed to protect the cargo. But they are not airtight, so a limited amount of air can get in. If you remain at rest most of the time, your air supply will be fine. Is there anything else?"

"When do I start?" Husam al Din shot her a hard look. "Allah is waiting for me."

Alicia Gomez shook her head in disgust. Even though she worked for al-Qaeda, she had no taste for martyrdom or murder. The money was good, and that was how she justified her connection to the terror network, but she did not agree with those who were anxious to kill themselves to prove their faithfulness. She was raised Catholic, and suicide and murder were sins. She knew she had to deal with that someday. Her professed shift to Islam was pure business – very profitable business – and for now that was all she cared about.

"The container is right over there," and she pointed to a distant corner of the warehouse. "As soon as you are ready, we will load the trailer inside."

"I am ready now," Husam al Din said.

"Very well. Do you have your device?"

"Everything I need is here," he said, patting the duffel bag.

"Then make yourself comfortable. We will close the trailer and load it into the container. Our people will bring the flatbed and truck within the hour. By tonight, you will be aboard the container ship *Desdemonda*. She leaves the harbor at three o'clock in the morning. You will need to conceal yourself in the hidden compartment one hour from now and not come out until the ship leaves. Do you understand?"

He scowled at her for sounding so condescending. He did not like someone talking down to him, especially not this woman who might suspect that he was afraid of close spaces. "Yes, woman, I understand," he growled.

"Hey," – she pointed her finger at his face – "don't you talk to me like that! You may be young and you may have decided to be some kind of hero, but I don't let anybody growl at me like that. Do you understand?"

His black eyes flashed and he showed her his teeth. "Do you understand that if I did not require your help, I would slit your throat? You cannot fool me, woman. You are a kafir. If you were truly Muslim, you would be ashamed to dress like this and show your eyes to me this way. You are lucky now, but Allah will have you in his hands one day and I will be there to testify against you."

"Oh my," she laughed, "listen to you. A suicide murderer who is going to testify against me at the judgment bar of God? Let me tell you something, He already knows my sins, and yours, so you better start thinking about what you are going to say to Him in your own behalf."

"I should kill you now," he snarled.

Alicia Gomez laughed in his face. "You talk brave for one who is about to die. Do you think maybe the sound of your own voice will give you strength? Silly boy." Then her eyes turned fierce and the green fire glowed. With fingernails like claws, she reached toward his throat, but stopped short. "Were you not going to your death by your own hand, I would kill you myself."

"Get out of here," he shouted. "You defile me and the place of my martyrdom!"

"With pleasure," she said, turning her back to him and stepping out of the trailer into the warehouse. "Lock him in," she yelled to her men.

They moved in and closed the trailer door, then a forklift was brought and hitched to the tongue. In less than five minutes, the trailer was pushed into the back of the shipping container and lashed to the tie-downs on the container walls. The empty space in front of the trailer was filled with cardboard boxes and plastic totes, all marked as household goods. Heavy web nets were draped over the boxes and lashed to the tie-down cleats, to keep them from shifting during shipment. The men stepped out and swung the heavy steel doors shut and threw the locking handles into place with a loud clash that echoed off the warehouse walls. The hoop of a sturdy padlock was dropped through the holes in each of the security handles and snapped shut. Forty minutes later, the truck arrived and the container was hoisted onto the flatbed and tied down.

"Here is the manifest," Alicia Gomez said, handing the driver the paperwork. "For the record, in the container are one RV travel trailer and household goods belonging to US Navy Ensign Hal Wadsworth who is transferring to Pensacola, Florida after a long and honorable tour of duty in the Philippines."

The driver nodded. "Sounds about right to me. Our guys at the loading terminal know that they're supposed to shuffle things around. This box will be loaded last so it will be one of the first off in Miami. Orders from Islamabad, I guess."

"Whatever makes the guy happy," she said. "Get this garbage out of here."

Inside the trailer, Husam al Din sat in the utter blackness, afraid to turn on the light and face the reality of his confinement. Sweat filled the palms of his hands and his breathing was quick and shallow. In an attempt at mental escape, he closed his eyes and sent his imagination to the high mountains of the tribal area, where the sky was wide open and snow blanketed the distant peaks. His mind saw soaring birds, free in the wind. He inhaled deeply to calm his racing heart, but the biting smell of formaldehyde from the trailer's cheap wood paneling stung his lungs and made him choke. Sweat dripped from his face and ran freely down his back. He fingered the button on his wristwatch until the dial lighted.

"One hour," he muttered into the darkness. "Only one hour until I have to climb into the coffin. This is worse than death. Allaahu, Akbar. Ashhadu Allah ilaaha illa-Lah."

Chapter Thirteen

October 13th – The Land Without Laws

Two hours after dusk, the wailing song of the call to prayer sounded across the tiny village, and all activity stopped. Josh Adams pressed his face close to the planks across the window and stared out into the cold blue light of early nightfall. As if in a hypnotic trance, all the villagers stopped what they were doing, and headed toward the dusty central plaza where the mosque stood. He knew from past experience that they would be there for most of an hour, and the streets would be empty. It was time.

It took only a few moments for him to remove the planks from the back window opening and step out into growing darkness. He tapped the nails back into place, then rushed across the narrow road and rapped on the door then put his ear against it. Sorgei called out from within.

"Josh?"

"Yes. It's time to get going. Are you ready?"

Josh heard the window boards move. "Here," Sorgei shoved a cloth bag at him through the opening. "Food and clothing."

Josh took the bundle and helped Sorgei climb through the window. The Russian had a worried look on his face as they replaced the planks. If they were lucky, nobody would discover that the prisoners had escaped until time for the morning meal. That gave them a ten-hour head start; and in this country, they needed it.

They looked left and right, but the street was deserted. "This way," Josh said, and the two of them scrambled across the road and ducked behind the house where Josh had been held. Extending to the horizon was nothing but empty wilderness – a dead-looking landscape of small rough brush and boulders. "Afghanistan is that way," Josh pointed toward a star that was just appearing in the night sky. "That's where we're going. We'll get back to my camp and we'll be safe."

"Maybe you will," Sorgei said, "but I don't think they will look too kindly at me."

"Leave that to me. I have a plan. But right now we've got to move. You just stay close to me. It's going to be a long, dark night, and you don't want to get separated from me. Okay?"

"Okay," Sorgei said, but there was reluctance in his voice.

Josh looked him in the eyes. "Listen, everything's going to work out." He pointed at the silhouette of a boulder pile in the distance. "We'll need to move as quietly as possible until we get to those rocks. Stay low, so you won't show above the horizon. Let's go," he said in a hushed voice, then took off in a crouched run.

Sorgei whispered a question as he bent and ran behind Josh. "How do you know where to go?"

"Trust me," he panted. "You just stick with me and I'll explain it all later."

Barely three minutes passed and they scrambled into the boulder pile and stopped to look back at the bleak village. Everything was dead still. Josh knew that the entire population was in the mosque, prostrated on prayer rugs that were turned to face toward Mecca – the same direction as the escape route he and Sorgei were on.

Chapter Fourteen

San Blas Islands – Eastern Caribbean

"So, how's it going this morning?" Dan Plover sounded particularly happy as he stepped into the hut that served as Sven's store. The Dane looked up from the large piece of paper he had stretched out across the counter.

"Ah," he said, "You guys are back from down south. How was it?"

"Man," Dan smiled, "I've never seen anything like it. We had the whole place to ourselves. It was just us and the birds and the monkeys. Perfect!"

"Well, I was just thinking about you," Sven said.

"Yeah? What about?"

"I've been looking at the chart. I love charts. When I study them, I can almost see what the ocean and the islands and the coastline look like. It's almost as good as going on the voyage myself."

"So which chart are you drooling on today?" Dan asked with a smile in his eyes.

"It's the one you will be using between here and the Rio Dulce. Won't be long now before you'll be heading out. The hurricane season has about to end. Unless something weird happens. A late storm ..."

Dan scratched his head, then tried to smooth down his permanently tousled hair. "That's why I'm here. Nicole wants to stick around for another couple of weeks, so the kids can have some more time with their friends, 'cause once we leave, who knows where we'll end up. We might not ever get back this way. At least not for a long time. And she wants to make sure we're not going to bump into a late storm. She has a sort of sixth sense about these things, women's intuition, I guess, if you believe in such things."

"Hmmm, just what's going on in here?" a female voice piped up. "You guys were talking about us girls, weren't you?"

Dan backed up and looked at Sven for help but got none, because Sven had his head down and was pretending to study the chart again. Dan tried to sound innocent. "I don't know what you're talking about."

"And don't you try to pretend that there's nothing going on here, either Sven." Grendel's tone was almost enough to prompt a confession.

He looked up from the chart. "Oh, hi honey."

"Don't 'oh, hi honey' me. We were standing outside and heard every word you said. These palm frond walls don't block the sound. What was that remark about intuition? It was a compliment, right?"

Sven shifted back and forth on his feet, looking for the right words. "Well, yah, sure honey ..."

"Yah?"

Nicole's face slowly melted into a warm smile. "You two should be lucky," she said, "to have such intuitive wives." Then she hugged Dan.

Sven turned to Grendel with a 'what about me' look on his face. She nodded, "Yah, I agree. You two are lucky. So, now, tell us what you were really talking about."

Just then, Jacob stepped into the room, with Kirsten right behind him. "Hi," Jacob said brightly. "What's up?"

"Well, uh," Dan said, "Sven and I were just looking over the charts and talking about how we're going to be sticking around here for another couple of weeks before we take off for Rio Dulce."

Jacob broke into a huge smile, "That's great. I love it here." He unconsciously glanced over at Kirsten, then realizing what he had done, he blushed. "I mean, this place is an awesome cruising ground. You know," he stumbled on, "we've got coconuts and palm trees and fish and ..."

Nicole rescued him. "We know," she said. "This is a pretty perfect place."

"But eventually we're going to move on," Dan said. "In a couple of weeks."

Jacob's face fell a little with the realization that there was so little time left. But he struggled to not let it show. "Oh, right. Of course. The Rio Dulce awaits. I hear that is a fantastic place." Then he turned and took Kirsten by the hand. "Come on," he said, "let's go for a swim." The two of them headed out the door.

"See ya later," Kirsten called back over her shoulder.

"You two be careful," Grendel shouted just loud enough to be heard as the kids walked down the beach. Kirsten waved her hand without looking back, so her mom knew she had heard.

"Well, all right." Nicole turned her attention back to Dan. "What do you two guys want for lunch? Grendel and I were just coming to see if you have any particular appetite."

"Umm." Dan grinned and wrapped his arms around his wife's waist. "I do have a particular appetite," he growled in a husky voice.

Nicole giggled. "I meant for food."

Sven broke into a hearty laugh. "I think he intends to nibble on you."

Grendel poked him. "You behave yourself. Don't go giving Dan any ideas."

Sven grabbed Grendel and swept her around, dipping her low for a dramatic kiss. "You're right. Let him come up with his own ideas."

A tiny giggle from outside caught the attention of the two snuggling couples. "Cadee, is that you?" Nicole yelled.

"Yep, it's me. But I can't come in there with you guys doing all that mushy stuff."

"It's okay, honey," Dan called out. "We'll be good."

Cadee stepped into the room, a slight blush on her face. "Jacob just told me the news." She bounced, excited. "Maria Elena and I can hang out together for another couple of weeks."

"That's right," Dan said. "I've got a little sail repair to do, and I want to scrub the bottom of the boat, and well, we'll wait for the weather to improve even more than it has."

"And besides that," Nicole piped in, "some of us women want to avoid any bad weather that might still be lurking out there. Isn't that right?" She smiled as she cast an accusatory glance at Dan.

"Well," Cadee said, "I'm like the weather to be kind of calm and nice."

"Good for you," Nicole put her arm around her daughter. "We women will stick together."

"Yeah, well," Cadee giggled, "looks to me like you and Dad stick together pretty well, too."

Dan moved in and threw his arms around Nicole and Cadee. "No man was ever luckier than to have two women like you in his life. We'll all stick together like this." He squeezed them in a bear hug and growled. "I love you guys."

"We're not guys, dad. We're girls."

Chapter Fifteen

October 15 – The *Desdemonda,* two days out of Manila …

As far as Captain Eric Sleagle was concerned, the day could not have been more perfect. Beneath an empty blue sky rolled an equally empty blue ocean. Farther than the eye could see from the height of the bridge deck, there was nothing except slowly rolling liquid azure that flowed in every direction to the distant curve of the horizon. The 48-mile radar showed the shipping lane empty ahead and behind, and the giant *Desdemonda* stood out like an island on an uninterrupted sea. She was, in fact, larger by far than many of the coral atoll islands that dotted some parts of the vast ocean. From the waterline to the top of her array of antennas above the bridge, she measured 118 feet. From bow to stern she was 887 feet, with a beam of 92 feet at the widest part. Two football stadiums could be built on her deck, with room left over for hot dog stands.

Her size was an advantage for deep ocean passages. With a grid of container cells in the cavernous hold below decks, most of the heavy cargo was carried low in the hull, which added stability to the ship and damped her motion on the water. Even so, once at sea, it didn't take long for the ship to begin her dance to the rhythm of the swells. Under fair conditions, the motion was gentle; a slow rise and fall of the bow, a peaceful roll to port then starboard; the kind of motion that put sailors to sleep as soon as their heads hit the pillow, like babies being rocked in a cradle.

In spite of her size there were times when typhoons turned the ocean into a nightmare of steep waves that sent green water over the bow of a ship – even one this large. When that happened, life aboard the *Desdemonda* was pure misery, as she bucked over mountainous waves, slammed into troughs, sending a thunderous shudder through the hull that sounded as if it were about to tear apart. In fact, that was a possibility. Large ships the size of *Desdemonda* sometimes ended up straddling waves, with nothing but air to support the hull in the area of the trough. More than one cargo ship had broken its back that way, straining the structure past the failure point, splitting the hull open, spilling her guts and then falling like a stone to the ocean floor.

But there was no such possibility today. Captain Sleagle stood at the helm and stared at the horizon ahead. Nothing but blue sky and gentle seas. He glanced at the gauges in the instrument panel, then picked up his pencil and made notes in the ship's log, indicating that the gauges were showing performance right where it should be, and everything about the *Desdemonda* felt perfect. He checked the GPS readings for latitude and longitude position, speed over ground, and course made good. He verified the course being maintained by the autopilot then stepped to the nav table to make notations of their position on the paper chart.

On Sleagle's ship, there was no such thing as depending entirely upon electronic navigation. Every half hour, whoever was on watch was required to annotate the chart, dead reckoning style, so the next man on duty would be able to track the ship's progress. It was a procedure as old as man's voyaging over the sea, and it was the best insurance against getting lost if the electronic navigation equipment failed – which it sometimes did.

The captain was satisfied with their progress. In the day and a half since leaving Manila, they had traversed more than 800 miles of the 8,944 nautical miles to Panama. He paused to think. The calculation came to him as easily as a simple sum. "Fourteen days to go," he mumbled to himself. "I can hardly wait to hit the Papagayo. I'm thirsty already."

Captain Sleagle looked forward, across the containers stacked and lashed down six high and eight wide on the cargo deck of the *Desdemonda*. The ship rolled gently on the swells, and the top of the stack swept back and forth in a wide arc across the horizon. The motion was unrelenting, but the captain loved the movement of a ship on the water. He was never more comfortable than when he felt the ship plunge and roll and yaw in ceaseless movement that brought a smile to Sleagle's face and put his heart at peace.

Sleagle had no clue that his ship was to be the carrier of a deadly virus. But Husam al Din was a man of the desert and mountains. He had no desire to be on a ship any longer than necessary to carry out his mission. He had insisted that the container in which he was concealed be loaded last, so it would be one of the first to be unloaded in Miami. That was the way he wanted it, and covert al-Qaeda operatives working at the dock made sure that it was done. But being loaded last put the container at the top of the stack on the foredeck, the spot farthest from the center of the keel, and that placed him precisely where the greatest movement was felt as the ship pitched and rolled and yawed. It was something he failed to consider.

Inside the blackness of the container, Husam al Din suffered a kind of sickness he had never known before. His mouth was dry as ash, his head spun, his gut cramped and his throat was raw from the continual retching. The smell of vomit hung in what little air there was in the trailer, and gagged him with every breath.

Chapter Sixteen

October 16th – Western Waziristan

A bitter wind howled past the entrance to the small cave where Josh sat looking out at the bleak landscape of rock and sparse forest that was just becoming visible in the cold light of dawn. The sky was brown with blown dust, and Josh couldn't help but think that it looked like a smoggy day in Pasadena – one of those days when you couldn't see the San Gabriel mountains a mile away. His gaze swept a distant ridge that was only barely visible through a thousand yards of dust-laden air. He and Sorgei had come over a shallow saddle in that ridge the night before, and finally took refuge from the bone-chilling wind in this small cavern among the rocks.

Suddenly, his eyes caught on something moving. A small puff of dirt, then another, rising from the ground behind the ridge, then blowing away in the wind. Strong and steady as the gale was, it would not raise individual puffs of dust like those he was seeing. Josh knew that something other than the wind was disturbing the ground. Then a round, black image topped the ridge, moving slowly with a steady back and forth motion. Then he saw another, and then a third.

"Sorgei." Josh shook the sleeping Russian's shoulder. "Sorgei, wake up. We've got to move."

"Whaa?" Sorgei opened his eyes slowly, rubbing the sleep away with his palms. "What is wrong?"

"Trackers." Josh pointed out the mouth of the cave toward the ridge. "Three men, black turbans. Taliban. They're hunting us."

"Are you sure?"

Josh looked at the Russian in disbelief. It was a stupid question, but he decided not to answer it directly. "You're a scientist. You know chemistry and biology. I'm a soldier, and I know how war is fought. These guys are after us. Just look at the way that one is studying the ground, searching for the next footprint while the other two are watching the rocks, looking for us. They're not out here for a pleasure hike."

"What are we going to do?"

Josh pointed at the men in black turbans. "Those two are watching for any movement among these boulders and caves. The other one is the tracker. See how he never takes his eyes off the ground? We need to get out of this cave and vanish into the boulder field. But we have to wait until those two are looking the other way. Gather your stuff and be ready to move on my signal."

Sorgei grabbed the cloth bag that held his extra clothing. The food he had saved on the last day at the compound was gone, but the bag of clothes made a good pillow and it was all he had to his name. "I am ready whenever you say."

There was no real trail for the Taliban trackers to follow – only the footprints of two men, one wearing boots with a combat sole, and the other wearing a pair of pirated knock-off Nike walking shoes that were popular in Russia. The two who followed the lead man, the one with his head down, carried Kalashnikovs at the ready, as if they were expecting to use their automatic rifles at any moment. The tracker's rifle was slung across his back. He led the way, studying the ground as if searching for a lost gold coin, sweeping his eyes left and right, often squatting to allow the shadow of the low sun to show an edge of the next footprint. The other two followed a few paces back and off to either flank, being careful to avoid making tracks that might mix with the ones their leader followed.

It was slow work, and Josh knew that these men were sent to find him and Sorgei the morning after the escape, when it was time for the first meal and the prisoners were discovered to be missing. While he and Sorgei took breaks to sleep, or just to catch an hour's rest, the trackers apparently kept to their work, doggedly pressing on without rest. With nothing more than the beam of a flashlight to help them see the small ridges and depressions made by footprints on dry soil, they persisted. One step at a time, moving from footprint to footprint across the vast wilderness, they came without stopping to rest, slowly gaining ground until they were now within striking distance.

"These guys are good," Josh whispered. "Too bad they're not a few hours later. Given more time, this wind would have wiped out our footprints."

Sorgei watched them over Josh's shoulder and nodded silently. Then he whispered, "They will find us."

"Yeah, I'm afraid so," Josh agreed. "We aren't going to be able to sneak away, now that daylight is coming."

"What are we going to do?" Sorgei asked with an audible quiver in his voice.

"Kill them."

"I am not trained to do that."

Josh stared at the Russian. "Maybe not one at a time, but you have been trained as a killer of men."

Sorgei lowered his eyes and nodded. "Perhaps you are right. But this is different. I have not had to look into the eyes of the man I destroy."

"I'll do the wet work."

"Wet work?" Sorgei asked, confused by the term.

"You'll see. But I'll need to have you distract their attention."

"I can do that," Sorgei said. "Tell me what to do."

"Okay, I have to get outside and hide so I can move around behind these guys. I'll let them approach the cave, and when they are in position I'll toss a small stone in here. It will be your signal. That's when you need to come out with your hands up, as if you are surrendering. I'll do the rest."

"Is that all?"

"If you're on speaking terms with God, it wouldn't hurt to pray."

With the plan laid, Josh watched the Taliban move slowly along the trail. Puffs of dust rose with each footstep, then blew away in the wind as they plodded down off the ridge into a low swale before starting to climb toward the cave. From where he watched in the deep shadows of the cave, Josh saw that there was one short stretch of trail where the cave entrance was invisible to the three men. He waited and watched as the black turbans slowly disappeared from view. Without hesitating, he used that narrow sliver of time to sneak on cat feet outside and into concealment behind a jumble of truck-sized boulders only a few yards away.

In three beats of his heart, he was hunkered down, perfectly still and listening. He heard nothing. *These men are good warriors,* Josh thought. *Great discipline. They move without sound. No idle chit-chat, just the business at hand.* He knew the reputation of the Pashtun warriors of Waziristan. Fighting was in their blood, and had been their legacy for a thousand years. In recorded history, no one ever defeated them. After a hundred years of trying, the British finally gave up the effort, licked their wounds and retreated, leaving Pakistan and the rest of their former Asian empire to fend for itself. Out-gunned, out-manned and facing the most powerful military force in the world, the Pashtun warriors fought to the death for their homeland and their traditional way of life. And Josh knew the three men coming after him were of the same breed.

Over the sound of the wind, Josh heard a soft footfall. Very slowly, he peered around the edge of the boulder. Guns at the ready, the three men were coming up the trail toward the cave entrance. Josh reached down to the heel of his right boot, loosened a rubber plug and then pulled it backward. An inch-wide by six-inch long ribbon of spring steel slid from its hiding place inside the boot sole. Half the length of the steel blade was honed to razor sharpness, and a wrap of black cloth tape covered the remaining three inches, forming a handle for this concealed knife that also served as the boot's shank.

With the blade in hand, Josh eased around the boulder to stay out of view as the three men moved past. From the debris of broken stone at the base of the boulder, he picked a pea-sized pebble. The backs of the three Taliban were toward him as the pebble whizzed past them and rattled into the cave. He heard a shout and a few seconds later Sorgei stepped from the shadowy depth of the cavern, arms raised, offering himself up as a prisoner.

While the three were distracted with Sorgei, Josh sprung from the cover of the boulders. He knew he had to be quick and agile to kill all three before they could kill Sorgei and then turn the guns on him. The sound of his movement was almost non-existent. Good as these Pashtun warriors were, Josh Adams was even better. Right now, he was fighting for a cause even more crucial than a homeland or a way of life … he was fighting for his very survival.

Before the man even knew Josh was behind him, the blade swept silently across the throat of the nearest Taliban, slicing deep enough to sever the windpipe and the carotid arteries. Almost in slow motion, Josh saw the muzzle of the AK47 coming toward him as the second man whirled at the sound of his dead comrade hitting the ground. Josh spun toward the weapon, stepped inside the arc of the rifle barrel, parried and clamped the fore-stock beneath his left armpit, and in the same motion thrust the razor up and across the throat of the second Taliban. In less than five seconds, two enemy were dead, their heads nearly severed.

The tracker was caught unprepared, his rifle still slung across his back. But at his waist was a dagger, and in a heartbeat it was in the man's hand. Josh crouched and with arms wide he started to circle to his left, staring into black, hate-filled eyes framed by bushy eyebrows and a full black beard on the snarling face of his enemy. The man said nothing, only gripped the dagger and circled, his eyes wide with anticipation. Twice, he lunged, and both times Josh narrowly dodged the edge of the blade.

On agile feet, Josh stepped left, and while his feet were crossed, the Taliban rushed in. It was just what Josh expected, and he whirled to avoid the point of the dagger, then smashed his opponent with a spinning back elbow that caught the man cleanly just below the temple. Josh heard the crack, as his elbow crushed the man's jaw, and the Taliban went to the ground.

Sorgei stood with his mouth agape, watching the two men fight. Not knowing what he should do, he did nothing – just stood there with his cloth bag in hand, trembling with the adrenalin rush of fear and excitement. He had never been in a fight before, and didn't really want to be in one now.

Josh was surprised that the Taliban fighter didn't stay down after the crushing blow to his head. With the nimble movement of a trained martial artist, the man rolled and came back to his feet, dagger in hand and a darker look in his eyes. "Now you will die, kafir," the man spit the Arabic words from lips that barely moved.

"I will die," Josh replied in Arabic, "but not today."

The Taliban lunged, and the point of the dagger caught Josh on the sleeve and sliced the fabric. White teeth glistened through the black beard, and the man circled again. "My dagger will find joy in your heart."

"Your dagger will be found among your bones and the bones of these your brothers, after the vultures and wild dogs feast on your flesh," Josh said, flashing a wild grin at his opponent.

They circled, hands wide but neither man making a move, and neither taking his eyes off his opponent. "You are a coward, kafir," the Taliban snarled. "Allah hates cowards."

"Then come ahead and send me to Allah," Josh goaded, trying to lure the man into making a move that he could counter. "Or perhaps it is you who are afraid?"

His black eyes flashed, as the Taliban lunged. Josh sidestepped and parried, slicing the forearm that held the dagger as it went past. "Aghh," the Taliban screamed, then instantly shifted the dagger to his left hand. When the warrior steadied himself, his back was toward the cave. Josh looked into the man's eyes and saw only murder and hatred.

Behind the Taliban, Josh noticed movement at the mouth of the cave. It was Sorgei, coming out of the darkness, a large rock held in his uplifted hands. In an instant, the Russian brought the stone down in a smashing blow on the back of the black turban. Cushioned by the pile of cloth, the blow to the head rattled the man but failed to knock him down. The dazed Taliban growled and spun around to face Sorgei.

It was the distraction Josh needed. He leaped forward and shot a knife-edge kick at the side of the enemy's knee. The man's leg folded with a snap, and Josh followed with a slash of the razor across the side of the man's neck, sending him sprawling into the mouth of the cave in a shower of gore. Sorgei caught the full impact of the falling man and was thrown backward onto the floor of the cavern, sending a cloud of brown dust into the air.

Josh rushed in to finish his opponent, but saw that the razor had already done its job. Sorgei was pinned beneath the lifeless Taliban, and Josh rolled the dead enemy to the side to free the Russian. Sorgei lay on his back, staring at the cave ceiling with a bewildered look on his face. A widening crimson stain soaked through the front of his clothing. The hilt of the dagger was wet with blood, and the blade was buried in Sorgei's chest.

Josh went to his knees beside Sorgei. "Hang in there. I'll get you out of this. Just hold on."

Sorgei slowly rolled his glazed eyes toward Josh, and swallowed hard. "I tried to fight. Tried to help you, but I think I will die here."

"You fought well, Sorgei. You did exactly the right thing."
****

A little after midnight, high on the northwest shoulder of Mount Preghal, Josh Adams sat in the complete darkness. It had taken half the day and half the night to get here from the cave. After dragging the dead bodies of Sorgei Groschenko and the three Taliban warriors deep into the cave, piling rocks over the corpses and doing all he could to sweep away the evidence of their struggle in case there were others who followed, he had set off across the wilderness toward this sloping mountain. In the growing darkness, unrelenting wind beat against him as he hiked, destroying any chance of hearing or smelling pursuers. An eerie feeling in the back of his mind kept him looking over his shoulders as he hiked, but he saw nothing.

Now, as he sat alone on the mountain in the deepest part of night, he removed his left boot, then lifted out the foot-bed. In a hollowed compartment in the sole was a tiny transmitter and a lithium battery. He assembled the components and pressed the switch. A red LED blinked. Eleven thousand miles up, an array of satellites captured his GPS locator signal with its individualized code, and sent it on to NIA headquarters in Titus, Maryland.

There was nothing for him to do now except wait. In the dark distance, the sharp clatter of a rock shifting against other rocks below him on the trail put him immediately on his stomach, as tight to the ground as he could get. *Someone's out there.* He held his breath and listened, but the only thing he heard was the droning of the wind. Then the wind carried the faint smell of dust. Then nothing.

What he feared most was a secondary search team that might follow up on his trail when the first Taliban failed to check in on their radio schedule. His imagination played the worst-case scenario. His ears picked up every sound and turned it into a threat, and his eyes transformed every hint of a shadow into an enemy. Out there in the darkness, there might be a squad of hunters combing the mountain side. They would scour every inch of the rugged terrain until they finally found him. Then they would fill him with AK47 rounds as he lay trapped in the boulders, unable to defend himself.

He heard another rock move, then heard their voices. This time, it wasn't his imagination. He heard them talking. Although he spoke and understood Arabic, these men were still too far off to distinguish what was being said. As the minutes ticked by and he listened, he thought he heard three different voices. They were spreading out across the slope, searching slowly through every rock pile. It was only a matter of time.

There was no place to go from here. If he moved, he risked immediate detection. The instinct to jump up and run, or even to try to sneak into a better position, was suicide. There was no real cover from bullets, and no place to hide himself other than to snug flat among the small boulders and remain as still as possible while the Taliban searched the area.

His mind raced through his options, but there were none. Then the thought came, and he decided to take a chance. It was either that or rely on slim luck that they would overlook him in their search. Quietly as possible, he gathered a couple of small stones in his hands, then rolled to his back and pitched one stone after another as far as he could throw them over a small ridge back up the hill. If could just divert them to another search area, he might have a chance.

An excited voice called the other two men to search over the ridge, and gradually, Josh heard the footfalls and voices move off, away from him. Still, it was too dangerous to risk moving to another position, so he hunkered down and hoped the hunters kept moving and were satisfied that they already searched the place where he was hiding.
****

Three and a half hours later, a stealth helicopter flying in whisper mode slipped across the border into Waziristan and eased up the northwest slope of Mount Preghal. In the distant sky, Josh saw the dark form blank out the stars before he even heard it coming. Only a faint red glow from inside broke the scene of utter blackness. Guided by the GPS locator, the chopper touched its skids on the high plateau less than 30ft from Josh, and gunfire erupted from just beyond the small ridge to his back. Small arms rounds hit the chopper four times before the helo lifted off and banked away, leaving him stranded and surrounded by Taliban.

Afraid the chopper crew would think they had been lured into an ambush, Josh hit the switch again on the GPS and hoped they understood. Suddenly, the sky lit up with a blinding flash, and the chopper swept the area with a HID searchlight. The high-intensity discharge beam nearly seared his eyes before he covered them. Knowing that the Taliban fighters were also blinded, he scrambled to his feet and waved, hoping the enemy didn't see him, but that the chopper crew did.

Within seconds, he felt the downdraft, and the chopper touched down next to him. Someone grabbed him by the collar and dragged him inside, and he heard the distinctive report of .50-caliber rounds from the door gun. Without hesitation, the chopper lifted off and was airborne again. A cluster of AK47 rounds whapped the side of the fuselage as the chopper banked sharply and headed west, out of range.

With Josh still unable to see, someone strapped his seatbelt and fitted a set of headphones on his head. He straightened them over his ears, felt for the mic and moved it in front of his mouth. "I'm on."

A familiar voice in the headphones said, "This is Curt at the farm. What's your status?"

"Alone, sir. Unfortunately. We have a situation. A very bad situation."

Chapter Seventeen

October 19th – National Intelligence Agency Headquarters, Titus, Maryland

"The cover worked flawlessly."

At 0500 hours, three days after his extraction, the man who had been known as Staff Sergeant Josh Adams sat in a soundproof room facing a cherry wood conference table that was surrounded by seven other NIA officers. "The villagers bought into my story about being dumped by my girl, and that I was sick of the army and ready to roll over. I let them think they were sucking me in and it worked like we hoped."

"Apparently, the backstory we created for you and your alleged girlfriend in Florida did the trick," Curt Delamo said. At 27, Delamo seemed young for this kind of work, but his short-cropped hair was already beginning to show some age. He had been in tough positions in field ops since his recruitment to the CIA at age 21, so he earned every strand of gray. And his experience behind the lines earned him this chair as leader of Team Foxtrot, in the Special Projects Division of NIA, a black ops subdivision of the CIA. This was dark territory, and what the team did was unknown to all but a few at the top in CIA leadership. It was to this team that they turned when help was needed with deep and deadly projects that might require methods beyond what was officially sanctioned.

Curt Delamo had the ultimate responsibility to conduct this mission, embedding Josh Adams with the Special Forces in Afghanistan, posing him as a deserter and traitor in an effort to penetrate the terrorist network to learn about upcoming plots targeting the United States. Information gleaned during interrogation of a prisoner at Guantanamo had triggered this mission: to infiltrate by means of allowing Josh to be kidnapped by the Taliban.

"I've got to hand it to him," Josh said, "Husam al Din did his homework. And fast. The astonishing thing is that the al-Qaeda network in the United States is not only alive and well, but also exceptionally effective.

Within a couple of days, they picked up every piece of evidence NIA had planted, and thought they discovered a gold mine in me."

"Our prisoner led us to believe that there was a Taliban unit that was hungry for just this kind of thing," Curt continued. "The set-up went well, I have to applaud all of you," – he made eye contact with each of the team members – "for baiting the hook so well. Josh, you played it just right. I'm glad we got you out of there alive."

"Husam al Din was convinced that he had orchestrated the whole matter of my treason. Of course, after he took off and left me sitting in the middle of Taliban Hell, it got pretty dicey. I wish I could have gotten Groschenko out too. He'd have been a valuable asset."

"Yeah, that would have been nice." Susan Vellum leaned forward and propped her elbows on the table while she nervously twirled a mechanical pencil between her thumb and forefinger. Her sandy hair was pulled straight back and trapped in a short ponytail that flipped enticingly every time she moved her head. That hair style, together with her black-rimmed glasses, gave her a secretarial appearance, but every time Josh looked in her sky blue eyes he ended up thinking of anything but office work. "Groschenko designed the bug, and he probably could have helped us defuse the thing, or at least understand how to deal with it better."

Bruce Wayonotte sat across the table from Josh. He was a burly man in his mid-forties with thinning hair and a thickening waistline, but he moved surprisingly fast. Before this most recent field op, Josh played racquetball with Bruce, and was beaten without mercy. "The thing I want to know is exactly what's coming at us, right down to the nuts and bolts. I know it's a biological weapon, but let's get to the details."

Josh reached for his glass and took a swallow of orange juice. "Okay, here's the lowdown. Sorgei Groschenko, you all know his background as a former Soviet biological weapons scientist. He developed a bacteria that Husam al Din intends to deliver to the Port of Miami inside a shipping container.

"I don't know exactly how the germ is to be released, but from what I gathered from Groschenko before he died, the plan is to disperse the bacteria among the dockworkers, who then carry the disease home to their families. Symptoms don't show up for a couple of days, and then it manifests as a severe cough and is spread naturally by the spray of saliva.

"But those who become affected think it's just a cold or the flu. Family members carry it to school, to the store, to church, anyplace they go, spreading the disease either by coughing into the air around other people, or by coughing into their hands and then touching other people. Heck, they can even leave it on the handle of a shopping cart or a gas pump or a door knob."

"Doesn't sound serious enough to raise any alarms," Jack Abernathy spoke up. "Happens every flu season."

"Exactly. Nobody will think it is anything unusual. That's the diabolical beauty of the plan. By the time the disease matures into its most virulent form, several days will have passed, and by that time it's too late. An infected person gets on a plane, travels to another city, visits friends, and the bug is transplanted across the country. The same scene repeats itself time and again until, within a few days, what began in Miami is in Los Angeles and New York and everyplace in between. And because it doesn't appear to be serious at first, nobody ever raises an eyebrow."

"So," Chris Banes broke in, "what did Groschenko say about what happens after the germ matures?"

"You've heard of necrotizing fasciitis – the so-called flesh-eating bacteria?"

Susan gasped. "You've got to be kidding!"

Josh shook his head. "Groschenko said this is even better."

"Better how?" Curt leaned forward, a grim look on his face.

"Better in that each generation of the bug disarms itself after four days."

"Why design the disease to do that?" Susan asked. "Sounds as if he wanted to limit its destructive potential."

Josh nodded as he swallowed a mouthful of orange juice. "That's right. Ordinarily it would appear that way. But the death of the former generation is what triggers each succeeding generation to mutate, so it can't be fought with conventional medical practices. Nobody will be able to get ahead of the problem fast enough to stop it. A person who gets the disease is dead within 72 hours after the bacteria matures and turns violent. Or not, but I'll get to that in a minute. If the victim dies, it'll look a lot like the progressive symptoms of necrotizing fasciitis. The patient suffers with vomiting, diarrhea, dehydration, a feeling of general malaise, weakness, muscle pain and fever."

"Still sounds a lot like the flu to me," Chris interjected.

"Exactly. But hang on. As dehydration continues, urination becomes less frequent, the blood pressure takes a severe drop, and the heartbeat becomes rapid and shallow. The bacteria are hard at work in the system releasing toxins. A rash suddenly appears over the entire body and then quickly develops into large, dark, runny boils that ooze pus. Within a few hours, toxic shock spreads through the body's organs and they simply shut down. The victim dies a very painful and ugly death."

"How did Groschenko know?" Curt asked. "He didn't do human testing, did he?"

"Actually, he did. Husam al Din provided a few infidels for experimentation. The whole thing was too much for Groschenko. He passed out like a schoolgirl when al Din suggested human lab rats. So the Russian worked in his makeshift lab and then al Din himself administered the dose to the prisoners. They were kept locked away in a sealed room underground some distance from the village, for observation. They tested the progress of the disease through two generations; then the bacteria died off and the place was safe again."

The room was quiet for a long moment. Then Josh broke the silence. "The only good news, if you can call it that, is that this bug isn't a hundred percent. Groschenko said some victims will suffer no more serious illness than a normal flu. He was working on a way to make it more effective, but Husam al Din was in a hurry and didn't want to wait."

"Well," Susan exhaled, "bless his heart."

"So, how can it be stopped?" The question came from the end of the table, where a noble-looking middle-aged gentleman sat. Ernie McFarland wore a pencil-thin mustache, slicked-down hair and a Jaguar green Ascot beneath his tweed jacket. Josh always thought McFarland would fit right into a 1950s British movie, playing the role of an ace flying a Spitfire in the big war.

"Total containment."

"You're saying we would have to shut down all travel in or out of the country?"

"A full-scale national quarantine. If anybody escapes across a border, the thing will keep spreading. For the sake of protecting the rest of the world, we would have to be willing to close our borders and absorb the full impact of the disease ourselves. Those who live through the pandemic will gain immunity from the mutant forms."

"We go public with this, and we won't need to worry about the disease," Chris said. "The country will explode with panic. Everybody will kill each other in a full-blown stampede to escape."

Josh nodded. "That's the convenient thing about terrorism. The rumor is as effective as the weapon."

Susan squirmed in her chair. "Let's get back to the disease. So you're saying that after four days of having been infected, the bacteria will either kill you or not. And if you live, you become immune and be safe from future outbreaks."

"That's what Groschenko told me."

Susan continued. "And that after several mutating generations, the bug will finally wear itself out and die?"

"Yes," Josh said. "But by that time, a large percentage of the population of the United States will be dead."

Curt Delamo sat back in his chair and stared at the ceiling. "Well, the way I see it, we have only two choices. Either we stop the shipping container from ever reaching Miami, or we evacuate Miami ahead of its arrival and then cordon the area and let enough time pass for the bug to die naturally. If we can manage to contain the bacteria, we will lose some people, but maybe not the whole population."

Denise Lund was the quiet one on the team and she had been listening as usual, and putting her thoughts together before speaking. "If we attempt to evacuate Miami, won't that be noticed by the al-Qaeda network? And if it is, won't they simply change plans and hit another port city?"

Josh nodded. "Denise makes a good point. Trying to empty Miami will tell the bad guys we're on to them and they'll just switch to another plan. They'll hit Houston or LA or San Francisco or Seattle. As much as Husam al Din wants to target Miami because he thinks it represents a lifestyle that is offensive to his theology, he wouldn't blink twice at having to take his weapon somewhere else."

Curt leaned forward again. "Do you know where the container is being shipped from?"

Josh shook his head. "No. But I do know that Husam al Din planned to be inside the container. He wants to become a martyr by delivering the weapon in person."

"All right," Curt said, "time to hit the streets. Josh, work with Denise and Ernie. You know what Husam al Din looks like, so put together a sketch. Get with the people upstairs. We need access to their assets in all the right places. Get that sketch into their hands and tap into the surveillance camera system at every airport Husam al Din might have used after he left Waziristan en route to a shipping terminal that has service to Miami. See if we can come up with a match.

"If I were a betting man, I'd say he headed for Indonesia or one of the other predominantly Islamic countries close by with major port facilities that can handle container shipping. Let's find that terminal and the ship he's on. Susan and Chris, get in touch with Infectious Diseases over at CDC and pick some brains without alerting anyone. We don't need to create any panic, but we need to develop a response plan. Jack, get with Homeland Security, the Coast Guard and the Port Authority in Miami to work up a port security program with enhanced inspections. If possible, we want to keep that container from ever reaching dry ground. I'm going to see the president."

National Hurricane Center – Miami

"Hey, Harlan, I think you should take a look at this. We've got us another one."

Steve Crossfield moved aside as Harlan Morehouse sat down in front of the monitor and watched the satellite playback of a weather system building off the west coast of North Africa. "Yeah, there she is all right. Just a baby right now, but give her time and let her feed on the 84 degrees water and she'll grow up to be a regular mama. Still too small and weak to merit any mention, but she'll bear some watching. Give her a week to ten days and then we might have something."

"Well, just in case, I'll get the paperwork together for the next name so we can christen her when it's time."

Harlan chuckled, "Yeah, we might as well be prepared. This has been one heck of a season, and I don't think it's going to end right on schedule. We could see a couple more of these before it's all said and done. Hopefully, no bombs."

"That's all we need," Steve agreed. "The whole coast from New Orleans to Pensacola still looks like a war zone. Maybe we'll get lucky and this one will spin off into the north Atlantic and leave us alone."

"Sure," Harlan laughed. "I believe in the Easter Bunny."

"Well, a guy can dream, can't he?"

Harlan slapped Steve on the shoulder as he was moving back to his own desk. "After you've been in this chair for a couple of decades, like I have, you'll come to accept that most of our dreams turn to nightmares. At least during hurricane season."

Chapter Eighteen

October 23rd – NIA Headquarters

An excited vibration in her pocket alerted Denise Lund that a call was coming in. "Denise, get Ernie and Josh and watch your monitor. I'll send the video footage via secure satellite when you're ready. From the sketch, I think this is your man. He went through here on the 11th, but as you'll see, he is no longer wearing a beard, and he's in western clothing." The man on the other end of the line was Rashid Singh, a NIA operative who ghosted through southeast Asia, changing his appearance and personal documents to suit his needs. A master of disguise and able to speak nine languages with perfect dialect, Singh had played the role of everything from a Dutch businessman to an elderly Indian grandmother to a British punk rocker. So it was easy for him to spot a man who was trying to change his appearance, as Husam al Din did.

"Hold a minute, Rashid. I'll get the guys in front of the computer."

A moment later, she was back on the line. "Okay, we're ready. I've got you on speaker. You can start the video feed. We'll download to a hard drive so we can do all the playbacks from here."

"This is footage from the international airport in Karachi at 0849 local time on October 11th," Rashid said. "Watch closely, because he passes by quickly, but still the picture quality is pretty good. I'm hoping Josh can make a positive ID."

The three of them crowded around the 36-inch monitor, scanning the crowd of travelers. "There," Josh pointed at the monitor as a man walked within camera range. "That's him."

"Are you certain?" Denise asked. "Tell me why you are so sure."

"It's his eyes. Back it up; I'll show you."

Denise reversed the hard drive in slow motion until the man came into view again. Josh walked to the monitor and pointed. "Stop there. Now, zoom in."

Denise typed the keyboard commands and the picture went to freeze-frame and then closed in for a tight shot on the man's face.

"Can you get closer on his eyes?" Josh asked.

"Yeah," Denise said, still fingering the keyboard, and the picture zoomed in to twice the former size. "How's that?"

"Good," Josh said. "Can we clean it up and sharpen the image?"

"Yes, but I thought you said you had a positive ID on this guy even though he was moving fast."

"Oh, I know it's him all right. I just want to show you two why I'm so sure."

"Okay," Denise said. "I'll have it in a second." She worked the keyboard and the image started to snap into clearer focus. "There you go."

"All right. Look there, above his left eyebrow. See that little diagonal scar? He was proud of that scar. He told me it was his first battle wound. Got it in the madrassa when he was a kid. A head butt from another kid that he had killed with his dagger. This is absolutely our man."

"Rashid, did you hear that?" Denise half shouted toward her phone as it sat on her desk some distance away.

"I did. Okay, now that I know for sure, I'll track this guy's movements from Karachi. I'll get back to you as soon as I have something."

Denise got out of her chair. "I'm taking a walk down to Curt's office. You guys want to come?"

****

At Karachi International Airport, Rashid Singh stepped up to the Indonesia Airlines counter, reached into his briefcase and pulled out a photo ID that showed him as an inspector for the airline. "I would like to see your passenger list from October 11th," he said to the smiling dark-skinned girl.

"Of course, sir." She smiled. "Please come this way." She led him down the counter to an opening where he could step through, then showed him the way to the office. "Please make yourself comfortable. I will summon the man who can help you."

"Thank you." Rashid smiled back at her and took a seat in a comfortable chair next to a potted tropical plant. *What a gracious young lady,* he thought. Only a moment passed before a door opened and a man in a western style suit approached him.

"What can I do for you?" the man asked, a cold tone in his voice.

Rashid stood up and reached out his hand. The man took it as gentlemen do all across the world. "I am here to inspect your passenger records. Particularly, I am interested in the flights on October 11th."

"What is this all about?"

"Well," Rashid said, "I am afraid it is confidential company business. All I can tell you is that we are trying to locate a fellow whom we suspect took something onto one of the flights that he was not supposed to have. The company is trying to keep it all as quiet as possible, as you might imagine. Word of this gets out, and the stockholders will start to worry."

The man in the suit did not return Rashid's smile. "Let me see your identification."

"Of course." Rashid smiled again, reaching into the briefcase. As he bent to retrieve the fake ID card, he heard a faint snapping thud, felt an impact in his upper spine and his hands went numb and started to quiver. The sound was familiar to him, but his brain didn't place it at first. It seemed as if time stood still. A strange, warm tingly feeling swept over his body. Then it came to him – the sound was the muffled noise of a silenced handgun.

Rashid Singh was dead before he hit the carpet.

October 25th – NIA Headquarters

Curt Delamo picked up the phone and pushed a single speed-dial number. One by one, each team member checked in alphabetically by last name. Even though this was a secure line, it was the check-in system he preferred, and he blamed it on his amateur radio network days. "Adams, Abernathy, Banes, Lund, McFarland, Vellum, Wayanotte." The roll call was complete, so Curt got right to the point. "Singh is dead. Meeting in one hour. My office."

An hour later, Curt broke the details. "Got a call this morning from Pakistan. Last night, a body was pulled out of a shallow grave beside a hangar at Karachi International. It was discovered by a maintenance guy. The police chief in Karachi reported it upstream, 'cause nobody seemed to know who the body was. Wasn't long until word was on the street about the strange body, and one of our field ops guys tracked it back to Singh. Bullet through the spine, just below C7. We've seen this before. It was a Pashtun hit."

"He was made." Jack Abernathy shook his head. "Somehow he was made. But I don't know how it happened. Rashid was too clever and too careful for that. He could have showed up for dinner and his own mother wouldn't recognize him."

"Well, if they got to Singh, they can get to any of us," Curt warned. "Somebody doesn't want Husam al Din to be followed."

"We know al Din flew out of Karachi on the 11th," Susan said, twirling her mechanical pencil in her fingers. "We suspect he was flying to a major port city with container facilities and routes to Miami. I say we jump ahead and see what we can find."

Curt drew a breath and thought for a moment. "All right. Get me a list of the most likely ports, and—"

"Already got it, boss," Bruce said, handing a sheet of paper across the desk. "And for my money, I'm betting on Manila. Don't ask me why. Just a gut feeling, and I do have a sizeable gut to work with. Not much hair," he chuckled, "but a substantial gut."

Curt scanned the list, noting the inclusion of distances and route vectors from each port to the canal at Panama. "Thorough work. Good job. But your substantial gut notwithstanding," – Curt shot a smile at Bruce – "I think we'd better split up and cover some territory. There are three ports of particular interest, and we better hit the ground running. We've got people in each of these places, and we'll put them on it immediately. Susan, I want you and Josh in Manila by tonight."

Susan sighed. "Major jet lag."

"Jack and Bruce, you're going to Jakarta. Denise and Chris, you're going to Singapore. Ernie and I will ghost behind each of you. I'm sure I don't need to tell you that Husam al Din is probably already in his container, halfway to Miami. We've got to find out where he departed so we can discover what ship he's on and exactly when it's due to arrive. Now, let's get out of here. I'm afraid we're running out of time."

October 26th – Inside the container on the *Desdemonda*

In the stench-filled gloom, Husam al Din pressed the button on his wristwatch to illuminate the dial, and noted the time and date. It had been thirteen days, according to the date block on the face of his watch; nearly two full weeks locked up in a dark coffin that never ceased to roll, pitch and yaw without mercy. At first the seasickness was so bad that he couldn't even think about food without vomiting, so he decided to forego eating altogether. Lack of nourishment took its toll, leaving him weak. While his body lost strength, his mind began to slide into doubt that all of this was worth it. Even without food, his gut still revolted at the constant motion of the ship, and the dry heaves were so violent that his eyeballs felt as if they were about to burst. After that, he decided that it was better to eat at least enough to allow his stomach to vomit comfortably.

With a weary hand, he reached up from his position on the bed, turned on the small overhead light and looked around at the mess. He prided himself on being a clean and orderly man, and the scene before him was disheartening. "What has happened to me?" he thought aloud, and the sound of his own voice came as a shock. It had been nearly two weeks since he heard any sound except that of his own miserable retching, and the constant *thrum-thrum* of the ship's engines vibrating through the steel walls of the container. And then it came to him – how long had it been since he heard the sound of Salaat, his prayers? How long had Allah gone without hearing the prayers of Husam al Din?

The thought stunned him, and he immediately rose from the bed to begin Niyyat, standing with respect and attention to put the world behind him. "Allaahu Akbar ..." he began, but the roll of the ship, and his own weakness toppled him and he fell in a heap beside the bed. He struggled back to his feet, intent on demonstrating to Allah that he had not forgotten. An excuse ran through his mind: *it is because I have been so sick*, he tried to justify himself. Then another realization crashed into his mind, and he fell to the bed and wept. "I don't even know which way it is to Mecca," he wailed. "How can I possibly pray when I do not know which way is toward Mecca?"

In his misery, he reached into the duffel bag and felt for one of the two flashlights that Asman Massud built for this special mission of jihad. He rolled it over in his hands, feeling the knurled aluminum barrel that made it look exactly like one of the expensive American flashlights he had seen in the picture above Massud's workbench. For a moment, he considered switching the light on and ending his wretched life. But he stopped, laid the flashlight on the mattress beside him and mumbled, "I am Husam al Din, the Sword of the Faith."

San Blas Islands

"You won't believe what I just heard on the SSB net."

Dan took the last two strokes of the oars and skidded the dinghy onto the beach where Sven was lying in the shade of a palm.

"This palm is too skinny. I have to keep moving every couple of minutes," Sven complained.

"Well, while you're whining about your inconveniently narrow tree, I'm frustrated as all get out."

"Why? What's the problem?"

Dan climbed from the skiff, pulled it half a boat-length onto dry sand and dragged the bow line up the beach with him. "The problem, my faithful Nordic friend, is that the National Hurricane Center in Miami is starting to make noise about another tropical depression that's meandering across the Atlantic, displaying intentions of heading our way."

Sven nodded at the line in Dan's hand. "You gonna tie that to something?"

"How about if I tie it around your neck?" Dan's voice rose, then he threw the line on the ground.

"Hey, I admit that I'm Danish and that we are known to be a powerful, not to mention good-looking, race of people. But wonderful as I am, I'm not in charge of the weather. Please don't spread that around."

"You said hurricane season was over."

"Almost over. I think I said almost over. Besides, this late in the season, weird things happen with the weather. Just get your brain back into cruiser mode. That means no stress; slow down to an idle, wear a big smile, life is good."

"That's easy for you to say. You don't have anywhere to go."

Sven grinned up at his friend. "Well, unless you want to go out there and play with a hurricane, I'd say neither do you."

"Yeah, well we did want to get to Guatemala, sail up the Rio Dulce, wander the jungle, take a tour to see the ruins up north. Stuff like that."

"Been there, done that," Sven yawned. "Rio Dulce has nothing that's better than this place, so just pull up a sliver of shade and relax. Sorry our trees are so skinny, but they'll have to do."

Dan flopped on the sand and stared at the palm fronds dancing on the breeze against a backdrop of perfect blue. "I guess you're right. It's just that sailing the Rio Dulce has been a long held dream of mine."

"Let me play psychiatrist for a minute, okay?" Sven said.

"Go for it. I already know I'm nuts."

"Being nuts is only part of your problem."

"Oh, thanks," Dan grumbled. "How much do I owe you for that sage diagnosis, Doctor Lutefisk?"

"Hey, don't let it worry you. We're all a little bit nuts."

"Especially those of us who pretend we're psychiatrists."

"Especially so," Sven said.

"So, what's the rest of my problem?"

"I don't know that we have time to cover that much ground." Sven shook his head in mock seriousness.

Dan sat up and started to get to his feet. "Right! Well, I guess this session is over. My check is in the mail."

"Okay," Sven chuckled, " sit back down. I'll give it to you straight."

"I can hardly wait."

"The whole problem can be summed up in one word – expectations."

"What's wrong with expectations?"

"What's wrong with them is that they don't always get fulfilled. An unfulfilled expectation is what causes stress. Stress is what causes heart attacks, ulcers and the kind of mental lapses that drive men into the path of a hurricane in an attempt to fulfill an expectation."

Dan laid back in the shade of the palm, laced his fingers behind his head and stared thoughtfully at the fronds and the blue. After a long moment, he rolled his head toward Sven. "Thanks Doc."

"I'll send you a bill."

Chapter Nineteen

October 27th – Colon, Panama

Captain Sleagle stepped from the sweltering humidity into the cool, smoky darkness of the Papagayo. A ceiling fan with fake palm frond blades thrummed with a low vibration as it circulated a cool breeze through the air-conditioned saloon. Old wooden chairs were tilted up against small tables scattered around the room, and most of the bar stools were unoccupied. It was early afternoon, so the place was almost empty. Here and there, the perennial drunk who paid no attention to time of day or night, sat in dazed silence and nursed a bottle. The Papagayo was relatively peaceful at the moment, but that would only last a few more hours until it devolved into the brawling chaos that erupted every night.

For a moment, Sleagle stood by the door and allowed his eyes to adjust to the darkness, then he spotted his favorite bar stool, empty, at the far end. He navigated through the maze of tables and chairs, pulled back the stool and took a seat. One glance at his wristwatch made him shake his head, disappointed that his time ashore was going to be so short.

"Ignacio," he called to the bartender, trying to make himself heard above the racket coming from the cluster of patrons apparently having a high time at the pool table. He had known Ignacio for more than fifteen years, and saw the skinny black-skinned man every time he came through Colon and made his traditional trek to the Papagayo.

"Aye, Capitan Sleagle, it is good to see you again."

"Is it me, or is it my money?" Sleagle laughed. "It's good to see you again, too, my friend. How is your family?"

"Ah, they are doing well. Now that Ramon has gone off to school, Solange has come to help me run this place. She takes care of the books, makes sure we don't run out of anything important, and keeps me in line."

"We all need some of that," Sleagle said. "I'll have a shot of El Fuego."

In two hours, he was due back on the bridge deck of the *Desdemonda* preparing for the final leg of the voyage, and he couldn't afford to have more than one drink in his belly.

"Coming your way," Ignacio said cheerfully. The shot glass of amber liquid slid across the polished bar and Sleagle caught it with a practiced hand and raised it to eye level as he quickly bowed his head. He couldn't count the times he had been in the Papagayo, sitting on this same barstool, downing this same drink, engaging in this same ritual.

Of all the places his career had taken him around the world, Panama was among his favorites, but not because of its scenery, and not even because of the Papagayo: it was the canal itself. The place seemed to defy the odds. Every time he transited the canal, he thought about the thousands of lives lost to accidents, yellow fever and malaria during its thirty-four years of construction. Of the 80,000 people who worked on the canal during the French and American construction years, nearly 30,000 died here. His great-grandfather, Cornelius Sleagle, was one of them. And yet, even with the losses, the project went on.

The human toll was huge, but while governments are sometimes capable of turning a blind eye to the cost in skin and bone and blood, they do not so easily ignore the financial expense. At more than $352,000,000 of 1914 US dollars, the canal was the most costly construction project the United States had ever undertaken up to that time. Money was poured into the job and, in spite of the rising death toll, occasional poor management, perpetual lack of equipment, and seemingly impossible engineering challenges, the canal was built. And now, just shy of a century later, abandoned by the ambivalent political interests of its American creator and left to the whims of local dictators and Chinese opportunists, the canal continued to live. No matter how many lives it claimed, the canal itself seemed to defy death. In the Papagayo, Captain Sleagle always bowed his head and raised his glass in a silent toast to the canal and to his great-grandfather.

Unlike many who prefer to toss back their shot of liquor, Sleagle nursed his, letting the warm liquid do its work slowly. Over the din of voices coming from the small cluster of people surrounding the pool table, he heard the word 'hurricane', and it immediately caught his attention. The word came from the television that was suspended near ceiling level in one corner above the bar.

"Ignacio," Sleagle called out. "Can you please turn up the volume? I want to hear this."

The barkeep nodded, wiped his hands on the thin apron hanging from his waist and reached for the remote control.

"... the track of Hurricane Yolanda is predicted to sweep into the Yucatan Channel, but we cannot say when that will happen. Right now, the storm has stalled south of Jamaica and is building strength. We will post the storm track hourly, because these things are unpredictable and she could start to move again at any time. In anticipation of what is to come, the entire coastline from Honduras to Cancun is under storm warning, and there is no indication that Yolanda, now at category 4 with winds of 135 miles per hour, will weaken before making landfall. Wave heights in the open sea around Yolanda are running nearly forty feet, creating extremely hazardous conditions. And now in other news ..."

Captain Eric Sleagle pushed the glass away from him without finishing his drink and left the Papagayo, walking toward the container ship terminal as fast as the heat and humidity would let him.

Waterfront warehouse district – Manila, Philippines

Rain pounded the streets of Manila and ran ankle deep in the gutters. Along the waterfront, tarped flatbed trucks came and went, spewing diesel exhaust into the sodden sky. Growls of forklifts and the occasional bark of a foreman filled the night air as the men on the graveyard shift moved pallets of cargo from trucks and into the warehouse. Under the cover of an overhanging eave, Josh Adams and Susan Vellum melted into the shadows, their eyes pinned to a metal entrance door at the end of the gray street.

Josh pulled back the sleeve of his raincoat and pressed the stem of his wristwatch. For half a second, the watch face lit up. "He's twenty minutes late."

Susan nodded slowly, and turned her eyes to scan up and down the street. "When you're on the warehouse gang, you're not always in control of your own time. Let's give him ten more."

"Antonio Almidori Filho," Josh rolled the name over in his mouth. "Has a nice ring to it."

"Well, if he's got what we want, he can quit his night job, 'cause the reward money will keep him in rice and beans for a long time."

From the end of the street, a split of light suddenly shot from the metal door. The silhouette of a man showed briefly against the light, then the door closed. They trained their eyes on the approaching man and listened to the quick splash of his feet on the flooded street as he jogged toward them. Susan's hand went into her pocket and her fingers tightened around the grip of her Beretta.

The man stopped running and stepped forward slowly, hands held open and palms forward at shoulder level. "It is I," the man whispered in a thick Filipino accent, yet with perfect English grammar. "Antonio Almidori Filho."

"We were told you have done work for us before. What do you have for us?" Josh asked.

"I have been one of yours for more than five years, working the waterfront and keeping my eyes and ears open. When word came that you were looking for a particular shipping container, I started poking about."

"What can you tell us?" Susan relaxed her hand but kept it in her pocket nonetheless.

"One of the drivers was in a bar about a week ago. Late into his drinking, his mouth loosened up and he started talking about a strange incident involving a container with an RV trailer in it. A woman named Alicia Gomez gave him orders to deliver the box to a container ship named *Desdemonda,* with specific instructions about how the delivery was to take place. Seemed odd to the driver. Under command of Captain Eric Sleagle, *Desdemonda* left the harbor on the 13th, headed for the Panama Canal and then on to Miami. That is all I know."

"That is all we need to know." Josh reached out his right hand to grasp the informant's hand. He reached out his left and handed over an envelope. "This is only part of it. If this pans out, you'll get the rest."

Antonio Almidori Filho took the envelope, stuffed it into his pants pocket, and bowed slightly. "Glad to be of service. Good luck on this." Then he turned and jogged back into the rain. In a moment, light showed around the perimeter of the door again, then it was gone.

"How would we ever do it without guys like that?" Susan put words to the very question that was running through Josh's mind.

"We couldn't," Josh answered. "Without native boots on the ground, our job would be impossible."

Susan finally pulled her right hand out of her pocket. "We can go after this Alicia Gomez later. Sounds like she's a figure around here and she's playing with the bad guys. Maybe, with the right kind of incentive package, we can put her to work for us."

"Yeah," Josh chuckled. "Make her a deal she can live with, or die without. She can cooperate and make a living as a double agent, or disappear the hard way."

"Works for me," Susan said, reaching in her pocket and pulling out a flip phone. She punched in a speed-dial number and waited.

"Delamo," the voice said on the other end.

"We've got it. *Desdemonda.* Left Manila on the 13th for passage through the canal and on to Miami. Target is inside an RV trailer being transported via container."

"Susan, stay in Manila and see if you can track down a container number and some more specifics about the shipment. I want Josh on the next flight to Panama. I'll pull the rest of the team back here and get on things from this end."

"Right, chief." Susan ended the call and turned to Josh as she stuffed the phone back in her pocket. "I stay here to chase paperwork. You go to Panama to chase the ship and the bad guy. Lucky dog."

"I already know this bad guy. Wanna trade?"

She smiled. "Not for a minute."

****

At NIA headquarters, Curt Delamo identified himself as a CIA officer, which was technically true, when he made his call to the Coast Guard station in Panama City. NIA was not known outside a small group of elite intelligence leaders inside CIA, so Delamo resorted to his link with the parent organization when working with other agencies such as the Coast Guard or Homeland Security. It was a fact that every NIA agent was also a CIA agent, the difference being that they were assigned to a black-ops Special Projects detachment that was known to only a select few.

In Panama, Captain Klaus Pfister picked up the line and listened to Delamo's request. Pfister was a hardline military type, trained to do things by the numbers and take no shortcuts. "Sir, can you give me a number where I can reach you? I'll need to kick this upstairs for approval."

"For heaven sakes," Curt almost yelled into the phone, but managed to hold it down to just a loud voice, "all I'm asking for is the status of one of the container ships coming through the canal. Is it there yet? Has it already passed through? That's all."

"With all due respect, sir, I don't know who you are. We live in a different age and work by a new set of rules since 9/11. Until I verify your identity, your request will go unanswered. Do you want me to proceed?"

Curt exhaled with a degree of exasperation. "Forget it. I'll just call the Port Authority."

"Begging your pardon, sir, but if you are really who you say you are, you might not want to involve them. Meaning no disrespect, but there is reason to be cautious with classified information, especially when dealing with the Port Authority in Panama."

"I appreciate your candor. This is a highly classified operation, and it needs the most urgent attention. What can you do for me?"

"I can do what I said and then get back to you. Is that what you want?"

"How long it is going to take?"

"I can't make promises, but I can say that I will personally see to it."

Curt understood bureaucracy well enough to know that it was futile to argue. "Then go ahead and do whatever you have to do. But please expedite." He gave the captain the number for a secure line into the CIA, a number to an upper echelon officer who would provide the right cover for Delamo. Then he hung up the phone.

Delamo's second call was to the Homeland Security, where he was put through to Secretary David Robinson. Robinson was already in the loop, so after brief pleasantries Curt got right to the point. "We think we have identified the ship. I am working on verification of its present location, and will notify you as soon as I have something more."

"Good," Robinson said. "Your people are on this, so we'll stand out of the way until it becomes a more domestic situation. But I'll start putting things into place in case we need to conduct a mass evacuation or go in and handle a decontamination-and-recovery mission."

"Thank you, Mr Secretary. I'll keep you updated."

Curt hung up, then placed his third call to Secretary Rick Keller at Defense. "Mr Secretary, I recommend that we put Seal Team Seven on standby and positioned for interdiction."

"I'll see to it," Keller said. "I'll have them stationed at Pensacola so we can conduct a fast attack."

"Thank you, sir."

Curt Delamo's next call was to his wife. "Honey, don't ask any questions. I'm not going to be home for a while. I want you to take the kids and go to visit your uncle Mick in Scotland."

There was a long silence on the phone, then finally Merrilee spoke. "You're kidding."

"No, I'm not. No questions. Just go. Plan for a long visit. I'll be in touch as soon as I can."

"Is tomorrow okay? I have things to arrange. Call Mick, for one. And the kids are off running around. It's not like I can just drop everything."

"Tomorrow will be fine. I need your support on this."

"Of course you have it. I'm sorry to be cranky. This caught me off guard."

"I know. Do what you need to do and call me from Mick's when you get there. Wherever I am, I'll be on the cell."

"Okay, honey. I love you."

"Love you, too. Tell the kids I love them. We'll talk soon."

The phone was barely back on the cradle and it rang again. It was Captain Pfister. "Sir, your request is granted. Here's what I have. The *Desdemonda* departed an hour and twenty minutes ago. Next port of call is Miami in approximately forty-nine hours."

"Thank you, captain."

"One problem, sir."

"What's that?"

"Hurricane Yolanda is dead ahead of the *Desdemonda*. The two will collide within the next seven hours."

"What's her strength?"

"She's at category 4 right now, sir. Winds are at 135 knots and rising. Sea state is at forty feet out of the southeast."

"A ship like the *Desdemonda* ... what can she take?"

"No ship is safe in those conditions, sir. Container ships are no exception."

"Can she be ordered back into port?"

"We have no authority to do so, sir. Aboard ship, the captain is the ultimate authority; the safety of the vessel and her crew is his responsibility."

"Why did he leave, knowing that the storm was coming?"

"I cannot speak for the captain, sir. But it is highly unlikely that he was unaware of the weather conditions. Perhaps he thought he could outrun the storm, make it into the channel and stay ahead of the weather."

"Racing the train to the crossing, huh?"

"In a sense."

"Stupid, if you ask me."

"I didn't ask, sir, but I have to agree."

"Thank you, captain."

"Think nothing of it, sir."

Delamo hung up the phone, thought a moment, then picked it up and called the National Hurricane Center in Miami. Noel Page took his call and started to read him the standard forecast.

"Mister Page," Curt stopped him in mid-sentence, "I can log into your website if all I want is the forecast. I want to know what this storm is really going to do. How bad will it get? Where is it going to make landfall? What would it do to a container ship caught in its path?"

There was a momentary silence on the line, and Curt was just about to ask if anybody was still there. Then Page spoke up. "Mr Delamo, I can't tell you with any degree of exactness what is going to happen with this hurricane. With the possible exception of my mother-in-law, there is nothing on earth as unpredictable as a hurricane."

"Isn't there anything else you can tell me?"

"We can make predictions based upon similar factors from past storms, but a hurricane is kind of like a serial killer: you can look at patterns of past behavior and make a guess about where he's likely to strike next and what he'll probably do, but you can't really know until after the fact. Wish I could tell you more."

"Yeah, me too."

Chapter Twenty

October 28th – The bridge deck of the *Desdemonda*

Desdemonda steamed north from Colon for more than fourteen hours, making 320 nautical miles before veering slightly to the northwest, well outside the hazards to navigation presented by the islands of Providencia. Captain Eric Sleagle propped himself against the helm station with feet wide apart and knees bent to absorb the ship's movement. He held a binocular to his eyes, scanning the southeastern horizon.

Solid overcast blanketed the sky, and the water was the color of new steel. A persistent swell from just ahead of the starboard beam rolled the huge ship slowly. It was a slow, lazy motion that was not yet uncomfortable for the crew on a ship the size and displacement of *Desdemonda*. Still, Sleagle was worried. This was not the usual swell, and he knew that it foretold the fury of a powerful storm still to the east and heading his way. The winds were already howling through the ship's superstructure. His instruments indicated a wind speed of 58 knots, gusting to 63. No, this was not at all normal for this time of year in the southwestern corner of the Caribbean Sea.

Sleagle was one of those men who had discovered his calling in life at an early age. He was a man of the sea, not only by career choice, but also as the fulfillment of a dream he held since childhood. He grew up reading sea tales, some fictional and some true. He was certain that, as with all tales of the sea, even the ones that claimed to be true, were embellished with a modicum of editorial license. Now, as he stood at the helm and considered what was coming at him, he recalled the story of a brigantine named *Tesoro do Rei* that was lost not far from here back in 1571.

As the tale went, the ship set sail for its home port in Portugal in late October, loaded with booty stolen or otherwise obtained from the natives of what is now Guatemala. Three days after weighing anchor and heading into open sea, a powerful hurricane ripped the ship apart and she sank with all hands.

The following year, men aboard another ship sailing toward the mainland saw smoke rising from a tiny island off present day Honduras. The captain ordered the sails down and sent a party ashore to investigate. They discovered Guillermo Ascente, former commander of *Tesoro do Rei,* living the life of a castaway in a primitive hut, wearing rags, skinny and almost lifeless, eating whatever he could scrounge from the jungle and the sea.

After returning to Portugal, Ascente became somewhat of a local hero as he told his story of surviving the hurricane that came to be known as 'O Gigante'.

"Sir," the voice of his first officer brought Sleagle back from his thoughts, and he turned to face the man.

"Yes, what is it?"

"A report from the deck crew, sir. They have checked all the tie-downs and found everything secure."

"Thank you. Carry on."

The bridge deck was elevated the height of a two-story building above the highest rank of containers, and was positioned near the stern of the ship, giving the skipper a commanding view of his cargo load. The bridge deck was a wide glass and steel hallway that stretched ninety-two feet across the ship, and was filled with the latest electronic monitoring, control, communication and navigation equipment. There were dedicated stations for the other members of his command team, consisting of his first officer and navigator. To port and starboard of the enclosed bridge, outside platforms offered secondary stations where the skipper could see up and down the length of the ship to either side and direct steerage and line-handling when docking, passing through locks, or when tugs were coming alongside. In some respects, the view from the bridge deck was like watching a football game from the owner's lounge through an expanse of windows high above the field.

Facing the command team were redundant arrays of monitors for the multiple radar and electronic chart plotting systems. Primary and secondary VHF and SSB radios, as well as the ship's intercom system, were centered on the command dashboard.

The helm station was home to the engine controls and the vast array of electrical and hydraulic systems controls. Rather than having a wheel, *Desdemonda's* manual steering was controlled by use of devices similar to computer game joysticks. Rudder angle indicators gave a visual feedback to the captain about how much steering effort was being made.

Manual steering was used for close-in work, but most of the time, the huge ship was steered by autopilot that was directed electronically by the global positioning satellite system, leading the vessel from one pre-designated waypoint to the next without the need for anyone to touch the controls.

On the open sea, the ship could literally tend itself while everyone on board went to sleep or fell overboard or died of carbon monoxide poisoning. Once the ship was underway and the autopilot activated, nothing would stop it from plowing ahead at full speed toward its destination. To Sleagle, all the electronic gadgetry came with both a bright and a dark side. It certainly eased the exhausting burden of having to manually control the ship hour after hour, day after day, as it had been done in earlier times before the advances of technology. But if the crew became complacent and lazy, the self-governing systems could carry the ship to disaster. Sleagle constantly reminded the command team that even with all the wizardry built into the control systems, it was still necessary, in fact it was the law of the sea, that the command crew maintain an adequate watch at all times.

"Machines and electronics are nice," he was fond of saying, "but they can't make judgment calls or respond to sudden emergencies the way a man at the helm can."

Much of the time, only one member of the command team stood watch. They worked by a three-on, six-off schedule leaving the off-watch ample time to rest and prepare for their shift. But today, as they prepared to head into the hurricane, all hands were on the bridge deck, and would stay there until the captain decided to shorten crew and resume the rotation schedule. This was one of those exceptional moments in the life of a container ship, when every set of eyes and ears was necessary for the next several hours as they sailed into harm's way.

The rest of the crew, consisting of twenty-nine men, were scattered throughout the ship, tending to cargo and mechanical equipment. A full team of ship's engineers stood round-the-clock watch on the engines and generators. Electricians and hydraulic specialists saw to the needs of the onboard electrical and hydraulic equipment. Others pulled shifts to maintain saltwater desalination units that provided fresh water for the ship. A mess crew kept everybody fed, and a gang of able seamen took care of general ship's maintenance, scraping and painting and fixing whatever needed attention.

Running all of this was a daunting task. In addition to commanding from the helm, it was Sleagle's job to make sure the entire ship was kept in top running condition, the crew well fed and cared for, and the cargo carried safely to its final destination. It took coordinated teamwork to make it all happen, and he was pleased with the team aboard *Desdemonda* for this voyage.

As he stared through the binocular at the gray scene before him, Sleagle called for Peter Moyes, his weather officer. A young man of slight build and a thinning wisp of blond hair stepped from a small room directly aft of the helm station. Without turning to acknowledge the man's presence, Sleagle asked, "What is the latest position of Yolanda?"

Moyes was twenty-three years old, had a weak chin, and his attempt at growing a mustache had failed miserably. The thin hairs on his upper lip were spotty and limp, but he persisted in letting the thing grow, to the amusement of the crew members who sported more substantial facial hair. Looking a bit more pale than usual, Moyes stepped beside the captain.

"The eye is located seventy miles distant at a relative bearing of one two zero and approaching at a speed of 12 knots and rising. We are under the leading edge and on a collision course, sir."

Sleagle raised his eyebrows. "Well, so much for being stalled. I guess it was too much to hope that she would sit still forever. I was hoping to get out ahead of her and beat her through the Yucatan Channel. The problem is that now that she's on the move, as the seas grow we're not going to be able to maintain our speed, so we can't outrun her. Eventually, we have to slow down and let her pass over us."

He turned to the chart table where, in spite of all the electronic gear onboard, the navigator still maintained a dead reckoning plot on paper charts – just in case the electronics failed. The captain scribed a line with his finger and tapped hard at one spot.

"We've got about four hours, I'd say, and she's going to run over the top of us right about here. What's the wind speed at the eye wall?"

Moyes swallowed a rising lump in his throat. "Reported to be 145 and rising, sir."

"Forecast storm track?"

"Miami is forecasting three options, sir."

"Let me guess. One is to sweep up this way," – he ran his finger across the chart – "through the Yucatan Channel and into the Gulf of Mexico. Another is to slam into the coast somewhere between Honduras and Belize, blowing the place to bits and wrecking the local tourism economy. And the third is to do something totally unpredictable."

"Yes, sir."

"Are they giving percentages?"

"Not yet."

Sleagle looked at his weather officer, as if waiting for something more.

Finally it came. "Not yet, sir," Moyes' eyes fell to the floor in silent apology for neglecting to be properly respectful.

"That will be all for now, Mr Moyes," Sleagle said. "Keep me updated every thirty minutes. But if there are any significant changes from what you've already told me, I want to know it immediately. Do you understand?"

"Aye, sir."

Moyes turned away and returned to the ship's weather station where he could monitor all the major forecasting stations, tap into satellite imagery, and receive real-time reports from data buoys and other ships in the region. A murmur stirred in his mind, but he was smart enough to never let it near his lips. He resented Sleagle and his constant demand for what he called 'proper military respect'. A quiet plan was growing, and he was more certain now than ever that this was his last voyage under the dictatorial command of Sleagle. In Miami, he planned to terminate his contract and find a nice, friendly cruise ship to work for. He'd seen the brochures. The food was undoubtedly better. There were parties every night. Rather than shipping containers, the decks would be lined with gorgeous babes. And maybe, just maybe, he could finally drop the 'sir' from his working vocabulary.

As ordered, Peter Moyes delivered weather updates to Captain Eric Sleagle every half hour. At each report, he addressed the man he despised with the hated word 'sir'. By the time he made his third report, winds were screaming at more than 70 knots, already at the first level of hurricane strength. Moyes knew that worse was yet to come as the center of the storm approached. Wind strength would increase steadily, doubling what they were already feeling, and perhaps even more than doubling by the time the eye wall slammed into them.

Desdemonda was rolling hard now, and every now and then there was a thunderous boom that shook the ship as the hull was hammered by a wave that was out of synch with the vessel's rhythmic roll and pitch. In calm seas, the ballast of heavy cargo was an advantage that helped keep the ship steady, but in conditions like this, the kinetic energy of half a million tons of swaying weight only amplified the movement. And with the cargo containers stacked as high as they were on *Desdemonda,* a great deal of weight was above the water line, raising the center of gravity and creating an inherently unstable load.

Like the swinging of a heavy pendulum, once the rolling motion started, the more the ship wanted to continue to roll, first to one side and then the other. Ballast in the cargo holds below decks acted as the far side of the teeter-totter, counterbalancing the weight above decks, but that concept was only good up to a point. Even sailboats with heavily ballasted keels were known to be rolled over in heavy seas, and *Desdemonda* was a far cry from having a sailboat's self-righting ability. Everyone onboard understood that, if the winds and seas continued to worsen, it was not inconceivable for the enormous ship to roll all the way over and never come up. There were no guarantees of safety just because she was a big ship.

Captain Sleagle had gambled on being able to outrun the storm. He stared out the expansive windows of the bridge deck and mentally kicked himself for his decision back in Colon. He could have stayed put and waited for the storm to pass. But sometimes a hurricane will progress so slowly that a fast ship can easily outmaneuver or outrun the danger. The report he had received from the weather service before leaving port showed that the storm had stalled for more than eight hours before beginning to move again very slowly, and he was counting on being able to outrun it and stay on schedule to Miami. But in the last dozen hours, it had picked up speed and was roaring like a freight train. He saw now that he was going to lose the race.

Moyes cleared his throat. "Wind strength is at 74, sir. Significant wave height is thirty-nine feet. Both wind and sea state are rising steadily, sir." He doubled up on the 'sirs' as a barely visible form of personal protest, but said the word through a clenched jaw. Maybe it was the stress of the approaching storm, or the fact that he was seasick and had spent the past twenty minutes bent over the toilet. But Peter Moyes was angry. He was sick and angry, and he wanted to be anywhere else but here. The last thing he wanted was to report to Sleagle.

Above the noise of the storm, the captain detected the difference in the way his weather officer talked to him. It wasn't just his imagination. The first officer and the navigator heard it, too. They looked up from their work, glanced curiously at each other and then stared at the captain and the weather officer.

"You don't look well, Mr Moyes."

"I'm not well, sir," Moyes yelled. "I'm sick to death of this ship and this storm. And mostly, I'm sick to death of you. Sir." He spat the last word. "You got us into this. We could have stayed in Panama and let the storm pass, but no, you had to be the hero."

Sleagle had seen this before: a young man who thought life at sea was going to be nothing but a grand adventure, seeing the world on somebody else's nickel and having a girl in every port; then the realities of it hits him square between the eyes, and he can't take it

"Well, son," – the captain put a hand on the young officer's shoulder, looked earnestly in his eyes and spoke with an almost hushed calm – "we can talk about my judgment later. But you are this ship's weather officer. Right now, you are one of the most important people on this ship and we are relying on *your* judgment to help get us through this."

The calm voice of the captain took Peter Moyes aback. He didn't know quite what to say, so he stood there with his mouth shut.

"We need you to be on top of your game right now. You must pull yourself together enough to be an asset to the command team. We're all depending on you. But I suggest that you go to my cabin, lie down, shut your eyes and rest for a while. It will make you feel better. I'll call for you when I need you."

"Your cabin, sir?" This time, the word 'sir' didn't stick quite so hard in his throat.

"Yes. My cabin will be the most comfortable place for you right now." He reached into his pocket, pulled out a key and handed it to the young man. "Go on. We'll handle things until you are back on your feet."

"Who will do the weather for you, sir?" The question was carried on a weak voice.

Sleagle smiled and patted the lad on the shoulder. "Don't you worry about that right now. When I got started in this business, I was a weather officer just like you. I think I can handle things."

"Just like me, sir?" Moyes' voice was almost a whisper.

"Uh-huh. Now you go rest. In an hour or so, we're all going to be extremely busy on the bridge, fighting to keep the ship. The command team will need you to be at full strength."

Peter Moyes turned and, on unsteady feet as the ship rolled to the waves, headed across the bridge toward the stairway that led to the captain's cabin. As he reached for the door, he turned back. "Captain Sleagle, sir …" When he saw the ship's commander turn to face him, he stood erect and snapped a crisp salute. "I'm sorry for what I said, sir." Then he turned and disappeared through the door.

Captain Sleagle felt the eyes of his first officer and navigator. He turned his head to face them and, perceiving their thoughts, decided to answer the question he knew was in their minds. "That was me twenty years ago," he smiled. "But don't you guys get any funny ideas about me being a pushover. And keep this to yourselves, okay? I've got a reputation to protect. Now get back to work. We've got a tough day ahead of us."

Almost in unison, the men sounded off. "Aye, sir."

Over the next hour, *Desdemonda* rolled and pitched to the waves. Wind screamed through the radio and radar antennas atop the bridge deck. Swells hit them from just aft of the starboard beam, maximizing their impact on the hull, and causing the ship to roll violently and shoving the stern sideways. It was the most dangerous way for a ship to stand to large oncoming waves, and it set the vessel into a slow, wobbling spiral motion with the bow describing a circle in a rhythm just opposite the circle being described by the stern. In a smaller vessel, the motion was called a death roll. It was uncomfortable, but there was no real risk of a ship the size of *Desdemonda* actually spiraling into a wave-driven broach. The danger was that, if the cargo got loose in the holds, the ship could become unbalanced or sustain hull damage from a container slamming around like a wrecking ball.

Driven rain slanted sideways, shutting down visibility to just beyond the bow of the ship. The world around them was slate gray and growing steadily darker. As if a sudden hill had appeared behind them, the stern angled up and the men on the bridge deck hung on to steady themselves as the ship rose and then fell off the back of the large wave. The whole ship shuddered under the impact, as the flat-sided hull slammed into the trough that followed the wave. Then she rose again and slammed once more, sending a shattering reverberation through the length and width of Desdemonda.

"That one was over sixty feet sir," the first officer shouted.

"Bring us about," Sleagle ordered. "We'll never survive unless we get the bow into those monsters."

"Aye, sir," the first officer responded as he laid the control stick over.

As the ship came beam-to, another wave hit, this one larger than the last, and the *Desdemonda* was rolled into a thirty degree list. Everyone grabbed for something solid, and everything not bolted down shot into the downhill end of the bridge. Sleagle held his breath for so long that it seemed as if time had stopped while the ship held steady on the extreme angle of heel. He knew that at a certain point, the weight of cargo above the ship's center of gravity would overwhelm the righting moment, with no coming back upright. She would just lay over on her side with cargo bay hatches bursting open and the ocean flooding in, sending them to the bottom.

While his officers strained to hold on, under his breath the captain prayed for the ship to right itself. After what seem an eternal wait, he felt the hull slide off the huge wave and fall into the trough. It was just enough to start the ship coming back up, but he knew the next wave was waiting to finish the job the first one started.

"I've got the helm," he shouted as the ship came level, and grabbed the joy stick and throttle controls. He rammed one control full forward and the other full reverse in a desperate effort to spin the enormous ship on its axis and get her pointed into the waves before the next onslaught.

Mercifully, there was a pause in the waves, and Sleagle knew that they had been slammed by a short series of rogue waves that were created by the unusual joining of two or three waves that combine their force and build to enormous height. If he could take advantage of the relative calm that followed those rogues, they might have a chance. But another set of rogues could come along at any time.

Slowly, *Desdemonda* regained her feet, and the giant propellers dug into the thrashing seas. Gradually, the scene before them rotated. Another wave slammed them, this time exploding across the cargo deck and drowning the bridge windows. A falling sensation followed the lifting of the wave, and they were back in the trough, but the ship was still turning. The next wave lifted them like a fast elevator ride, then they fell again, and this time the bow went down first.

"We're getting there, men!" the captain shouted. "Just a little more!"

The next wave broke over the bow, sending a mad river of foam raging toward the bridge windows from more than 800 feet ahead. It smashed into the glass and the bridge shuddered under the impact. Captain Sleagle thumbed the joystick and adjusted the throttles to bring the ship into a quartering position that would save them from taking the waves directly on the nose.

"Sorry, men, but I don't think we're going to find a comfortable way to ride this one out."

Through the thick glass of the bridge windows the scene was ghastly. As far as the eye could see, mountainous gray-green cresting waves, shredded by violent wind, fought their way toward the ship, each seeming to shove the other aside for the privilege of being first to punish the *Desdemonda.* Captain Sleagle exhaled deeply, wiped the sweat from his brow and turned his thoughts inward. He didn't want to tell his men just how close they had come to disaster.

He never believed it was possible to suffer such a pounding in a ship this size, but now all doubts were gone. It was a freak of nature, this late-season hurricane, and he knew he was staring down the throat of a monster that can tear a container ship apart.

Chapter Twenty-one

October 29th – Panama

"I understand your request, but we're not flying a chopper into that storm." Captain Pfister's graying flat top hair bristled, as the commanding officer of Coast Guard Sector Panama tightened his jaw, planted his palms firmly on the desk and glowered at Josh Adams.

"Do you understand that this is a matter of national security of the highest magnitude?"

Pfister leaned back, exhaled and tried again. "Mr Adams, I hear what you're saying. I've already been in contact with Mr Delamo. But it is a physical impossibility for us to put you on the deck of that container ship right now. The ship you're chasing is caught in the middle of one of the worst hurricanes this sector has ever seen, and there's not a thing in the world we can do about it until the storm moves out of the area. Then we can go in and see what's left of the ship."

Josh pushed back from the desk, straightened up and reached for his cell phone. "Thanks. I've got some calls to make. I'll get back in touch with you later."

"Just for the record," – Pfister brushed back his bristled hair – "it wouldn't matter if the president himself ordered us into that storm right now."

"Are you saying you would disobey an order from the president?"

"Not saying that at all, sir," the captain was quick with his reply. "But if we followed those orders, nobody on the mission would live to tell about it."

"Well, I'm not calling the President. And I don't expect you to put lives at unreasonable risk. Just keeping the chain of command informed. Unless they send me elsewhere, I'll be around, and I'd appreciate it if you let me know the minute we can board that ship."

"The captain stood and offered his hand. "Will do, sir."

San Blas Islands

Sven and Dan stood on the beach staring with focused attention at a solid shield of grey sky to the northeast. "See, I told you so," Sven said. "When will you learn to listen to the Danish genius?"

"Yeah, well I have to admit that you called it right this time. As far as genius goes, I'm not buying it. Just luck, I'd say. But I suppose it's enough to fool the girls."

Dan felt a pinch on his bottom and yelped.

Nicole retracted her hand and grinned. "You boys aren't talking in disparaging terms about us girls again, are you?"

Dan spun around. "Geez, Nicole, where did you learn to sneak up on me like that?"

"Nice try, buddy." She eyed him like a shopper checking for bad fruit. "Don't go trying to change the subject. Were you, or were you not, saying bad things about us girls?"

"Not," Dan tried.

"Strike one." Nicole shook her head. "You know what happens after strike three? Wanna try again?"

Sven was enjoying his friend's sudden trouble. "I think you're busted. Might as well confess and throw yourself on the mercy of the court." He turned to Nicole. "Your honor, if it please the court, this man is guilty as charged. And to add to his offense, he was also making disparaging remarks about my Danish genius when it comes to weather forecasting."

"Genius, huh?" Grendel stepped out of the hut waving a sheet of paper. "Is that what they call a weather fax these days? Here's the latest." She read from the paper: '*The eye of Hurricane Yolanda is at 15 degrees 4 minutes north latitude, 81 degrees 19 minutes west longitude. She's gaining strength and is expected to generate wind speeds in excess of 155 miles per hour. Forecasters are warning of landfall somewhere along the coast of Guatemala, although she could turn north through the Yucatan Channel into the Gulf of Mexico.*'

Dan lowered his eyebrows at Sven, "Weather fax, huh?"

Sven took a step back and stammered, "Well, uh …"

"Well, uh, indeed!" Grendel threw the paper at Sven. "So, mister Danish genius, can you tell us all what Hurricane Yolanda is going to do next? Maybe you can make it sound so convincing that you can even fool us girls." She turned her icy glare at Dan.

Dan held up his right hand. "I solemnly swear that from this minute forward, I will never say another bad thing about you girls. You're the greatest. After all, you defrocked this Danish fraud." He turned an evil eye on Sven.

"Ah, come on," Sven complained. "It was all in good fun."

Dan put his hand on Sven's shoulder and looked him in the eye. "There is a path to forgiveness, my friend, but it leads through your secret snorkeling hole so we can catch some dinner."

"Agreed. Let's go grab our gear."

Grendel put her hands on her hips and stamped her foot as the boys walked away. "Nicole, have you ever noticed that whenever our men get in trouble, they seem to solve it all by going fishing?"

"I guess it could be worse. At least we'll get another seafood dinner out of the deal."

Aboard the *Desdemonda*

With her bow quartering into the raging seas, the *Desdemonda* pitched, rolled and yawed violently. Everyone on board was forced to live by the rule of 'one hand for the ship and one hand for yourself', maintaining a constant grip on some kind of handhold to keep from being thrown down and injured.

Peter Moyes steadied himself in the doorway leading to his office. "Sir, the latest report from Miami." Moyes held out a computer printout for Sleagle, who was seated at the helm station.

Sleagle kept his eyes on the instruments. "Read the pertinent stuff to me from there, if you will. No need to risk crossing the bridge deck just to hand me the report."

"Thank you, sir," Moyes breathed. "The essence is that they're predicting movement of the eye up into the Yucatan Channel by 0600 tomorrow. Finally, we'll be on the backside of this hideous monster and it will be shifting away from us."

"Hideous monster? Are those their words?"

"Uh, no, sir," Moyes stammered. "Those are mine."

"A pretty fair description, I'd say. Thank you for the report, Mr Moyes. I'm glad to see you're feeling better. It's nice to have you back with us on the bridge deck."

Moyes flushed. "Sorry, sir, for leaving you without a weather officer for so long. Thanks for allowing me to use your cabin. Sir." This time, there was no hint of resentment in the use of the word 'sir'.

"Did you find the meds in the head cabinet?"

"I did, sir. But if you don't mind my asking, why do you carry seasickness medication?"

Sleagle turned toward Moyes. "For seasickness, of course." Then sensing the young officer's reluctance to ask the next question, the captain went ahead and answered it. "Yes, even I suffer from *mal de mer* sometimes. All it takes is the wrong set of circumstances, and anybody, even an old salt, can get seasick. Nothing to be embarrassed about."

"No, sir."

"Hang on!" the first officer shouted, "here we go again. Another big one."

The ship plunged into a canyon that had opened a gaping maw in the sea. The bow fell for what seemed like forever, then slammed into the trough at the bottom. The weight of the bow in a freefall continued down, like a diver cutting a clean hole in the water. Moyes gasped and clung to the doorway, sliding to the floor as his legs gave way. To him, it felt as if the ship would just keep going down and never come up. But a long moment later, the ship came up slow at first, then faster and faster until it broke out over the crest of the next enormous wave. Then it plunged again and slammed with a shuddering violence into the bottom of the trough.

"I'd say some of these are above 70 feet, sir!" the first officer shouted above the noise of the storm.

A deep metallic groan sounded from the bowels of the hull, as if something big and important were giving up life, and a worried look crossed captain Sleagle's face. "Damn," was all he said. But it was enough to swing the eyes of the navigator and first officer toward their captain. They knew Sleagle was shaken.

Moyes began to whimper like a puppy that is suddenly lost and afraid.

Sleagle grabbed for the microphone, thumbed the button and shouted, "All hands. Secure yourselves, we're in for a nasty stretch! Deck and cargo hold stewards, survey and report conditions in your areas!" He hung up the mic and turned to the officers on the bridge deck. "You guys okay?"

"Yes, sir," the first officer and navigator said, almost in unison, but in spite of their words, they really thought the ship was in serious trouble. "Moyes?"

"Sir?" the weather officer asked with a quiver in his voice.

"You okay?"

Peter Moyes cleared his throat, took a deep breath and tried to quiet the quaking he felt inside. "Yes, sir," he lied, "I'll be fine."

"Good. I haven't lost a ship or a weather officer to a storm yet, and I don't intend to start now."

Moyes closed his eyes, smiled weakly and exhaled, as if he had just been relieved of a terrible burden. "That is wonderful news, sir,"

****

Inside the topmost container on the *Desdamonda,* total blackness surrounded Husam al Din. His eyes were wide, but he intentionally kept the light turned off so he wouldn't have to see the chaos that filled the trailer. Everything that was not part of the RV's permanent structure was strewn about the floor. When the ship plunged and slammed into the trough, the refrigerator door flew open just long enough to eject everything, then on the next roll, it slammed shut again, extinguishing the dim, momentary light that glowed from inside. Cabinet doors and utensil drawers burst open and threw their contents out. Even in the darkness, though he couldn't see it, Husam al Din knew the mess was there, and it troubled him deeply. To him, the piles of scattered refuse symbolized the wreckage of his life at this moment.

"Allaahu akbar," he choked in a broken whisper, then redirected his prayer to ask a question that had been worming about in his mind. "Why will you not help me?"

Deep in his heart he felt abandoned, and as that reality rose to his conscious mind, he fought it with prayer. "Allaahu akbar," he began again. Before another word could be whispered, his stomach leapt to his mouth as the ship fell into a deep wave trough and everything in the container and inside his trailer became nearly weightless. He clawed at the bedding, where he lay on the mattress, trying to hold on in a plunging pitch darkness that felt as if it would never find bottom. Then came the violent shudder, as the hull slammed into the next rising wave, and Husam al Din thought he heard a deep, metallic groan, as if the ship itself were calling out to Allah to save it from destruction.

The sensations of falling, then being thrust back up, then rolling and falling again were more than he could take. His head swirled, his throat and nostrils felt the burn and stench of acid and partially digested food rising from his stomach, and there was nothing he could do to stop it. He vomited again. Where it went he could not tell in the utter blackness of this place that had become a prison to him.

Again, falling, rolling. This time, not quite so hard, but hard enough that he grabbed for the mattress and hung on to keep from being pitched to the floor. His hand found a slimy wet pool, and he knew what it was. The thought of it turned his stomach over again, and he wretched, ejecting the rest of his stomach contents into the mattress in front of his mouth. The ship hit the bottom of the trough and began the sudden rise, thrusting Husam al Din's face into the fresh warm pool of stinking filth.

He came up sputtering and spitting, vomiting uncontrollably with dry heaves as his stomach was now empty. Then he stopped. In the darkness, the chaotic turmoil suddenly gave birth to a moment of fierce resolve.

"Allah," – he wiped his face in an effort to be clean before presenting himself to God – "I am Husam al Din. Sword of the Faith. You may test me all you want, but I will not be broken. My life is for jihad, and I will carry out my mission if you will but let me live."

The final words of his prayer were swallowed by the sound of wind screaming through the ranks of containers at the top of the stack on the bow of the mighty ship. Even inside the container and inside the trailer, the sound of the wind could not be stopped. A piercing shriek had for hours split the darkness with its desperate, warbling scream, fading only momentarily when the ship dropped into a hole between the waves.

Hour after hour, the constant thrumming of the hurricane drummed against the metal containers without letup. The noise and violent movement became a torture that Husam al Din accepted at the hands of Allah. If only he understood why … but then, he knew that it was an affront to challenge Allah's wisdom. *There must be a purpose in this,* he thought. *Perhaps it is only to make me stronger.*

Something hard slammed against the side of the container, jarring him where he lay and sending the sharp noise of tearing metal through the trailer. Not knowing what to expect next, Husam al Din quickly turned himself around to face the other end of the mattress, away from the filth. Holding on as gravity once again failed and his stomach stampeded toward his throat, he strained against the sickening impulse and listened. Then a new sound surrounded him. It was the sound of water.

****

On the bridge deck, the intercom came alive. "Captain Sleagle," a voice shouted above the background of howling wind.

Sleagle grabbed the mic, "Aye, this is the captain."

"Sir, this is Yarmouth on forward deck watch. It appears we've lost a couple of boxes from the top of the forward stack, starboard corner."

Sleagle steadied himself as the ship dove though the next trough and green water climbed over the bow and exploded in white foam, swallowing the forward third of the ship. He reached for his binocular and raised it to his eyes, straining to see through the glass in front of him that was streaming water in spite of the windshield wiper. His right index finger turned the focus wheel as he scanned the stack of containers nearly 800 feet ahead. The ship thundered again, as another mountainous wave boarded the bow, and Sleagle pulled the binocular down and massaged his eyes.

"Brock," Sleagle called out to his first officer, "do you see what Yarmouth is talking about? Have we lost boxes off the starboard bow?"

The man at the far right side of the bridge deck took up his binocular and studied the cargo containers. "Hard to tell from here, sir. Could be, but the boarding seas are making it a tough call. Yarmouth is a lot closer than we are, so maybe he's right. Wouldn't be the first time."

"I know, I know," Sleagle mumbled. "But I hate losing people's stuff."

"Not your fault, sir," Brock replied. "Some days old man Neptune just gets greedy."

"Yeah, well," the captain said, "just the same, I hate it."

"Take it up with Neptune, next time you see him, sir." Brock had crewed for Sleagle long enough that he felt comfortable as he chided the captain.

"Not today," the captain retorted. "I don't want to see the old man in person today. Seems he's in a bad mood."

"Aye, sir," Brock said. "Maybe a small offering will be enough to quench his appetite."

Sleagle looked into his first officer's eyes from across the long bridge deck and said earnestly, "The way this storm is shaping up, we'll be lucky if we get out of here with just a small offering."

Chapter Twenty-two

October 30 – Coast Guard Station Panama

"Have you heard anything yet?" Josh Adams wasn't all the way through the door before he asked the question.

The Coast Guard officer looked up from his desk with a grim countenance and shook his head. "Nothing."

"How does a ship the size of *Desdemonda* vanish?"

Pfister pushed aside his computer keyboard and leaned back in his chair. "In a storm the size and power of Yolanda, anything can happen. It's a big ocean. Big and wide and deep." He stood up and walked to the window, propped his arm against the frame and stared out into the glare of sunshine. "Who knows, maybe we'll find her. I wouldn't hold my breath, but like I said, anything can happen."

Josh reached in his pocket and brought out a folding knife with a black four-inch blade. The tang on the blade allowed him to open and close the knife with one smooth movement of his thumb. It was an old habit, opening and closing the blade repeatedly, to burn off nervous tension.

"How many search planes are up?"

"Three." Pfister pushed away from the window and returned to his chair. "They've been flying patterns since first light. I don't have time to give you a whole course on search-and-rescue mission planning and conduct, but I'll give you the one-minute version. Pull up a chair." He swiveled his computer screen around so Josh could see it.

Josh settled into the seat and leaned forward toward the monitor.

Pfister pointed at a spot on the screen. "Radio communications were lost here." Then he shifted his finger to another point. "But this is what we consider the LKP – the last known position of the ship. It was a full two hours after loss of radio contact. Coordinates at this position were derived from the GPS integral to the ship's EPIRB – the Emergency Position Indicating Radio Beacon. The EPIRB can be activated manually, or it fires automatically if submerged. Calculating the time of eleven hours, eighteen minutes from the LKP, and factoring the prevailing sea current set and drift and the wind speed and direction, we extrapolated the predicted position of the ship at the time the search was initiated, which is where we began the search. There has been no radar contact."

Josh looked up from the monitor "What took eleven hours and eighteen minutes?"

A weary look crossed Pfister's face. "Yolanda is what took eleven hours and eighteen minutes, Mr Adams. We don't send SAR teams into the teeth of a hurricane to chase an EPIRB signal, which may or may not have been set off accidentally. We wait until conditions allow us to initiate the search without undue risk to our personnel or equipment. The patterns of search are designed to give us optimum visual coverage of the ocean surface, but I've got to tell you that the sea state is still very boisterous and it doesn't take much of a wave pattern to hide stuff."

"Stuff as big as a container ship?"

"Mr Adams, did you ever hear of the *Edmund Fitzgerald*?"

"Of course," Josh said. "A big ore-carrying ship that went down in a storm on Lake Superior back in the 70s."

"Tenth of November 1975. She was 726 feet overall. Almost as big as *Desdemonda*. Up until 1971 it was the largest carrier on the Great Lakes. The storm that killed her brought winds that were relatively mild. Averaged 42 knots with gusts a few knots higher. Seas were eight to fifteen feet. Nothing a ship like the *Fitzgerald* should have been concerned about."

"So, how did it happen?"

"There are a couple of theories. The most accepted one is that some deck hatches were either damaged or left unsecure and they allowed boarding waves to flood the cargo bays. When she got low in the water, she plunged headlong into the trough of a large wave, and as the water came over her decks she couldn't recover. It took her down in just a matter of a few seconds. Nobody had a chance to escape. All twenty-nine of her crew perished in a heartbeat. Nothing was ever seen of her on the surface, even though there was another ship close by and a search was conducted almost immediately after losing communications."

"So what's the other theory?"

"It's somewhat speculative, but research into the cause of catastrophic shipwrecks involving large ships has led to a line of thinking that sometimes a ship can be too big to handle the conditions of a storm. The *Edmund Fitzgerald,* it is thought by some, had such a long hull that as the waves built up, her bow and stern might have been supported by crests while her midsection span was left insufficiently supported over troughs, and she broke her back."

"Just curious, but is there any evidence to support that one?"

"Since there were no survivors or eyewitnesses, those who believe the broken hull theory cite evidence on the bottom of the lake. Divers eventually went down on the wreck and found that the mid-ship structure had disintegrated and that the stern section came to rest upside down on top of the disintegrated middle portion of the ship. Now, some say that could happen as the bow plunged into the floor of the lake and the cargo shifted forward, shearing off the stern section. But I don't know. I'm just telling you that strange things can happen in a bad storm, and being in a huge ship does not necessarily guarantee your safety. And that was not an ocean and a relatively small storm, nothing near the strength of a hurricane the size of Yolanda."

Josh sat back, having seen enough of the computer monitor. "So what you're telling me is that we might never find anything of the *Desdemonda?*"

The Captain nodded. "Might not. Then again, we might. We wouldn't have search planes out there if we believed that there was nothing to look for. Perhaps some of the containers on the cargo deck broke free and we can find them."

Josh's eyes brightened. "That's exactly what we're looking for. I can't explain everything, but the container we are after was loaded last, so it was atop the stack on the cargo deck."

"Well, there's certainly a better chance that a container on the cargo deck would be recoverable than one that was in the hold. If the ship broke up and went down fast, she would take to the bottom everything that was inside. But don't get your hopes up. Some containers float around for years without being located. Others sink, and some lie just below the surface and present a hazard to navigation. There have been tragic accidents in which boats have struck semi-submerged containers and sunk."

Josh stood and extended his hand. "Thanks. Please let me know if anything is found. And I need you to keep this quiet. It is a matter of utmost national security."

"I understand, Mr Adams," Pfister shook Josh's hand and then sat back down as Josh let himself out of the office.

November 1st – San Blas Islands

Cadee walked slowly, her feet dragging on the soft sand as the idle wavelets danced around her ankles. Maria Elena chatted brightly, trying to cheer her friend. "Don't worry, Cadee, we will see each other again. I know we will."

Cadee broke into a sob, "I don't know how that will ever happen. When we sail away from a place, we don't ever seem to go back again."

"Maybe this time it will be different. Maybe your parents will want to come back here sometime."

"I don't think so," Cadee moaned. "They keep talking about all the places they want to go, but they never talk about going back to places they've been."

"Well, you must honor your parents. I remember the time my mother and I were sent to get drinking water from the river. I was little, then, and the water was so heavy. My mother never complained about the burden, but I did. We stopped along the trail and she tried to cheer me up. I didn't want to be cheerful, and I asked her how she could be happy about having to carry such a heavy burden."

Cadee stopped walking, wiped her cheeks and looked at Maria Elena curiously. "What did she tell you?"

A smile crossed Maria Elena's brown face. "I will never forget it. She told me that each morning when she arose, she decided that she was going to be happy."

"Yeah, but what if you're not happy?" Cadee whined.

"She told me that being happy is something that comes from inside, not from outside. If we let outside things control our happiness, then we are slaves to those things."

"But I don't want to be happy right now."

The little Cuna girl put her arm around her friend's shoulder. "Then that is your decision?"

"No. It's my parents' fault."

"How do you want them to make you happy?"

"Stay here, so I can be friends with you."

"Can we not be friends if we are apart?"

"Well, sure, but I'll miss you."

"And I will miss you. After you are gone, I will think of the things we did together, and it will bring a smile to my heart."

Cadee threw her arms around her friend and sobbed. "Oh, how can you be so strong?"

Maria Elena hugged Cadee and whispered, "If we are not strong, we do not survive." She stepped back and held Cadee at arm's length by the shoulders, and looked at her with moist black eyes. "Let us make a promise that we will be together again someday."

"Okay," Cadee whimpered. "When?"

"I want to go to college in the United States. I read about the college named Stanford, and that is where I want to go. Maybe we can be room-mates."

Cadee wiped her face. "It'll be ten years before we're ready for college."

"So, in ten years we will be together again. From now until then, we will be friends in our hearts, no matter where we are. We will be bigger then, and more beautiful. The boys will chase us, and maybe we'll let some of them catch us."

The thought made Cadee laugh. "Yeah, that will be fun. By then maybe I'll be ready to let a boy catch me."

"It is good to hear you laugh. There will always be time enough for tears, so we must cherish our moments of laughter."

Cadee looked at Maria Elena as if she were seeing a different person. "Who taught you these things?"

"My mother. Her life has been hard, but not as hard as her mother before her. All the women have passed down the wisdom of their time. I am lucky. I will be the first from my family to be able to go and see the world. I have decided to be happy."

But Jacob Plover wasn't happy. He swallowed hard, his mind racing to come up with a way to say what was in his heart, but his mouth was reluctant to form the words. The plastic bow seat felt hard beneath him, and he gripped the stainless steel rail with a white-knuckle death grip. He stared off at the palm trees that lined the beach seventy-five feet across the shallow water from where their boat was anchored. His heart pounded, and he wished it would quit, because he was sure Kirsten could hear it thumping.

Jacob turned his eyes on Kirsten and saw her head down, her face hidden behind by the cascade of silky blonde hair. More than anything, he wanted to go over and kneel before her and take her hair in his hands and lift her chin and look into her crystal blue eyes and tell her exactly how he felt. But the thought terrified him. What if she laughed at him and told him he was just being silly? He could never live with that. It was easier, he decided, to live with a silent burning for her than to risk the rejection. He turned his face back toward the beach and let the breeze dry his eyes.

Kirsten sat fourteen feet away, on the opposite bow seat, looking at her hands as she kneaded them in her lap. She looked to be filled with a kind of sadness Jacob had never seen before. He wanted her to know that he was not just another transient sailor's son who is here today and gone tomorrow. Jacob realized she had taken root deep in his heart, and now the prospect of never seeing her again caused him to breathe deeply to try to calm the ache.

Kirsten stopped knitting her fingers, drew a deep breath and exhaled quietly, then wiped the palms of her hands on her knees. She tossed back her hair and lifted her gaze toward Jacob.

The teenagers' parents were chatting about other things. Smoke rose into the night sky, and the glow from the fire lit a small circle around the two families. "Sven, I've got to hand it to you," Dan smiled as he reached out to take his friend by the hand, "you've got yourself a little slice of heaven here."

Sven drew Grendel closer to him with his left arm around her shoulder. "Palm trees, pristine beaches and perfect weather all year round don't make heaven." He hugged his wife with clear intent.

"No," Dan agreed, "but those things don't hurt, either."

Nicole gave him a light punch in the ribs. "Hey, buddy, you know what he's saying."

"I know. And I agree. There is nothing on earth that can replace a loving wife and kids." Then a boyish smile sneaked across his face. "Of course, a well-trained dog ..."

He winced as Nicole punched him again, this time not so softly. "You are in so much trouble."

He chuckled as his arms shot out to embrace Nicole. "Trouble is my middle name."

Sven stirred the coals with a stick, sending a fireworks display of sparks skyward. "Well, Mr Dan Trouble Plover, I guess tomorrow is the big day."

"Guess it is," Dan said, a hint of sadness in his voice. "I'm going to miss this place, but we've gotta move on."

"Why, dad?" Cadee piped up. "If we like a place so much, why leave?"

Jacob glanced over at Kirsten, then found his voice. "Yeah, dad. I think we're all happy right here. I know I am." He blushed, but in the evening darkness nobody noticed. But Kirsten nodded slowly, her own face glowing a little redder than the firelight.

Nicole came to Dan's rescue. "Now children …"

Jacob said it first, but Cadee's mouth was already open with the same words. "Mom, we're not children anymore."

Nicole's hands went into the air. "I'm sorry. I truly am. No, you are not children anymore. The last couple of years, you two have grown up to maturity beyond your age. We love you and respect you for who you are. But, we all agreed in the beginning that we wanted to cruise the entire Caribbean. We just barely got through the Panama Canal and stopped here. We haven't even seen the Caribbean yet, except for this one tiny spot."

Cadee raised her hand, in a most mature and controlled manner. "Yes, Cadee," Nicole said.

"Well, I, for one, have decided that I'm going to be happy, no matter what."

Dan's eyes focused on his daughter with a hint of suspicion. "Have you been listening to my Earl Nightingale behavior modification tapes again?"

Cadee's lips spread into a smile, and she said in her most adult voice, "Actually, my behavior doesn't need modification. But thanks for asking."

"You're right," Dan said. "Maybe I should listen to those tapes."

Nicole cupped a hand over her mouth to stifle a yawn. "Maybe we ought to turn in, so we can all be rested when we cast off at first light."

"I'll stay and put the fire out," Sven said.

Grendel snuggled close to him. "I'll stay with you."

"Me too," Kirsten said as she leaned against her dad.

Dan helped Nicole to her feet, and Cadee got up and wiped the sand off her bottom. Jacob sat on the log, saying nothing.

"Jake," – Dan nudged him – "you coming?"

"In a minute."

"Well, okay then. Good night you guys," Dan waved as he and Nicole and Cadee headed for the dinghy.

Jacob slowly stood, brushed the back of his shorts with both hands, then reached into a pocket and drew out a folded piece of paper. "This is for you," he choked out the words as he handed the note to Kirsten. Then he turned and ran after his family.

Kirsten stared at the paper, then lifted her eyes to follow Jacob as he disappeared into the darkness. A hint of dampness filled her eyes as she looked up at her parents, then she rolled the tightly folded note over twice in her hands and stuffed it into a pocket.

Chapter Twenty-three

October 31st – Panama

Josh felt the buzz in his pocket before he heard the soft ring of his cell phone. He flipped the phone open and heard the voice of Captain Pfister. As he listened, he brushed a napkin across his mouth, laid his fork aside, pushed back the chair and waved for the waiter to bring the bill. Just before snapping the phone shut, he said, "I'm on my way. I'll be there in thirty minutes, ready to fly."

The sun was high and bright, and the glare made him squint as he left the restaurant and slipped a pair of sunglasses over his eyes. Across the street was the hotel, and he trotted carefully through traffic to the far curb, then pushed through the glass door and headed for the elevator. There were things he needed from his room – a camera, a voice recorder, a notepad.

While he gathered his stuff with one hand, he flipped the cell open with the other and dialed the agency to alert Curt Delamo that the Coast Guard had found the *Desdemonda*. "I don't know what we'll find out there. I'm on my way to the Coast Guard station to catch the helo. Soon as I know something more, I'll get back to you."

"Do you need back-up?" Delamo asked.

"Not unless you are craving some hot tropic nights. This place is sweltering. Besides, there's a crack Coast Guard team on my six. As soon as I have boots on the deck and see what we're dealing with, I'll be back in touch. We might need to prepare a hazmat team, but right now I have no clue. Job one is to locate the container, then I'll work on job two."

"What do the Coasties know? What have you told them?"

"Absolutely nothing. Captain Klaus Pfister is my contact here. He knows only that this is a matter of highest national security, but I've given him none of the details."

"Good. I've talked to him, as well. He was the one I contacted while you were on your way from Manila. You know the drill. Let the guys backing you up know that you're looking for one guy in a container and that he might need to be shot dead on your signal. That's all. Can't have this info leaking out."

Josh had his stuff in hand and closed the door to his room. On the run down the hall toward the elevator, he signed off. "Got it. I'm gone."

"Godspeed," Curt said.

"Thanks man." Josh flipped the cell shut and tucked it in his pants pocket, pushed through the lobby door and hailed a cab.

Captain Pfister was at the guard gate when the cab arrived. Josh stepped out, paid the cabbie, then he and Pfister walked quickly toward a Coast Guard staff car that was waiting to take them to the airfield. As they approached, the driver snapped a salute, and Pfister returned it, then ducked through the door that was being held open for him. Josh followed, and the door was shut behind him. Finally he had a chance to ask the questions that were circling his mind like buzzards over a wounded beast since receiving the call half an hour earlier. "How did you find the ship? What condition is it in?"

Pfister held up a hand. "One at a time. First, we didn't find her. One of the hurricane hunter C-130s passed over her about an hour ago while on routine patrol in the wake of Yolanda. One of the crew was shooting digital aerial photos, and when he reviewed the images, he saw what looked like part of a container ship peeking out from under a cloud band. It was just a corner of the ship, but we had alerted all aircraft to be on the hunt, so he called us immediately."

A pleased look crossed Josh's face. "Good work."

"Sometimes we get it right," Pfister said. "Anyway, we ordered a fly-by and more photos. This is what I've got," he handed a folder to Josh, "these will help answer your second question about her condition. What you see here is all we know so far."

Josh opened the folder and pulled out a stack of 8x10 images printed on glossy photo paper. Sent from the computer aboard the C-130 to the computer at the Coast Guard station, they were only minutes older than real-time. "Excellent," Josh whispered as he flipped through the images. "How far out is she? And how did she get lost from all contact?"

"You are the master of follow-up questions, aren't you?"

"Sorry. One at a time, I know."

Pfister chuckled. "Well, I shouldn't be so hard on you. I need to remember that you're only a civilian."

"Oh, that was a nasty dig," Josh shot back. "I'm only sort of civilian. I'm in the intel business, and I get anxious to have it all at once."

"I understand. Well, to answer your first question, she's about 320 miles from here. We'll need to do a refuel aboard a cutter with a helo platform mid-way. The HH-65A doesn't have the range for an out and back without a pit-stop going each way."

Josh tucked the photos back in the folder. "How'd she drop off the chart?"

"From the look of the antenna array on top of the bridge, I'd say she got pretty badly torn up by the storm, which is why we could not make radio contact. Our radar from ground stations doesn't reach much beyond the horizon, so once the storm hit and we grounded all our airborne radar assets from flying near Yolanda, there was no way we could see the ship."

"What about the EPIRB?"

"It's only speculation, but either someone onboard thought it was time to activate the distress signal, so that if the ship went down we would have her GPS coordinates for SAR, or one of the units got knocked overboard. These devices are engineered to float free of a sinking ship, activate itself and then float on the surface so it can keep sending a GPS and ship identification signal to the satellite system. A container ship the size of *Desdemonda* has several of these in brackets positioned around the outside of the bridge."

The lengthy explanation made Josh smile. "I know," he said. "I carry a mini PLB. Same thing, almost. Except it doesn't float free and turn itself on if I sink."

The car rolled to a stop. In the background, the sound of rotors and the whine of a jet helicopter engine could be heard. Captain Pfister opened the door. "We're here."

Fifty-one miles out of the San Blas Islands

"I've got an idea." Nicole Plover spread a chart of the western Caribbean across the dinette table in front of Cadee and Jacob. "We're right about here." She pointed to an empty spot of blue half an inch north of the San

150

Blas Islands. "We'll be passing by these islands in a couple of days." Her finger traced an imaginary line between Honduras and some dots of brown surrounded by blue. "Maybe we can visit some of those islands, buy postcards and send them back to Maria Elena and Kirsten. What do you say?"

"You're just saying that to cheer us up, right?" Jacob, still in his pajamas, had a dour look on his face. After helping hoist anchor at dawn, he'd gone back to bed and slept until now. He didn't bother to comb his hair before coming to the main salon, and it was the worst that Nicole could remember since they arrived in the San Blas months earlier. Of course, she reminded herself, he never used to comb his hair in the morning until he met Kirsten. The thought made her chuckle.

"No," – her mind returned from its muse about Jacob's hair – "I was just thinking that it would be nice to stay in touch with our friends."

"Did I hear somebody say something about touching?" Dan bounded through the cabin door, the autopilot remote control in his hand and an oversized smile that bordered on being a mischievous grin. He slid into the dinette seat beside Jacob, intentionally crowding his son, swarming over him with a hug. "I'm here to touch someone, and I'm starting with you, little buddy."

"Ah dad," Jacob protested, trying unsuccessfully to shove his dad away. "You're not exactly what I was hoping to hug today."

Dan jumped back. "Ooh!" He feigned surprise with wide eyes and brows raised. "Not soft enough for you, huh?"

Dan moved on to Cadee, swallowing her up in a bear hug. "And how are you this morning, my little angel?"

"I decided to be happy," Cadee said. "But I sure do miss Maria Elena."

"I know, honey," Dan consoled her, "but you've still got me."

Cadee put her arms around her dad's neck and kissed his cheek. "I love you, dad. You're the best."

"Spread the word," Dan chirped. "I don't think this guy over here believes it."

Jacob sat up, put his elbows on the table and rested his face in his hands. "Yeah, I do. You're the best dad there ever was. You're just not much of a girlfriend."

Dan slid in beside his son. "Man, I'm glad to hear you say that. Girls come and girls go, but of dads you have just one."

"Hey," Nicole said. "Watch it. Some girls come and don't go. Some stick around forever."

"Yes, and I am lucky for that." Dan reached across the table and took Nicole by the hand. "Forever sounds good enough for me."

Jacob took his face out of his hands. "Dad, all I want is to be as lucky as you are."

For the first time, Dan realized that his son was growing up fast. Too fast. It wouldn't be long before Jake was looking for the love of his life. He was a thoughtful and tenderhearted young man, and if Kirsten were the right gal for him, who was Dan to throw up roadblocks or to tease his son about it?

He reached for Jacob's hand and gave it a squeeze. "Sorry, son. Didn't mean to make light of something so important to you. Will you let me off the hook this time, kind of like catch-and-release fishing?"

Jacob laughed. "Sure, dad." Then with mock seriousness, "Just don't let it happen again or you'll have to spend some time in your room."

"It's a deal." Then Dan's eyes opened wide and he stood up. "Oops, I better get back out there. The autopilot can steer, but it can't see what's up ahead or make life-saving decisions. That's the job for super-skipper."

He stepped out through the door, called back to his family, "Glad to see you're all up by the crack of noon."

"He is such a character," Nicole told her children.

"He sure is," Jacob said. "How did you two ever get together? You're so … um, so normal."

"Well, just for the record," Cadee piped in, "I wouldn't want to have a normal dad. Too boring."

The sound of his family's voices drifted through the open cockpit door and Dan's eyes filled. He sat at the helm and looked up, as if checking the mainsail, but he was looking far beyond the top of the mast. Under his breath he whispered. "Thank you, God. I am such a lucky man."

Manila, Philippines

"We've got numbers." Susan Vellum held the cell phone close to her head and cupped her other hand over the ear to quiet the noise of the airport. "I finally cracked Alicia Gomez, and I've got all I can get here."

152

Curt Delamo leaned back in his office chair, tossed his pen onto the desk and smiled. "Finally, something's going right. So, what did it take? Nothing for the media to wring their hands about, I hope."

"Nope, just a little heart-to-heart girl talk." Susan laughed. "I'll give it all to you later. I'll be sending across a flashcrypt right after this call, with all the pertinent data. I know this is a secure line, but somehow I still trust flashcrypt more."

"Fine, I'll go pick it up. What's your sense now?"

"I have a package to deliver, if you know what I mean, and I think she'll be an asset."

"You want to bring her here?"

"I think she'll be useful to us if we keep her very close. Besides, she won't last the night if we leave her here. She knows that. It's one of the things that convinced her that a long and relatively easy life working for us would be better than the slow and painful razor-and-acid torture and death that waits for her if we leave her behind. Let me tell you, she is more than anxious."

"So, you kind of went public with her?"

"Only to a few key players. But her gig is over here."

"When are you leaving? I'm concerned about your safety."

"Boarding the plane right now, boss. Don't worry about a thing. Gotta go now."

"All right, be safe. Call me when you can." Delamo put the phone back on the cradle and worry lines crept across his forehead.

Susan pushed the button on her cell phone to end the call, then keyed in the code for a flashcrypt and sent an encoded message containing the container description and serial numbers via secure satellite to a receiver in the NIA office in a fraction of a second. Then she closed her cell phone and tucked it inside her purse. Over the airport intercom, the call went out announcing her flight from Manila to Los Angeles. She turned to face the beautiful, dark-haired woman sitting alone in the corner of the waiting area. Somehow, Alicia Gomez didn't look so dangerous now. In fact, as she stood, her face revealed a hint of fear.

"Don't worry," Susan said, taking her by the elbow as if escorting someone who was unable to walk without assistance. "I'll get you through this."

"You don't know these people," the woman with the auburn hair and green eyes said.

"Well, I don't think they can reach us now. The airport is secure and once we're in the air you will have nothing to worry about. Trust me, your future is brighter than if you stayed in this business."

"I only worked for them because the money was good. For a girl like me, the choice was either that or prostitution. I was good at what I did. But I never really converted to Islam. My grandparents were Catholic. My parents were Catholic, and I am Catholic. It was only for the money."

"Prostitution probably would have killed less people," Susan said as they handed their tickets to the woman at the gate, then walked down the enclosed boarding tunnel.

At the door to the plane, Alicia Gomez hesitated. "I think I know that woman," she whispered to Susan. "I am not certain, but I think I recognize her."

The airline hostess welcoming passengers into the plane wore a friendly smile and nodded at Susan and Alicia as they approached. "Welcome to Philippine Airlines. Please make yourselves comfortable. We are almost finished boarding and will be taking off in just a few minutes."

"She looks safe enough to me," Susan whispered to Alicia.

"Perhaps so. It was only an impression. I just thought her eyes hung on me too long."

They stepped through the doorway and turned right into the aisle leading to their seats. "Do you mind if I take the a window seat?" Alicia asked. "I will want to bid farewell to my homeland."

"You got it." Susan stepped aside and let Alicia seat herself first.

The entry door was shut and latched, and the high-pitched sound of jet engines revving up filled the airplane. An announcement came over the speaker system telling passengers to observe the flight attendants as they demonstrated the seatbelt procedure and other safety information. Susan looked forward and saw the flight attendant who had greeted them at the door. She was saying something into a hand-held radio, and for an instant they made eye contact. A second attendant was making announcements into the intercom microphone and a third held up a sample seatbelt buckle for all the passengers to see. Susan had long since memorized the process, so she buckled up, laid her head back on the seat and closed her eyes.

A sudden crack and the impact of something wet and sharp against her face stunned her. Instinctively, she reached a hand to shield the side of her head, but it was too late. Blood, brain tissue and bone fragments filled her hand. Just before losing consciousness, the last thing Susan saw was that Alicia Gomez had been shot through the head from outside the plane.

Chapter Twenty-four

The bright orange HH-65A Dolphin helicopter sped across the open ocean at 120 knots for ninety minutes before falling into a circling pattern and lining up for a landing on the platform of a 210-foot WMEC Coast Guard cutter. In addition to carrying out drug interdiction missions, the fast cutter was equipped both for carrying and servicing the short-range helos when they were on extended flights. Even though Yolanda was more than 200 miles to the northwest, the residual wind and waves that followed in her wake for the next day and a half made landing on the moving platform a tricky operation. Winds buffeted the chopper, and the turbulence was like a ride over a very bad stretch of road.

"New Jersey," Pfister said into his helmet's mouthpiece.

The two flight crewmembers grinned and nodded agreement, but Josh didn't understand what he had heard through the helmet earphones. "Why do you say that?"

A smile crossed the Pfister's face. "Have you ever driven through Jersey City?"

"Ah," Josh said. "I get it. Are we going to make it down okay?"

"Oh yeah." Pfister shook his head emphatically. "I told these guys that they better take care of me, or else."

"Or else what?"

"Trust me, there is even worse duty than Colon. Besides, these guys are the best in the business. They'll get us down."

It took two passes, but finally the chopper touched down on the pitching and rolling platform. Two Coasties sprinted from their safe positions and attached tie-downs to the Dolphin, and the rotors slowed and then stopped. With one finger, Josh pushed the mouthpiece up in front of his lips. "Now what?"

Pfister was already unfastening his seatbelt. "Everybody off while she's being refueled. Safety regs."

Josh and Pfister exited the helicopter, followed closely by the pilot, co-pilot, engineer and rescue swimmer. They were shown the way forward along the ship's side deck, climbed a flight of stairs and stepped into the nav station. The pilot busied himself with the logbook from the chopper, and the rest of them were handed cups of coffee by one of the young crewmembers.

The crewman who had led them to the nav station approached Pfister. "Fifteen minutes, and we'll have you back in the air, sir. We've begun refueling already."

"Very good," Captain Pfister said, lifting the steaming cup to his lips. Then he turned to Josh. "We're half way there. The Dolphin's operational range is 360 nautical miles. Of course, that's with a built-in safety factor. It'll get us to the *Desdemonda* and then back here for another refuel."

"Not knowing what we're going to find out there," Josh said, "I might need as much as a couple of hours."

"No problem. We'll shut down the chopper and strap her down on top of the most stable-looking stack of containers. From the aerial photos, it looks like most of the cargo is still in fairly good shape. She's on the back side of the storm now, and even though there's still a lot of wave action where she is, we probably won't see waves above ten or twelve feet; a ship that size will have a pretty slow rate of pitch and roll."

"Do we just show up unannounced?"

"Of course, we haven't been able to contact the ship's commander by long-range communications yet. But when we get within five miles or so we'll try to raise the captain by VHF. They should have some hand-held marine band VHF radios on the bridge, and those units will still be intact, since their antennas are built in. Failing that, when we circle the bridge a couple of times he'll get the message that we're going to come aboard."

"What will they do about their radios?"

"Now that the storm has passed, I expect that the ship's engineer, communications officer and electrician will be working on repairs to the antenna array. I have no idea how much damage was done to the rest of their navigation system. They might need to be escorted back to Colon for major repairs."

The door swung open and the young crewman poked his head inside. "All set, sir. You can board when you wish."

Pfister tossed the empty foam cup into the waste bin, straightened his cap and nodded to Josh on his way out the door. "Time to fly."

More than an hour into the second leg of the flight, Pfister pushed the helmet mic up in front of his mouth. "Mr Adams." Josh looked up from the packet of photos he was studying. "Everything I said back there was assuming that there are still people alive on the *Desdemonda.*"

The thought struck Josh like a clap of thunder. "What are you saying?"

Pfister shook his head slowly. "Wouldn't be the first ghost ship in these waters."

"Ghost ship?"

"Maritime history is full of them, and every one is a mystery that leads folks to speculate about piracy or mutiny and abandonment of the ship. Or maybe a horrible storm that batters a ship so badly the crew are lost overboard while trying to escape in a life raft and they all drown. Or they are injured and die aboard, and by the time the ship is found there's nobody left alive."

That was all he said, then he leaned back and looked off into the distance as the sea rushed by below, leaving Josh to dwell on the subject of ghost ships. There was nothing to see. Cloud cover overhead was high and broken in places, and the drone of the rotors began to put Josh's mind into a trance. Without warning, the earphones in his helmet suddenly crackled to life with the pilot's voice. "I'm showing a ship-sized blip on the radar, sir."

Pfister pushed the mic to his mouth. "How far out?"

"I'm on the 48-mile scale, and it just showed up. Time to target?"

"Twenty one minutes, sir."

"At fifteen miles out, begin trying to raise the bridge on VHF. Maybe there's a hand-held turned on."

"Aye, sir."

Josh pressed his helmet against the window, but couldn't see forward well enough to spot anything, so he sat back and waited. The chopper bounced in turbulence caused by residual wind behind the great storm. The eye was more than 100 miles away and moving to the northwest, but the chopper was gaining on the powerful swirling winds and the closer they got, the bumpier the ride. The helmet came to life again. "Sir, I've got contact with the C-130. They're circling and shooting more photos."

Pfister moved the mic again. "What's their report?"

"No visible signs of life on board. The ship is not moving, it's just sitting in place, except for the drift of current."

"Maybe they lost their engines, damaged the wheels or lost steerage. Has the C-130 done a low and slow fly-by?"

"I'll ask, sir." The pilot switched off his intercom and talked with the pilot of the C-130. In a moment, he was back on the helmet phones. "No, sir. The closest he's flown is half a mile at an altitude of twelve hundred feet."

"Tell him I'm requesting a low and slow, and as close in as he can safely maneuver. I want to wake up whoever is onboard that ship."

"Aye, sir. We're at twenty miles now, sir."

Josh looked at his watch. In ten minutes they'd be circling the container ship themselves, and with any luck a few minutes later he'd be standing on deck. A buzz in his cargo pocket alerted him to an incoming call, and he dug for the satellite phone, flipped the antenna up and looked at the display. It was Curt Delamo. He quickly stripped off the helmet and held the phone to his ear. "Curt!" Josh shouted above the sound of the rotors and jet engine. "What's up?"

"Where are you?"

"In a chopper, just about to land on the deck of the *Desdemonda*. What have you got for me?"

"Good news and bad – the worst." Delamo's voice trailed off.

"Bad first, then," Josh shouted.

"Susan's hurt. Alicia Gomez was blown away. A head shot. Susan caught the bullet after it exploded Gomez's head. Luckily it was a small caliber round. We figure it was a soft hollow-point that was crosscut to be more lethal. It flared when going through the window, flared more as it passed through Alicia Gomez's head, but still had enough momentum to do considerable damage to Susan. She's expected to live, but she might lose her left eye."

Josh reeled at the news. He and Susan had been together for a long time, and their relationship went well beyond their work. He dropped his head into his hands, overwhelmed.

"Josh, you there?" Delamo's voice came over the phone.

Slowly, Josh raised the phone back to his ear. "Yeah, I'm here."

"The good news is that she's still alive. I'm betting the terrorist shooter thought he got them both. It was bloody, and they were both down in the seat. So the sniper evidently left the scene thinking he killed Susan as well."

Josh could hardly catch his breath. He threw his head back and forced himself to inhale deeply, then he blew it out and talked into the phone again. "I'm glad she's alive. But when we catch the bas—"

"Don't let it get personal!" Delamo's voice was sharp. "You do that and you'll lose focus and end up making mistakes. I know how you feel about Susan. But don't let this tear you down. Do I need to bring you in and send out a replacement?"

The chopper banked and started a low circle around the ship. From the window, Josh saw the bow and the disorganized pile of containers that were once stacked precisely and locked together. He exhaled hard. "No. I'll be fine. Who's taking care of Susan?"

"She's in the army hospital in Manila. They're doing the best they can. I think she's out of danger of anything more serious than losing her eye, though we're not entirely sure about that yet. The doctors are hopeful. I'll keep you informed of her progress. In the meantime, the other news is that I have the numbers for the container you're looking for. Susan relayed them to me just before she and Alicia Gomez boarded the plane. Are you ready to receive them?"

"Yeah, go ahead."

"Okay, here they are. Bravo, alpha, one, one, mike."

"Bravo, alpha, one, one, mike," Josh repeated for verification.

"That's correct. The container is rust red in color. The lettering is white. That's what you're looking for. The loading manifest listed the container as the last one loaded, and it should be in the top row on the starboard bow. Questions?"

"What did the manifest show as cargo?"

"Personal items, including an RV trailer belonging to a navy man being transferred to Pensacola from Manila. Needless to say, the guy doesn't exist. The navy's never heard of him. Anything else?"

A deep sigh escaped his lungs. "None for now. We're circling the ship. The bow is a mess of tumbled containers. I'll be on deck in a few minutes and I'll get back to you with what I find."

"Right," was all Delamo said.

"If you can get a message to Susan, tell her ..." He paused to think of what was appropriate to say by way of his boss.

"Don't say it. I know what to tell her. You just take care of yourself. We'll do everything we can for Susan."

Josh pressed the button to end the call, flipped the antenna down and stowed the phone in his cargo pocket. He pulled the helmet down over his head and immediately heard a voice in the earphones.

"Bad news?" It was Pfister, and he was looking at Josh with concern. "I can read bad news a mile away."

"One of our people, was, um ..." he lost his words.

"How bad is it?"

Josh felt the wetness in his eyes, so he reached up under his sunglasses and brushed them as casually as he knew how. "It's bad."

"Sorry to hear that," Pfister said. "These are dangerous times. Your people and mine, and some others like us are all that stand as a barrier to protect the innocent ones back home. If not us, then who?"

"I know," Josh whispered. He looked up into the eyes of the captain. "You a praying man?"

A smile crossed Pfister's lips. "Humph. Are you kidding?"

Josh didn't quite know how to take that, but decided to go ahead anyway. "Well, if you were ..."

"If I were?" Pfister challenged. "Of course I'm a praying man. I don't leave my room in the morning without checking in and requisitioning some special favors."

"Do you mind adding a name to your prayer list, then? Her name is Susan, and she's really going to need some help."

"Consider it done. I believe in miracles, and I know just who to ask."

The helmet earphones clicked and the pilot was suddenly on the intercom. "We're on final approach. Touch down in thirty seconds."

The chopper bobbed and weaved, fighting turbulence created by powerful wind swirling around the ship's structure. From the window, Josh saw the bridge of the huge ship, tilting first one way and then the other as the chopper struggled to find a level spot to set down. He spoke into the mic. "Was there ever any VHF contact? I was on the phone at the time."

Pfister shook his head, "No joy."

From beneath the seat, Josh felt a solid impact, then another, as the landing gear slammed onto the upper rack of containers halfway between the bridge and the wreckage at the bow. They were down. While the rotors slowly coasted to a stop, Josh stared out the window at the desolate vision of a ship adrift on the open sea. Scrambled containers at the bow looked as if they had been tossed there by the hand of a giant who was throwing a temper tantrum.

"Sir, we've got company," the pilot said over the intercom. Through the window, Josh saw three men walking across the top of the containers, heading toward the chopper. The side door slid open and Pfister moved past him and jumped onto the container deck.

Even though the rotor height was well overhead, all three men instinctively ducked as they met below the slowly swirling blades. With a hand extended, Pfister introduced himself in a loud voice that carried above the declining whine and whirr as the chopper's engine and rotors slowed. "Captain Klaus Pfister, United States Coast Guard. How can we be of service?"

"Captain Eric Sleagle, sir," The captain yelled, as the men shook hands. "Thanks for coming. We're in kind of a mess."

"How about your crew?"

"All accounted for and in good shape. We were lucky in that regard. This is Bill Keith, my first officer, and Steve Flynn is our navigator." The men shook hands all around, then the captain continued. "But we have sustained quite a bit of damage. All communications were lost when a rogue wave broke across the bow with such force that it swept over the bridge. Never seen anything like that before. Stripped our array completely off, including radar and satellite antennas. I'm afraid we've lost a few containers overboard, and one of them apparently damaged our rudder as it went under the ship. We're basically dead in the water."

As the rotors coasted to a stop, Josh climbed from the helicopter and Pfister made the introduction. "This is Mr Josh Adams. He's here on official business. We can help you with your ship, but I think you need to hear what Mr Adams has to say before we do anything else."

Josh stepped forward and extended his hand. "Captain Sleagle, is there someplace private we can talk?"

The ship captain's grip was powerful, his smile engaging. "Of course. Follow me. We'll go to my cabin."

As they made their way toward the bridge, the flight crew scrambled to attach tie-down straps to secure the helo to the platform created by the containers. The ship rolled slowly through a series of deep troughs, and movement on deck was just enough to make it difficult to walk a straight line. The chopper shifted side to side on its landing gear as the crew fought to ratchet the straps tight. The men had not taken a dozen steps before the tortured sound of metal against metal coming from the bow stopped them in their tracks. In unison, every man turned to look forward. Against the backdrop of heaving seas, it was difficult to determine what caused the awful sound, but Josh knew from what he had seen while circling the ship that the pitching and rolling bow was a wrecking yard of tumbled containers. While they watched, the noise came again and, like a sudden avalanche, the precariously piled cargo gave way, launching at least two containers off the starboard side into the water.

"How many have you lost?' Josh asked.

"Not sure. We lost a couple yesterday, just as the storm started to really hammer us. We've been in survival mode for the past twenty hours. It's been impossible to deal with that load on the bow. Before the storm, that forward stack was two boxes higher all the way across than the stack you landed on. Take a look. You can see that the starboard half of the stack has been torn away, leaving some of the boxes jumbled like a child's toy blocks. I'm not sure how many we've lost altogether. The ship has been too unsteady to risk sending my men into that pile to have a look. I figure at least another twenty-four hours before the seas will be calm enough to start working around that mess."

A moment later, they turned and headed toward the bridge again, and Josh knew that he couldn't wait another twenty-four hours for the seas to calm down enough to satisfy the captain before sending his crewmen into harm's way. Josh would have to go in by himself. And he'd have to do it soon.

Chapter Twenty-five

In Sleagle's office, Josh bent over the table and checked the manifest and cargo grid diagram that showed where each container was stacked. "The one I'm interested in is a red 40-footer with the serial number bravo, alpha, one, one, mike. According to what I've been told, it was one of the last containers loaded."

"Then it would be right here." The captain pointed to a spot on the grid map, and crosschecked against the manifest. "Yep, top of stack, starboard side. Right there in the front corner." He looked up from the papers spread out on the table, straightened his back and exhaled hard. "The one you want was at ground zero, right where it looks like a bomb went off. I'd be surprised if that wasn't the first box off the ship when we were smashed by that rogue wave yesterday."

"Is there any possibility that it's still on the ship? Maybe it collapsed into the crater when other containers beneath it tumbled out of the stack."

"Well, anything can happen, Mr Adams, but if was I a betting man I wouldn't lay too much on the table to back that theory."

"Just the same, I'd like to have a look."

Captain Sleagle drew a breath. "Must be important cargo." He eyed Josh, hoping to jog a clue out of him. "Mind telling me who you work for and who this cargo belongs to?"

"The answer to both questions is the same. The government. I'm asking your permission to explore that pile of wreckage to find out if my container is there."

"If the government is involved, I have a hunch you will do it with or without my permission. Be my guest. But, Captain Pfister, I want you to stand as a witness that I am released of any liability related to this venture."

Pfister nodded. "If it ever comes to that, I'll testify. You're on your own, Mr Adams."

"Can I have a copy of the grid map and manifest, so I can make sense of what I'm seeing down there?"

"No problem," the captain said, handing the papers to Josh, who folded them and stuffed them inside his shirt.

"Can I get a few men to stand by with ropes, just in case I need a hand?"

"We are short-handed, and my primary responsibility is to get this ship back in shape to continue the voyage. But I'll send one man from my forward deck crew, and a hundred feet of five-eighths double braid. That enough?"

It was less than Josh hoped for, but with a practiced poker face, trained to not show disappointment, he said, "I'll take it. Have him meet me at the chopper. If you gentlemen will excuse me, then."

Josh showed himself out of the bridge, down the ladder, and across the platform to where the helicopter was lashed. From his duffle bag, he retrieved a short-barreled Berretta, pulled back the slide just enough to verify that there was a round in the chamber, slid the clip out to check that it was full, then slammed it home and thrust the gun into the cargo pocket of his pants leg. Into a breast pocket went a short, rubber-coated flashlight, sized right for holding in his teeth.

By the time he was ready to go, the deck crewman was there with a coil of rope over his shoulder. "I hope you know what you're getting into," the man shouted over the noise of the wind.

Josh reached out a hand. "Hi, what's your name?"

"Romero."

"Well, Romero, If I'd known what I was getting myself into, I'd have become an actuary."

Against the roll of the ship, the men scrambled forward the distance of a football field before coming to the edge of the wreckage. From up close, it looked worse than it did from the air or from the bridge. The forward stack had once been two levels higher than where he now stood on a ship-wide platform made up of containers stacked four high above the main deck. The bow stack was once eighty feet from front to rear, being composed of a mixture of 20- and 40-foot cargo boxes laid together like bricks.

Now, half of those top two rows were missing along the starboard side. And like a landslide, when the boxes on the right front corner collapsed overboard, the stack below was yanked out of position, and several of those lower containers had also disappeared, dragging the boxes next to them down into the crater. What stood before Josh was a huge hole filled with an avalanche of railroad car-sized steel boxes, thrown every which way.

"Let me have the rope," Josh said. "You ever belay anybody before?"

Romero nodded. "Oh yeah, around here, rappelling is sometimes the quickest way to get from one place to the other."

Josh quickly tied a bowline around his waist. "I'll try to avoid rappelling, but I'll use this as a safety rope. Let me have slack to move, but be ready in case I go over. I'll yell if I fall."

"Got it," Romero said, taking the rope around the back of his waist, moving to a spot where he could take a seat with his heels propped against a ridge in the platform. "Belay on."

"On belay," Josh answered, then walked to the edge and disappeared over the side into the crater. He moved easily down the side of the first container, came to the bottom of the first descent, then turned and stared into the jumbled mess. The cargo boxes had tumbled sideways at angles that left small openings between them, leading into black holes.

A large wave pounded the ship from the side, and salt spray rained down on Josh. On the sharply angled wet metal, his feet slipped, and he went down hard, grabbing at the ridges on the side of the container, but unable to get a grip. The rope tightened around his waist, and he stopped.

"You all right down there?" a voice shouted from above.

Josh struggled to get his feet back under him. "Yeah," he yelled back. "Sorry about that. Just a slip."

"Thought you were going to let me know if you fell."

"Well, let's not count that one as a fall. Okay, give me slack, I'm going in."

He pulled against the rope until he had enough slack to allow free movement, then he ducked through a small triangular space formed by containers lying helter-skelter. Deep in the narrow opening between tangled boxes, he came to a corner with markings on it. He turned on the flashlight and studied the serial number. With the other hand, he pulled the grid map out to study container numbers and positions. From the numbers, he could see that the container that formed the angled roof directly above him had been loaded at the top of the stack and three rows inboard from the position shown for BA11M.

I need to look farther to the right.

He refolded the map and crawled into the open. "Need more slack," he called, then pulled the rope to him as he scrambled around the end of the next container that was lying at a severe angle.

"Three rows," he muttered, digging his fingers and the toes of his shoes into small nooks on the wet steel walls and clawing his way toward the outboard side of the crater. *Should have brought my Mad Dogs.* "Slack," he yelled, tugging again at the rope. On his rare days of leisure, he enjoyed recreational rock climbing, and his Mad Dog shoes fit his feet like a second skin, and had soft, sticky rubber wraparound soles that let him climb like a spider.

For the next ten minutes, Josh scrambled around the wild canyon of steel, repeatedly pulling the grid map out of his shirt and beaming his flashlight in dark crevasses to study serial numbers and compare them with what he was seeing around him.

"One more to go," he whispered into the air as he crouched to duck through another dark chamber leading, he hoped, to the final row on the starboard side.

On hands and knees, with the flashlight in his teeth, he pulled at the rope and crawled forward. He felt the ship list heavily to starboard and knew a deep trough was passing beneath the hull. A heartbeat later, a solid flood of seawater cascaded through the black tunnel, catching him by surprise, filling his mouth with the sharp taste of salt, and washing him backward on the slippery metal.

An ugly groan, deep and low, like the warning growl of a predatory beast about to attack, echoed from the trembling pile. Something shifted, but at first, Josh couldn't tell if it was just the movement of the ship, or if the pile was edging sideways. He tugged at the rope, but it wouldn't budge. "Slack!" he yelled, but the roar of the next wave sweeping over the bow drowned out his words. He tugged again, but the rope was tight as a steel bar. With daylight just a few feet ahead, he didn't want to have to back forty feet through the tight tunnel to retrace his steps. His fingers whipped at the knot around his waist, tugging at the loop and the running end, and in a matter of seconds he had it undone. The ship rolled again, and the containers groaned, louder and closer this time.

Throwing himself forward, Josh scrambled for the daylight and caught his fingers around a door latch bar that was a perfect handhold. With all his strength, he pulled himself out of the tunnel and was instantly inundated as the next swell sent seawater exploding over the bow. With a sickening growl, the unstable pile of containers shifted under the weight of the flood, knocking him off his feet, and the tunnel he had just escaped from slammed shut like a giant trash compactor.

The containers were shifting, and steel walls pressed toward him. An open slot offered itself, and he dodged into its protective airspace. A sliding cargo box narrowly missed him as it gained speed and thundered into the box behind him. Together, the two containers shifted toward the edge of the ship, then stopped as the ship rolled to port on the crest of a swell as it passed beneath the hull.

Seconds later, Josh felt his feet going out from under him again as the ship dropped into the next trough, and the container behind him disappeared into the sea. Two more of the huge metal boxes rushed toward him, but then the ship rose on the next swell, and their momentum stopped.

I've got to get out of here!

There was nothing behind him now but air and the open sea, and the wind clutched at his clothes, tearing at him, dragging him toward the edge. Over his shoulder, he saw nothing but an endless series of foam-topped waves lining up to punish the ship. On the next roll of the ship, a container knocked free from the pile shoved its way toward him, and he had no place to go but to grab the latching handle and hang on. The hull rose on the next swell and the box stopped, but not until the end of it was cantilevered over the open sea, with Josh dangling by his fingers.

Below him, swells reached up to snatch at his legs. Into the next trough and over the following swell he held on, but his hands were weakening. He knew it was only a matter of time before he was swept away, plummeting along with the falling container. To his left, he spotted a container that was jammed tight in the stack, like a stuck puzzle piece. It was now or never. He jammed his toes onto a tiny ledge and heaved himself upward, throwing his left hand out to catch a knobby door hinge.

One inch at a time, he edged up and sideways until he could grip the corner of the cargo box with his left hand, then he waited for just the right moment. At the peak of the next crest, as the ship momentarily paused before falling off into the next trough, he let go his right hand, braced both against the corner and then threw himself out into space, hoping to come down on something solid.

From somewhere that sounded like the bowels of hell, the horrible noise of metal grinding against metal split the air. The containers shifted again, this time violently, and the one Josh had been clinging to moments before, slid over the edge and fell into the sea.

Regaining his feet, he clambered to the next container aft and to port, as far away from the starboard edge as he could move. Ahead of him, the rope dangled, and above it Romero stood watching.

"On belay!" Josh shouted as he grabbed the rope. "Haul me up!"

Romero grabbed rope, backed away, and the line shot upward. Josh gripped the rope with both hands, leaned back slightly, planted his feet and started climbing. When he reached the edge, he flattened his palms on the surface and pushed himself up and over. For a moment he lay on the platform breathing heavily, then he rolled over and looked at Romero.

"Did you find what you were looking for?" the crewman asked.

Josh grinned. "I found a whole new meaning to the concept of living on the edge. Other than that, no, I didn't. Thanks for being here for me. Got kind of rough down there."

Half an hour later, as the chopper lifted off, Josh placed a secure satellite call to Delamo. "It's not onboard the *Desdemonda*. I went into the jaws of the monster looking for it, but it's gone. What's the news about Susan?"

"She's out of surgery and in stable condition. There is hope that her eye will recover." Delamo didn't say anything more for a few seconds, giving Josh a moment to digest the good news.

Josh pressed back against the chopper's seat, relieved to hear the positive prognosis "That's the best thing I've heard all day. The rest of my life is in kind of a mess. *Desdemonda* lost a lot of containers over the past thirty hours or so; I'm thinking nine at least, but we're not sure exactly how many yet. It's going to take some crane work to straighten it all out so they can take inventory. These things could be spread out over a couple hundred thousand square miles of the southwest Caribbean. It's going to take a major search effort."

"It's likely that some of them will sink, and we'll never find them."

"I know, but statistically some will stay afloat. And, personally, I'm not willing to bet the future of the United States on whether or not bravo, alpha, one, one, mike is going to be a sinker or a floater."

"I agree. I'll get some CIA assets in the air to augment the search already underway by the Coast Guard. You sound a little exhausted. I suggest you take a couple days off in exotic Colon. I'll keep you posted about the search as it gets underway."

"And about Susan?"

"Of course."

Josh flipped the satphone antenna down, crossed his arms and laid his head back against the webbing of the seatback. His eyes drifted shut, and a moment later he was asleep, rocked comfortably by the movement of the helicopter, and droned into unconsciousness by the rhythm of engine and rotors. It wasn't until they landed on the cutter, and he had to get off the chopper to follow safe refueling procedure, that he realized just how exhausted he was as he dragged himself up to the nav station.

The physical requirements of his work, he could handle. But the emotional stress of hearing about Susan's injuries had knocked him down. He loved her, and he was sure she loved him. There was something in the way she looked at him, and he wanted to see that again. As he stood gazing out over the fueling platform and drinking a cup of coffee, he thought how ridiculous it was for them to play this silly game. *When I see her again, I'm going to tell her what I've been meaning to say all these years.*

He finished the drink and reached to toss the foam cup in the trash bin when he heard the first low *whump*. "Get down," someone yelled, and he instinctively hit the floor just as a yellow ball of flame filled the windows and he heard the distinctive sound of a ship's siren.

Chapter Twenty-six

When he came to, Husam al Din couldn't tell exactly where he was, except that it was dark and he was pinned under something heavy and soft. Gradually his head cleared, and he backtracked through his mind, trying to figure things out. He wasn't sure how long he had been unconscious, but the lights inside his brain were only slowly coming back on. The last memory he came up with was of being inside a trailer, sealed in a cargo container on a ship named *Desdemonda,* on his way to Miami to deploy a biological weapon of mass destruction.

He reached for his left wrist, found the watch and pushed the button to illuminate the face. It read Nov 1 and the hands showed that the time was 8:41, but he didn't know if that was morning or night. Not that it mattered very much. It had been weeks since he lost contact with the five-time each day ritual of his prayers. Not knowing which direction it was to Mecca, he had fallen into almost total neglect of the very thing that held his life together since childhood. The thought made him sad and angry at the same time: sad about what Allah must certainly be thinking about him now, and angry at the situation that brought him to this regrettable point.

The weight pressed down against him, and he pushed back, bracing himself against whatever the hard object was behind him, and shoving with arms and legs. The soft heaviness that weighed him down moved easily. With his fingers, he probed the surface until he found an edge, and then he recognized it as the mattress. *I am against the ceiling and the bed is on top of me.*

In his mind, he rehearsed the layout of the trailer. The bed was all the way at one end, with the bathroom, then kitchen between him and the living room at the other end. Beneath the weight of the mattress, he turned and crawled toward the open space. His feet were surrounded by rubble, and he kicked it aside and stood in the utter blackness, reaching out to steady himself as his world pitched and rolled. The motion was different somehow – faster and more pronounced. Through the walls of the trailer, he thought he heard the sound of water sloshing about.

His hand found the rocker switch on the wall, and he flicked on the lights. The scene was chaos, and it took a moment for his mind to adjust to his inverted world. Down the hall, he saw the cabinet and sink, suspended from what appeared to be the ceiling. He opened the door next to him, and stared at the upturned toilet, and paper unrolled and swimming in six inches of sewage that apparently found its way back through the plumbing from the holding tank.

He pushed the door shut, thankful that the wall above the top of the jamb would constrain the filth of that room. Down the hallway ahead of him, the rest of the trailer looked like a junkyard. But even though the trailer was upside down, and everything in it had been thrown out of place, he decided that he could make do. The food and water would still be okay, he reasoned, and the small table and the comfortable living room chair could be turned over and used on the ceiling, which was now the floor. If his watch was correct, and it was now the first of November, he would soon be in Miami. *But what has happened to the ship? Why is the trailer upside down?* The thoughts troubled him, but without any answers and without any control over the situation, he could do nothing except wait to see what happened next.

He gritted his teeth. "Nice trick!" he yelled into the darkness. It was his first informal communication with his god, and he hoped that even though he was not facing Mecca and perhaps the time was not according to tradition, Allah would hear him. "But I will not be broken. I am Husam al Din, Sword of the Faith. It is my destiny," – he slammed his fist against the thin lauan wall, driving a hole through the paneling – "and I will carry it out. Test me if you must, but I will not fail!"

Chapter Twenty-seven

Captain Klaus Pfister looked up from his desk, as the door opened and Josh was escorted in. "Sorry we lost a day, but I'm just glad that's all we lost."

Josh took a seat. "Yeah, I got the report."

Pfister nodded. "No serious casualties. I guess that's why the refueling team wear their fireproof space suits. The chopper can be repaired, and the cutter is undergoing a refit. And there's the obligatory investigation into the cause of the fire. I think they'll come up with a grounding problem and an errant static spark, but we'll see."

"The ride back on the cutter wasn't all that bad," – Josh flipped open a notebook – "but it gave me a whole new appreciation about being a land mammal. Here, my boss requested this." He handed a small stack of papers across the desk.

Pfister quickly leafed through them. "Yeah, I ordered the same stuff from NOAA. Trying to figure out the set and drift of normal currents is pretty straight forward, but things get all out of whack when a storm the size of a hurricane comes into play. It's going to be a crapshoot. The play of wind against whatever portion of the container is still above the waterline has to be factored against the influence of currents below the waterline. Not having reliable data about either of those factors will make the task exceptionally difficult. Some of the data buoys were destroyed, either blown off station or sunk outright. We're doing all we can to determine where any surviving containers might have drifted, but we'll need a large dose of luck."

"Well, this is all we have to go on right now. I've been following the reports about Yolanda. Sounds like she hooked north and scrubbed the west end of Cuba pretty hard."

"The good news is that when she headed across land she lost strength and came out the other side a marginal category 2 and dwindling. Looks like she's going to continue to downgrade before finally going ashore south of Tampa."

"The Gulf Coast dodges another bullet. After Katrina, everybody along that coast holds their breath when a southern Caribbean storm heads up through the channel."

"Yeah," Pfister said, "It'll take years to recover from that one."

"Well, to help prevent any further disasters, I'd like to get in the air as quickly as possible."

A serious look crossed Pfister's face. "Last time I took you anywhere, one of our choppers nearly blew up. You think I'm going to trust you again?"

It took a moment, but Josh finally detected a crack in the captain's straight face. Looking as serious as he could, he retorted, "Last time I let you take me anywhere, you dang near killed me. You think I'm going to trust your airline again?"

"All right, I guess that makes us even. Go grab a helmet. I've already got a pair of C-130s flying patterns based on the best LKPs we could extrapolate for the string of containers lost in the 30-some-odd hours *Desdemonda* was fighting the storm. We might as well fly a third pattern in a Dolphin."

November 2nd

"Hey dad?" The voice came from over his shoulder, as Dan sat on the wide captain's seat scanning the horizon with a binocular.

"Yeah, Cadee, what is it?"

"I'm just looking at the chart plotter and I noticed that we're heading toward San Luis Miguel."

Without taking his eyes off the horizon, Dan absently fielded the question. "Yeah, so what?"

"Well, I hope we're not going to land there."

"Why not? I thought it might be a good place to refill our water tanks."

"Maria Elena told me that there are pirates in these islands, and that we should stay as far away as possible."

Dan put the binocular down. "Now how could that little girl know such a thing?"

"She said they steal everything, even children, then sell them. She told me that they will kill anybody who tries to stop them. They have machetes and guns, and she said they have no soul."

"Pirates without a soul? Sounds grim," he said, then grabbed her for a hug. "I won't let anything bad happen to us. I'm the master and commander, remember?"

"Yeah, but dad ..."

He picked up the binocular again and stared out across the water. "No yeah buts, I promise we'll be careful. Besides, Maria Elena might just have a very active imagination."

"I don't think so, dad. She's very mature for her age."

"No doubt. I'm sure life in the San Blas Islands will make a girl grow up and take responsibility a lot faster than girls her age in the cities."

"Maybe she even knows things about these islands. You're always telling us how important it is to get local knowledge about the places we're sailing."

Dan laid aside the binocular and swung around to face Cadee. "Local knowledge is very important, honey. That's why I spent so much time with Sven. He knows this part of the Caribbean better than anybody I've met. He kept us out of that hurricane we've been hearing about on the radio. But he didn't say anything to me about pirates."

"Well, maybe he doesn't know everything."

Dan laughed. "No, I'm sure he doesn't know everything." He saw from the look in her eyes that Cadee was worried. "Okay, I'll tell you what, if it will make you feel better we'll skirt this island group and conserve on our water supply until we get farther north. How does that sound?"

Cadee's eyes brightened, and she threw her arms around his neck. "Thanks, dad. Maria Elena would be very happy about this. She was really concerned, and even made me promise to mention it to you."

"Well, we don't want to disappoint Maria Elena, now do we?" He winked. "If you'll stand watch for me for a few minutes, I'll go down to the nav station and work out a new set of waypoints that will take us around San Luis Miguel."

She hopped up into the captain's chair. "Can I take it off autopilot and bear to starboard a few degrees, so we don't get any closer?"

"If it will make you feel better."

With the manual override system, the autopilot released control as soon as she took the wheel and gave it a turn. The wheel turned easily in her hand, and the catamaran responded immediately. On the new course, the wind played over the sails a little differently, so she reset the autopilot to hold the new course, stepped to the traveler to ease the main sheet, and then to the winch to ease the genoa. A smile of pride filled her face as she craned her neck to look up at the sails, now full and taut and the telltales flying straight back.

As Dan ducked into the cabin, a thought struck him, and he called out to Cadee. "I was watching something about thirty-five degrees to starboard and maybe a couple miles off. Keep your eye out so we don't run into anything, okay?"

"Sure, dad," she said as she climbed back into the seat. "I turned us only about ten degrees, but I'll watch for it." She picked up the binocular and scanned the horizon in an arc to the right of their course, looking for whatever it was her dad had been watching.

A moment later, she poked her head into the cabin. "I see it, dad. The radar picked it up, too. I'm on the eight-mile range right now, and the object is reflecting a strong signal and is only half a mile away."

Dan came up from the port hull nav station to take a look. Cadee handed the binocular to him and jumped down from the seat as he slid into position behind the wheel. A quick study of the radar screen gave him a relative bearing on the object, and he aimed the seven-power binocular that direction. The commotion brought Jacob out of his aft stateroom. In his hand was the sign language book he was studying.

"What's up, dad?"

After a quick glance at his son, Dan smiled and nodded at the book. "Great literature, don't you think?"

Jacob grinned. "Spoken like a true author, dad. But hey, it's not bad. Even I can understand it."

"There's something floating out there." He handed the binocular to Jacob. "See what you make of it. Where's your mother?"

Cadee bounded through the cabin door in search of Nicole, and found her in the galley preparing sandwiches. "Found her," she called back toward the cockpit. "Hey, mom, dad's found something."

Nicole wiped her hands on a dishtowel. "What is it?"

"We don't know.

It took only a few seconds for Nicole and Cadee to join the men in the cockpit. Dan had switched off the autopilot and was closing in on the mysterious object, now only a few hundred yards away.

Jacob lowered the binocular. "Looks like a half-submerged shipping container, to me."

Nicole took the binocular as Jacob moved to the traveler to adjust the mainsail. "Well, I'm glad you guys spotted it before we ran into it," she said. "That thing could have sunk us if we hit it at speed." She looked at Dan, who was steering the boat closer. "What are you doing? Let's stay away from it in case a swell catches us and we smash into it."

"We're okay, honey," Dan tried to calm her. "I just want to take a closer look. Jake, will you please lower the outdrive and lock it down? Then furl the headsail and I'll start the engine. We'll just circle it under power, so we've got good directional control and can stay out of harm's way." He emphasized the last part for Nicole's benefit.

He switched on the glow plugs for half a minute, then fired the diesel. It started immediately, and he set the autopilot to steer them away from the container and directly into the wind. "I'm going to drop the main," he told Nicole, in keeping with their standard safety procedures at all times when someone left the cockpit to go up on deck while underway.

"Be careful, daddy," Cadee called out.

In a matter of minutes both the headsail and the main were stowed, and the boat was a few hundred yards past the floating cargo container. "All right, gang," Dan said with a note of adventure in his voice, "let's go see what we've got here."

"What we've got here," – Nicole didn't sound amused – "is a huge metal object that can sink our boat. What the heck are you thinking?"

"Well," Dan said in a soothing voice, "what I was thinking was that maybe we've found ourselves a grand treasure. Who knows what might be in that container? It might be a Rolls Royce—"

"Oh sure," Nicole interrupted. "Well, did you notice that the container is upside down?"

"Or maybe it's a load of Nike shoes, or computers, or money."

"Or maybe a bunch of motorbikes," Jacob interjected with a smile.

"Or clothes," Cadee chimed in, looking hopeful.

"Or just somebody's junk." Nicole shot a warning glance at Dan and planted her hands on her hips.

"Well," Dan said cheerfully, "we'll never know until we take a look"

"And just how do you propose to take a look?" Nicole asked. "You can't open that thing up out here in the middle of the ocean, and we sure can't tow it ashore."

"You've got a point there," Dan said. "Any ideas from the crew?"

Silence filled the cockpit, and Dan was almost ready to give up his treasure hunt when a thought entered his mind. His eyes brightened. "I've got it."

"Stand back, kids," Nicole mocked, throwing her arms wide in front of the children, "I don't want you catching whatever it is your father has."

"Now come on," Dan encouraged them, "a little support from the crew. At least hear me out."

A look of resignation crossed Nicole's face. "Okay, what is it?"

"Well," Dan said, "I admit there's nothing we can do with that big box by ourselves. But maybe we can hire somebody to salvage it for us. Haul it to shore so we can see what's inside. What do you say?"

Jacob got a big grin going. "Yeah, just think what we might find inside. Maybe we'll be rich."

"I don't know," Nicole said. "Where are you going to get a salvage company out here? Besides that, how much do you think it'll cost to hire it done?"

"Don't know 'til we try to find out, right?" Dan was almost gleeful.

Jacob was all encouragement. "Right, dad, let's go for it."

"Cadee, what do you say?" Dan asked. "We've got to take a vote, before we spend any of our cruising kitty."

Cadee looked at her mom, worried that their disagreement about this might turn into a serious argument. "I don't know," she stammered, her eyes on Nicole.

Nicole sensed her daughter's insecurity, and knelt to look her in the eye. "Hey, it's okay, kiddo. No big deal here."

"Really?"

"Yeah, really," Nicole assured her. "What's your vote?"

"Well then," – her face lit up – "I vote to see what's inside. It's like a giant Christmas present."

"So, since it's only early November, does that mean we have to wait a couple months?" Dan teased.

Cadee clapped her hands. "Okay, late Halloween,"

"So let's see by show of hands," Dan said. "Only unanimous votes are moved upon, so we don't go against the wishes of anyone."

Cadee's hand went up first, followed quickly by Jacob's. "You know where I stand," Dan said, looking toward Nicole, who still had her hands firmly planted on her hips.

"Come on, mom," both kids pleaded in unison. Jacob offered the final encouragement, "At least we should find out what it costs to salvage it."

"So where's the nearest salvage operation?" Nicole asked.

Dan picked up the VHF radio microphone. "Reach out and touch someone." He shrugged. "If everyone agrees, I'll see if I can raise someone on the radio who can give us a lead to a salvage company. Who knows, maybe there's someone right here in the islands."

After a moment of holding out, Nicole relented. "Okay. Let's at least make the call."

Chapter Twenty-eight

Susan Vellum stood at the door to Josh Adams' hotel room and knocked quietly.

He heard the faint rapping, looked at the clock on the nightstand and shook the sleep from his brain. "Three in the morning? What the heck is important enough to wake a man at three in the morning?" He threw back the covers, grabbed his robe and walked to the door. "Who is it?"

"It's Susan." The voice was intimately familiar, but it made no sense that Susan was here in Panama. Wasn't she in a hospital in the Philippines?

He threw off the chain lock, flipped open the deadbolt and swung the door wide. Susan melted into his arms, and they kissed deeply.

A bioelectric shock from somewhere in his nervous system shot through his body, and he jumped, waking himself from the dream. He was sweating. His t-shirt was wringing wet around the collar, and his breathing came hard and fast. In the distance, he heard a knock at the door and wondered if his dream had written itself in his brain at the speed of neurons, to make rational sense of the knock; a rational sense that was acceptable to him – even longed for.

"Who is it?" he called out.

"Mr Adams," a young male voice responded in perfect American English, "Captain Pfister sent me to get you. They've located a container."

Josh reached for the lamp and switched on the light. "I'll be right there!" he yelled through the door, then scrambled into his pants and shirt, tucking his pistol into the back of his waistband. In less than a minute he was out the door and heading down the steps behind a young man in a Coast Guard work uniform. They got into a car that had been left at the curb, and raced off into the night.

"What's the situation?" Josh asked.

"Don't know the specifics, sir," the young man answered. "Only that a report came in from a cruise ship that they had hit a hard submerged object. Turned out to be a container."

Minutes later, they checked in through the security gate and drove to the captain's office. Through the window, Josh saw Pfister talking on the phone.

"Thanks for the lift." He got out, slammed the car door and waved as he headed up the steps.

The door opened as he was reaching for the handle, and the captain stepped into the night air. "You ready for a ride?"

"You're asking if I'm ready to cheat death again?"

Pfister grinned. "A Carnival cruise ship hit something hard and metallic about an hour ago. They hit it so hard that it punched a triangular hole the size of a Volkswagen just below the waterline."

"You figure they hit the corner of a container?"

"Looks that way. After they sealed off the damaged compartment so the whole ship wouldn't flood, they trained spotlights on the water to see if they could spot what caused the damage. There it was, about ninety percent submerged, a shipping container."

"Color?"

"Your favorite and mine, red lead."

"Were they able to see a serial number?"

"Not that lucky, I'm afraid."

"Well, I'd say let's go have a look. Can we land a chopper on the ship?"

"Oh yeah," Pfister said. "I've already deployed a cutter, but the chopper will be faster for us. And the cruise ship is equipped with several full sets of scuba gear onboard, so we can go down and check the serial number from under water, if necessary. You're certified, I assume?"

"Since I was eleven years old. Got certified with my dad, so we could spend some quality father and son time getting a nitrogen fix."

"Good. By the time the cutter arrives to take the container in tow, we'll already have some answers."
****

The sun was still below the horizon when Josh spotted what appeared to be a Las Vegas hotel with all the lights on, floating on the black sea below them. The chopper circled, then fell into an approach toward a helipad on the stern of the ship. The skipper met them at the pad and handed them off to a crewman who showed them down seven flights to the equipment room where the scuba gear was stowed.

"I'll be right behind you," the skipper said. "Just have a few things to take care of first. I have a skiff waiting for your use on the swim platform. It'll save you having to swim a couple hundred yards to get to the bow."

"Is the container still at the bow?" Josh asked.

"Yes. Actually, it hung up in the penetration, so we know exactly where it is."

Moments later, Josh buckled his weight belt and took a suck on the second-stage regulator to check the system and make sure the air was clean. Even the slightest hint of an oily taste indicates a compressor problem that would fill the tanks with lung-damaging contaminated air. He switched on the dive light to check its operation, then turned if off again.

"I'm almost there," he said. "Just got to spit in my mask and I'll be ready."

"Here," – the equipment room steward handed him a small plastic bottle – "we don't encourage our guests to spit in the masks. Use this anti-fog, instead."

"Hey, my spit's clean," Josh said in mock protest.

The steward rolled his eyes, showing no sense of humor. "Right."

With fins in hand, Pfister and Josh followed the steward down the hall, through the door leading to the swim platform where the skiff waited with a driver aboard. The pilot pushed the throttle forward and two minutes later, they were at the bow of the ship. Looking up from the skiff, Josh thought it was like sitting at the base of an enormous white skyscraper that slanted out overhead to block part of the sky. Lights from more than a thousand staterooms shimmered from the black water like a sea full of silver mirrors.

Under the skillful hands of the skiff pilot, the small boat hovered effortlessly in the corner created by the ship's hull and the container that was still loosely stuck in the penetration. The two men made eye contact, gave the 'okay' hand signal, placed a palm against their masks and rolled backward off opposite sides of the skiff.

In the dark water, the rust red color of the container was an ugly, vague form that seemed to grow as an appendage from the white hull of the cruise ship. Josh swam to the corner that penetrated the hull, and saw that the connection was tenuous. *We're lucky it hung on this long.* A quick examination of the wound showed that extricating the container would be fairly easy, with a tug line pulling from the cutter. But this cruise was over. The ship would have to return to Panama for professional repair, and all the passengers would get full reimbursement to cover the cost of their ruined vacations. *An expensive bump in the night.* Josh thought about the millions this little accident was going to cost the cruise line.

There was no serial number painted on the corner nearest the ship, so Josh caught Pfister's attention and pointed at the far end of the container that angled down to a depth of forty feet. A quick knife action at the waist cocked his body and he kicked into the darkness below. Pfister followed, and in a few moments they hovered at the deep end of the container and stared at the painted serial number. Disappointment was in their eyes as they looked at each other and Josh shook his head then jerked his thumb upward. Pfister nodded, and they slowly began the ascent to the 15-foot level where they paused for a safety stop before hitting the surface.

Back in the equipment room, Josh stripped out of his wetsuit. "One down, eight to go."

"Yeah," Pfister agreed. "But you saw how low in the water this one was floating. Some of them might have gone to the bottom by now. We might never find all of them. In fact, I would bet against it."

It was a grim reality – the ultimate quandary of the rock and the hard place. Josh knew they might never find the container with Husam al Din and his weapon inside. But he also knew that he could never breathe easy until they did.

140 miles south – Off San Luis Miguel Island

An hour before sunrise, Dan looked up from the book he was reading and stretched. Night watch in the cockpit was a lonely job, but he didn't mind too much. The quiet emptiness of the open ocean brought peace to his soul. He had relieved Nicole at two o'clock and spent his time alternately reading and keeping an eye on the floating container, now two hundred yards off. He didn't want to be too close, but didn't want to lose sight of it either. That big metal cargo box might hold a treasure, or it might just be somebody's household stuff being shipped across an ocean to a new residence. He didn't know, but it really didn't matter. It was the adventure of the whole escapade that counted.

From far away to the west, the deep, chugging sound of a diesel engine suddenly disturbed the early morning air. *Well, it looks like the man gets up early.* Dan picked up the binocular and stepped to the rail. It was still too early to see much through the dim morning light, but the throaty growl of the motor carried across the water with unmuffled clarity. The sound of that motor, Dan hoped, was coming from the barge of Senor Juan Baptista de la Vega, a salvor from the island of San Luis Miguel that he contacted by radio the evening before.

"Si, senor," the man had assured Dan, speaking fair English with a heavy Spanish accent. "I can salvage the container for you. I have a barge with a crane, and can lift the container right out of the water. Please, senor, give me your coordinates, and I will come to you in the morning."

The whole thing sounded almost too easy.

Nicole poked her head out through the cabin door, her eyes still sleepy. "How you doing? I thought I heard something."

Dan pointed toward the island. "I think its de la Vega. Sounds like an old diesel that is badly in need of some attention. Out here in the middle of nowhere, that's what I would expect."

"I'll get dressed. I think we can let the kids sleep."

Twenty minutes passed, and the sound of the distant engine grew louder. Finally, through the binocular, Dan was able to see a dark spot on the horizon and a column of black smoke rising and then drifting apart in the morning breeze. Nicole stepped into the cockpit, her hair in a ponytail and wearing a flowered calf-length dress.

Dan whistled, "Wow, don't you look nice!"

"Well, it isn't every day we get visitors on board. He sounded so nice over the radio, talking about his grandchildren. I thought it would be nice to clean up a bit to welcome him. Do you think I should prepare some breakfast for Mr de la Vega?"

"I don't know about him, but I could use some."

"I've been thinking," – Nicole put an arm around Dan – "if that container is full of valuable things, maybe we should try to notify the rightful owners, so they can come and get it."

A frown built on Dan's face. "If it's anything valuable, the insurance will pay off the owners."

"Then we should notify the insurance company," Nicole said.

"What about finders keepers?"

She shrugged. "I'm just trying to do the right thing."

"Well, I think the right thing is for us to claim salvage rights. It's the law of the sea. Senor de la Vega is charging us a thousand bucks just to haul that thing to the island so we can open it up. The least we can do is consider it an investment and feel good about keeping whatever we find inside."

Nicole frowned. "It's nothing but a gamble. How can you call it an investment?"

"Look, anybody who knows anything about Wall Street will tell you that all investing is the same as gambling. You put your money into something that you hope will pan out. Maybe it does, and maybe it doesn't. It's all a gamble. We're just buying this big box and hoping that when we open it we'll find something good. Same as investing."

"So you feel good about it?"

He looked stunned. "Of course I feel good about it. Are you kidding? There might be a sports car in there, or a load of jewels that somebody's shipping halfway around the world."

"And if that were the case, what would you do with it?"

He was almost speechless, but finally stammered a response. "Why, why, I'd ... I guess I'd ... well, actually I'm not sure. I don't need anything else." Then his eyes brightened, "But wouldn't it be great to have all that kind of stuff?"

Nicole patted him on the arm. "Dan. Get a grip. Listen to yourself."

"Why, what do I sound like?"

"Greed. Lust, envy, covetousness, pride," – she wrinkled her forehead – "but mostly lustful greed."

"I don't think so," he protested. "It's for the kids."

"They don't need anything else, either."

Dan stood silent for a moment, thinking about Nicole's words. The smoke and noise from de la Vega's boat were closer now. "Are you saying that you don't want the container?"

Her eyes danced as she broke into a grin. "Are you kidding? I was just giving you a hard time. Of course I want it. There might be a whole load of mink coats in there, or pearls, or oriental dolls. Wouldn't those look nice in our living room? Maybe there will be some expensive paintings."

Dan turned toward his wife so he could look her in the eyes. "Nicole Plover, are you playing with my psyche?"

She giggled. "I was just trying to send you off on a guilt trip. Don't worry. What woman wouldn't want to open a 40-foot gift package that dropped right out of the blue? My gosh, my gosh! I can hardly wait."

A sigh escaped Dan's lungs. "After all these years of marriage, I still don't know how to read you, sometimes."

She pinched his cheek and winked. "If I weren't a mystery, life would be too easy."

He tweaked her nose. "Well, I do love a challenge."

"Ahoy there!" a shout rang out across the water.

They looked up and saw a dirty old platform made of wood that looked as if it had been salvaged from derelict dock pilings. Toward the rear of the barge stood a rusted crane, a spool of cable and an engine that appeared to have been yanked out of a dead tractor. A small tug was positioned behind the barge, pushing it ahead, and apparently straining under the load, as Dan looked at Nicole's pretty dress then nodded toward the captain of the little tug. A cloud of black smoke belched from the exhaust stacks.

"I think maybe you have overdressed. Levis might be more suitable."

Behind the wheel was a gray-haired old man, bent with age, wearing ragged clothes of dark, indistinguishable color. Between his few rotted teeth he held a limp cigar, dripping saliva from its unlit tip.

Nicole's face reddened a shade. "I think you might be right." She hurried off, down the steps into the starboard hull and then into the main stateroom.

"Senor de la Vega?" Dan shouted and waved toward the tug. "Thank you for coming. Have you had breakfast? I think my wife will be fixing something, if you want to join us."

"A pleasure," the old man shouted back. "I have had nothing to eat since yesterday. May I raft up to your boat after I set my barge adrift?"

Dan moved to the lifelines. "I will place the fenders and catch your lines."

It wasn't long before the boats were lashed together, and the old man climbed into the catamaran, leaving the barge to drift a few hundred yards away on the calm morning sea. Presently, Nicole came into the cockpit wearing Levis and a baggy t-shirt that had obviously been used for painting the bottom of the boat. She handed each of the men a glass of orange juice, smiled at Senor de la Vega and asked, "Now, what may I fix for your breakfast?"

Chapter Twenty-nine

A light swell rocked the boats gently as the men finished their breakfast and their negotiation. "Ah, senor," Juan Baptista de la Vega droned, "the thousand dollars is my fee to come out and find you and survey the situation so I can see what I can do for you. It is a lot of trouble to hook up my barge and tow it this far, and fuel is very expensive."

"I think I hear some bad news coming," Dan said and exhaled loudly.

The old man didn't pause to listen to the complaint. "Of course, it is customary in the salvage industry that after we get the container back to the island I will expect to receive a percentage of whatever is inside. I know that I am taking a very big chance, because it might be nothing of value. But we are in this together and it is only fair, do you not think?"

No, Dan did not think it was fair. "A deal is a deal," he argued. "We agreed on a thousand dollars for you to salvage our container. You never said anything about a percentage, and I expect you to be a man of your word."

"Oh, senor," – the old man bowed his head as if ashamed – "I am sorry that you think such a thing of me. I am grandfather to twenty-two, father to nine, husband to three … or was it four, I can no longer remember. It cuts me to the heart to hear you say that you think I am not a man of my word. I weep to hear such a thing."

"Dan," Nicole whispered loudly through the cabin door, jerking her head for him to come and speak to her.

Irritation was in his voice as he said, "Excuse me, Senor de la Vega. My wife wants a word with me."

"May she be more kind with you than you are with me," the old man lamented. Then he held out an empty glass. "When you return, please bring me some more orange juice."

Dan took the glass and shook his head in disgust as he rose from his place on the cushioned cockpit bench and went to the door. Nicole had a hard look in her eye. "What the heck are you doing? You trying to break this old man's heart?"

"I'm negotiating," Dan explained in a hushed voice. "He's trying to rip us off."

"Well, don't be so hard on the poor old man. Look at him, he has nothing. And all he's trying to do is support his family. My gosh, nine kids and twenty-two grandkids? Think how hard that is. It won't hurt for us to be a little generous with him."

Dan handed her the glass. "He wants more orange juice."

She took the empty glass and stared at it. "I'll have to make some more. He already drank all we had."

Dan shot her a sour grin. "We're trying to be generous, right?" He returned to his seat and Nicole closed the cabin door and headed for the galley. A moment later, she heard Dan exclaim at the top of his voice, "Sixty:forty! That's robbery!"

As she reached the top of the steps leading from the galley, she heard de la Vega state his terms. "Senor, I am an old man, and my barge might not look like much to you. But it is the only barge within 200 miles. If I go away from here, you will have nothing. And, if you think about it, I can always come back and take this treasure for myself after you are gone. But if I help you, you will at least have something. We will both have something. It makes good business, no?"

"Dan," Nicole's voice called from the cabin door again.

"Por favor," – Dan broke away from the negotiations again to talk with Nicole. "What now? Did you hear what he is demanding?"

She handed him a full glass of orange juice. "I did. I think the whole Caribbean did. It woke the kids and they're wondering what's going on. I don't think all this arguing and bickering is good for them."

"So? What do you want me to do?" His voice was tense with frustration.

She looked at him with a question in her eyes. "Are we doing this, or not?"

"You think we should take the sixty:forty split?" he asked, his voice rising to a near falsetto.

She shrugged. "Well, I don't know. Let's see, last time I checked, sixty beat zero all to heck."

He looked hard at her for a long moment, and she stared back without flinching. Seeing that she wasn't softening, he relented. "Oh, all right." He threw his free hand into the air, nearly upsetting the glass in his other hand, then he turned and went back to his seat in the cockpit, handing the glass to de la Vega before he sat down. The next thing Nicole saw was Dan reluctantly shaking hands with Senor de la Vega.

"Okay." The old man clapped his leathery hands then held one out, palm up.

"What's that?" Dan asked.

The old man closed his hand and rubbed his thumb across his forefinger, the universal sign language for 'pay me'.

"You want your money in advance?"

"Senor, I have already spent several hours of my time, burned a lot of fuel and put wear and tear on my equipment. It is only right that you pay me for my services."

"And what have I gotten for my thousand dollars?" Dan protested.

"You need not worry, senor. I will load the container on my barge and take it to the island, as promised." His palm was still out.

The door to the cabin opened, and Nicole stepped into the cockpit. Dan went to meet her and she handed him a stack of $20 bills that she had taken from their onboard safe. "Here," she said as she approached de la Vega and held out her hand. "Half now, the rest when we have the container safely ashore. I think that's only fair, don't you?" She smiled sweetly as she folded then tucked the rest of the stack of bills inside her blouse. "I'll just hold the rest right here," – she patted her chest – "for safe keeping."

For a moment, she thought she detected a flicker of anger in the old man's eyes, then he took the bills and his expression changed. "Thank you, senora. My wife and children and grandchildren will bless you." He grunted as he leaned forward to rise from the seat, bracing his hands on his lower back and wincing as he straightened up. "Ah," he gasped, seeing the concern on Nicole's face. "It is an old injury from a hard life at sea. But I will be all right. You will not be disappointed. I can still work hard. Did I hear you say you have a son?"

Dan nodded. "We have two kids. A daughter who is 11, and a son who is 17."

"That is good. I am an old man, and you can see that I am crippled with age. It will go faster if you and your son can help. Why don't you get him ready for work, and I will go get the barge and come back for you."

De la Vega struggled to climb over the side into his tug. After a few moments, he started the smoky engine, cast off the dock lines and motored away toward the drifting barge.

Dan let the noisy tug move some distance away before he spoke. "Half now, half later, huh?"

She smiled. "Hey, if we'd given him the whole thousand, what would keep him from chugging away with all the money and then coming back later for the container after we were gone? This way, he's got some incentive to keep his end of the bargain and get the rest of the money."

"You're a smart cookie." He hugged her.

"Of course, I'm a smart cookie," she said, "I'm a woman."

"Your brilliance has never been in doubt," Dan chuckled. "After all, look who you married."

"Neither my brilliance, nor my mercy." She gave him a peck on the cheek. Then she turned quickly and disappeared into the cabin, leaving Dan to ponder that last remark.

Twenty minutes later, the tug was back, pushing the barge before it. Dan and Jacob scrambled aboard and waved goodbye to Nicole and Cadee, as Juan Baptista de la Vega throttled the controls and they chugged north beneath a growing black cloud of diesel smoke. In the distance, the dark profile of the container was silhouetted against the horizon, rising and falling with the swell.

"How are we going to do this?" Dan shouted over the noise of the engine.

"It is not easy," the old man said, "but I have done this before. There is a big looping current that sweeps around these islands." He waved his arms in a large circle as he spoke. "It reaches all the way from Panama to Nicaragua and far out into the main current that flows up toward the Yucatan Channel. It pulls in things from way out in the Caribbean Sea. Every now and then, something like this container shows up. So I have experience with this.

"That's good," Dan said. "But you'll have to tell us exactly what to do. We've never done anything like this before."

"No problem," the old man said. "We will pull the barge alongside and tie up to the container using those ropes," – he pointed to two piles of line, one on each end of the barge – "then you and your son will climb on it and I will hand you some chain that you must hook to the corners.

There are hooks on the ends of the chain, and all you have to do is find a good place to attach it at each corner. We are lucky, because this container is floating pretty high and all the corners are there for us."

"Then what?" Dan shouted the question.

"Then we will bring the middle of each chain together and I will lower the big hook on the crane cable to you."

Dan nodded. "Okay, I get it. It'll form a lifting bridle."

"Si, senor."

When they were alongside the container, the old man shook his head. "It is upside down."

"Is that a problem?" Dan asked.

"It is better for us if we turn it over out here on the water. It will roll over easily. Then, when we open it up, whatever is inside will be sitting the way it was loaded."

"Okay, just tell us what to do."

The old man directed them, and Dan and Jacob each took a rope and passed it through a tie-down point on the metal walls, then back to cleats on the edge of the barge. With the box secured, Dan boosted his son onto the container, then climbed up behind him. Juan Baptista de la Vega shuffled across the wide platform, dragging a chain in each hand.

"On each of the far corners, you will find a place to attach the hooks," he told them. "Then I will lift with the crane and the container will roll."

The job was easier than Dan thought it might be, and half an hour later the old tractor motor was growling and the big cable drum was turning. An inch at a time, the crane started to lift the upright container out of the water. As it came clear of the surface, a steady flow of water ran out from beneath the doors.

"Watch out," the old man warned them, as he pushed a control lever that started to swing the crane around. "This is how I became crippled twenty-five years ago. You men move back to the tug."

Dan and Jacob were happy to comply with the skipper's orders. Under the weight of the container, the barge tilted steeply to one side, but the old man stood his ground at the controls and swung the crane in a wide horizontal arc. The floating platform straightened itself as the crane and its load came across to the center, and de la Vega lowered the freight box.

"Good job," de la Vega shouted after he shut down the motor. "Now you men tie her down to cleats from each corner, and I will start the tug. I will take you back to your boat, and you can follow me to my home on the island of San Luis Miguel."

Lunch was ready when the men arrived back at the catamaran, with the barge carrying her load. As they ate in the cockpit, Nicole stared up at the container and suddenly felt dwarfed by its size. "Wow, that thing is bigger than our whole boat"

"Longer, yes," Dan agreed. "But we're nearly twice as wide."

"Yeah, but look how it towers above our cabin roof," Cadee exclaimed.

"Okay," – the old man straightened his back as he stood – "I better get started. I will be going slowly, so you will have no trouble following me." He climbed over the side to the tug and fired up the motor.

"Go ahead and take off," Dan shouted above the noisy diesel, using the boat hook to push the old boat away. As the tug motored off toward the island, he turned to his family, "Well guys, there's our treasure chest. Won't be long now."

"I hope it's full of Japanese motorcycles," Jacob said eagerly.

"Whatever it is," Nicole said, "I have no idea how we're going to stash it on this boat."

"Well, if it's something really good, maybe we'll just have to get ourselves a bigger boat," Dan said. Seeing Nicole's expression, he changed the subject. "Okay, kids, let's clear the cockpit of all this stuff. I'll help mom wash the dishes and you guys straighten up the rest of the boat. We can let the tug get a head start, 'cause we can go a lot faster than he can. I figure in an hour we'll fire up and follow."

Everyone jumped to their duties, and in no time, the boat was ready to go. Dan kept an eye on the distant column of black smoke, still showing clearly against the sky, even though the tub and barge had dropped below the horizon.

The hour came and went, and finally it was time. Everyone was anxious to get underway. "Jake, please lower the outdrive." Dan said. "I'll get this puppy humming so we can follow the barge."

For the next nine and a half hours, they tagged along behind the barge, keeping a respectable distance and maneuvering slightly upwind, so the smell of the diesel smoke would blow away from them. Two and a half knots made it seem almost as if they had dropped anchor and were standing still, yet that was all the barge would do. San Luis Miguel was a little over twenty-three miles distant when they started, and appeared to get no nearer, even after hours of progress. At first, only the two highest points of the island were visible over the horizon, and with each passing hour they were able to see a little more of the island's shape come into view.

Dan pulled out the chart covering the area around San Luis Miguel and studied the hourglass shape of the land formed by two prominent hills, connected by a narrow waist, creating harbors on opposite sides of the island. On the chart was a thin line that ran down the side of one hill, curving out of the jungle and into the deepest part of the harbor on the east side of the island. *A river,* Dan thought as he studied what was before him.

Jacob came into the cockpit and sat next to his dad. "Look at this." Dan outlined the island with his finger. "San Luis Miguel is claimed by both Colombia and Nicaragua. I've heard of places like this where two countries dispute ownership for decades, maybe even centuries, but neither makes a move to occupy the territory."

"So what happens?" Jacob looked more closely at the chart.

"Nothing. Without the political will to establish an undisputed claim to ownership through occupation, the land sits empty. These countries probably have no budget for a military or law enforcement effort. Think about it, this little spot of land is hundreds of miles from the countries that claim it, and it's probably considered not worth the trouble or the money that's necessary to defend their claims."

"Well, how do people like Senor de la Vega end up there?"

"He, and whoever else is there, probably just moved in and set up house, made their own rules and basically run their own little kingdom."

They sat in the cockpit studying the chart, and the tropical night came quickly. In the distance, lights began to appear at the base of the dark, jungle-covered island. With the final glow of dusk fading, Dan noticed a cluster of small, boxy forms that he presumed to be houses or buildings of some sort. He had the binocular to his eyes when Nicole stepped out into the cool night air of the cockpit.

"Ah, there you are," – she gave Jacob a hug – "I made some cookies for you and Cadee. "They're on the counter, cooling."

"Great," Jacob beamed and went inside. Through the cockpit window, he flashed a series

of hand signals to his dad: *thanks for the history lesson.*

Dan signaled back: *you're welcome. We can talk more about it later.*

"You two seem like you were having a good time."

"So, where's my cookie?" Dan teased.

"I brought you the cook and left the cookies for the kids."

He patted the seat, inviting her to sit next to him. "I'll take the cook anytime. Still, I hope the kids leave a cookie for dear old dad."

She laughed. "I can always make more. See anything interesting?" Nicole peered off into the night.

He handed the binocular to her, "Nothing that I can make out. We're still about three miles off. Doesn't look like much of a village to me."

She studied the scene for a few moments. "Do you think this is a good idea?"

"A little late to be asking."

"Not really. We could just let the old guy have the container and go on our merry way to Rio Dulce."

"You serious?"

"I don't know what it is, but there's something that feels weird about all this."

A somber expression crossed Dan's face. "When we got married, Reverend Lofgreen gave me some counsel. Do you remember? He said, 'Mr Plover, you wear the pants in the family, but Mrs Plover has the hotline.' I think he was telling me that I need to listen to your intuition. So, are you having one of those intuition moments?"

"I'm not sure. Maybe it's just that we've never done anything like this before and it makes me kind of nervous. I don't want a sudden windfall to affect how the kids view life. That's one of the reasons we came on this cruise, so we could get back to the basics and help them understand what is and what isn't important in life. Sudden wealth that is not earned can destroy people. You've see that happen. And this is kind of like winning the lottery."

He stepped behind her and wrapped his arms around her waist, pulling her back into his chest. "Or maybe it's like winning a load of somebody else's dirty laundry. We have no idea what's in there. Doesn't it intrigue you?"

195

"Sure it does. But …"

"If it makes you feel any better," he interrupted, "I understand how you feel about this. I've been having some of the same feelings myself. Maybe it comes from being married to you for so long."

"I think we need to sit down and talk with Jacob and Cadee."

She had barely finished her words when the kids came out of the cabin. "Mom," – Cadee's voice was soft and apologetic – "I'm sorry. We weren't trying to eavesdrop, because I know that it's rude, but we heard what you and dad were saying."

"Yeah," Jacob said, "we're mature enough to see what's going on here. Finding a treasure at sea might be great, but it isn't real life. Cadee and I have been talking. None of this matters."

"So, should we just let it go and head north for Guatemala?" Dan asked.

There was a brief moment of silence, as Nicole, Cadee and Jacob looked at each other and stumbled over their words. Then in unison, the decision was made. "Nah," they all said at once. Laughter erupted, and Jacob spoke for them all, "Hey, we all know it would kill us to leave now and never know what was inside that container."

"Then we follow the barge?" Dan asked, and they all nodded like a bunch of energetic bobble-head dolls. "We'll pay the guy his thousand bucks, so his family will have some money, and we'll give him his forty percent?" They all agreed. "And maybe we'll let him have the whole mess?"

Silence cloaked the cockpit, as the thought sank in. Nicole was first to speak, "Well, maybe I'll take just one mink coat."

Before she finished, Jacob was already voicing his opinion, "How about just one motorcycle?"

Cadee folder her arms and shook her head. "You guys are pathetic." She held her pose for half a minute, but then broke down. "It wouldn't hurt to have just a little bit of whatever is in there, would it?"

"You all have a point. I'm just trying to figure out where to park a new Ferrari on deck," Dan said.

A loud blast from an air horn made them all jump and look forward. The island was much closer now, and they could faintly see through the darkness what appeared to be a cluster of small wooden buildings scattered along the beach in front of the backdrop of jungle trees. A dark gap opened before them like a deep, black concert hall. The opening was bordered along both sides by jungle growth.

"Hey Jake," Dan said, "this must be the river we saw on the chart."

The barge glided slowly into the mouth of the river beneath a dense canopy of limbs that had grown across it, creating a seventy-foot high tunnel that seemed to reach into the heart of the jungle. A short distance upriver, lights moved about on shore, illuminating a wooden dock that ran parallel to the shoreline. At the far end of the dock, a flash of reflected torchlight gleamed from the windshield of a small runabout. Dan couldn't help thinking how out of place the sleek boat looked in this primitive jungle setting.

Dan looked at his wristwatch. Five minutes to ten. It had been a long day, and darkness had shrouded them for nearly the past three hours. He was tired, but his heart was pumping fast with excitement for what lay ahead.

Juan Baptista de la Vega maneuvered the barge up to the pier and half a dozen torch-carrying men appeared out of the darkness to tie the boat to the pilings. A sudden chill raised the hair on the back of Dan's neck as he studied the scene through his binocular. *So, where are all the wives and children and grandchildren the old man spoke of?* The thought passed almost as quickly as it arose, as he considered the time of night. *Ah, they must be in bed already.*

A space at the end of the pier was the right size for the catamaran. Dan turned a wide circle and spun the boat around so it faced out toward the open ocean. Docking with the bows facing the onshore breeze and swells coming into the river from the open water was more comfortable and safer for the boat.

On an impulse, Dan turned to his daughter. "Cadee, I'd like you to go below for now."

"How come?"

"I'm not sure," he said honestly, "but something doesn't feel right. Just give me some time to check things out. I'd be more comfortable if you were in your cabin." He winked at her.

She winked back. "Okay, daddy," as she disappeared through the cabin door.

Jacob laid the fenders over the side on his way forward to handle the bow line, and Nicole had the stern line in hand as Dan maneuvered the boat into a cushioned landing against the wooden dock. Four men spaced themselves out along the pier, and two of them took the dock lines. The other two held shotguns, and they were pointed directly at Jacob and Nicole.

Chapter Thirty

Juan Baptista de la Vegas leapt from the barge and strode down the length of the dock toward the catamaran, looking for all the world like a man half his age. With a glowering face he yelled at Dan, "Let me introduce my family." Then he roared with a gutteral laugh, whirled around and threw his hands in the air as if to accept an applause, and all his men laughed with him.

"What's going on?" Nicole whispered.

"I'm not sure," Dan said, "but I don't think de la Vega is the grandfather he said he was. He's a fraud. We've been suckered."

Suddenly, the old man did not appear to be so old. His bent back was straight and strong as a tree, and his crippled legs carried him easily as he marched proudly up and down the wooden dock accepting the backslaps of his men. With machetes raised, half a dozen men gave a shout.

"Julio," de la Vega yelled into the night, "Tiago, bring the beer. It is time for celebration."

A moment later, out of the darkness, a man trotted onto the torch-lit dock, carrying an old beat-up picnic cooler. "Set it down there," de la Vega ordered, and the man did as he was told. "The first and the coldest one for me," de la Vega shouted, looking around at his men, "unless there is anyone here who wants it some other way."

All the voices went silent as the old man stared from man to man. "No complaints? Then I will have the first and the coldest." He reached into the box and pulled out two bottles of beer, twisted off the cap from one and raised it to his lips. Without pausing to take a breath, he drained the bottle, sucked out the last of the brew, wiped his mouth on his sleeve and smashed the bottle against the rocks at the edge of the dock. As if he had accomplished a great feat, he threw his hands into the air, and a cheer went up from the men. He turned to Dan and held out the other bottle, then snatched it back. "The best plunder so far was the yacht with the generator and ice-maker."

Dan looked around. "I don't see a yacht."

"It is now in Nicaragua, wearing a new name."

Out of the crowd, one voice rose above the rest. "What have you brought us tonight, boss?"

"It is in there," de la Vega pointed at the container, "and it is in here," he pulled a wad of $20 bills out of his pocket and waved it in the air. The men erupted in a wild cheer, but he stopped them with a raise of his hand. "That is not all." He stepped aboard the catamaran, grabbed Nicole by the hair and yanked her head back. She screamed and Dan lunged toward de la Vega, but a bearded giant of a man jumped into the cockpit and laid the sharp edge of a machete to his throat. "Do not be so stupid," de la Vega spit at Dan and glared at him with icy eyes. Then he reached a grubby hand into Nicole's blouse, smiled wickedly and pulled out the other half of the bills that she had hidden there.

"You leave my mom and dad alone," Jacob screamed from the bow, but the man with the shotgun stepped in close and with a powerful thrust drove the barrel into Jacob's stomach. The staggering blow knocked the breath out of him and he collapsed in a heap on the deck.

The old man shoved Nicole to one side and she stumbled into the far corner of the cockpit. The crowd exploded in a cheer worthy of a bullfight, as de la Vega waved both hands full of $20 bills. Like famished vultures, the men moved in, clawing over each other, trying to be the first to grab some of the money.

"Easy there men. Back up," Vega yelled, pocketing the money so he could pull a pistol from his belt and fire a round into the air. The men stopped where they stood and he waved the gun at them. "Don't make me shoot any of you. You know how I don't like being crowded." Then he laughed as he put the gun back in his waistband, and slowly the men began to laugh with him.

"That was a good joke, boss," one yelled.

De la Vega shouted above the uproar, "You will each get a share of this, and you will each get a share of what is in the freight box."

"What's in there, boss?" one of the men asked.

"I don't know. We will find out soon. But whatever it is, it's ours now," de la Vega said. "Ruiz and Javier," he ordered the ones holding weapons on Jacob and Dan, "take these people and lock them away until I decide what to do with them. Juanico," he called to a third man, "there's a little girl inside. Get her. The boy, I think we can sell him to the Colombian cartel to work as a drug mule. I am sure we can get a good price for the girl in Aruba. The woman …" his rotted teeth showed as his lips spread wide, "… I have my own plans, for her. And the man, tomorrow we can turn him out on the island and hunt him for sport. Lock the kids in one hut and the parents in the other." He motioned toward a pair of wooden sheds just beyond the trees in the clearing toward the larger buildings.

Nicole struggled as a man with a nasty scar across his face pulled her arms behind her back and bound her wrists with a rough rope. "Dan," she yelled, "do something!"

"Yes, Dan, do something," the bearded man named Ruiz held the machete to Dan's throat, and showed his yellow teeth. His breath smelled like the bottom of a garbage disposal as he pressed his face in close and sneered, "I beg you to do something. I haven't killed anybody yet today, so go ahead and do something so I can be happy tonight."

Dan choked on the foul breath. "I'm sorry," he apologized to Nicole. "There's nothing I can do."

The taste of acid rose in his throat and he felt weak and sick inside as Javier and Juanico pulled his children off the boat. Cadee cried so hard she could hardly stand up to walk, so Juanico grabbed her by one arm and dragged her over the rough wood of the dock. Jacob flashed a defiant look and jerked back and forth as he was led away.

"Be strong, Jake," Dan called out. "Comfort your sister." Then the kids were led away into the shadows. Nicole broke into tears and Dan's heart ached as he helplessly listened to Nicole's sobs and Cadee screaming in pain and fear in the distance.

Juan Baptista de la Vega stood before Dan and Nicole, a proud look on his face. "Give me the combination to your safe. You will have no need for the money. There is no way for you to get off this island, and there is no point in refusing my demands."

Dan looked the old man in the eyes. "Why should we make it easy for you? You make it sound hopeless for us, so why should we cooperate?"

"That is a good question, senor. You are looking for incentive, are you? As you have seen, I am in charge here, and I can command my men to do as I please. For example, I can command that your little girl be released unharmed on Isla de la Juventude, a small island that belongs to Cuba. There she will be cared for and adopted into Cuban society by people I know. Or, I can sell her into the white slavery trade on Aruba and she will grow up giving pleasure to whoever will pay. Or I could simply tell my men to do with her as they wish." He stopped in front of Nicole, looked her in the eyes and spoke in a slow, evil voice. "Some of my men are not … how should I say it … they are not normal, when it comes to children. I assure you that what they wish to do to a little girl like her is not a pretty sight. But I leave it to you. It is your choice."

"Look," Dan begged de la Vega, "please let us go. There is nothing to be gained by harming any of us, especially the children. What satisfaction would that possibly bring you?"

"You make a good argument, senor." De la Vega showed the gaps in his rotted teeth as he grinned at Dan. "You want your freedom, is that right? Is that all you want? Just your freedom?"

"Freedom for our family, for all of us, yes, that is all I want," Dan said. "You can keep everything. Just let us sail away from here with our children."

"Ahhh," the old man looked deeply into Dan's eyes, "yesterday you had your freedom, and you had your children. But you wanted more than that. You wanted a treasure that you found floating on the sea. And now suddenly you are no longer interested in the treasure? Now you are willing to trade everything you have just to get your freedom and your children back again?"

"That's right. You can have our money, you can have the container and everything that is in it. We don't want any of it. What would you gain by not letting us go?"

The old man thrust his finger at Dan's face. "I gain the fact that you will never be able to lead authorities to this island. And I also have a nice new catamaran to go with my nice new runabout." He nodded toward the sleek boat tied at the dock beyond the barge and chuckled. "Haven't you been wondering where that boat came from?"

The words escaped Dan's mouth before he could stop them. "You are pirates!"

"Ha!" de la Vega laughed, "Pirates, are we? Hey," – he glanced at Ruiz – "he says we're pirates. How about that," and the two men burst into laughter. Then suddenly de la Vega stopped laughing and growled through clenched teeth. "You're right. We're the deadliest pirates that ever took these islands, and there's nobody for a thousand miles who dares to get in our way. Now I want the combination to the safe on your boat, or I'll tear it out of there and blow the thing wide open. One way or another, I'm going to get all your money, and there's nothing you can do about it."

"I'll give you the combination," Nicole snarled, glowering at the old man, "but if anything happens to my children, I'll come back from the dead and tear your heart out through your throat."

"Hot dang, boss," Ruiz blurted, "she's a live one, ain't she!"

De la Vega backed up a step and looked long and hard at Nicole, his eyes serious. "This is a real mother." His words were quiet and sounded almost reverent. "Not that I have known it personally, but I can respect a mother's love for her children. Perhaps if my own mother …" His words trailed off and lost themselves in bitter thoughts of his childhood.

Nicole noticed a change in the old man's countenance, and softened her tone, "What happened to you as a child? What did your mother do that filled you with so much hatred of people?"

A wave of anger and sadness crossed de la Vega's face. He had not told his story to anyone, and was unsure why he would tell it now. But he looked at Nicole and the words started coming.

"I was four when my mother sold me for a bottle of whisky. The man who bought me to work as a slave in his bar beat me with a strap every night before I was sent to sleep under the porch with the dogs and share their food and water. Ticks from the dogs sucked my blood until they swelled up this big," – he held his finger and thumb in front of her face, an inch apart – "they sucked my blood until they got too big, then they burst and my blood was all over me.

"When I was seven, I crawled out from under the porch one night, ran away to the waterfront, stowed myself on a freighter and hid under the canvas cover of a lifeboat. I had nothing to eat for three days, and to drink I had only the stale saltwater trapped in the bottom of the boat. I thought I would die if I didn't get off of that ship, so I jumped overboard in the middle of the night when I saw lights on shore in the distance. I didn't know how to swim, but it was swim or die, so I kicked and thrashed my way toward the lights and finally came ashore on Isla de la Juventude.

"I broke into people's houses to steal food and lived like an animal in the jungle for six years. Then I fell in with Castro's revolutionary brigade. They took me in because I was tough and could live like a rat in a garbage dump. They taught me all I needed to know about taking what I wanted from those who had more than I did. But years later I saw that Castro's government was nothing but a lie, so I got out, stole a boat and came here to set up business."

"Sounds like a hard life," Dan said.

De la Vega blinked and shook his head, as if to remove the memories. "You have no idea." Then a cold grin spread across his mouth. "But you're about to find out." Turning to Ruiz, he gave the order. "Throw them in the hut. Lock it solid. If either one of them tries to get away, kill the other one. We'll deal with them tomorrow. I'm tired." Then he strode off toward the end of the dock and ducked into the darkness of the trees.

Ruiz pointed the machete at Dan's stomach and shoved Nicole with his other hand. She stumbled back, caught her heel and fell, her arms pinned behind her, and she cried out in pain.

Anger filled Dan's heart. "You son of a—"

"Shut your mouth," Ruiz ordered. "Get up and get moving," the bearded pirate snarled at Nicole. She struggled to her feet and felt Ruiz's powerful hand shove her forward. "You next," Ruiz growled at Dan, spinning him around and planting the point of the machete against his spine. As prisoners, Dan and Nicole walked the length of the dock then followed a trail into the shadows of the jungle before emerging a moment later in bright moonlight at the edge of a clearing. There ahead were two small huts, and Ruiz pressed the machete into Dan's back to move him faster.

Dan winced, and under his breath, he whispered to Nicole, "I'm working on a plan."

"Shut up," Ruiz snarled, digging the point of the machete into the flesh beside Dan's spine. "Why wait for the hunt? I should kill you right now." The sharp pain nearly made Dan's knees buckle, and he felt blood ooze from the wound and run down his back.

Chapter Thirty-one

Thirty feet into the clearing the first hut stood in bright moonlight like a black tool shed. It was made of rough wood planks, hammered together with rusty nails and tied with bits of rope or braided vines where nails had no purchase. At first glance, it looked flimsy, but Dan could see that with an armed guard outside it was strong enough to serve as a temporary prison.

"Get in there and shut up or I'll beat your brains in," Ruiz threatened them as he shoved them through the door and slammed it shut. From inside, they heard the metallic sound of a lock snicking closed through a latch. *Why would they need a lock on a tool shed?* The reality of it settled in. *We aren't the first prisoners to be held here. I wonder what happened to the others?* But he didn't even want to bring up the subject to Nicole.

"Back to back," Dan whispered. "Quick, let's get these ropes off." They moved together, leaning back against each other. "I'll do yours first," he said and started fumbling with the knot lashed around her wrists. It took only a few minutes and her hands were free. A moment later, she had loosened the rope restraining his arms. He rubbed his wrists to restore circulation, then in the darkness felt his way over a pile of unidentifiable rubble on the floor until he reached the side of the hut and pressed his face to a narrow slit in the wall.

Twenty feet away, he saw the hut that held Jacob and Cadee. Through the thin wooden walls and across the short distance, they heard Cadee whimpering and they heard Jacob's voice trying to console her.

"If it's the last thing I do, I'll kill de la Vega if he hurts you or the kids," Dan swore under his breath.

From fifty yards farther on, the sound of slurred men's voices roared through the night air. To Dan's ear, nothing sounded more pathetic than a bunch of drunks baying at the moon, but tonight, it was the music he wanted to hear, the louder the better. "Listen to that," he whispered to Nicole. "That might work to our advantage."

"What, a bunch of drunken pirates?"

"Yeah, I just hope they keep on drinking."

Dan searched along the wall until he found a wider slot between two planks and pressed his eye to the wall. Across the clearing, he saw the other hut. The moon was bright, and sharp shadows were cast on the beach grass that covered the ground. Beyond the hut, he saw a larger building with lights burning inside. Through the bare window he watched shadows of men moving about, raising bottles of booze to their mouths, and he listened to the boisterous singing and yelling and cursing. "Keep slopping it up, you filthy pigs," Dan muttered.

In the moonlight, Dan noticed that there was no guard standing by the hut where the children were confined. Apparently, Ruiz was expected to guard both huts, figuring that the kids would stay put in the locked shack and cause no trouble, as long as their parents were being held as prisoners.

"Hey, son," Dan yelled, and a crashing blow thundered against the door from outside.

"Shut up!" Ruiz yelled, but it was too late. Dan saw his son's hand reach out through a slot between the planks of the far hut.

"Yeah, dad?" Jacob yelled back. "We're okay."

"Shut up, you kids," Ruiz threatened at the top of his lungs, "or I'll kill your mom!"

Cadee howled when she heard that, and the verbal torture was more than Nicole could take. "Listen, you stinking animal, you shut your mouth, or after I'm through with your boss I'll hunt you down and rip your tongue out by its root."

Dan raised his eyebrows and stared in surprise at Nicole. Her eyes were glowing with anger and she was puffing her breaths like a fighter getting ready for battle. He'd never heard her talk this way before, but decided to go along with it. "Ruiz," he called through the door, "you'd better listen to her. She's a karate master and she's already killed a man bigger than you."

Ruiz yelled back, "You're lying," but his voice sounded a little unsure. "You just be quiet in there, or the boss will have my head."

"You afraid of your boss?" Dan thought he detected a weak spot that could be worked.

"Are you kidding? I ain't afraid of nobody."

"I don't know," Dan said with obvious doubt in his voice. "Sounds to me like you are."

"I ain't afraid. I'm just smart." The pirate tried hard to sound convincing. "I know where my money comes from."

Dan moved against the back wall, shoved his shoulder against a plank and felt it give. One more shove and the slot opened a little wider. He stuck his hand out and waved it toward the far hut, and Jacob waved back. *Good, he sees me.* In a flurry of finger movements, Dan flashed sign language into the night. A moment later, Jacob's hand started moving and Dan read the message.

"Listen, Ruiz," Dan called out, wanting to keep the attention of his guard, "if you're so smart about money, why are you going to split the treasure in the container with all those other men. How many are there?"

"Hey," Ruiz shouted, "I'm not stupid. I know what you're trying to pull. You want me to tell you how many men we have here."

"No, that's not what I was trying to do." Dan rolled his eyes at Nicole. "I was just thinking of how many ways you're going to have to split all that money. And here you are, standing guard all by yourself while everybody else is in there, drinking up your share of the booze and having a good time. Why should you have to split the money with them when you're doing all the work? You'll only get, what, a tenth or a twentieth?"

"We split everything," Ruiz responded. "It's the rule."

"Yeah, but who made the rule?"

"De la Vega makes all the rules," Ruiz shouted "He's the boss. Now shut up."

"Yeah, and how much does he take?"

"You don't listen very well, do you?" Ruiz growled.

"You afraid to even talk about it?"

"I told you, I ain't afraid of nothing."

"So why not tell me how much de la Vega takes?"

Ruiz huffed. "The rule is that he gets half, and the rest gets split nine ways between us."

"So," Dan continued quickly, not wanting Ruiz to realize what had just happened, "if we're talking about a million dollars, the boss gets half a million and you end up with a little over fifty thousand? Does that sound fair to you? I don't think so."

Ruiz was silent for a long moment. "Are you saying there's a million dollars in that container?"

"I know exactly how much is in that container," Dan lied. "And better yet, I know how to open it. But I'm not going to tell anyone who is such a fool that he lets himself get ripped off by some guy just because he says he's the boss and wants to make all the rules."

"The boss says—"

"Listen man, the boss is only the boss as long as you let him. He's ripping you guys off. What would you do if you were the boss?"

Ruiz started talking in a lower voice, as if he were afraid to be overheard having such a conversation. "I'd split it all even."

"Now that sounds fair to me," Dan said. "I can work with a boss like that."

"You?" Ruiz sounded unbelieving.

"Heck yeah," Dan said. "I figure our chances are better if we cooperate with you than if we fight you and end up getting ourselves killed. Yeah, I'd work with you, if you were boss."

Ruiz was quiet, and Dan hoped it was because the man was thinking about what had been said. Greed and power are temptations that can tear a man away from his foundation, and Dan knew that if he lured Ruiz into his trap, it might give him a chance to save his family. If he failed, it was likely that by tomorrow he would be dead, with Nicole in bondage to de la Vega and the kids sold into white slavery.

Dan stuck his hand back out through the slot and pressed his face to the opening, then signed again to Jacob. A moment later, his son's fingers began moving. He understood, and he pulled his hand inside. After a few minutes, the sound of Cadee's crying stopped, and Dan was hopeful that it was because her brother had shared the plan with her and gave her a job to do that her dad said was important.

In the distance, the drunken party was louder than before. "Ruiz," – Dan moved next to the door so he could speak in a low voice – "listen to them in there, having a good time while you're stuck out here. I think you'd be a better boss that de la Vega. You deserve something better than the measly little bit he is going to give you. You ought to be in charge."

"Perhaps, you are right, senor," Ruiz said in a hushed tone. "What do you propose?"

NIA Headquarters

Curt Delamo's phone rang and he looked at the caller ID display, then reached for the handset. "Josh. What do you have to report?"

"Sorry to call you so late," Josh said, "but we're going to need to pull out all the stops here. We need more C-130's looking for containers. Only three have showed up so far, and none of them is the right one. It's still out there somewhere."

"I talked with Secretary of the Navy, Bob Avery, this afternoon. The president has authorized him to dispatch a carrier out of Pensacola as soon as the storm gets out of the way. Probably another day or two, but as soon as possible we'll get a ship loaded with planes down there to help with the search. At least Husam al Din is no longer on his way to Miami."

"Until we find the container, I'm not willing to assume that. I know this guy. He's a fanatic, and I won't rest until I know he's caught or dead." Josh replied. "In the meantime, is there anything you want me to do other than keep the Coast Guard company."

"When you have a minute, you might stop by one of those little gift shops and buy a get-well card to send to Susan," Curt suggested.

"I've been sending those every day since I heard the news."

"Thought you might."

"What's the latest?" Josh asked.

"She's going to keep her eye."

Josh stroked his forehead. "Ahhh, that's good," he exhaled hard.

"They're releasing her tomorrow morning. Chris Banes is on his way to take up where she left off. Whoever it was that shot Alicia Gomez and wounded Susan is still out there, and we want to find him."

"You sure it's a him?"

"Not sure at all. Who would have guessed this Gomez woman would have risen to the level she did? But Susan has some information for Chris that might help track down the shooter, or at least someone close to him."

Josh nodded silently, unsure what else to say. Then it came. "Tell Chris to take good care of her."

"He knows," Curt ended the call.

San Luis Miguel Island

"Ruiz," Dan spoke quietly through the thin door. "As a show of good faith, I'm going to tell you what's in the container."

From outside, the pirate answered in a hushed voice. "How do I know you will tell me the truth?"

"You don't trust me?"

"Why should I trust you, senor? You are a prisoner, and soon you will be dead."

"Yeah, well, I don't want to be dead. I want to make a deal with you."

"What kind of deal?"

"You get everything that's in the container. You don't have to split it with anybody."

"What about the boss?"

"If you've got the guts to do this, you don't have to worry about him anymore."

Ruiz was quiet for a long moment before speaking again. This time, his mouth was very close to the door and he was speaking just above a whisper. "Before I will listen to your plan, I need to know you can be trusted."

"All right. You know de la Vega was after the combination to the safe on our boat?"

"Yeah."

"Well, I'm going to give you the combination. There's $4,000 still in there. You go open the safe and keep the money for yourself. Then you'll know you can trust me."

"I can't leave here," Ruiz complained.

"Where the heck are we going to go?" Dan sounded frustrated. "You've got us and our kids locked up. Are you going to do this or not? If you don't have the guts for it, forget it."

"I got the guts," Ruiz protested. "What's the combination?"

"Okay, the safe is under the sink in the galley. Spin the dial twice to the right, then stop on twenty-two. Turn it back to the left all the way around once and then to thirty-two, then back to the right to fourteen. Go check it out. You'll see that I can be trusted."

The sound of footsteps walking away brought a sigh of relief to Dan, and he moved to the rear of the hut again. "Nicole, I need your help pushing this old plank out. We've got to hurry. He'll be back in a few minutes."

Together, they shoved against the loose plank until it fell away from the side of the hut. He squirmed out through the opening and raced to the other hut, kneeling in the shadow at the rear corner. "Jacob, Cadee, it's dad," he whispered loudly.

"Dad," both kids said in unison.

"Shhh," he cautioned them. "You guys shove while I pull on this plank." In a moment, they had it loose. He reached in and stroked Cadee's hair, then grabbed Jacob's hand in a wrist wrestler's grip. "You two just stay put until I get my plan going. Watch for my signs. Then you know what to do."

"Got it, dad," Jacob said, referring to the sign language instructions received earlier.

Dan swung his eyes toward the dock. "I've got to get back. Wait for an opening, then do it." He kept low and sneaked back to his own hut, crawled in through the opening and repositioned the plank. A few minutes later, footsteps sounded from the direction of the dock, and Ruiz took up his position again in front of the hut.

"You told me the truth, senor."

"Well, that's just the beginning," Dan said through the door. "You can have everything that's in the container for yourself, or you can split it up with your gang anyway you want. You'll be the boss."

Ruiz sounded more friendly this time. "What is in the container, senor?"

Dan's mind flashed back to what he saw painted on the container as they first approached it with their boat. In his mind's eye, he could read it perfectly, but he wanted to buy some time and give Jacob and Cadee a chance to make their move. Dan whispered through the door. "I'm going to talk quietly. We don't want the rest of the men to hear what we're talking about, okay?"

He heard Ruiz squat down next to the door. "Here's what I want you to do, Ruiz," Dan whispered. "Walk down to the container and look at the top corner. You'll see some letters and numbers painted on it. It's a code that tells what's inside. And I know what it means."

"How do you know these things?"

"I used to work in the shipping business. Container codes were part of my job." He decided to test Ruiz, "Hey, I just gave you the combination to our safe. You trust me, don't you?"

"Uhmm." Ruiz sounded as if he were not completely sure.

"Look, what have you got to lose? Just go down there and read the serial number. You'll be amazed when I tell you what it means."

"If you know what it means, you tell me what it says. Then I'll go check."

"You're a stubborn man, Ruiz," Dan argued.

"If I am going to be the boss, I can be stubborn if I want to."

"You're right," Dan agreed. "The boss is always right. Okay, the serial number you will see will say BA11M. Go see for yourself, then I'll tell you what it means."

Again, the footsteps faded away into the shadows. Dan thrust his hand out through the opening and caught Jacob's eye. His fingers worked quickly, and Jacob returned a sign of understanding. In the moonlight, Dan watched as the children crawled out the rear of the hut and scrambled across the clearing and into the shadows of the jungle.

If all went as planned, this would be the first step in their escape. If not, there was no doubt in his mind that it would be the first step toward all of their deaths.

Chapter Thirty-two

Nicole took Dan's hand and whispered, "What have we gotten ourselves into?"

Dan breathed deeply. "I am sorry for all of this."

"The kids ..." she began, but at the sound of distant footsteps on the wooden dock he put a finger to her lips.

"You've got to get out of here. Jacob knows what to do. They're waiting for you in the shadows beside the trail to the dock. When Ruiz comes back here, you all sneak aboard the catamaran and hide below. I'll get there as soon as I can. Now go."

She squeezed through the small opening at the back of the hut, crouched low as she sprinted across the clearing and disappeared into the shadows.

From way off, Dan heard the rhythmic rush of low waves breaking on the exposed shoreline. A mild breeze blew through the openings in the hut, and Dan felt suddenly more alone than he had ever felt before.

A few moments later, Ruiz rapped on the door and whispered, "There were letters and numbers. It said BA11M, just as you told me. So now you tell me what that means."

Dan put his mouth close to the door so he could whisper. "Listen carefully. We don't want anybody else to hear this. You're in luck, my friend. The BA in the serial number stands for Bank of America. When the bank has large amounts of money to ship around the world, they pack it in large bales, wrap it in plastic sheeting, put it in plastic totes and use containers like this one to ship it. There's nothing but a huge load of raw cash in that container."

"American dollars?" Ruiz whispered the question.

"Yes, but the best part is how much. The numbers 11 and the letter M tell us that there's $11 million in there."

"Eleven million!" Ruiz said out loud, and Dan hushed him through the door.

"Quiet. You don't want everyone else to hear you."

"Eleven million," Ruiz said again, this time in a breathless whisper. "Are you sure?"

"Do you want to open the container and see for yourself?"

"Yeah," Ruiz breathed, and Dan heard the lust in his voice. "Yeah, I do. If I could get my hands on eleven million, I could—"

"You could be the boss of this place," Dan reminded him. "If you have that kind of money in your hands, you can tell the others that you will share it equally with them, not like what de la Vega does. They will come over to your side just like that." Dan snapped his fingers with a loud click. "Then you'll be the boss, and you'll also be very rich."

"Yeah," Ruiz breathed.

"But the thing is that when banks ship money, they use special security locks. I know how to break them open. But I want in on this," Dan said. "I want to be an equal partner."

"Special locks?"

"Heck yeah," Dan said. "You don't expect them to ship that kind of money without special security locks do you? There are four of them. One on each of the vertical latching bars. But that's no problem for me."

"You get me inside that container, and I'll make you my right-hand man." Ruiz laughed under this breath.

Carried on the breeze, the raucous noise of the drunken party in the distant house sounded louder than before. "Listen to that," Dan said, "now is the time to make your move, while everybody else is getting drunk. You and I can break into that container, and you'll have the money in your hands before any of those guys wake up. By sunrise, you'll be in charge of this place."

The metallic sound of a key being forced into the lock brought a sigh to Dan's throat. The door swung open and the shadow of a giant of a man stood before him. "Get out here," Ruiz demanded. "Your kids stay in that one," he pointed toward the other hut, "and your wife stays here until we're done. You got that?"

Dan nodded, "Yeah, I got it."

Moonlight flashed in front of Dan's face, and he saw the blade of a large knife in the hand of his captor. "Don't do anything funny," the bearded pirate warned, "or I'll slit you open and take your wife for myself." Ruiz quietly closed the door and snapped the lock back in place.

"Hey, I thought we were going to be partners," Dan protested.

"We'll be partners after we get the eleven million."

"You don't trust people very easily, do you?" He glanced over the big man's shoulder toward the dock and thought he saw three crouching forms duck over the side of the catamaran and disappear.

"I don't trust people any more than I think they should trust me. Now let's get going." They crossed the moonlit clearing and entered the dark trail leading to the dock. As they stepped onto the wooden planks, Dan snapped his fingers as if he had a sudden thought.

"We need a couple of tools. Do you have a hacksaw and a bolt cutter, by chance?"

"Yeah. They're on the boss's tug."

Dan smiled at the big man, "Good. Grab those and I'll go have a closer look at the locks."

Ruiz stared at his prisoner, hesitated and then decided that he had the situation under control. "Just don't get any ideas," he threatened, waving the knife.

Dan held up his hands. "There's nothing to worry about. I'll just be right over there." He pointed toward the barge. Sixty feet farther down the dock, Dan glimpsed Jacob's face peering at him from the shadows of the cockpit, and his hands went to work. Jacob saw the signals and signed back, and Dan saw his son quietly slip the aft dockline off the double horns of the cleat, leaving the eye of the line hanging to the cleat by a single horn.

A noise behind him turned Dan back toward the tug, and he saw Ruiz coming. In his hand was a large bolt cutter. "This what you need?"

"No hacksaw?"

"Couldn't find one."

Dan took the bolt cutter and stepped onto the barge. "Well, let's see if this will do." He walked around behind the container and Ruiz was right behind him. Dan swung the handles wide to open the jaws, then turned to Ruiz. "Give me a little room to work. Stand over there. This is going to take a minute."

Ruiz stepped back and Dan clamped the bolt cutter jaws over the lock and pretended to squeeze as hard as he could. Nothing happened. He gritted his teeth, grunted and squeezed again, but still he was not able to break the lock. "These special security locks are made of hardened steel," he looked sheepishly at Ruiz, "I don't think I'm strong enough to break it. That's why I wanted a hacksaw."

Ruiz stomped forward. "Get out of the way, you're too weak." He grabbed the bolt cutter and shoved Dan aside, who made a point of tripping and falling on his side in full view of the catamaran. Quickly he flashed a sign into the night.

Ruiz gripped the bolt cutters in powerful hands, clamped the jaws on the lock and pressed the handles together. Snap! "Hah!" he said, pointing at the broken lock and admiring his work, "nothing to it."

Dan flashed a sign and, in the distance, the sound of a diesel engine came to life. "Congratulations," Dan yelled, scrambling to his feet, "the money is all yours." He jumped from the barge to the dock and ran toward the catamaran. Jacob was already at the bow line, releasing the eye from the cleat.

"Go, go!" Dan yelled as he ran. Jacob took the wheel, shoved the throttle forward and the catamaran started to move. As it cleared the end of the dock, Dan leapt and landed on the starboard hull swim-step, grabbed the stainless steel railing and climbed up into the cockpit.

"Good job, son."

"Thanks, dad. I did like you said and told Mom and Cadee that you wanted them to go below and stay out of sight."

"Let me take the wheel. Go below and tell your mother and sister that it's okay to come up now." He scooted onto the captain's seat, and Jacob reached for the cabin door. From the main salon, a scream pierced the night.

Nicole's cry was suddenly muffled as de la Vega stumbled through the door with his hand clamped tightly around her mouth. In his other hand was a machete, and he waved it threateningly. "Don't try annathin," he slurred, obviously deeply soused, "or I'll kill her."

The old man wobbled on his feet, as the boat took a small wave against the beam. It was all the break Dan needed, and he lunged for the machete, knocking it from de la Vega's grip. Nicole broke free, and a noise from behind caused the old man to whirl. When he did, the last thing he saw was a heavy crystal pitcher shattering into his face. Cadee stood, feet apart and ready to swing with her fist if the pitcher didn't do the job, but de la Vega had crumpled to the deck.

"Sorry about your pitcher, mom," Cadee broke down and cried. "I didn't know what else to do."

Nicole took her daughter into her arms. "Oh, sweetheart, you did just the right thing. I can get another pitcher, but I'm so proud of you."

"What do we do with him now?" Jacob asked. Cadee and Nicole held each other and shivered, even though the night was very warm. Tears and quiet moaning came from the women as they clutched each other in mutual comfort.

"He goes over the side," Dan said without a bit of indecision in his voice.

"He'll drown," Jacob protested.

"He might," Dan agreed, "if the sharks don't eat him first. But that's exactly what he gets for taking us hostage, stealing our money, threatening to kill us all, and just a minute ago threatening to kill your mother. If he drowns, so be it. Come on and give me a hand."

With that, Dan and Jacob hoisted de la Vega's limp body and dragged it to the edge of the cockpit, where they could toss him over the side.

Just then, a weak voice spoke with a slurr, "Pleash doan kill me. I sorry." De la Vega raised his head and stared with glassy eyes into Dan's face. "Por favor."

"Dang," Dan cursed beneath his breath. Then to Jacob he said, "Son, turn the boat around. We'll take him back close enough that he can crawl ashore."

"Dad, a man can drown in six inches of water. Let's take him back, toss him onto the dock and then leave."

"Thash a goo idea." Vega grinned a senseless and mostly toothless grin. "I sorry, you know," his head bobbed up and down.

A few minutes later, the catamaran eased silently up against the ageing wooden pilings of the decrepit dock and Dan and Jacob muscled the mostly limp body of the old man over the rail and onto the planks. Juan Baptista de la Vega no sooner hit the dock than he bounced to his feet and started yelling for his men to come running.

"Quick, you low down dogs, they are getting away. Come quickly."

In the distance, the door of the larger building banged open and yellow light poured out. Three men came stumbling as fast as their drunken legs could carry them, trying as they ran to pull up their pants, put on shoes, and take another swig on a tall bottle.

"Quick," Dan said to Jacob, "get her turned around and off the dock. I'll try to stop them," and he jumped over the rail to face de la Vega. "You are a lying rascal," Dan accused the old man. "We should have thrown you over."

"Yes, I am a lying rascal, but you are a fool, senor. You have been a fool twice, and now you will die this night, and so will your children. And after I have finished with your lovely wife, she will join you. I will still have your money and this fine sailing vessel and all the treasure that is in that container over there." He exhaled a hearty laugh as he motioned toward his barge.

The three men were running and stumbling, and two more were coming out of the building. Dan knew he didn't have much time. "Get going, son," he shouted to Jacob. And then he threw a punch that landed squarely on the old man's jaw. Juan Baptista de la Vega had a very hard jaw, and Dan's fist felt pain all the way to the wrist, but the old man's knees buckled and he went down.

Baptista hit the dock hard, but he rolled and came back up quickly, grappled Dan at the knees and tackled him. The two men rolled on the rough planks of the dock, and Vega delivered two punishing blows to Dan's rib cage. Everything went momentarily black as Dan lost his wind, but in the edges of his consciousness he heard the low rumble of a Westerbeke diesel and he knew Jacob could get the family safely away. But for some reason, the boat was not moving.

"Go Jacob, take off, now!" Dan yelled the order.

"No dad, I'm not leaving you," Jacob protested.

Dan scrambled to his feet, being quicker and more nimble than Vega. He looked hard at his son, caught his eye and gave a signal with his hand. Jacob responded with a nod and a hand signal of his own, then thrust the throttle forward and the catamaran moved away into the dark.

Just then, the three other men surrounded Dan, grabbed him by the arms and threw him hard on the dock. One of them stepped on the back of Dan's neck, and cursed. He recognized the voice of Ruiz. "You stupid idiot. You ain't goin no place but to perdition." Then he turned to de la Vega, "Should we go after 'em, boss?"

Juan Baptista de la Vega got to his feet, straightened his back, rubbed his jaw. "Naw. We ain't none of us in condition to go out there tonight. We'll go get 'em in the morning. I can outrun 'em with my fast new boat. Let's just get this gringo back to the hut. Only this time, he ain't gettin away again, you hear?"

"Yeah, boss," Ruiz agreed.

De la Vega wobbled on uncertain feet. "I came down to the boat to get away from all that drunken bellering at the house. Then, all of a sudden, there's the woman. She walked in, right past me, 'cause I was passed out in the aft cabin. But when the motor started, I thought I'd better get up and see what was happening." The old man stared at Ruiz. "I thought I left you to guard the man and his family." His tone sounded accusatory.

"Right, boss," Ruiz grinned at the old man. "But I tricked him into telling me what was in the container and how to break in. I made him think I was going to cut you out and take over."

De la Vega closed one eye and stared hard at Ruiz with the other. "But you would never do that, right?"

"Right, boss."

"And then what, you just let the bunch of 'em go?"

"Naw, I gotta admit that he tricked me while I was busy with the lock.

"Well lock him up tight this time," the old man slurred. "I'm going to bed."

Dan watched in amazement as Juan Baptista de la Vega stumbled a crooked line down the dock and into the shadows. "How can he fight so well when he's so drunk?" he asked Ruiz.

"He's old and dangerous. He's got a lot of years of experience, and somehow being drunk doesn't slow him down when it comes to fighting." Then Ruiz shoved Dan along the dock. "You get back in your cell, mister. You dang near got me killed here tonight, listening to your stuff about me becoming the boss."

As they walked down the dock, two other men stepped in to surround Dan. "The boss said we need to stay out here with you."

"What!" Ruiz protested, "He don't trust me?"

"We're just doing what we're told," one of the men said.

"That's a fine thing!" Ruiz spit. "He figures it takes three of us to watch one prisoner?"

Knowing the answer before he asked, Dan put the question to Ruiz in front of the other men, "So, did you see what was inside?"

"Didn't have time, what with all the ruckus down at your boat."

"What's he talking about?" one of the others slurred. "What did you see where?"

They arrived at the hut, and Ruiz shoved Dan through the door and slammed it, then set the lock. "It ain't nothin'," Ruiz dodged the question. "Just sit down and help me guard this guy. You two don't look too good."

Chapter Thirty-two

Dan pressed his ear to the door and listened as the men began to argue. "Maybe we better listen to Ruiz," one of them said after a while. "It's the best chance we'll ever have to make it big."

"I don't know, Pacheco," the third man said. "I don't know about killing the boss."

"Well, if we don't kill him," Pacheco said, "he'll come after us and kill us. For his cut of eleven million dollars he'll sure do that. And this world won't be big enough to hide in."

"Well, I never did like him," the first voice answered. "And besides, here we sit guarding this stupid gringo, and they're all in there sleeping like babies, or maybe drinking more rum." Then, in a low voice the man growled, "I say let's kill 'em all and take the money and run."

"We don't have to run. Just take the money and stay here," Pacheco argued.

Ruiz spoke up, "Listen you two, if we do this, then I'm gonna be the new boss. And that means you two follow my orders. Right?"

Through the thin door, Dan heard two mumbled voices that sounded as if they were agreeing. "Okay," Ruiz spoke again, "then it will just be the three of us. We will split the eleven million fair and square. That's the kind of boss I'll be."

"What about the rest of them?"

"We've gotta kill 'em all," Ruiz whispered. "I'll take out de la Vega. You each take out three. But you gotta be quiet about it. Slit their throats while they're sleeping off their drunk."

"So what about this guy?" Pacheco asked. "Do we kill him too?"

Dan sat closer to the door and pressed his ear to the wood, wanting to hear what plans they had for him. "He ain't a threat to us," Ruiz said, and Dan exhaled the breath he was holding. "I say we just leave him here, locked up, until we're done. We can deal with him later. Right now, we got some murdering to do."

"Just who are you planning on murdering?"

The booming voice belonged to de la Vega, and suddenly the door exploded. Ruiz tumbled through the splintered wood and sprawled on the dirt. The huge bearded pirate rolled and looked up. Vega stood over him, feet spread and one fist clenched around the neck of a bottle of rum.

"You thinking about killing me and taking all the loot for yourselves? Don't lie to me," he threatened, "I been standing in the shadows and listening long enough to know your plans."

He strode into the hut and bashed Ruiz across the skull with the bottle, sending a hail of broken glass and a slurry of booze across the room. Ruiz crumbled like a dead man. Carlos fled like a rabbit, and Vega turned toward Pacheco. The younger man, seeing that his time had run out, dove for Vega's midsection, knocking him back into the far wall. And then the slugging began. Dan had to hand it to Vega – for an old guy, he held his own in a fight, even when he was drunk.

Dust rose from the floor as the two men grappled, crashing through boxes and knocking over other items that were stored in dark confines of the hut. Dan stepped carefully out of the way, while the men grunted and slugged, and he slipped to the back of the hut. In the darkness, he found the loose plank and pushed it aside, then sneaked out into the night.

At first, he crouched as he crossed the bright clearing, then as he reached the shadows at the edge of the jungle he stood and ran at full speed, ducking vines and jumping over obstacles on the ground. His breath came hard and fast as he sprinted, and he didn't stop until he had penetrated the jungle for what he thought to be at least fifty yards, then he squatted and sat dead still. Through a clearing in the trees, he took bearings from the stars, then checked his watch. It was 2:15 in the morning. Hoping to get free, he had signaled Jacob to circle around the island to the far side, where he intended to meet the boat in a cove on the opposite side at three o'clock – only 45 minutes.

"Two miles," Dan whispered through heavy breathing. "Two miles and no trail. That could take two hours or more." From his study of the chart, all he knew was that the low pass between the island's two major hills led to the natural harbor on the far side. With no clear indication of a trail, he would have to bushwhack.

Far behind him, Dan heard shouting. It was de la Vega, and he sounded furious. "Mutiny is it?" he yelled like a wounded bear, "I'll show you what mutiny brings." Three shots rang out, then there was silence.

"Look, the rest of you men," Vega roared, "the traitors Ruiz, Pacheco and Carlos got what they deserved. Who else among you wants to join them?"

The voice of the old man thundered through the trees and he sounded boiling mad, ready to shoot any who defied his orders. From the silence among the men, Dan surmised that Juan Baptista de la Vega had regained control of the rest of the men.

"Now look at what has happened," the old man's voice boomed again. "The prisoners have gotten away. But do not worry. I do not think the woman will leave her husband behind. I do not believe the children will leave their father. They will be back for him. And when they come, we will have him and we will use him as bait to capture the woman and the children. I will kill the man, sell the children, and keep the woman for myself. Now, get out there and find him!"

A cheer went up from the semi-drunk crowd, and loud talking followed as the men scattered to search for Dan.

At the sound of the cheering and Vega's threat, Dan's blood ran hot. "Over my dead body," he muttered, then glanced skyward once again to check his direction and pushed quietly through the jungle foliage.

Gradually, the sounds of voices and men breaking through bushes faded behind him as Dan periodically looked at the sky to maintain direction while he picked his way through dense forest growth. Half an hour passed, and it felt to him as if he were making good progress over the ground. Beneath his feet, the land had inclined for more than twenty minutes until it reached a natural crown and then the terrain started to drop away and he knew he had passed over the saddle between the two hills and was descending into the lowland on the far side of the island.

The trees and underbrush were thinner and drier on this side of the island, allowing him to see through natural openings. Ten minutes farther on, he saw a glimmer ahead, and as he stepped into an opening the moonlight on the water brought a smile to his face. He checked his watch then pressed on. The land was falling away more steeply now, and as he reached out to grab a branch to steady his descent a thunderous blow crashed down across his arm. Unable to stop the scream of pain, he cried out, lost his grip on the branch and tumbled down the trail, landing in a heap in the bushes below him. Shaking off the pain, he looked up and saw the silhouette of a man standing above him with a club in one hand and a machete in the other.

Juan Baptista de la Vega belched out a cruel laugh. "Ah, senor, I knew I would find you here. And look," – he pointed out toward the cove, where the catamaran was at rest – "there they are. I will have all of you. You should not have tried to defy me."

Dan glanced at the boat and saw Jacob and Cadee in the cockpit. It looked as if they were staring into the jungle watching for him to come to the beach. At this distance, it was hard to tell but it looked as if the dinghy was gone.

De la Vega stepped closer, and Dan rose to his feet. "What? You expected us to just give up without a fight? You don't know the Plover family very well, mister."

"I don't care who you are, you will not prevail against Juan Baptista de la Vega. I take what I want, I use who I want, and I kill who I want. There is nothing you can do about it."

The old man lunged down the hill at him, holding the machete high and swinging the club. Dan stepped to one side and ducked. The club whistled over his head, missing by inches, and Dan snapped a knife-edge kick that caught Vega in the ribs. The gun flew from his waistband and vanished into the underbrush.

The old pirate grunted out his breath, stepped away and grinned. "Is that all you've got?"

"Not by a long shot," Dan answered, then turned and dove through the bushes, rolling to his feet four yards farther down the trail. Pushing bushes aside as he ran toward the beach, Dan yelled to his family, "I'm coming", but Vega was only five strides behind him.

Dan flew through the last line of bushes and onto the beach. The dinghy was there, pulled halfway up onto the dry sand, and he stopped in his tracks. *How did that get here?*

De la Vega crashed out of the jungle with the club and machete held high and a fierce look in his eyes. The old man charged like an enraged bull, a growl roaring up through his throat, sounding like a rabid beast about to devour its prey.

Confused by the empty dinghy, Dan whirled to face the onrushing pirate, and that was when he heard Nicole's voice. "Hey mister," she shouted.

Juan Baptista de la Vega planted his feet and whirled toward the feminine voice. Ten feet away, Nicole stepped out of the shadows. Vega lowered the machete to gut level and sighted down its gleaming blade toward Nicole, then aimed the point at Dan. He swung the club in a circle to his side as he stepped closer to Nicole, an evil grin spreading across his nearly toothless mouth. "I will have her now, senor," he snarled, "and you will watch. Then I will kill you both."

Nicole took two steps forward, raised her arm and sighted down the barrel of an orange flare gun. "Don't ever threaten my family," she hissed. Then she pulled the trigger and watched the night light up as the brilliant red rocket covered the distance in less than a heartbeat and found its target deep in the old man's throat.

Chapter Thirty-three

Under cover of darkness, the Plover family quietly sailed north, away from the horrors of San Luis Miguel. The night wind was steady and with the main and genoa taut in the breeze, the GPS was showing a speed over ground of seven and a half knots. For more than an hour, Dan tried to raise someone on the VHF radio, but it seemed no one was listening. Finally, he hung up the mic and decided to wait until morning.

"Someday, we've got to get a single sideband," he muttered into the night.

Nicole nodded absently, without saying a word, and he wasn't sure she even heard what he said. She sat at the helm station, but wasn't really steering. The autopilot was keeping them on course, and she was staring idly at the moon-glimmered seas and occasionally looking up the mast to check sail trim. She couldn't sleep that night, so she volunteered to take the final watch, to be alone with her thoughts.

Dan stretched out on the cockpit seat behind her, to be nearby if she needed him. The past eight hours had been nothing short of hell on earth, and she had walked deeper into the fire than any of them. She had looked into the face of evil, spit her defiance, and then destroyed it. It was a heavy burden to bear – heavier than anyone should ever have to carry. But it was kill or be killed. The threat was not to her alone, but to her family, and that was unacceptable. She was left with no choice. Right now, there was nothing Dan could say that wouldn't be an intrusion into her private suffering, but at least he could lie down close by so she didn't feel totally alone. It would take time, he knew, for her to heal emotionally – maybe forever. But he would wait forever for her, if that's what it took.

Three hours later, the morning's red orb balanced on the horizon for only an instant, before breaking free and floating alone in the sky. The hot color of sunrise brought Dan's eyes open, surprising him with the sudden realization that he had been asleep. He looked toward Nicole. She was still sitting in the double captain's seat, still staring out across the broad ocean, still quiet. He sat up, rubbed his eyes, stepped to her side and ran his hand across her shoulders then down her spine. He curled his fingers and started a gentle scratch, and she hunched her back and turned to face him.

"Ooh, that feels good," she whispered. Her eyes were red and swollen.

"How about I give you a massage this morning," he offered. "Then you can take the rest of the day off. Buzz can steer." Buzz was their name for the autopilot, because of the low hum the unit made with each steering correction.

"I wish I was tough, like you." Her eyes returned to the distant horizon.

He rubbed her shoulders. "If I had to do what you did back there, I'd probably be puking my guts out from the trauma. I think you're plenty tough."

"He had it coming," she muttered.

"Yes, he did. I'm only sorry that you're the one who had to deliver it to him."

"He would have killed you." She looked deeply into his eyes. "I couldn't let that happen."

"Thank you for saving me."

She turned to look at the sea again. "Then he would have come after the kids and me." Her words had a haunted sound. She stared for a long time at the horizon, then turned again to Dan. "But I've killed a man."

He cradled her face in his hands and kissed her on the forehead. "You saved a man. You saved a woman and two children. You saved a family. De la Vega killed himself by what he was trying to do to us."

She lost herself in thought and Dan said no more, knowing that emotional recovery would be a long and slow process. In the silence of the morning, the only sounds were the wind filling the sails, the watery sluice of the wake, and a periodic hum as Buzz kept them on course. They had crossed thirty-eight miles of ocean, and San Luis Miguel had passed beyond the horizon behind them when she finally spoke again. "I think I'll sleep," her voice sounded like an exhausted whisper as she stepped down from the captain's chair. They embraced, but he knew her heart wasn't in it, and she quickly stepped into the cabin and disappeared into the forward stateroom.

Dan picked up the mic and switched the radio on. As he turned up the volume, he heard the final words of a message. He listened a moment, but heard nothing else. Then, suddenly, the radio crackled into life again.

Whoever he was hearing was close enough for the transmission to come through, but he was hearing only half of the conversation because the other party was too far away. He gave it a minute, then thumbed the mic. "Break, break."

A moment later, he heard the words, "Come back, breaker."

"This is *Whisper*, over."

"*Whisper*," a British sounding voice on the radio came back. "This is *Borboleta*. What can I do for you?"

"Do you have a single sideband or ham radio? I need to relay a message to the Coast Guard in Panama."

"We're heading that way ourselves," the voice said, "but yes, we can relay by radio. What's your message?"

Dan gave his latitude and longitude, heading, speed and intended destination, then told *Borboleta* what happened on San Luis Miguel. "Please let the Coast Guard know about this. And for your own safety, give that island a wide berth."

"Thanks for the warning, *Whisper*. I've read about pirate activity in these islands. Glad you got out of there with all your kit. I'll transmit this message to Panama as soon as we end this chat," the man on *Borboleta* promised.

"I appreciate it," Dan responded. "Unfortunately, all our kit, as you put it, doesn't include our cruising kitty. They took it all. But we're happy just to survive."

The signal started to break up, as *Whisper* and *Borboleta* were heading in opposite directions and VHF line-of-sight signals are good for only about twenty miles from boat to boat. Dan signed off and hung up the mic. He studied the GPS and chart plotter, then walked back to the transom hammock and stared at the wake, running in an undeviating line toward the far horizon. Three shots were fired, he reflected back to the moments after his escape. Ruiz, Pacheco and Carlos were murdered. Then Juan Baptista de la Vega lost the fight on the beach. *Four down, out of ten,* he thought. *I wonder what's going on now.*

Chapter Thirty-four

Hours earlier, the island had become a place of murder in the chaotic dark hours of morning. Ruiz, Pacheco and Carlos lay dead. Six exhausted men gathered in a clearing and flopped on the ground to rest.

"Any of you see the boss?" Juanico asked as he approached the men, but his question was greeted only by shaking heads. "Anybody been all the way across to the other cove?" Again all the heads shook in the negative. He turned and headed for the faint trail Dan had taken. "Don't nobody do nothing. I'll be back in a couple hours."

In the hour it took Juanico to return from finding Juan Baptista de la Vega dead and nearly headless from the fire in his skull, he had formulated a plan. He came out of the jungle directly behind the main house, went inside and loaded a pistol then tucked it into his waistband. With Vega's machete and club in hand, he walked into the cluster of lounging men. "The boss is dead," he announced. "I'm in charge now."

Five ugly, bearded faces turned to stare at him. Tiago got to his feet, took two steps toward Juanico and adjusted his slouchy hat. "Who says?"

Juanico reached to the small of his back, drew the pistol and fired. The bullet smashed into Tiago's chest and the man pitched back and fell like a tree, dead before he hit the ground. "Any more questions?" Juanico looked from man to man, but no one said a word or made a move.

"Now, here's the deal," Juanico began. "I was sneaking around last night and heard Ruiz talking with the guy we took prisoner. I got good ears, and I heard the man say there's eleven million dollars in the box over there." He waved toward the container. "All we gotta do is go in and get it."

Every man sat up and looked intently at Juanico. "I went to have a look while everybody was out hunting in the bushes, and it looks like Ruiz had cracked open one of the locks. The bolt cutter is still there, laying on the barge where he dropped it." He swung the pistol around, aiming at each man in turn. "Now, we're going to work together, and nobody is going to get any more than anybody else. There's five of us here, and we're gonna split the loot square. I ain't like de la Vega, to take more than my share. But I'm the boss now," – he paused to stare them down one at a time – "unless any of you thinks otherwise."

Flies were gathering in the bloody wound on Tiago's dead body as it lay in the heat of the rising sun. Without a word, the men got to their feet and followed Juanico to the barge. "As the boss," Juanico said, tucking the pistol back in his waistband, "I think it's only right that I work right along with you boys. We work together and we share the treasure. Any complaints about that?"

A mumbled chorus of agreement sounded through the crowd. Juanico smiled. "Then I'll take my turn right now." He picked up the bolt cutters and spread the jaws around the next lock. After snapping the jaws through the lock, he handed the cutters to the next man. It took only a moment to break each lock, and quickly the men gathered around to throw open the four vertical latching bars that held the container doors shut.

With a creaking, metallic squeal, the latches were released, and a shallow stream of water poured out as the doors were swung wide. The men rushed toward the opening, but Juanico pulled the pistol and fired a round into the air. "Back off, men," he yelled. "One at a time, and I'm first." He stepped up into the chaotic mess inside the container. A nylon cargo net was draped across a jumble of boxes and plastic totes, but many of them had burst open and there was stuff strewn about under the net. Juanico released the net from the tie-down hooks and kicked a few boxes out to make room for him to move around inside.

The men tore into the crates as if they were treasure chests. After clearing away a few of the water-soaked cardboard boxes and plastic totes, Juanico ripped into one box after another, hoping to discover bales of plastic-wrapped money. Finding nothing but household goods and clothes, he fired off a nonstop string of cuss words in Spanish until all the men stopped what they were doing and stared at him.

"Hey, boss," one of the men said. "We ain't found the money yet, but even this stuff will be worth something. We can take it around to other islands to sell."

Juanico stopped cursing and stared at the man, as if he had lost his mind. Then he thought about it. "You're right. Lay this stuff out on the barge. Organize it in piles, according to what it is."

"Where's the eleven million, boss?" one of the men shouted.

Juanico shook his head in bewilderment. "I don't know. But I ain't done looking yet."

For the next ten minutes, he continued shoving one box after another toward the open doors, and the men formed a bucket brigade of sorts to move the cargo quickly onto the barge to be sorted into piles. After he had made his way ten feet into the container, he could see something different behind the wall of boxes and totes. It was yellow and white and looked like corrugated metal siding.

"There's something else in here," he called out. "You two," – he pointed quickly to the men closest to him – "get in here and start moving this stuff away. Time for me to take a break." He stepped out of the container and wiped his arm across his sweaty forehead. Already the day was hot, and there was no air movement inside the container to cool things down. Even beneath the shady canopy of overhanging trees, the tropic air was stifling.

With two men working, all the boxes and totes were quickly moved away, revealing the front wall of the travel trailer. "Hey, boss, now what?" one of the men asked. "This thing is so wide we can't go any farther."

Juanico hopped up to take a look, and could see that the trailer filled the interior of the container from wall to wall. "We gotta pull it outside." He looked around and saw the crane winch at the front of the barge. "Antonio, bring the winch cable in here," he ordered, and moments later the cable was strung to the trailer's hitch A-frame. "Okay, start it up." He stood at the lip of the container opening and waved his arm up and down. The winch whirled to life, and the cable became taut. "Back off, everybody," Juanico shouted, and the trailer started to roll toward the doors.

"Maybe the money's in there, boss," somebody said, and Juanico just shook his head, hoping for the best. But in the back of his mind, he knew this didn't look like a shipment of baled greenbacks from Bank of America.

"Whatever it is, we share it equal," he shouted above the noise of the winch, and all the men cheered.

The winch cranked and the trailer slowly dragged forward until the hitch jack reached the lip of the container. Juanico raised his hand and rotated it in a circle above his head. "Keep going," he shouted, and the jack slid off the container floor, throwing the trailer nose down on its frame with a crash. "Keep going." Juanico spun his hand overhead again, and the winch kept churning. Fifteen minutes after starting the process, the forward half of the trailer hung outside the container. It was enough to allow entry through the side door, and to Juanico that was enough.

Four rough-looking men gathered around Juanico as he twisted the door knob and pulled. Cocked at an angle, the trailer walls flexed enough to jam the door tight. "Somebody bring me a pry bar," Juanico yelled, and one of the men broke ranks and ran to the tool shed. In a moment, he was back with a long bar. Juanico stood aside. "Go ahead," he ordered, "open it up." The man with the bar slammed the chiseled end into the crack between the door and the frame, pulled back and the door popped open.

"Santo!" the man shouted, throwing his hand across his face and moving back so quickly that he tripped and fell over. "It stinks. Something died in there."

Weeks of vomit inside a hot metal box had created a stench like the bottom of an old grave. All the men moved away from the trailer, fanning hands in front of their faces to clear the air. "We will let it air out for a while," Juanico said. "Let's go have breakfast and we will come back later."

He turned to walk away, but the lure of eleven million dollars was working in the minds of his men, and none of them wanted to leave the trailer behind. Without hesitation, he drew the pistol and fired a shot at the container. The round ricocheted into the tropical sky with a whine, and every man jumped off the barge and walked quickly down the dock toward the main house. "I don't deal well with disobedience, men," Juanico shouted. "That's the last warning you'll ever get."

In the dim recess of his bleary mind, Husam al Din thought he heard the sound of a bullet ringing somewhere. He felt half dead, but dragged his aching body from the corner where he had fallen and was covered by an avalanche of a stinking mattress and a pile of filthy blankets. How long he had been there, he had no idea. He rubbed his face and blinked. *Is that light I see?* Yes, there was daylight in the trailer. *Maybe I'm in Miami and they've off-loaded the container.*

He dug through the debris covering the trailer floor and found his duffel bag, grabbed the web handles and headed toward the light.

Chapter Thirty-five

A wave of fresh air met Husam al Din as he reached the open door to the trailer and squinted into the bright sunlight. He inhaled deeply. Thick, warm and humid as the air was, at least it smelled fresh, and he was thankful to have something to breathe other than the putrid stench that had been locked inside the foul container. The clean air stimulated his lungs, and as he inhaled again and again, oxygen began to awaken his mind. His eyes adjusted to the brightness of the day, and for a moment he stood just inside the trailer, taking advantage of the shadow for concealment as he tried to make sense of what was around him.

This is not right. Why is the trailer lying at such an angle, half in and half out of the container? It was a puzzle. The scene outside was clearly not the container yard at the Miami shipping terminal. In the distance, he heard voices trailing away, and he quietly peered in their direction. Through the trees he saw a cluster of men walking away from him, heading toward a small building a few hundred yards distant across a clearing. With duffel bag in hand, he leaned out the doorway and looked up at the canopy formed by high branches of tropical trees that lined both banks of the river. *Where am I?*

After the men entered the building and were out of sight, he stepped down onto the barge and studied his surroundings. A small tug was tied behind the barge, and beyond that was a red and black boat that looked fast. Without a sound, he moved first to the tug and stepped inside the cabin to look for charts that would tell him where he was. A quick look told him that this was an old work vessel, but it was equipped with a GPS. He pressed the button to turn it on, and waited as the display indicating satellite linkage blinked on and off. *It's the trees. They're blocking satellite signals.*

A short distance down the dock from the tug, a sleek 26-foot powerboat was tied bow and stern. Before leaving the tug cabin, he watched and listened for the men he had seen earlier, but there was no movement and no noise coming from the direction of the house. He felt his energy returning and he moved swiftly to the powerboat, climbed aboard and placed the duffel bag on the floor at the foot of the driver's seat.

The dash was equipped with a VHF radio, a full complement of gauges, and a chart plotter. He spotted the small, mushroom-shaped GPS antenna next to the radio antenna on the stainless steel targa arch. A pair of 225-horsepower outboard motors stood ready for action, and the keys were in the ignition. A cuddy cabin stood open, so he ducked below to see what he could find. Held to the roof overhead by a pair of bungee cords was a plastic tube. He pulled the tube down and shook out the rolled paper chart, then spread it on the small forepeak bunk. It was a chart of the western Caribbean, showing Panama to the south and a cluster of islands along the eastern coast of Costa Rica, Nicaragua, Honduras, Belize and the Yucatan Peninsula. In the upper right-hand corner was the western tip of Cuba, and as he studied that part of the chart, he knew that he was getting closer to accomplishing his goal because Miami was not far from Cuba.

He stepped back up to the cockpit and tossed the rolled chart on top of the dashboard, then turned the ignition key to start the port engine. It jumped to life and settled into a quiet rumble as he let the motor warm up at idle. Over his shoulder, he glanced at the building, but there was no movement. He stepped onto the dock and untied the bow line, coiled it quickly and tossed it onto the foredeck, then released the stern line. With a gentle push, the boat floated away from the dock and he scrambled aboard, spun the wheel and pushed the throttle. The boat responded instantly, turning out into the center of the river channel and gliding past the tug and the barge.

A moment later, he was clear of the overhanging trees, and the GPS indicated strong signals from six satellites. By the time he left the mouth of the river, Husam al Din had his coordinates. *This is where I am.* He drew an imaginary line on the chart with his finger. *And that is where I am going.* He turned the starboard ignition key and felt the second engine roar to life and brought the starboard throttle equal with the port throttle, then threw both throttles all the way forward. The boat came up on plane and leapt ahead.

Station Panama, Coast Guard Communication Center.

234

"Station Panama, Station Panama, Station Panama, this is *Borboleta,* over."

"This is Station Panama, over."

"This is *Borboleta.* I have an urgent message to relay from *Whisper,* a catamaran sailing in the vicinity of San Luis Miguel."

"Go ahead with your relay," the young communications officer said. Over the next several minutes, the owner of *Borboleta* gave a description of the *Whisper* and the Plover family, the container, the piracy incident and their escape from Juan Baptista de la Vega.

"*Borboleta,* is anyone aboard *Whisper* currently in danger or in need of medical attention?"

"Negative. To my knowledge, they are all safe now and are proceeding toward Rio Dulce in Guatemala. But, I say old man, they've had a bugger of a time. They are citizens of your country. Perhaps you could do something for them."

"Thank you for your report. I will process this information through the proper channels. Station Panama out."

No sooner had he ended the radio transmission than the communications officer picked up the phone and pressed a speed-dial number. "Captain Pfister," the voice on the phone said.

"Sir, this is Gable in com. I've just received a report of a container being found near San Luis Miguel. And there was a piracy incident involving an American family."

The news brought Pfister bolt upright in his chair. "I'm on my way. Have all the details printed out for me in ..." – he looked at his watch – "... six minutes."

"Aye, sir," Gable said, and the phone went dead.

As soon as he had a dial tone, Pfister punched in the numbers for Josh Adams' cell phone. It rang twice, then a voice answered. "Josh here."

"Mr Adams, another player just came into your game. Meet me in com as quickly as you can get there."

"Ten minutes?"

"I'll have a helmet ready for you."

San Luis Miguel Island

Antonio Souza was out of breath when he reached the small house. "Juanico, the boat is gone."

Irritation flooded Juanico's voice, "What boat?"

"The red and black boat. The boss's pride and joy. It's gone."

"How could it be gone? It was there just a few minutes ago." Juanico shoved his wooden chair back and it fell with a clatter against the wall. He headed out the door, walking fast and swinging a machete with one hand. "Get all the men," he yelled back toward Antonio. "Maybe those people came back and stole our boat while we weren't looking."

"What are we going to do?"

Juanico stopped in mid-stride and turned, "I don't know yet." Then he shook the machete at Antonio. "Just you quit talking about the old man as the boss. I'm the boss now, and that boat is my pride and joy."

"Sorry, boss,"

"That's a fast boat. We'll never be able to catch them. But we gotta do something. Nobody comes into our backyard and steals from us!" He stomped away toward the dock. Behind him, he heard Antonio yelling to the other men to come to the dock.

By the time all the men came running, Juanico stood staring at the empty spot along the dock where the sleek red and black powerboat had been tied. He walked back and forth along the vacant platform and shook his head in disbelief. "How could this happen?"

A small, heavily bearded Brazilian pushed through the cluster of men. "Boss," he said.

"What is it, Andre?'

"Do not worry. We can take the tug to go find the boat."

"We can never catch that fast boat with this tug. It barely moves."

"Yes," Andre agreed, "but it will move, and the other boat will be dead in the water soon. It's almost out of gas. The boss ..." – he stopped and looked sheepishly at Juanico – "... the other boss, he told me to fill the tank yesterday, but I forgot."

A grin spread across Juanico's face. "Well, we will just let them run out of gas. How long will it take?"

"Only a couple of hours. That is a fast boat, but one that is thirsty."

"Then we will let them run out of gas for the next couple of hours, and then we will go get our boat. In the meantime, we have a treasure to find.

Who is brave enough to go into that stinking trailer to look for the treasure?"

A chorus of voices sounded and everybody's hand went up. "Okay, to be fair, I will send you in two at a time and you can search for fifteen minutes. Bring out whatever you find, and then the next two will go in. That way everybody will have a chance. Andre, because you brought me the good news about the boat, I will send you first. Choose someone to go in with you."

"I will take Antonio."

Juanico flicked his hands at the men. "Go then, the time is counting."

Andre and Antonio sprinted to the barge and jumped up into the trailer. "Whew!" Andre yelled, "It still stinks very bad in here. Smells like vomit."

"How would vomit get inside a locked container?" Juanico asked.

"I don't know, boss, but I know the smell of vomit and that's what this is."

"Your time is running out."

Andre pulled his head back inside the trailer and he and Antonio started tossing things out the door onto the barge platform. "Whew," Andre yelled as he threw a couple of blankets out the door. "I think I found the puke." Next out the door was a mattress.

"You men," – Juanico pointed to the other two who were just standing around with hands in their pockets – "pull that stuff aside and make room."

A moment later, Andre poked his head out the door and he was wearing a grin. "Look at this, boss," – he waved something black. "I didn't find any money yet, but we can get some good money for this."

"What is it?" Juanico walked toward the barge.

"It is one of those expensive American flashlights made of aluminum. The kind the cops carry. It was on the floor under the mattress and blankets."

"Here," Juanico held out a hand, "let me see it." Andre handed it to the boss, and ducked back inside to continue his hunt.

From the heft of the flashlight, Juanico could tell it was well made. He looked into the lens, found the switch with his thumb, and pressed. In the palm of his hand, he felt a dull thud, but the light didn't come on. He shook it then thumped it against his leg, and looked into the lens again while thumbing the switch on and off. Nothing. Then he noticed that from the butt of the flashlight there was a faint mist that looked like smoke curling through his fingers. He sniffed at the mist, but it didn't smell like smoke, so he handed it off to the man standing next to him.

"Here, what does this smell like to you?"

The man sniffed at the flashlight and shook his head. "I've never smelled anything like it, boss. Maybe the batteries are bad."

Juanico took the flashlight back. "Yeah, maybe that's it. Well, the rest of the thing looks okay, so we'll just replace the batteries." He yelled into the trailer, "Hey, Andre, look for batteries."

From deep inside the trailer came the response, "Okay, boss."

Panama Coast Guard Station

Three hundred and fifty miles south, a C-130 rolled down the runway and lifted off. Through the headphones built into the helmet, Josh listened to Pfister. "We've got the cutter *Victory* on her way at max speed, but we'll fly some air surveillance first and shoot some photos. According to the report we got from the *Borboleta,* the folks who found the container contacted a salvage operation to help rescue the thing. Turned out to be a band of cut-throat pirates that took the family hostage, threatened to sell the kids into white slavery and murder the man. You can guess what they intended to do with the woman."

"But the family managed to escape?"

Pfister laughed and related the story to Josh. "Yeah, they broke out and the dad distracted the bad guys while the rest of the family got away on *Whisper*, their catamaran. Dan Plover, the dad, made a run for it across the island, where he had signaled his son to meet him an hour later with the boat. But the pirate leader, a piece of garbage named Juan Baptista de la Vega, caught up with Dan and was about to hack his head off with a machete when Nicole, the mom, showed up with a flare gun and ran a rocket down de la Vega's throat."

"Geez," Josh grinned, "wish I'd have been there to see that!"

"Yup, then the family sailed off heading north until they could make radio contact with someone to report the incident. *Borboleta* was heading south, picked up *Whisper*'s call and had a SSB radio that got through to us, and that's how we found out about all of this."

238

"Did they verify the serial number on the container?"

"They did. BA11M

"How long until we're over San Luis Miguel?"

Pfister checked his watch. "About another hour and fifteen."

"And the *Victory?*"

"About twelve hours."

"What's the plan?"

"If we can locate and verify the container, I have orders to quarantine the area and a hazmat team will be brought in from Homeland Security. Right now we're just trying to isolate and secure the container." Pfister looked at Josh. "And if this is the one, what are your orders?"

"I'll be with hazmat. In fact, I'll be the first one into the container."

"I don't envy you, Mr Adams."

"You're a smart man, captain."

Chapter Thirty-six

Sixty-eight miles north of San Luis Miguel, the red and black powerboat flew over the ocean with only the rear one-third of the hull touching the water. Both tachometers read 4500 RPM, and the huge outboards were screaming. Husam al Din stood with the wheel gripped in both hands, his eyes blurry from the wind. He had been confined too long to be satisfied with sitting now, so his legs were spread and his knees absorbed the motion of the boat as it skimmed the endless blue surface. It felt good to have the wind blowing through his hair.

On his face was a fresh beard that had grown to its previous glory while he was imprisoned in the container. It felt good to be bearded again, and he wore the mask of an Islamic man proudly. His t-shirt and blue jeans were draped across the passenger seat, drying out after having been washed clean of the stench when, earlier in the day, he had stopped the boat for more than five hours. The pause took a long time, but to him it was worth every minute. Besides washing his filthy clothes, the break gave him a chance to take a salt-water bath to purify himself through the wudu ritual ablution. Then he took a compass bearing to the east, the direction toward Mecca, half a world away. On his head, he wore a black turban, and a long robe covered his body, clothes that he had brought in his duffel so he could feel properly dressed for Salaat, the ritual prayer, and for the moment of his jihad.

From the duffel, he unrolled his prayer rug, then, standing erect with his head down and hands at his sides, he recited his own personal call to prayer. "Allaahu Akbar," it began, and was repeated four times. "Ashhadu Allah ilaaha illa-Lah," twice repeated, bearing witness that God is great and that there is none worthy of worship except God. He begged forgiveness for his weakness and for missing so many prayers. For good measure, he performed wudu and recited the Salaat five separate times to make up for some of those he had missed. Allah, he hoped, would understand and bless him on his mission. The five hours lost from his voyage left him feeling renewed and clean again.

In the hot tropic afternoon, the t-shirt and blue jeans were soon dry, and he dressed again in the chameleon clothing that he hoped allowed him to pass unnoticed among the people where he was going – Miami, Florida. It was the place where he intended to begin his holy war. Once started, it would spread quickly across America, and engulf the Great Satan in a deadly disease. Too bad – the thought made him shake his head – I left one of the flashlights in the trailer. But I still have this one; he gripped the weapon and smiled as he folded his turban and placed it into the bag. And I still have this; he pulled the dagger from its sheath, admired the gleam of sunlight from its razor edge, then slid it back in its case and placed it in the duffel.

With his purification and prayers behind him, he had stirred the big outboards back to life and raced for an hour across the open water. He scanned the chart plotter, noted his course line and turned the wheel a little to port to correct his route. While studying the instruments, he suddenly noticed the fuel gauge and gasped. Immediately, his hand went to the throttles and he pulled them back. The boat dropped out of plane and the ocean grabbed the hull, bringing it to a halt as surely as if it had brakes.

His eyes were pinned to the fuel gauge needle, and he watched it bob a little, dangerously close to the empty mark. He turned the ignition keys counterclockwise, and the engines fell silent. *I must find a place where I can get fuel.* He scanned the chart plotter, but the GPS indicator showed that he was in open water and a long way from the nearest island.

In a compartment next to the wheel, he found a binocular. Land might be too far away, he figured, but perhaps he could find another boat out here and beg some fuel. It was his only chance of continuing on.

For four and a half hours, he let the boat drift northward on the powerful Yucatan Channel current while he fingered the binocular's focus ring and swept the horizon. The tropic evening was closing fast, and yet there was nothing. He was alone on a huge and empty sea, nearly out of fuel and with no way to get any, unless another boat passed by.

A pink veil covered the western sky and the light was fading. Before long, it would be too dark to see, but he pressed on, using the last available daylight as he panned the binocular. Suddenly, an image caught his eye and he steadied the glass to the northwest. There, perhaps three miles away, almost invisible through the dim light and the hazy marine layer, he saw the faint profile of a sailboat. He braced his elbows on top of the windshield and watched the distant boat ghosting along under white sails with a black stripe slashing down the rear of the headsail. The light was almost gone when he turned the ignition key for one engine, pushed the throttle forward and watched the tachometer needle rise, then he swung the wheel toward the distant sailboat.

On the *Whisper*

"I hear something."

Nicole looked up from the hammock seat that was perched between the dinghy davits. Sailing at seven knots was a peaceful experience; quiet except for the giggle of the wake as it passed beneath the stern of each hull. With almost no noise to disturb the silence of the evening, she immediately heard the low, throbbing tone of an outboard motor. To sailors, the sound of a power boat is irritating. And noise carries almost unimpeded across open water, so Nicole noticed what she considered to be a nerve-grating racket. "That's an outboard. I can tell by the sound. Who's out here at this time of night?"

"Drug-runners, maybe," Dan said as he grabbed the binocular and stepped up on a cockpit bench for better visibility. "Of course, we're out here and we're not running anything illegal." He pointed off the starboard quarter, "Still too far away to identify, but I'd say it's coming from right over there. I can see a small dark spot, and from the continual rise in tone, it's obvious that it's coming toward us."

Nicole sat up and looked where Dan was pointing. Even though the night was warm, she suddenly shivered and hugged her arms around herself. Worry lines furrowed her forehead, as she stepped onto the cockpit bench. "What are we going to do?"

"We've got no place to duck into." Dan continued to stare at the spot on the horizon, as it grew in size and the noise became more distinct. He lowered the binocular and looked at Nicole. "Go below and make sure the kids are all right. I'll see what this is all about." Seeing her concern, he hugged her. "De la Vega is dead. He can't hurt us anymore."

She looked up into his eyes. "Yeah, but what if it's his gang of pirates?"

"What would they want with us? Ruiz got all our money. They've got the container, and they're probably back there trying to break in and get to the eleven million dollars I said was in there."

"You told them there was eleven million dollars in the container?"

He smiled. "Yup."

"How did you come up with that?"

"After you left the hut, Ruiz came back and told me exactly what I knew he would, that the serial number on the container read BA11M. I told him it was a code used by Bank of America to indicate that there was eleven million dollars being shipped."

She smiled, and he was glad to see an expression other than sadness and fear on her face. "That's not bad, Mr Plover." Then her attention turned again to the approaching sound. "So, who do you think that is?"

"Whoever it is," he said, "I'll take care of it. You go below and be with the kids. We've all had more adventure than we need today. I'm sure they'll appreciate you being with them right now."

For fifteen minutes, Dan watched the dark spot grow. It was coming faster than they could possibly escape, so there was nothing for him to do but stand and watch. With the memory of Nicole's heroic action fresh in his mind, he loaded the flare gun and tucked it into the waistband of his shorts in the small of his back. Then he stood with the binocular to his eyes and let Buzz steer the boat to the apparent wind. In his gut was a sinking feeling of being totally alone and vulnerable. An image flashed through his mind of a priceless crystal goblet that had fallen into the path of stampeding bulls, and there was no one around to pluck it out of harm's way. That was his family – a delicate and irreplaceable treasure. *Why did I bring them here? Why risk everything like this?*

Even though night was falling fast, the low-light binocular magnified and brightened the image, and what he saw astonished him. It was the same boat that had been tied alongside the dock at San Luis Miguel. His right hand closed around the flare gun while he continued to hold the glasses with his left. As the boat approached, he saw a man he had not seen before standing behind the wheel of the red and black powerboat. The man's face bore a full dark beard, and he was wearing a white t-shirt. That much Dan could see. And the man was waving. The face was not one from the island, and none of the pirates wore a white; they were a grubby lot, and their clothes were dirty. The shirt on the man in the boat was very white, almost as if it were new.

Dan relaxed the grip on the flare gun and returned the gesture. "I need fuel," Husam al Din yelled across the distance as the boat came closer. "I am almost out of gas. Do you have some that I can purchase?"

"Just keep your distance," Dan yelled and made a pushing motion with his hands. "First of all, we don't use gasoline. Our engine is diesel. And second, I want to know who you are. I saw your boat on an island. We were taken by pirates," – his hand went back to the flare gun – "and I don't want you to approach our boat until I know who you are."

"Ah." Husam al Din smiled and wiped his brow as a gesture of relief, then he launched into a lie that he made up even as he spoke it. "If you have been on that island, then you must know that my boat and I were hijacked by some bad men. I was taken hostage. But this morning, I was able to escape and get my boat going. But they left it without much fuel."

The story sounded plausible to Dan. De la Vega and his gang could possibly have pirated this man's boat, just as they had done to their own. Perhaps in the chaos of their own escape this morning, the other man was also able to escape from wherever they were holding him. It was possible.

"Well, I'm sorry," – Dan wagged his head – "but we don't have gasoline on this boat. But we should be able to send someone to help you as soon as we get into our next port. I'll mark your latitude and longitude and send someone to find you. How's that? Do you have enough food and water to hold on for a couple of days out here?"

Husam al Din shook his head sadly. "They left me with nothing."

Dan thought about it for a moment. "Well, I can't tow your boat. It's too big and heavy for our sailboat to tow. But I can't leave you out here without food and water. You stay right there," – he pushed his hands to tell the stranger to back away from the catamaran just a little – "and I'll put together some food and water for you. Then I'll send someone who can bring you some gasoline. I'll be right back." He ducked into the cabin, leaving Buzz steering and the other boat following.

Just inside the doors to the main salon, Dan bent down and looked in the refrigerator. He pulled out a few things, gathered them into his hands and stepped into the galley, then slid open the cabinet where canned foods were stored. Over his shoulder, he called out, "Nicole, can you help me put together a package of food and water for this fellow? He's out of gas and ..."

"I'll be right there," Nicole answered as she stepped out of Cadee's aft cabin, but the sudden look of terror on Nicole's face stopped Dan in his tracks.

"What is it?" He spun around just in time to see the sweep of a fist driving into his temple, and then everything went black.

Chapter Thirty-seven

The sun was high when the C-130 banked into a long clockwise turn and Josh moved to a window to look outside. More than a mile below, he saw the green hourglass shape of a tropical island, resting like an emerald on a cobalt blue jeweler's cloth. *A beautiful sight. Like a bit of paradise.*

After circling once at a high altitude, the airplane began a slow descent. Of what he could see from his view through the window, there was no activity on the ground. But that didn't surprise him. Only the edges of the island and a couple of clearings were visible all the way to ground level, the rest of it was veiled by a dense canopy of trees. Still, as they circled again at a lower altitude, he saw no boats and no people.

"Maybe we ought to take a low and slow flyby," he suggested to Pfister, received a nod of agreement and the captain relayed an order to the pilot.

On the next pass, the C-130 was less than a hundred feet off the water and moving just fast enough to stay airborne. Josh planted his face against the window and studied every shadow. "There," he pointed, as they followed the contour of the east harbor, "see it?"

Pfister stared, then slowly nodded. "Yeah. Looks like a dock back under the canopy where that river emerges." He moved the helmet mic in front of his mouth and spoke to the pilot, then switched the mic off and turned back to the window. "I ordered another pass, this time right up the mouth of the river at tree-top level. We'll have high-speed cameras going. Maybe they'll pick up something we aren't able to see."

"It's going to be the middle of the night before the cutter arrives?" Josh asked.

"Yeah. We'll sort out what we can see from the photos on the onboard digital monitor, then go back to Panama. If the container is here like the message from *Borboleta* said, we'll fly you out on a chopper to join the cutter crew before they arrive. That is, if you don't mind making a refueling stop along the way."

Josh rolled his eyes, "You do know how to tempt a guy."

The plane leveled off just above the water and headed straight for the mouth of the river. Suddenly, the pilots revved the C-130 engines and

Josh felt the aircraft begin to climb. Outside, the flash of green treetops became a blur as the plane rose through the saddle separating the two harbors. A message came into the helmet earphones.

"Anything else before we return to base, sir?"

"How about one more go-round," the captain said. "I don't think Mr Adams has gotten his money's worth yet."

"Aye, sir," the pilot said, and he tipped the wings on end as the plane banked sharply to the right.

Eight minutes later, after a second pass up the mouth of the river and over the saddle, the C-130 pulled up and leveled off toward Panama.

"They're ready, sir," the words came through the headset, and Pfister motioned for Josh to follow him. In a forward cabin just aft of the cockpit bulkhead was a computer screen with the image of a wooden barge carrying a rust-colored container. Josh took a seat beside the computer operator and pointed to the corner of the screen.

"Can we move in on that?"

"Yes, sir." The operator dragged the mouse over the photo and zoomed in on the requested spot.

"Can we clean it up?"

The operator typed on the keyboard, brought up a menu, gave the commands, and the image sharpened.

"Can you take it another step?"

"The image will begin to pixilate, sir, but I'll do whatever you want."

"I just need to be able to read the serial number."

"Aye, sir." The operator manipulated the image to bring a higher level of sharpness and contrast. "How's that, sir."

Josh stared at the screen, then blew his lungs empty through pursed lips. "Perfect. BA11M. There it is. We've got it." He turned to Pfister with fire in his eyes. "Soon as we touch down, I want to be on my way to that cutter. Nobody can go ashore ahead of me. Is that clear?"

Pfister sat back and studied Josh's face, then scanned the faces of the two crewmen in the room. A look of surprise and expectation formed their expressions, and they glanced at each other and waited for the inevitable. The captain dragged his chair closer to Josh, then raised his voice and launched into a tirade.

"Have I been retired while I wasn't looking? Did somebody put you in command of my Coast Guard? Let me tell you something mister," – he pointed his finger at Josh's chest, and Josh backed up – "this is my C-130, that's my chopper and my cutter and my men. And, quite frankly, Mr Adams, I don't like people, especially civilians, giving me orders and asking me if that's clear. Is that clear?"

Josh looked away, exhaled and gathered his thoughts. His voice was low, when he spoke. "Yeah, sorry. I got carried away. I understand the military chain of command and protocol. It's just that I've been chasing this guy halfway around the world." The tone and strength of his voice grew, and his eyes cut a hole in Pfister. "You don't know what's going on, but trust me, this is probably the most dangerous situation the United States has ever faced." He gritted his teeth, leaned in close to Pfister and snarled, "So forgive the hell out of me if I get a little excited. Okay?"

The two men stared at each other for a moment, and Pfister knew the ball was back in his court. Finally, his upper body began to rock and his head nodded very slightly. "Yeah, I'll forgive the hell out of you. After all, you're the one who's going to have to face whatever is down there. So I guess you can be forgiven for losing it once." He pressed toward Josh until their noses almost touched, tightened his jaw and growled, "But, mister, you've had your once." The captain stood up and left the room. Josh looked at the two crewmen. Both were wearing grins.

"Touchy," Josh said.

"Mister," the computer operator answered, "consider yourself lucky. The old man doesn't like new dogs trying to mark his territory. Meaning no disrespect, sir."

"None taken."

Josh closed the door behind him and returned to his seat by the window across from Pfister. For the next hour, neither man spoke. Josh sat looking out the window, trying to imagine what he was going to find when he got on the ground at San Luis Miguel. Pfister seemed to have lost himself in paperwork as he sat making notes on a clipboard and occasionally going forward to relay messages to the pilot that he apparently didn't want Josh to hear. It was the longest hour Josh could remember, but finally the landing gear touched down and the plane taxied to the terminal.

"The chopper is waiting," Pfister finally spoke, but his words were cold. "You'll have two stops on the way out, the first for refueling and the second will be the *Victory*. They'll still be many hours from the island, when you arrive." Then, without offering a handshake, the captain turned on his heels and walked away.

Josh grabbed his flight bag and was met by a crewman from the chopper who led him aboard. At 2330 hours, Josh stepped out of the chopper onto the landing pad of the 270-foot WMEC *Victory*.

"We're three and a half hours out, sir," the crewman said. "Do you want to get some shuteye before we make landfall?"

No matter how much adrenaline was coursing through his veins, Josh had to admit that he was tired. "Sure. Lead the way." He followed into the sleeping quarters and was shown a narrow steel bunk.

"Sorry, sir, this is all we have," the crewman said.

"It'll do just fine. I've slept in a lot worse places, believe me." He tossed his flight bag onto the foot of the mattress, removed shoes and socks, stripped off his shirt and pants and crawled into the bottom bunk. It was too hot for covers, so he just turned his face to the wall to hide from the red night vision light and closed his eyes.

A puff of warm breath raised the hair on the back of his neck, but before he had a chance to turn, he felt soft arms wrap around him and then Susan whispered, "Josh, be careful. I love you."

The next thing he knew, someone was shaking him awake. "It's time, sir."

Chapter Thirty-eight

A thunderous pain pulsed in Dan Plover's head, as consciousness started to return. At first, everything was a blur that faded in and out of double vision, then finally began to clear, but his brain shut down again and he closed his eyes. His world rolled over in a dizzy spin and he couldn't quite remember what happened. In the darkness and the whirl, he forced the thoughts to come. *I was talking with Nicole, and ...* Then it slowly flooded back. *The man with the thick black beard, the one who asked for gasoline ...* Yeah, it was coming to him. His eyes opened again and this time, as his vision cleared, he saw the bearded man, and he was holding a dagger to Nicole's throat.

"You will do exactly as I say, or I will slit her throat." There was no emotion in the man's voice. For all appearances, he was not the least bit excited or worried. It was all just a matter of simple fact: if Dan did anything wrong, Nicole would die, and there was no question about it.

"What is it you want?" Dan asked from his position on the floor, afraid to move enough even to sit up.

"You will take me where I want to go." He pulled Nicole's head back and pressed the blade deeply against her neck.

"Whoa," Dan yelled, "hold on there, mister. No need to get excited. I'll take you where you want to go. Just back off with that knife a little. There's no reason to hurt anybody here."

Husam al Din eased the blade from Nicole's throat, but held her head back tightly into his chest and the dagger was still only a breath away. "You will take me to Miami."

"Okay," Dan said, "I can do that. But it's several days away from here at the speed we are able to travel. If you want to get there, we can't sit here like this the whole trip." He glanced around the main salon, but from where he lay on the floor of the starboard hull, he couldn't see if Jacob and Cadee were there.

"You have children on this boat."

It was a statement, not a question, and Dan wondered how the man knew about the kids if they weren't in the main salon. "I can smell them," he

250

answered the unasked question. "I want them out here, right now, in front of me so they can see the danger their mother is in. Then they will know that if they don't do exactly as they are told, their mother will die."

"Jacob … Cadee," Dan called, not wanting to display any hesitation before this madman. "Come here, please. Don't make any sudden moves."

From the port aft cabin Jacob emerged, and the sound made Husam al Din whirl around, the blade still at Nicole's throat.

Cadee came down from the forward stateroom and saw her dad lying on the floor. "Dad," she cried out, "are you okay?"

"I'm okay, sweetie. This man has taken us hostage and is demanding that we take him to Miami. We are going to do exactly as he tells us, or he says he'll kill mom."

"It is not just that I say I will kill her," Husam al Din snarled, "I will kill her. And after that, I will kill you," – he pointed the dagger at Jacob – "and then I will kill you," – he aimed the blade at Cadee. "You," – he looked at Dan – "I will keep alive, because I need you to sail me to Miami. You will do it. How many members of your family die along the way is up to you."

Dan held up one hand. "Well, just relax. I'll take you to Miami, but …" he lowered his eyelids half way and stared at the man, "… I'll tell you something. If you kill any one of us, this voyage is over. You'll have to kill me, because I'll be on you like ants on a picnic and I won't stop until either you or I are dead." He looked at Cadee and then at Jacob, "Kids, if that happens, you go overboard. Your mom and I will see you beyond the veil. We're a forever family and we'll be there waiting for you. I promise you that."

Cadee broke into tears and fell to her father's side, hugging his neck. "I don't want anything bad to happen," she wailed.

"None of us do," Dan consoled her. "But if this man kills your mom, for any reason," – he turned to face Husam al Din – "I will no longer cooperate, and he's going to have to kill me next because I won't let him come after you unless he kills me first." He pointed a finger at the bearded man, "I hope you understand that, mister."

Without any change in his expression, Husam al Din slipped his forearm around Nicole's neck, laid the blade against her cheek and pulled her backward out through the door to the cockpit. "You and you," – he nodded toward the children – "sit there." He pointed to the dinette. Then he looked at Dan, "You get up and come out here."

Jacob and Cadee looked at their dad, and he nodded. "Everything will be all right." He rose to his feet, climbed the steps into the main salon and then ducked out through the companionway door.

"Sit there," Husam al Din commanded, and Dan slipped into the captain's chair. "Now, we will go to Miami."

"What about your boat?"

"That is not my boat. I do not care about it."

Dan looked up at the sails, then at the apparent wind gauge and turned the wheel to adjust coarse. "Why don't you just take our boat and leave us in that one? Eventually, someone will come along and find us. Just give us some food and water, and take our boat."

"I know a lot of things, but I do not know how to sail. I will keep you alive only for that."

Dan nodded. "I see. Are you going to hold a knife to her throat all the way to Miami?"

"If I must, I will."

Dan turned to face the man. "Look, I already told you that I will take you to Miami, and my word is good. I have no interest in interfering in your business, if you're running drugs or whatever it is. My only interest is in keeping my family safe. So you can put your knife away. We aren't going to fight you. But I can't sail this boat by myself. Everybody has a job to do to make the boat operate, and if you want us to take you to Miami then you're going to have to let us do our jobs."

Husam al Din held his arm around Nicole's neck, the blade to her face, but Dan saw his eyes start to shift and knew the man was thinking. After a moment, he relaxed his arm just a bit. "You are a man of the book?"

"A man of the book?" Dan asked.

"You believe in the Bible?"

"Yes,"

"You believe in eternity?"

"Yes, of course."

"And you believe that your family will be together in eternity?"

"That is one of our beliefs, yes." Dan responded, setting Buzz to steer, then turning to face the bearded man. "And do you believe, as well?"

"There is no God but Allah. That I believe."

"I don't care what name you use for God. Allah is fine with me," Dan said.

"Most of your people do not believe." Husam al Din looked at Dan.

"That's their loss," Dan said.

"And you are not afraid to die, or to have your family die?"

"Death is part of life. Without it, we cannot return to God. No, I'm not afraid to die. But I don't want to die tonight."

"That is what separates us." Husam al Din stared at Dan with black eyes. "I am ready to die right now."

"I want to live as long as God will allow," Dan said, "but when He wants me to come home, I will go."

"If you are a believer, then you should be a man of your word," Husam al Din said, with no change of expression.

"I am."

"Will your family follow your commands?"

"I don't command. That is not the way of a good husband or a good father. But when I make a decision for the family, they all support me."

Husam al Din relaxed his arm from Nicole's neck and removed the blade from beside her cheek. "Then make a decision for your family and make sure they understand it well, and you all may live."

Nicole rushed to Dan's side and he swallowed her in his arms, leaving Husam al Din standing at the far side of the cockpit. "We have been through enough, already," Dan said to their captor. "We do not want any more trouble. I have made a decision for the family. We'll take you to Miami, and my wife and children will support me in this decision."

"Very well." Husam al Din sat on the far cockpit bench, facing Dan. "Then go about your business of sailing to Miami. How long will it take?"

"I'll do some calculations. We weren't intending to go there, so I don't know the numbers without checking the charts."

"Then check your charts and make your calculations. I will wait."

****

Through the night, they sailed north toward the Yucatan Channel, strong current boosting them along and adding miles to their progress. Nicole and the children occupied the bed in the forward stateroom, but none of them slept. With the cabin light off, they lay on their backs and watched the stars through the deck hatches, and Nicole whispered a bedtime story to calm their nerves – her own as much as the kids'.

"With a sailboat," Dan explained, "it is impossible to say exactly how fast we will be able to travel. We still have more than 700 nautical miles to Miami. Right now we are making almost eight knots, but the wind can change."

"You have an engine."

"We do," Dan admitted, "and about forty-five gallons of fuel, between what is in the tanks and in the jerry cans. On flat water and not fighting a current, at the most efficient cruising speed, that will take us about 350 miles at seven knots."

Husam al Din did the math in his head. "So, if you can sail at least half the time, and you have to use the motor the other half of the time, we can still make it all the way to Miami without refueling."

"Under perfect conditions, we can make the trip in roughly a hundred hours – a little over four days. But there are no guarantees. We may end up facing contrary currents, or another storm could catch us. We may lose the wind altogether and not have enough fuel for the whole trip."

"You speak too much of problems." Husam al Din frowned. "You must learn to be more positive."

"I'm just telling it like it is." Dan shrugged. "I don't want you to be disappointed in our progress and thinking that I'm doing something to intentionally hold us back."

Husam al Din rose from his seat and stretched. "You are an honest man?"

"My father taught me to be," Dan answered.

"I must sleep. I want your word as an honest man that you will not do anything to slow our progress toward Miami. On the life of your children."

"My honor is good enough," Dan bristled. "You have my word. I am not interested in any harm coming to my family."

"I will sleep there," Husam al Din pointed to the dinette seat. "I want to be close."

"The table can be lowered to make a bed," Dan offered.

"Not necessary. My comfort is not a concern."

Dan noticed that the man with the beard never let the duffel bag get very far from his grasp. Everywhere he went, even to use the bathroom, the

duffel bag went with him. Now, he took it into the cabin and placed it on the floor beneath the dinette table as he stretched out on the bench seat to sleep. A curious question kept nibbling at Dan: *I wonder what is so important in that bag?*
****

Just before dawn, Dan heard the bearded man snoring deeply. With Buzz tending the steering, Dan quietly removed his sandals and stepped through the companionway door. He saw the duffel bag under the table, not more than six feet away from where he stood watching the man sleep and listening to his heavy, slow breathing. Without a sound, Dan slowly knelt to the floor. Beneath the dinette table, he had a clear view of the sleeping man's face, and now the bag was less than four feet away. With a little shift in his position, he could almost reach it.

The boat rolled gently on long, low swells, and Buzz hummed as it turned the wheel to keep the boat angled properly to the wind. Dan leaned toward the table, ducked under and reached. Buzz hummed, and the sails slatted in a wind shift, then tightened again and were quiet. Only a foot to go. Then suddenly, his hand tightened around the handle loops and he lifted the bag just high enough to clear the floor.

Quietly, an inch at a time, Dan pulled the bag to him. Like a shadow, he moved back into the cockpit and placed the duffel on the captain's chair. Over his shoulder, he glanced again at the man sleeping on the dinette seat, then turned his attention to the bag. He wrapped one hand across the zipper to muffle the sound of its opening and with the other he pulled the tab slowly.

Without turning on the cockpit light, for fear it would awaken his captor, Dan reached into the bag to feel what was there. Soft cloth met his touch. *Clothing.* He dug down through the gauzy material and his fingers touched something hard. With fingers trained to Braille, he felt the length of the hard, metal tube. Most of it was textured in a crosshatch pattern. Near one end, he felt a groove that ran all the way around the tube, as if it were a place of joining two pieces together. In his mind he was drawing a picture of what his hands felt. Beyond the groove, the tube was closed off. *An end cap.*

His fingers explored the surface of the cap and he detected a tiny circle, then another. He felt around the end cap and found seven identical circles that felt like small holes. Satisfied with his examination of that end of the tube, he moved his hand along its length to the other end, where he discovered a flared bell-shape. Across the face of the bell, the surface was smooth as glass, and the picture was clear in his mind. *A flashlight.* His fingers moved back down the barrel and found a soft rubber button. *The switch.* He paused at the switch and ran his fingers across it, pressing lightly.

Chapter Thirty-nine

Josh Adams rolled out of the bunk and pulled his clothes on, then followed the crewman topside. When Josh came through the door to the bridge, the coxswain was scanning the island through a binocular. In the light of the moon, the silhouette of the island stood off the port bow, perhaps a half mile away and downwind. Without revealing details of his mission, Josh had advised an upwind position, but was careful not to say that it was to avoid the chance of contamination from a wind-borne toxin. To Josh, the container bearing the serial number BA11M was a toxic zone and was to be treated with the same respect that a nuclear site would receive. But he was not to make any of this known to the men on the ship. Until he determined otherwise, the container was one of the most dangerous places on earth. But it was also one of the most important secrets, from a national security standpoint.

"What do you see?" Josh asked the coxswain.

"See for yourself, sir." The coxswain handed him the binocular and he pressed it to his eyes.

"There's the river," Josh said. "Leads back into the overgrowth like a dark tunnel. No lights anywhere, and nobody moving around."

"No, sir." The coxswain took the binocular back and continued his watch.

"I must go ashore alone," Josh said. "I'll need night vision, one of your hazmat suits and a Zodiac."

"Carter," the coxswain said, and a young crewman stepped forward.

"Aye, sir."

"Take Mr Adams down to the small boat launch platform."

"Aye, sir,"

Without looking away from the binocular, the coxswain said, "Everything is ready for you. Captain Pfister gave us our orders."

Seven minutes later, Josh stepped aboard the waiting Zodiac, adjusted the headband for the night vision scope, pulled the hood down and sealed his hazmat suit, and cracked the throttle only slightly so he could pass quietly into the night toward the mouth of the river. Several minutes later, with a hundred yards to go, he cut off the ignition and the Honda outboard fell silent.

Standard issue with every Coast Guard inflatable boat is a set of oars, and Josh swung the oars around, dipped the blades quietly into the water and pushed, allowing him to face forward as he guided the boat silently into the calm river. Jungle trees formed a thick canopy at a height he estimated to be at least sixty feet overhead, and soon he was deep in the black, moonless cavern beneath the ceiling of branches. Ahead, on the left, he spotted the dock. The barge was there, and the container was on the barge. He rowed silently to the side of the container, looked up and saw the serial number he was searching for. With the small inflatable boat tied to the river side of the barge, he figured he was shielded from view of anyone ashore. But the bright view of the landscape through the night vision scope revealed no one anywhere around.

Very slowly, he pressed down on the edge of the barge with his hands and eased the weight of his body onto the floating platform to prevent it from reacting abruptly to his climbing aboard. He shielded himself along the container's end wall until he could see around the corner and scan the full length of the dock. Cardboard boxes and plastic totes were scattered and a mattress lay half on the barge and half on the dock. Blankets were piled as if they had been thrown without care of where they landed. Amid the junk strewn on the dock, Josh saw something that took his breath. Sprawled along the wooden platform were the bodies of four men. It looked as if they had fallen clumsily, with legs and arms in awkward positions, as though they had died on their feet and dropped suddenly.

"Whoa," he whispered.

He drew his 9mm short-barreled Glock 26 from the pocket of the hazmat suit, stepped onto the dock and walked toward the bodies. Even in the darkness, the night vision scope gave him a daylight view of the scene. He bent over the first man he came to, and jumped away as maggots flooded out of the mouth of the corpse. The dead man's blotchy black flesh was a mass of large red boils oozing dark yellow pus.

In the man's hand was a metal flashlight, and Josh pocketed his pistol then pried the flashlight from the man's stiff fingers. His rubber gloves picked up a smear of pus as he thumbed the switch and noted that the light did not turn on. He rolled it over, examining both ends, and noticed a pattern of holes in the bottom cap. *Something about this is not right. This isn't the real thing.* Then it dawned on him. *This is the delivery mechanism.* He set the flashlight on the dock, standing upright so it would be easy for the forensic hazmat team to see when they arrived.

He moved along the dock from body to body, and found each of the men in the same condition. At the far end of the container, he saw that the doors were open and the trailer was halfway out, hanging at an angle with the wheels still inside the container and the tongue jammed down onto the barge platform. He stepped around to the side of the trailer and saw another dead body just inside the open door.

Josh shoved the dead body out of the way and climbed into the trailer. The chaos inside revealed nothing of the missing terrorist. He was not there. None of the men he had seen so far was Husam al Din. So where was he?

Back on the dock, Josh walked toward a break in the trees that he saw ahead. The trail led onto a bright moonlit clearing where there were two small shacks. He pushed open the door to the first and inspected the interior. Nobody. The second hut held the bodies of three men, each shot once in the head. Beyond the second shack stood a larger building with a single window. It was dark inside. Josh moved cautiously across the clearing toward the building, but suddenly drew to a stop. There on the beach grass lay the body of another man, and closer inspection showed that this one had been shot in the chest. *Nine, so far, four dead of gunshots and all the others from something else. And no Husam al Din.*

He approached the main building with gun drawn, the night vision scope showing the way. The door was open, and he went in. From room to room he searched, but found no one else. *What happened here?* He pondered the question on his way back to the dock, but couldn't come up with an answer that seemed to fill all the empty spots in the puzzle. *Pirates, loot, greed. Grabbing for guns. All that I can understand, but that only accounts for four dead. What about the others? And where is Husam al Din?*

Twenty minutes after his arrival, Josh was finished. He untied the Zodiac, pushed away from the dock and motored out of the river. He pressed the handheld VHF radio to his mouth and contacted the ship.

"I'm coming in. Have the decontamination team ready to hose me and the boat while I stand off from the ship. Then I'll strip down, leave everything in the Zodiac and swim to the ship. I'll need to be decontaminated again before I board, just in case I touch anything while trying to get out of the boat. Have a crewman ready to burn the Zodiac and everything in it."

"Aye, sir. We're ready for you," came the reply.

Forty minutes later, light was just beginning to show over the horizon when Josh stepped out of the hazmat suit and jumped overboard. A team in a second Zodiac stood by with a can of gasoline that they threw into the boat Josh used, then set it ablaze. As Josh trod water below the boarding ladder, the decontamination team hosed him with antibiotic solution; then he climbed aboard and took a shower.

The skipper met Josh as he stepped out of the shower. "Damn lot of precautions you're taking, mister."

As he toweled dry, Josh cut to the chase. "We need to secure this area. Until the hazmat team arrives, nobody goes to that island, I don't care who they are or what country they're from. And I suggest we back off a few miles and stay upwind."

"The old man was right about you," the skipper said. "You act like you run this show."

"As a matter of fact, right now, I've got to place a satellite call to Captain Pfister, the old man, as you call him."

"He isn't going to like hearing a phone ring this early," the skipper warned.

Josh smiled. "It's okay, I'm already on his crap list."

From the foredeck, Josh placed the call. When he heard Pfister's voice, he said as cheerfully as he could, "Good afternoon, captain. How has your day been going so far?"

"Afternoon? It's zero five thirty. Is that you Adams?" Pfister's voice was rough and carried no hint of humor.

"Indeed it is, sir. I need a favor."

"You need a court martial."

"I'm a civilian, remember?"

"Then you need to be keel-hauled."

"You sound in fine spirits, sir. But what I really need is to make contact with the owner of *Borboleta.*"

"Why?"

"Just covering all the leads. He took the call from the family that was held by the pirates on San Luis Miguel. Then he relayed the information to the Coast Guard. I'm betting he knows more than he reported, and I need to know everything he can tell me."

"Your target went missing?"

"Yes, sir. The situation here is ugly with a capital U, and my man is nowhere to be found. That means he's still out there, and I want to talk with the man whose family was being held on the island. The owner of *Borboleta* is my first step to finding them."

"All right, let me see what I can do. I'll call you back when I have something."

"Thank you, sir." Josh ended the call and dialed again.

"This is Curt." The voice sounded more awake than Pfister had, but not by much.

"Curt. Josh here."

"What have you found?"

"Found the container on the island of San Luis Miguel, about 370 miles north of Panama. The box had been salvaged, hauled ashore on a barge, and opened."

"Was Husam al Din there?"

"No. But I found nine dead. Four shot to death, and the rest died of something bad that had nothing to do with bullets. We need a forensic hazmat team on the ground right away, and a bio weapons tech to try to figure this thing out."

"Anything else?"

"Yeah, I need an official thank-you card sent to Captain Pfister at Station Panama. He's been a huge help, but he's feeling a little pinch in the ego department right now. He's not used to non-brass button types taking charge of anything. Maybe you could have the president sign the card."

"Is that all?"

"How's Susan?"

"She's out of the woods. In fact, she'll be on a flight home this afternoon."

"Tell her I said hi."

"Hi? That's all?"

"That'll do for now. I'll tell her the rest myself later."

Thirty minutes later, the satellite phone rang and Josh set his cup of tea aside and answered. "Mr Adams," – the voice sounded businesslike – "I have the information you requested."

"Ah, Captain Pfister. I've been thinking of you."

"No wonder my bowels have been running."

"Great sense of humor, sir."

"You can reach the owner of *Borboleta*, a fellow named Nigel Marsh, at the number I'm about to give you. It's a hotel in Colon, where he's staying while having some bottom work done."

Josh copied the number on a slip of paper, thanked the captain and disconnected the call. Immediately, he dialed the hotel and connected to the room of Nigel Marsh, forgetting the early hour. A sleepy voice answered, "Alo?"

"Mr Marsh?"

"Yes, who is this?"

"My name is Josh Adams. I work with the American government, and I'm trying to follow up on an incident involving a sailboat that was taken by pirates on the island of San Luis Miguel."

"Ah, yes," – the voice sounded more awake – "Pity the filthy dishwater those folks got themselves into. How are they doing?"

"Actually, I'm hoping you can tell me a bit more about them. We're trying to track them down so we can find out how they're doing."

"Mighty nice of you, if I do say so. You Yanks are good to your own. So, how can I help you?"

"Start at the very beginning. Tell me every word that was said."

"Okay, well, let me see. It's early, you know, and my brain isn't fully engaged quite yet, but I'll give it my best. Okay, let me see, I got the call on the VHF, channel sixteen it was, and this chap named Dan Plover wanted to know if I had a single sideband and could contact the Coast Guard in Panama. I told him I did and I could and I would."

"Dan Plover? Did he mention the names of anybody else on board?"

"Said his wife was Nicole and they had two kids, Jacob and Cadee, ages 17 and 11 respectively."

"Did he say where they were from? Their home port?"

"Yes, he did. Said they were from Seattle. Boat name is *Whisper*, and it's a 34-foot cruising catamaran, a Gemini 105Mc, if I remember right."

"Where were they heading?'

"Said they wanted to go to the Rio Dulce. Well, I said, that's a nice area. I had just come from there myself, and I told them all about it. But they were anxious that I report the piracy incident to the Coast Guard."

"Did they tell you any details about the island?"

"Actually, yes, they did." And he related the story to Josh. Besides the barge, he added, there was a very fast looking red and black boat with a pair of big outboard motors at the dock.

Red and black boat? It wasn't there this morning.

"Did Mr Plover tell you how many men were on the island?"

"He did indeed. Said there were ten, including de la Vega himself."

"Ten," Josh repeated.

"Yeah, that's what he told me. Ten."

"Did they open the container?"

"Not while the Plovers were there. Oh, it sounded like a horrible plight they were in."

"But they never saw the container opened?"

"No, sir. They got out of there as fast as they could and counted themselves happy to leave the container behind, no matter what was in it."

Josh had what he needed. "Well, Nigel, I want to thank you for your help. Good luck on your voyage."

"Oh, you're welcome. When you see the Plovers, will you tell them that I did as they asked me to? And give them my best."

"I'll do that. Goodbye." Josh disconnected the call, sat back and looked at the notes he had been furiously scratching. Then he dialed Curt Delamo again.

"I need one more thing."

"Sure," Curt answered, "what is it?"

"I need all the intel I can get on a Dan Plover. Wife's name is Nicole. Two children, Jacob and Cadee. They live someplace in Seattle, and they're sailing a Gemini 105Mc catamaran named *Whisper*. I need to know everything I can about them and their boat."

"I'll go to work on it. Do you think you've got a lead?"

"Yeah, maybe. Anything on the hazmat team yet? I've been on the island and can brief them about what they're going to find in the way of body count, structures and the general layout of things. I think I located the delivery mechanism. It's a bogus flashlight. I left it on the dock where the team can see it when they arrive."

"Good," Curt said. "I'll alert them."

"Tell them that the toxin isn't working exactly the way Groschenko planned. Might be the hot tropic temperatures have altered the bacterial activity or something. But the dead bodies on the island died real fast, not the lingering illness we've been led to believe. Tell the team to be ready for something real grotesque."

Curt groaned. "Well, if the toxin has altered in that way, it might have changed in other ways, too. Like maybe it won't die off when there's no live host."

"That's what I'm afraid of. McCarthy's the best biotoxin man we have. Let him know what we're thinking and that he's going to have to be looking for mutations, or at least altered states from what we originally thought."

"Will do."

"By the way, there's apparently one more body that I didn't see. It's on the other side of the island from where I landed. Seems Nicole planted a hot kiss down the windpipe of the chief pirate with a 12-gauge flare."

"Good for her!"

"One other thing."

"What is it?"

"Do you think you can arrange for an image satellite to search for a boat?"

"Can do. What's the target?"

"A red and black runabout powered by a couple of large outboards. It was at the island when the Plovers were there, but it was gone when I went ashore this morning. If Husam al Din made it off the island on that boat, he might have another delivery device with him. I've got a bad feeling."

Chapter Forty

The sun was high when Husam al Din opened his eyes, and his hand fell instantly to the duffel bag. He rose and stepped into the cockpit, looking east toward the sun. It was late, but even a late prayer was better than he had been able to do for the past couple of weeks. Jacob was at the helm. "Your father trusts you to guide the boat?"

Jacob looked at Husam al Din with dark, angry eyes then turned to look forward and did not answer.

"Ah, I see. You are a defiant one."

Jacob grabbed the binocular, stepped out of the captain's chair and walked forward to the bow, then proceeded to scan the horizon ahead. Husam al Din followed, and Jacob reacted. "Stay away from me," he growled without a hint of fear in his voice.

"Your father would order you to your death. And you would follow that order?"

Jacob turned to face the bearded man, and spit his anger. "My father would die before allowing any harm to come to us. And, yes, if he couldn't protect us, he would have my sister and me deny you the pleasure of having us for yourself. It's called courage, mister. Something you probably know nothing about. You're just a slimy, no-good drug-dealer, kidnapper and murderer."

"You are wrong. I am a man on a mission of mercy, to save my people from a corrupt infidel nation."

"Yeah, well if you're on a mission of mercy, why did you hold a knife to my mom's throat?"

"I am a desperate man, and I will do whatever it takes to accomplish my mission."

"Well, you just stay away from me, or I'll go overboard. I'll die before I'll let your filthy hands touch me. And that will reduce your power over my father."

"You have a strong spirit," Husam al Din said with a note of admiration in his words. "Too bad you are a kafir. Now, I need a place to pray and I want to be alone." He reached into the bag and pulled out his prayer rug and laid it flat, facing east, on the wide deck. He placed the dagger across the top edge, then stood erect with his head bowed and began the Salaat.

"Perfect," Jacob retorted, and he turned away from his captor and followed the narrow side deck along the port rail back to the cockpit. "You just stay right here and be alone all you want."

Dan and Nicole were coming out of the cabin when Jacob stepped down into the cockpit. "Dad," Jacob whispered, "can't we do something?"

"What are your thoughts?" Nicole asked. Jacob, at 17, was nearly a man, and had a good head for problem solving.

"We could activate the DSC piracy message on the radio."

"A good idea, son," Dan whispered. "But the VHF is good for only about twenty-five miles. We'd have to hope for another DSC equipped boat to relay the message to the Coast Guard. The thing I'm afraid of is a reply coming in over the radio. It would let that guy," – he nodded toward the front of the boat – "know that we've called in the posse. No telling what he will do if he feels threatened."

"How about the EPIRB," Jacob suggested. "It's quiet. No voice reply to let him know we've activated it, and eventually somebody will show up to rescue us."

"I wonder what he would do if a plane suddenly started circling overhead, or a rescue boat pulled up next to us?" Nicole asked. "What did he say to you, up there on the bow?"

"Said he was a desperate man on a mission of mercy to save his people from an infidel nation."

Dan and Nicole exchanged anxious glances. "A Muslim extremist," Dan whispered. "He's no pirate or drug-dealer. He's a terrorist!"

Nicole finished his thought. "Guys like him are suicide bombers. They're not afraid to die, in fact, they're looking forward to it. They expect a big reward in heaven if they die in battle. He's got nothing to lose, and that makes him incredibly dangerous."

All three of them looked through the forward cabin window toward the bow. Husam al Din was kneeling on his prayer rug, facing east. "What are we going to do?" Jacob asked.

"Take him to Miami," Dan said. "My first priority is to keep my family alive. Anything we do to make him think we're working against him will put you guys in jeopardy."

"But," Jacob argued, "if he's a terrorist, we can't deliver him to Miami. Personally, I'd rather die than help him kill other Americans."

Dan placed a hand on his son's shoulder. "You have the heart of a hero, you know that?" He turned to Nicole. "Eventually we've got to feed him. Do we have any poison onboard?"

She wagged her head. "Sorry, but I neglected to bring the cyanide. Besides, if that guy has any brains at all, he'll make me sample the food on his plate before he eats it."

"I don't know how much of a terrorist he can be. I checked out his duffel bag while he slept. All he's got in there is some clothing, his dagger and one of those nice metal flashlights."

"Maybe he's part of a bigger operation and he's just trying to sneak into Miami to join the rest of his group," Nicole said.

"Could be. But I gave him my word that we wouldn't try to stop him from reaching Miami. I think I convinced him that he can trust me. That's the only reason he's letting us be free to move around the boat. I don't know what to do."

Nicole wrapped her arms around Dan and Jacob. "We'll think of something."

Chapter Forty-one

The satellite phone rang and Josh lifted it to his ear and listened to Curt Delamo.

"Dan and Nicole Plover, ran the Plover Clinic for the Hearing Impaired in Lynnwood, just north of Seattle. He's 43, she's 39. Two and a half years ago, they left the clinic in the care of a partner and embarked on a voyage down the west coast, through the Panama Canal and into the Caribbean. After doing the Caribbean for a year, they were going to turn around and head back home.

"The kids, Jacob age 17 and Cadee age 11, are being home schooled through the Viceroy System. Bright kids, from what I see of their grades. Their boat is a 2004 Gemini 105Mc catamaran, thirty-four feet long, fourteen feet wide, and draws eighteen inches with the centerboards up or six feet with them down. She's white with black trim, the mast height is forty-six feet above the water. Power is a single 27-horsepower Westerbeke diesel married to a Sillette Sonic Drive leg.

"Cruising speed is about seven and a half knots. Fuel capacity is thirty-six gallons divided into two tanks, giving a practical range of 250-plus miles, depending on conditions. Of course, they might be carrying extra fuel in jerry cans. That's typical of cruising sailors. After this call, I'll satellite e-mail a floor plan and manufacturer photos, along with the specs."

"Speaking of satellites, how are we coming with a satellite image so we can find that red and black runabout?"

"We're moving the bird into position right now. I'm thinking that within half an hour you should be able to receive a tracking image that's clear enough to read the name on the boat."

"Once we find her, I'm going to need a way to stop her."

"Now that Yolanda's out of the way, we've got a carrier moving down into the Yucatan Channel. I'll send a long-range chopper for you. There's plenty of firepower on the flattop to stop that runabout."

"I'm not sure we want to do that. I want to take Husam al Din alive."

"For interrogation?"

"Exactly. He's a resource. He may not know who killed Rashid Singh and Alicia Gomez, but he knows other terrorists in al-Qaeda, and who knows where it will lead. We have ways to get that information, and it's a waste to let it slip away by blowing him off the planet."

"We need to get our hands on the weapon, too," Curt added.

"You read my mind. After what I saw on San Luis Miguel—"

"What's your plan?"

"I'm still working on it. But I need to have you ship me a replacement Glock 26. Mine was destroyed in a Zodiac fire."

"What?"

"Story for another time, but I don't want to go in without at least a little firepower. Right now, I'll get off the line and wait for the e-mail and the satellite tracking image."

After disconnecting from the call, Josh pulled out his laptop computer and strung a Firewire cable to the satellite phone. Moments later, the e-mail came through and Josh pored over the drawings, photos and specifications while waiting for the satellite images.

He didn't have to wait long, as a flashing icon notified him of the link. He worked through the menu and suddenly a photo appeared on the monitor. It was a wide overview of the ocean covering a distance of more than a hundred miles to the north of San Luis Miguel. He called up a menu and increased the target selectivity. Several small squares popped onto the screen, each indicating that the satellite was detecting something other than water. Most were far to the east, not the direction he was expecting the red and black boat to head if Husam al Din were trying to get to Miami by the quickest route.

One by one, he selected the squares and zoomed in. When he pulled up the fifth one at a distance of nearly eighty miles and due north of San Luis Miguel, he whispered "Bingo!" and ran the image up to maximum zoom. The high-resolution digital image gave him a clear view of the boat. It appeared to be dead in the water and there was nobody visible in the cockpit or on deck. Switching to infrared mode, he scanned the boat for a heat signature that would indicate someone in the cabin below deck. Nothing. *So, what's an empty boat doing in the middle of nowhere? Especially this boat?*

Working fast, he commanded the computer to give him a latitude and longitude, and the numbers came up on the screen. Then he looked at his watch and worked a calculation backward. *If the Plovers escaped at 0300 and sailed north at seven and a half knots, and if Husam al Din made his escape the next morning when the pirates opened the container ... hmmm. It's possible. With this boat sitting here empty, it's possible.*

He turned back to the satellite image and shifted the view one quadrant to the north. With an increase of selectivity, a scattering of small squares appeared, and he started the process again, examining each hit, one at a time. There were no catamarans fitting the profile, so he shifted the satellite view another hundred miles north and began again. This time, there was a hit. Near the top of the screen, in the open waters of the Gulf of Mexico, a catamaran was sailing northeast, and it looked identical to the overhead photo Curt had sent him. He zoomed in to maximum, angled the view and read the name, *Whisper,* on the starboard hull. *Right boat, wrong place, if they were heading to Rio Dulce.*

At NIA headquarters, Curt answered the phone and listened as Josh explained. "I found *Whisper.* Husam al Din must be aboard because the Plovers were supposedly heading to Guatemala, and now they're 200 miles north of where they should be. They're already north of the Yucatan Peninsula and are heading northeast. They're making good time toward Miami."

"Got a plan?"

"We can't risk showing our hand. If we show up in force, Husam al Din is just crazy enough to activate his device, kill himself and the Plovers and anybody else who is around. I've got to get on *Whisper.* If I can take Husam al Din alive and get the device before he activates it—"

Curt cut him off before he could finish his sentence. "What do you need?"

"Send an Apache chopper for me, and I'll meet it halfway. I'll have the Coast Guard HH-65 Dolphin lower me onto the runabout by cable. The Apache's fast, so have it pick me up there and take me to the carrier. Then I'm going to need to borrow a Needlefish two-man sub and one guy to operate it."

"The Navy doesn't operate Needlefish yet. It's still experimental. There won't be one on the carrier."

"Well, I need one. It's light enough to be slung below a MH-53E Sea Dragon chopper for deployment. Where can you get one?"

"Let's see," Curt thought out loud, "I'll call Pensacola Underwater Experiment Station."

"Have it delivered to the carrier as fast as you can. And while you're at it, I need a new set of clothes. These Coast Guard duds remind me too much of the military. There's stuff in my locker."

"What happened to your clothes?"

"I burned them along with my Glock in the Zodiac."

"I can hardly wait to hear the rest of that story."

"Later. We're running out of time, and I've only got one chance."

Chapter Forty-two

"Where is the little girl?" Husam al Din took the plate of food from Nicole, sat at the dinette table and shoveled food into his mouth. He fed himself with his hands, and bits of food caught in his beard. To Nicole, his piggish manners were disgusting, but he didn't seem to notice, or if he noticed he didn't seem to mind. He was hungry and here was food. That was all that mattered.

"Why do you want to know?" Nicole's eyes couldn't hide the contempt she felt for him.

"Perhaps I just want to know that your husband has not thrown her overboard." He flashed a cruel smile. Then he lowered his eyebrows and scowled. "If I want her, you cannot hide her from me."

"You stay away from her." Nicole slammed a plastic cup on the table, bouncing his food from his plate. "She has done nothing to you."

He was enjoying the control he had over Nicole's emotions. "Take my word for it, girls grow up and disappoint their parents. You might as well let me kill her now, before she dishonors your family."

"Listen, mister," Dan came through the companionway door from the cockpit where he had heard the conversation, "if you want to get to Miami, you better shut up and stop talking like that. I won't have it."

"You won't have it?" Husam al Din rose from his seat. "There is very little you can do about it."

Without a word of argument, Dan spun around and went out to the cockpit, released the genoa sheet and grabbed the furling line and hauled it in hand over hand. Then he vaulted to the cabin roof and went to the mast, released the main halyard and let the sail fall into the lazy jacks. The boat glided to a stop. He jumped down from the side deck and faced Husam al Din, who had come into the cockpit to see what was going on. "You told me you don't know how to handle a sailboat. Well, now you either apologize to my family and then shut your mouth, or I won't take you another mile. Nobody's going anywhere."

Shick ... Dan heard the sound of the dagger coming out of its sheath before he saw it. The bearded man lowered his head like a crazed dog

272

about to charge and held the knife out to one side, carving little circles in the air with the point. Through the open doorway, Dan flashed a hand signal to Nicole, but to Husam al Din, it looked like nothing but the quivering hand of a frightened man.

Nicole raced down the steps into the starboard hull, pushed open Cadee's cabin door and gathered her daughter into her arms, then fled to the forward cabin where Jacob was resting. "We go now," she whispered.

Husam al Din swung the blade back and forth as he slowly approached Dan. "I will not apologize, but neither will I kill you. I will injure you only enough that you can still run the boat, but by the time I am finished with you, you will lose your desire to disobey me."

Dan backed away, stepping up onto the rear deck where the davits held the dinghy over the transom. From his position, he saw the forward hatch open and Cadee climb out onto the forward deck. "I will not have you abuse my family anymore," he said as he reached for the davit line and released it from its cleat and held it in a tight grip.

He glanced forward and could see Jacob on deck now, taking the ditch bag from Nicole as she climbed through the hatch. With quick steps, Dan scrambled to the other davit and released the line, then opened his fist and the dinghy dropped into the water. Husam al Din lunged, but Dan stepped back and fell into the water next to the dinghy, leaving his captor standing alone in the cockpit, waving the dagger at nobody.

Three splashes from the front of the boat told Dan that his family had gotten safely away and abandoned ship. He grabbed the dinghy rope, jammed it in his teeth and towed the small boat bchind as he swam away from the catamaran. Fifty feet from the *Whisper*, the family came together and he helped boost Cadee into their 10-foot Walker Bay sailing dinghy. Nicole swung the waterproof ditch bag into the small boat, and Dan helped lift her over the side. Jacob climbed aboard next and Dan followed.

"You cannot leave me here," Husam al Din screamed from the cockpit.

"Tough luck, buddy," Dan yelled back, as he and Jacob rigged up the mast and sail. "I told you not to mess with my family."

A few minutes later, the breeze filled the sail and the dinghy moved away smartly. "Now what?" Nicole asked.

Dan squinted into the sun, held one hand above his eyes and pointed with the other. "I've always wanted to sail to Cuba. Can't quite see it from here, but according to my last chart entry, it's over there about sixty miles or so."

"We can't go to Cuba, dad," Cadee said. "It's against the law. Won't we get in trouble?"

Dan heaved a sigh. "Look around, sweetheart. We're already in trouble."

Chapter Forty-three

Beneath his feet, the aircraft carrier felt like a steel building on solid ground compared with the cutter Josh had been on for the past couple of days. He stared into the screen of his laptop and studied the dim night satellite image of the *Whisper*. During the time it took for him to be flown to the runabout and dropped by wire so he could transfer to the fast attack helicopter for his flight to the carrier, he wasn't able to keep an eye on the progress of the catamaran. And now, strangely, it stopped moving, except for a bit of drift on the current. The infrared scan indicated only one person onboard, and that worried him. He had no doubt that it was Husam al Din, as he watched his target go to the foredeck, spread a prayer rug and kneel. Josh wondered what this madman had done with the Plover family.

His phone rang. It was Curt. "The Needlefish will be on deck in three hours." Josh checked his watch. "Emile Nunez is your pilot. He's the best there is with this little sub. He can thread the eye of a needle."

"Well," Josh answered, "if he can thread the space between the hulls of a catamaran in the pitch dark of 0130, that's all I ask. My plan is to rig it under a chopper and drop in ten miles from the catamaran, so the sound of the rotors won't alert Husam al Din. We'll make the final approach at periscope depth."

"And just what is your plan once you're aboard? You can't wear a hazmat suit in that sub. There's barely room to inhale."

"Yeah, well, I'll just have to wing it, I guess. Have you seen Susan?"

"Only briefly. She's on leave for the next little while."

"How is she doing?"

"Ummm." Curt sounded as if he didn't want to talk about it.

"Curt, you there?"

"I'm here. I just think it's better for you to decide that for yourself after you get back."

Chapter Forty-four

Under a black overcast sky, the Sikorsky MH-53E Sea Dragon helicopter lowered the Needlefish sub into the water without so much as a splash, and the four cable attachments disengaged. The trip from the carrier reminded Josh of an extreme ride at Six Flags, except they didn't get upside down. Emile Nunez switched on the intercom and asked, "All set?"

"I'm ready," Josh answered, a bead of sweat trickling down his forehead. He hated closed spaces, and he had never been in a tighter enclosure in his life.

"It'll take us about an hour for the approach," Nunez explained. "That will put us right under the target. Then I need to work us into position, which can take some time."

"You just do what you do best," Josh said. "The important part is that the guy on that catamaran never knows we're there."

"I can put you under that boat quiet as duck down floating on a summer breeze."

"Wake me up when we get there. I'm going to close my eyes for a while. Nothing but black to see outside right now anyway. Black outside, black inside. I might as well take a peek behind my eyelids."

Nunez chuckled. "A bit tight in here for you, huh?"

"My skin is looser than this thing." Josh closed his eyes and listened to the faraway hum of the electric motor spinning a stealth prop. The sound drifted away behind him and became almost imperceptible. It seemed like only a few minutes had passed when the intercom crackled in his ears. Josh flicked his eyes open and looked at his watch. It read 0137.

"We're on target, sir," Nunez said quietly. "We're thirty feet down, and holding. My upward facing sonar shows us directly below the space between the hulls. Where do you want me to surface?"

Josh cleared his throat. "At the bows. This boat has a solid foredeck, so if we can come up in the space below the foredeck and between the bows, that will give me the best cover. This late at night, he won't be on deck saying his prayers. I'll swim a lap from there to have a look-see. You should submerge and stand by."

"Aye, sir."

A moment later, the clear plastic dome over Josh's head quietly broke the surface directly between the bows and beneath the solid foredeck. He felt for the Glock in the holster under his left arm, tugged it out and pulled the slide back just far enough to check for a round in the chamber. Double checking was an old habit, even though his firearm always carried a round in the chamber. Satisfied, he snugged the gun in its holster, then quietly released the overhead latches and slid the dome back on its glides. Without a sound, he wiggled up out of the seat and eased himself over the side into the water, careful to make no ripples or splash. He reached up and slid the dome forward and latched it from outside, and the tiny sub dropped away beneath him.

Using silent dogpaddle techniques, he swam without disturbing the water back between the hulls toward the stern. Bridge deck clearance was low at the rear of the boat, leaving barely enough airspace for his head to remain above water as he approached the transom. The Sillette drive leg was in the up position, with the propeller out of the water. From above him, Josh heard footsteps, then the sound of an aft compartment being thrown open. Almost as background noise, he heard Husam al Din's Arab accent. "Allaahu Akbar. Allaahu Akbar, Allaahu Akbar," over and over like a broken recording that had fallen into a never-ending continual loop. The words were spoken out of breath, as if the man had been running, but there was no place to run on the small boat. *He's in a panic.*

After a few minutes, the footsteps and the muttered beginning of the prayer receded to the cabin, and Josh moved to the swim-steps that led down to water level at the rear of the port hull. A moment later, the footfalls returned, and this time the voice was louder, almost as if he were shouting the repetitious prayer to catch the attention of a god who was not responding. Josh ducked back under the transom and listened to the sound of metal against metal, then something hard and heavy was dropped on the fiberglass floor of the engine compartment. The way it hit the floor, it sounded like a wrench falling among a clutter of other tools. *I bet he's trying to figure out how to lower the drive leg so he can use the engine to drive the boat. But he's working in the wrong compartment.*

Again, footsteps moved away from the stern and into the cabin, and Josh took the opportunity to muscle himself onto the stairs and climb into the cockpit. From somewhere inside the cabin, came a noise that sounded as if Husam al Din were rummaging through tools that were apparently stored beneath the bunk in the aft starboard cabin. Without a sound, Josh moved to the side deck and melted into the shadows forward of the hard bimini that covered the cockpit. And there he waited.

"Allaahu Akbar, Allaahu Akbar, Allaahu Akbar," the words became louder as Husam al Din stepped out of the cabin, strode to the transom and bent over the engine compartment once again with tools in hand.

"Allah isn't going to help you with this," Josh said from the shadow, and Husam al Din whirled around, still on his knees, straining to see where the words came from. In the dim light from the cabin, the Arab warrior looked fierce. His bloodshot eyes stood out like red lasers against his dark face, and his teeth showed a white growl framed by the black beard. Josh stepped from shadow and onto the cockpit bench.

"Sergeant Adams!" Husam al Din sounded astonished. "What a surprise."

"I'll bet it is." Josh jumped down to the cockpit floor and stood with feet apart and hands spread and ready. "So, how's your jihad going, so far?"

"How did you find me?"

"You left a trail of blood and destruction that was easy to follow. It ends here."

Husam al Din sneered, "If you try to stop me, your blood will spill next."

"Maybe. Maybe not. The only thing certain is that it ends here for you."

"Who are you?"

Josh held his finger to his lips and mocked the terrorist. "Shhh, it's a secret. Don't tell anybody, but I'm not Sergeant Adams and I'm not in the army."

Husam al Din eyed him suspiciously. "But our intelligence …"

"Your intelligence found only what we wanted them to find. We're way ahead of your people. Ask yourself how it is that I am here right now, in the middle of the ocean on a dark night, and you never knew I was coming."

A look of angry understanding flared in al Din's eyes. "Of course. CIA?"

"Close."

"It does not matter. What do you think you can do to stop me now?"

"If you resist, I'll kill you. But I would rather not. Either way, I'll recover your weapon so we can study it."

"Not a chance." Husam al Din rose to his feet gripping tools in both hands. "I am not easy to kill, but I will not be taken alive."

Josh pulled the Glock from the holster and aimed it at the terrorist. "Never bring a wrench to a gun fight." He nodded toward the tools in al Din's hands. "I don't really care one way or the other. I'm more than happy to help you accomplish your precious martyrdom. If you die right here, right now, it will save us all a lot of time and money."

Husam al Din stepped slowly to his right, his eyes fixed on Josh. "I do not think you will kill me. If that were your purpose, you would already have done it. I think you want to take me alive, so your people can interrogate me. I know all about your infidel brutality."

Josh shifted one step to his right, as Husam al Din continued to move slowly. In the closeness of the cockpit, if they had reached out they could almost touch each other, but each kept a cautious distance. Too late, Josh saw what Husam al Din was after. The Arab suddenly threw the screwdriver and a fistful of wrenches and rushed for a duffel bag on the captain's seat. Josh threw up his arms and ducked as the hail of wrenches pelted him, but the butt of the screwdriver got through and smashed him in the right eye. He felt the socket break and he was instantly blinded. A stinging blow hit his right wrist, and the Glock flew from his grip and disappeared over the side.

Still blinded, Josh crouched and instinctively swept his arms in front of him in a blocking maneuver. His right eye throbbed and when he forced it open, blood and fluid drained into his hand, but the vision was gone. Squinting his left eye, he saw Husam al Din with a dagger in one hand, and in the other was a black metal object that looked like a flashlight.

"I saw a device just like that on the island where you escaped from the container."

The Arab was silent. A dark, brooding mood overcame him as he intently focused on Josh's every move. It was stupid of him to have left the second device. But his mind was not in focus when the container doors swung open. Weeks of seasickness left him dehydrated and malnourished from vomiting almost continuously. The device that he momentarily thought about using to commit suicide had simply been cast aside among the rubble in the trailer. He could almost forgive himself for forgetting it in his rush to escape. But not quite.

"I'll tell you this, your weapon doesn't work the way you think it will. Groschenko was wrong."

"I don't believe you." Husam al Din waved the flashlight and moved his thumb to the switch. The dagger carved small circles in the air in front of him. "Groschenko is the best at what he does. He tested it, and it worked."

"Maybe," Josh said, "but something has changed with the toxin. Maybe it's the tropic heat. Sorgei ran his tests in the cold mountains, not the hot tropics. What I saw on the island was instant death, not a slow, progressive disease. You pop that and *bang*," – he snapped his fingers – "we both die that fast."

Husam al Din grinned wickedly, as he circled to the right. "I am ready to die. I have been ready all my life."

Josh took another step to his right. "That's the difference between us. To me, life is a gift from God. Something to be protected as a way of honoring him."

"And to me," Husam al Din said, "life is a gift to give back to Allah, as I do his work. That is how I will honor him."

Trying to buy some time while he scrambled to think of a way to get the weapon away from the Arab, Josh argued, "Think about it. If you die here, your jihad will end in failure."

"My jihad will be a success, if I kill even one American. And you will do just fine." Husam al Din lunged with the dagger, and Josh reacted slowly because of his limited vision. He stepped back just a fraction too late and felt the blade pierce his chest. A spreading red blotch appeared on his shirt, and he felt a burning weakness where the blade penetrated.

The shock of the impact knocked Josh back, and he stumbled onto the cockpit bench. Husam al Din rushed him, but even from his fallen position, Josh unleashed a flurry of straight kicks that forced his attacker to back away. He scrambled to his feet, but the Arab caught him with a withering roundhouse kick to the temple on his blind side, and Josh crumbled in pain.

"You are not much of a fighter," Husam al Din said. "I thought your government trained its agents better."

The words were barely spoken when Josh shot a sweeping leg kick from his position on the floor. The kick caught Husam al Din just above the ankle, and both legs were chopped from under him. He hit the floor on his back but rolled and came up quickly. Josh was on his feet and met Husam al Din as he was coming up, landing a left jab then a hooking right punch low on the ribcage. The air went out of the bearded warrior, and he backed away to catch his breath, still gripping the flashlight and waving the dagger.

"I underestimated you, kafir. I will not do so again."

"Too late." Josh exhaled, stepped in and threw a knife-edge kick that caught Husam al Din in the solar plexus, driving the wind out of the man. He followed with a spinning back-kick aimed at the Arab's wrist and the flashlight flew from his hand.

It was a mistake, but Josh watched the black metal tube tumble through the air and hit the water. As with most mistakes, the distraction cost him. A crushing blow to the ribs knocked him off balance, as Husam al Din tackled him. The force carried both men out of the cockpit and, as they crashed onto the aft deck, the dagger sliced into Josh's lower abdomen.

Pinned by the Arab who straddled him, Josh stared into an ugly face that was twisted by rage. Husam al Din lunged, and Josh felt the blade again as it sliced into his shoulder. The Arab followed with an elbow strike that caught Josh on the blind side. He never saw it coming, and the blow blacked him out for a heartbeat, leaving his mind a foggy haze.

Husam al Din jerked the dagger back and lunged again, but Josh instinctively arched his back and kicked upward, knocking his attacker off him. Both men rolled to their feet. Josh was bleeding badly. He stumbled back and braced himself against the stern pulpit.

"I have to hand it to you," he wheezed, "you're good with a knife."

"I am Husam al Din, Sword of the Faith. And I will kill you with my short sword." He rushed again, the dagger held in a forward grip, swinging upward, aimed to penetrate just below the sternum and tear into Josh's heart.

With sweeping hands, Josh deflected the blade, broke his attacker's grip and spun the dagger around backward. When the full weight of Husam al Din thundered into Josh, the dagger was between them, and the point sank into soft tissue. The momentum of the rush carried both men over the rail, and a red slick spread on the water.

The wounds had taken their toll and the impact with the water knocked the breath out of Josh. Blackness swept a dark cloud over his conscious mind and he suddenly felt very cold as he sank into the deep. Beside him, drifting toward the bottom of the ocean, was his mortal enemy, Husam al Din, Sword of the Faith. His eyes were wide, disbelieving. His lips moved, but there was no sound except the gurgling hiss of air escaping from his lungs. Just below his sternum, the dagger of his childhood was buried to the hilt in the hollow of his chest.

Chapter Forty-five

Something bright surrounded Josh, and he remembered stories he had read about people dying and finding themselves traveling through a tunnel of light. Then he heard a sound. Soft footsteps, the whisk of cloth rubbing against itself. He opened his eyes just a slit, and immediately groaned in pain. His right eye was blind, the protective bony structure of the eye socket had been crushed. The left eye saw only a gauzy white light.

"Ow," he complained out loud.

"Welcome back," a soft female voice caught his attention.

"You an angel?" he choked. "I thought it wasn't supposed to hurt in heaven."

"What makes you think you're in heaven?" This time it was a man's voice.

"Hell?"

"We've been called lots of things, but heaven and hell aren't among them. Actually, though, I think Miss Devon has been called an angel before. She's your primary care nurse. I'm Doctor Bishop. You're at Bethesda."

"Bethesda," Josh mumbled. "What happened. The last thing I remember …"

"Not another word." Josh recognized Curt Delamo's voice from the corner of the room. "I'll debrief you when we are alone."

"Curt?"

"Yeah, I'm here. Been here for the past …" he glanced at the clock on the wall, "… I guess seventy hours, give or take. We'll talk later. In the meantime, is there anything I can do for you?"

"I could go for a Ruggiero's deep-dish pepperoni with extra cheese, olives, sausage and anchovies."

"You must be feeling better," nurse Devon said.

Curt scrunched up his nose. "I don't know. There's something permanently wrong with anybody who like anchovies on a pizza."

"And a root beer. A double-huge frosty mug." Josh smiled. Then he groaned again. "Man, it hurts even when I smile. Why can't I see anything?"

Nurse Devon moved to his side, cradled his head and shifted the gauze wrap to uncover his left eye. "Because the movement of our eyes is connected, when one eye is injured we generally cover them both to keep them both quiet so the injured one can heal. I'll remove the bandage from the left if you promise to just lie still and keep your right eye quiet. Don't go looking around the room."

"Promise," Josh whispered. "Can I have that pizza now?"

Nurse Devon smiled and shook her head. "I'll have something sent up, but don't be too disappointed if it isn't pizza."

"Hospital patient food? I'd almost rather starve."

"You need some nourishment. This IV drip isn't much of a meal," Curt said. "I know. I've eaten it before. Even the hospital food is better."

Josh heaved a sigh. "Okay. But make it a double. I'm hungry."

"That's a good sign," the nurse said as she left the room and shut the door behind her.

With the door closed, Curt pulled a chair close to the head of the bed so they could talk in hushed voices. "That was a close one, my friend," Curt said. "We almost lost you this time."

"All I remember is going over the rail, hitting the water and watching Husam al Din disappear below me with a dagger through his heart."

"Yeah, that's pretty much how Emile Nunez described it. He was sitting about thirty feet down when the flashlight device hit the water. Initially, he went after it, trying to catch it with the Needlefish's grab tool before it sank out of sight. Then he saw the two of you hit the water. He could tell that you were not in good shape. Basically, you were unconscious and bleeding badly. He looked at the flashlight disappearing below him, then looked at you and made a choice."

"I'm glad he made the right one," Josh chuckled.

"Actually, he got fired over it."

"You're kidding!"

"Hey, that weapon was important to us. National security and all." Curt looked serious, then slowly a smile replaced the straight face. "Nah, I'm joking. Actually, he's up for commendation for saving your life."

"Well, I'm putting the man on my Christmas card list. How'd he do it?"

"He's good with that Needlefish. He just came up below you and maneuvered so you were lying across the hull like a wet rag. Then he surfaced and called for a chopper."

"And the device?"

"Gone. The water's more than eleven hundred fathoms deep over a silt bottom where it went down, and the current was running. By the time it hit the bottom, it could have been anywhere, and it's too deep to go looking for that needle in a haystack."

"So we're just going to leave a bio-weapon lying on the bottom of the ocean?"

"Afraid so. We can hope that the pressure at that depth doesn't cause the thing to release the toxin. Or if it does, that the salt water will deactivate it. Or that the cold at that depth will kill the bacteria. Or that—"

"Yeah, you can stop now. I get the picture."

Curt shrugged. "I don't know what else to tell you."

"What about the Plover family? What happened to them?"

"In their ditch bag they had a personal locator beacon with a built-in GPS that gave their exact location. The navy sent a boat to pick them up and bring them to the carrier. They needed some time to rest before we started our debriefing, so they stayed on the ship for two days. Then they were delivered back to their catamaran, and they promptly turned her around and headed for the San Blas Islands. Said they've got friends there they want to get back to."

"How did they handle all the trauma?"

"They handled it better than I expected. But it's still going to take some time for the emotional healing to happen. From what they told me about their friends in San Blas, I think that's the best place they can be right now."

"You met them?"

"Oh yeah. I debriefed them. When Nunez brought you up, I caught an F-14 hop to the carrier."

"Huh," Josh grunted, "I didn't know you cared."

"Don't get a big head. I didn't want anybody to talk with you until I had a chance to debrief you."

"Oh, thanks a lot, my pal. Can't trust me to keep my mouth shut?"

Curt grinned, and Josh knew he'd been had again.

A knock came at the door, and Curt pushed the chair back, drew the curtain around the bed and went to answer. The door clicked open, and Josh heard him say, "Come on in. I'll leave you two alone for a few minutes." Then he went out.

When Susan pushed back the curtain, Josh smiled weakly and blinked his uncovered eye. "That was a wink, in case you missed it." He pointed to his face. "You're sure a sight for sore eye."

"You, too." She smiled. "Always the tease. But I like your humor."

"Hey, that's cute," – Josh pointed at her – "we have nearly matching face wardrobes. You don't mind if I call you Patch, do you?"

Susan bent over his hospital bed, cradled his face in her hands and moved in as if she were about to give him a kiss. He wetted his lips, closed his good eye and puckered up. She stopped six inches short, grabbed his nose and whispered, "You might think you've faced death before, buster, but keep it up and I'll show you what real suffering is."

"Okay, I'll be good," he promised and she released his nose and stepped back. He massaged his nose, pretending it hurt, then smiled at her, cleared his throat and softened his voice. "I have been wanting to ask you a question."

Her face brightened. "I'm listening."

"Would you ..." his words caught in this throat and he choked.

"Would I what?"

He grinned. "Would you sneak me a pizza?"

"What?" she almost yelled, then caught herself. "What kind of question is that?"

Josh grinned. "Nah, actually, I had another question in mind. But you know what they say about the way to a man's heart."

"Yeah, yeah, I've heard. So what's your real question, Mr Adams?"

"Well, if pizza is out, would you, uh ..." he stammered, "would you dance with me?"

She stepped back with surprise. "Dance with you?"

"Yeah," he choked again. "Would you dance with me at our wedding? Please say you will. I love you, Susan."

Her lips softened and a warm smile slowly spread across her face. She bent and hugged him, then kissed him tenderly. "Mr Adams, what am I going to do with you?" When she straightened up, he noticed a tear on her cheek. She grabbed a tissue from the bedside box and said, "I'll be right back."

As she walked away, he half sat up, but was too weak and plopped back on his pillow. "Where are you going? Don't leave me now. I want another one of those kisses."

She reached for the door handle, turned to face him and smiled. "I'll be back. I'm going after that pizza."

Epilogue

Bill Martin turned away from the computer screen, rubbed his eyes and looked at Fenster Roberts, his partner in the *Molly B* treasure-hunting boat. "I think we're searching in the wrong place. We've been over this grid a hundred times. If Captain Guillermo Ascente's account of the *Tesoro do Rei* is right, that ship should be on the bottom, right out there." He pointed out the cabin window at the wide Caribbean Sea. "But it isn't."

"So where is it?" Roberts barked his frustration. He jumped up from the table and strode out the cabin door, turning to shout over his shoulder. "Where do we go from here? We've tied up six years, not to mention a lot of money."

Martin sank back in the seat and sighed. "I know. But I've got a hunch. I've been studying these NOAA current charts, and I think I know what happened. We've got to head north. Follow the path a wounded *Tesoro do Rei* would take if she were driven before a hurricane. She might have stayed afloat after Ascente abandoned her, then gone down later. I'm betting she's on the bottom, somewhere between here and here." He poked his finger at the chart and moved it between two spots.

Roberts stepped back into the cabin and looked at the chart. He waved his arms in resignation. "Why not! Couldn't be any worse than this place."

Three days later, Martin squinted at the monitor. "The metal detector is picking up something. Nothing on the screen yet. Only the signal from the magnetometer."

"How high is it set?"

Martin looked away from the screen. "High. At this depth, it needs to be high. Especially to read something that's buried under centuries of silt and muck."

"Well, chase it down and see what it is. If we can find a cannon, or even a cannon ball, or maybe part of the anchor or chain ..."

"It isn't a strong enough signal for any of that," Martin said. "It could be nails in a plank or something. If it's anything that's part of the debris trail, we can track it to the main wreck." He pushed the joystick, and the ROV moved toward the sea floor. "Still can't see anything, but the signal is getting stronger."

"Good." Roberts leaned in and watched the monitor, as Martin manipulated the ROV to zero in on the signal.

"I'm on it," Martin shouted. "Signal is strong. Still can't tell what it is, though."

"Can you get it in the scoop?"

Martin twitched the joystick back and forth, and a cloud of silt rose from the sea floor, obscuring the view through the ROV camera. "Can't see a thing. I'll have to feel my way along." A moment later, Martin whispered, as if he were afraid that a loud voice might disturb the ROV. "Got it."

"Bring it up. I'll get the big net ready."

Bill Martin stayed at the controls, his eyes riveted to the monitor. Fenster Roberts stepped outside to the aft deck and moved the boom into position. A moment later, the bright yellow underwater pod broke the surface. Roberts swung the big net below the ROV and lifted it aboard.

His job finished at the controls, Martin stepped onto the rear deck and found Roberts bent over the ROV. "What is it?" he asked. "What did we find?"

Roberts stood up, a look of disappointment on his face.

"Nothing but this flashlight."

About the author

Richard H. Johnson is the author of *Rich Johnson's Guide to Wilderness Survival* as well as *The Ultimate Survival Manual,* and *Rich Johnson's Guide to Trailer Boat Sailing.*

Rich is one of America's best-known experts on wilderness survival, urban suvival, disaster survival, emergency preparedness, and sailing. As an Army National Guard Special Forces veteran, he developed his outdoor skills further while living off the land and off the grid for a year in wilds of southern Utah with his wife Becky and two young children.

He has been a regular columnist for *Outdoor Life* magazine and has published hundreds of articles on outdoor subjects. Find him at *www.facebook.com/rich.johnson*

Printed in Great Britain
by Amazon